KEEPERS OF LIGHT

CHRISTOPHER SALMON

ARCADIA
press

Arcadia Press

Keepers of Light

© Copyright Christopher Salmon 2014

Published 2014

ISBN 978-0-9871625-4-0

Published by Arcadia Press
www.arcadiapress.com.au
Country of publication: Australia
Cover design James Terry, Arcadia Press design studio

For Donna.

Be not forgetful to entertain strangers for thereby some have entertained angels unawares.

(HEBREWS 13:2)

CHAPTER ONE

HE Southerly flew angrily towards the coastline, whipping salt spray into his face. It stung him like the needlepoint prick of a sea urchin. The sea clawed its way over the rocks, coating them with a slippery sheen that made footing almost impossible. His drenched cotton pants clung to him like another layer of skin. In rhythm with the ocean's surging, torn fibres of the three-inch mooring rope slackened then rubbed hard against his left hip. It gouged his skin and exposed his flesh.

Ben Douglas lunged at the rope in front of his son and smothered it in his hands. "Hold on, Best! Just hold on!" he yelled above the crash of the waves.

The lurching seas engulfed the sixty-foot-wide rock shelf whose shape rimmed the southern headland like the brim of a Digger's hat. Best stumbled; a torrent of water consumed him. When it withdrew, it dragged him closer to the shelf's edge. Molluscs, sea urchins, and sea snails – always objects of curiosity – lacerated and punctured his skin. He raised his head and screamed, but his cries were robbed by the unceasing roar of the ocean.

Ben Douglas heard nothing, felt nothing. For a split second, he was contained within that surreal space where fear and shock blunt the senses. He was blind to the massive seas and stood mute as blood seeped from his large, leather-like hands. As if slapped across the face by the Southerly, he jolted back to life. His eyes followed the rope from his hands as it trailed off and snapped about like a giant snake slithering madly into the water. His years as a lighthouse keeper had honed his vision to detect any deviations from what was normal. Foreign debris floating on the surface of the ocean from entombed shipwrecks were always hazards that had to be located and displaced to shore. He had spotted dots against the horizon when all others just saw endless sea. But he could not locate the end of the rope that held his drowning wife while his son, Best, was attached to her as if by an umbilical cord. Within seconds, the sea swallowed Best's mother and turned her into a millstone that slowly drew Best towards it.

Everything was clear now. He saw the fear in Best's face as his small limbs windmilled about against his white shirt soaked with salt water and blood. Ben Douglas crouched to his knees to wait for a lull in the ocean's beat – that almost musical pause as waves recede back to gain momentum for the next crescendo. As the swell loomed towards the rocks, he strained back on the rope. The sheer volume of water coupled with the ice-like surface of the shelf bowled him from his feet. He dropped awkwardly inside one of the shallow rock pools, moving to break his fall with his left hand while gripping the rope with his right. He did not flinch as the pin-like heads of several urchins penetrated the callused pad of his hand and embedded themselves deep into his skin. He straightened his legs and fixed the soles of his leather boots against the side of the tiny pool. He lunged forward then stretched back as if rowing a dinghy. Three times, to the tempo of the sea, he fought for Best's reprieve. But it was only temporary. He knew he could not hold out against the steadfast will of the ocean.

The decision was monumental, and made quickly, and like many great decisions, would be subject to desperate, anguished examination for years later. He located a small sharp rocky crag that formed part of the lip of the rock pool. As he'd done many times before to sever snagged fishing lines when his knife was out of reach, he began to work the rope back and forth against the serrated edge.

Best cracked his head against a jagged rock, the last obstacle between him and the rising sea. And as blood trickled down his face into his eyes, blurring his vision, his last image before falling unconscious was that of his father trying to cut his umbilical cord.

IT was dark, and ominously quiet. The wind funnelled around the rim of the Hole, creating a low whistle that echoed downwards, losing intensity as it descended until the sound disappeared completely near the sandy bottom. Best's shirt was tattered and stained red from the wound that wept from his hairline. He was shivering. Sand rained down on his face. Tiny grains irritated his eyes, obscuring what little light his engorged pupils were trying to capture. The form stood over his crumpled body. He tried to speak, but seawater dribbled from his mouth. Then the voice. It pounded against his head. Then he awoke.

*

THE sun's rays shot through the window in fragments, diffused by salt stains left by sea spray. Eyes still shut, Best fumbled instinctively for his spectacles, forgetting in the haze of waking that they had been lost to him for well over two years. Still, at his age, time was subjective, going faster for some people, and slower for others. His right eye opened tentatively, balking at the dawn sun. He rubbed his brow in an effort to orientate himself, smudging beads of sweat that had formed during his fitful sleep. With his eyes now open, he gazed through the window, and was mesmerised by the orange gleam cast by the sun over the smooth surface of the ocean. The natural glow was a reassuring light-force that reflected medicinally onto that fortunate humanity who rose every day to seek its treatment. It was responsible for giving Best's face a vital radiance in total contrast to the pasty-faced residents of the Home's western rooms, which were mostly illuminated by fluorescent lighting. Early morning joggers and walkers moved along the shore, sometimes dancing as the gentle sea dribbled indiscriminately over their feet. Surfers in the water before sunrise took advantage of the glass-like surface and three-foot peaking waves. A group of Malibu riders clung together at Greensands while the short boarders were scattered along the rest of the four mile beach. With his arthritis-riddled left hand tucked securely by his side, he pulled the lapels of his terry towelling dressing gown together with his right to overcome the draft wafting underneath the door. He disliked the way it chilled his clammy skin. He wrestled himself from the bed and dropped awkwardly into the wheelchair. He squirmed and rubbed his left hip as he tried to erase the dull pain that had migrated to the top of his bum.

*

TIPODY'S lithe hand reached forward and gently fingered the engraving. He was careful not to stain the tip of his fingers with the green residue that had resulted from years of oxidisation. The tarnished copper plaque was tucked behind an undisciplined limb of one of the front garden's frangipani trees, and was only fully visible in the dead of winter, once the tree had shed all its shrivelled leaves and shrunken white flowers. He mouthed the name softly:

Saint Bede's

He glanced up at the polycarbonate yellow sign, perched above the arched entrance like an afterthought, a stark reminder of the lost art of craftsmanship. Although only added in the last five years, most of the yellow pigments had been bleached out by the harsh ultra-violet rays of the sun, making the sign more cream than yellow. As a result, it was lost against the rendered white walls of the Home.

Thurrough Nursing Home

As Tipody lunged up the stairs, he wasn't sure which of the Home's names to bestow fame on; both were succumbing to age and the elements, much like those residing inside. It wasn't an important detail. The Home was only a bit player. He would be front and centre.

His soft leather shoes kissed the polished linoleum as his lanky stride glided stealth-like down the shaded corridor. He nodded officiously to the orderlies who had marshalled to distribute powdered scrambled eggs, sinewy bacon, soggy toast, concentrated orange juice, and lukewarm tea to the early risers. He compared the room numbers to those on his manifest. Four doors down, one room was now empty – a death or transfer, he reckoned. He made his way to the office undisturbed. Most of the residents were still sleeping, dreaming of younger, freer and more nimble days. Others, who did not dream, thought of nothing at all; their minds permanently incarcerated in a prison from which there was no escape. They hung on to their occupancy by the barest of threads.

As he sat impatiently awaiting the arrival of the Superintendent, he took out the files and laid them on the desk. For the past six months he had carried the entire histories of the residents of Thurrough Nursing Home around in his Stamford briefcase. He had no need to pass the time perusing the details. He had memorised them all. He rubbed his roman nose, more as an instinctive reflex than from the urge to itch. He noticed that the desk was surprisingly bare, save for a few pens and pencils stuck inside a stained Styrofoam coffee cup. He leaned closer and delicately selected four HB pencils. He studied them closely before returning them to their station. The pencils were exactly the same length, and he deduced they had never been used. He glanced around the office. The pattern of the linoleum that ran seamlessly into the corridor and the unusual placement of the power points seemed to indicate that the room was once home to one of the residents and that the Superintendent spent little time here.

"I didn't expect you 'til later," the Superintendent offered in surprise as he walked in to find the doctor waiting.

Tipody shook his hand without getting out of his seat, displaying a smugness that the Superintendent found off-putting.

"I was keen to get started," said Tipody.

The Superintendent approached an old cabinet that used to contain a porcelain washbasin. He flicked the switch of the percolator perched on its flaking bench-top. "A kick-starter?" he asked.

Tipody shook his head. "No," he answered curtly before adding a little more warmly, "I'm a tea drinker." He didn't want to seem too sanctimonious. After all, he would still need cooperation.

The Superintendent made his way to the door. "I'll get you one from the kitchen."

Tipody rose to his feet. "No," he responded abruptly before forcing himself to sit back down. "That's all right," he added calmly. "As I said, I'm keen to get started."

Tipody examined the Superintendent as he sat down opposite. He prided himself on his observations. Through his years at medical school, he was one of the smartest students and had developed an arrogance that came with this knowledge. He always finished academic tasks ahead of other classmates and thus spent a good deal of time in the study of his fellow students. Like most young men, he lusted after several females in his class, but was soon dismayed to find that such feelings were not reciprocated and were instead directed to other males who Tipody would then scrutinize enviously. He gave his intellect more credit than it deserved and struggled to comprehend why the opposite sex didn't find that aspect of his personality more attractive. His distorted self-image failed to see that oily hair, which seldom tasted shampoo, a rather large nose, along with a withered frame, and his habit of stooping to compensate for his lanky height, were not qualities that young women found particularly appealing. As a result of his lack of social interaction with females, and the jealousies that hampered his relationships with males, he became further withdrawn. Long after graduation, and as

CHAPTER ONE | 9

the years went on, he became obsessively devoted to his work and to forming judgements about others who he began to interact with more as specimens than human beings.

His eyes narrowed as he studied the Superintendent's face, noticing that it was mined with broken capillaries. In a predominately coastal shire, this could be caused by years of constant exposure to the sun, or as in the case of the Superintendent's swollen nose, alcohol, concluded Tipody. He glanced across at the cabinet. There was a lock on the bottom door. That's where the booze would be, he reckoned.

The Superintendent tapped his fingers on top of the oak desk. Tipody's eyes darted to the tips of the Superintendent's index and middle fingers. They were stained an unhealthy shade of yellow. He was obviously a smoker. Within seconds, Tipody had discovered two of the Superintendent's vices and briefly wondered how many more he'd unearth if their time together was prolonged.

Tipody refocused. He eyed the manifest. "Have there been any changes to the listing?"

The Superintendent sat more upright. He wanted to be helpful. He was now guarded, but still aimed to be helpful. After all, those had been his brief instructions. He picked up the phone. "Can you print off today's resident manifest, please?" he asked someone.

"It's imperative it's current," said Tipody.

"It will be," responded the Superintendent.

There were several seconds of uncomfortable silence as they waited.

"The Home's fifty-five-years-old next month," the Superintendent remarked.

Tipody nodded his head and didn't attempt to feign interest.

"It was started during the Second World War by a Catholic priest," the Superintendent added. "Mainly for injured and infirm returned servicemen."

Tipody glanced towards the door. He was getting irritated. He had little patience for anyone, which not only partly explained why he never married, but also why he could only ever work alone. "I'm aware of that," he replied.

"The priest called it Saint Bede's after –" The Superintendent was interrupted by a male orderly who entered and dropped a file on his desk with the same level of sensitivity he showed towards the removal of corpses from rooms. It was the orderlies' primary task during the night when relatives were not around to be shocked by just how roughly the dead bodies of their loved ones were handled.

The Superintendent scanned it quickly. "There's been one transfer since – Pemberton."

Tipody located the name on his manifest and struck a line through it.

"And one deceased," he added before half-whispering the name.

Tipody applied the same censure to that resident, forever removing the memory of both of them.

"I've some questions regarding certain individuals," mentioned Tipody, as he retrieved several of the papers on the desk, which the Superintendent was doing his best to ignore.

"Questions?" asked the Superintendent.

"Medical conditions. Mental acuity," explained Tipody.

The Superintendent shifted uncomfortably in his seat. He began tapping on the desk once again. Tipody caught him looking longingly towards the liquor cabinet. Tipody glanced at his watch. It was just past 8:30am. He was a hard case all right.

"As you can appreciate," began the Superintendent, "I don't have much to do with the residents. The position's purely administrational. We've doctors on call, but you'd be better off talking with the nurses."

Tipody smiled unsympathetically. "I understand." He had been told all about the Superintendent: how a botched surgical procedure years ago had led to him being struck off the Medical Practitioners' register.

Tipody rose from the chair and gathered his files. The Superintendent followed and met him by the door, half blocking his exit. "I have your letter of appointment from the Department of Health, but as it's not a medical appointment, I'm not exactly sure what the nature of your tenure is –?"

Tipody confidently flicked invisible lint off the lapels of the jacket that draped from his shoulders as though it was still on a coat hanger. "Research."

"What kind of research?" asked the Superintendent.

Tipody's false grin disappeared. He had lost all patience with the probing of the lowly Superintendent. "Important research."

As Dr Richard Tipody awkwardly brushed past him, the Superintendent was left with a feeling of despondency that he couldn't quite explain.

CHAPTER TWO

BEN Douglas' face glistened in the noonday sun. Sweat ran down his forearms and mingled with the slick substance that had migrated to his hands from the wood. He groaned loudly as he hauled the last of the barrels from the storage room underneath the stone staircase. The rest of the oak vessels were lined up like soldiers against the southern sandstone wall of the cottage next to where the old vegetable garden used to be. He rubbed his palms against his canvas pants, which were already soaked with whale oil. He hugged and levered the last of the tubs across the lawn and avoided stumbling over the igneous rocks that had pushed through the surface of the soil like icebergs.

"Think it'll work?" asked Best as he stuck their clay mugs under the dribbling tap attached to the tin rainwater tank.

Ben Douglas dropped to his haunches and gratefully received the water, gulping most of it down in seconds and pouring the rest over his head. "Abraham Gesner," he managed to reply as he rubbed the residue into his crop of ginger hair.

"Who?" asked Best, always fascinated when his father revealed such knowledge.

Ben Douglas glanced up. Fluffy cumulous clouds created by rising warm air inland moved in a civilized and orderly way across the sky. The north-easterly pushed them gently, not impatiently and irately as southerly winds did. There were no signs of the cirrus pre-frontal cloud that normally advertised the imminent arrival of the Change. The seas would be calm tonight; a good day to convert to the new fuel.

"He tested it at the Maugher's Beach Lighthouse," he eventually responded after completing his assessment of the weather. "It worked a treat."

As Best poured his father another mug of water, he glanced across at the lemon tree planted ten years ago just outside the southern facing window, grown not only to produce fruit but also to protect that particular window from the onslaught of howling southerly winds. His father consumed his second round of rainwater. He didn't complain about the hardened taste of the drinking water that Norah used to dilute with a squeeze of lemon juice. As Best screwed up his mouth, he was certain his father was also missing the lemon, missing her. He plopped on top one of the barrels, not concerned that his pants would become soaked with the oil. He was used to being dirtier now. That's just the way it was.

"Where's that?" asked Best.

His father could never rest for long. He sprung back to his feet and moved towards the new tin tanks resting in the shadows of the lighthouse wall. "Up north," he yelled back.

"Queensland?" probed Best.

Ben Douglas laughed. "Bit further north. Not far from where that big ship went down a few years back. Remember her name?"

Best racked his brain. "Ti... Titan?"

"Titanic," his father corrected.

"The lighthouse mustn't have been that good then," assumed Best.

"No light where she went down. You know what they said about her?

They said that even God couldn't sink her."

Best stared at him with saucer-like eyes. "You think he did?" he asked solemnly.

Ben Douglas laughed. "No," he replied as he ruffled Best's untidy weather bleached hair. Best was still uncomfortable when his father showed affection and he cocked his head away slightly. "It was an iceberg," Ben Douglas added.

Best was relieved. His concept of God was one that stayed in Heaven, not one who intervened so drastically in the affairs of men. "We only have the Thurrough Reefs to worry about," said Best.

"Just as deadly," Ben Douglas commented soberly as he looked out across the peaceful navy blue of the ocean: a sleeping giant whose reefs had claimed numerous ships over the years.

Best shielded his eyes as the sun reflected violently off the new metal containers that were in total contrast to the dull brown of the barrels that housed the whale oil. "What's the new stuff called?" he asked.

Ben Douglas unscrewed the cap from one of the containers and took a deep whiff.

"Kerosene… Smells like rotten whisky." He turned to see dust spiralling skywards from the dirt road that wound through the sparse gum trees that blotted the three-mile-long Thurrough Peninsula. "We've got company."

Best was enthralled by the motor vehicle. He hadn't seen many of them, and none had yet made the journey out from the township of Thurrough; their owners not prepared to subject their delicate new toys to the dirt and numerous potholes of the unsealed road. Best stared at the bonnet and craned his head to listen to the chugging noise underneath the metal flaps, which was drowning out the steady vibrato of the cicadas nestled in the Peninsula's trees. He slowly circumnavigated the car.

"Thirty-five horsepower," stated Kent Lawrence proudly as he stepped from the new black Buick.

Best gently touched the shiny charcoal steel of the wheel's mud protectors.

"Don't do that," said Lawrence sternly.

Best withdrew his hand, stung by the command.

Ben Douglas laid a protective arm over his son's shoulders. "It's just a bucket of bolts," he commented.

Kent Lawrence plucked a white handkerchief from his breast pocket and proceeded to rub away a mark. "An expensive bucket," he countered as he folded the makeshift chamois and returned it to his pocket, content he had removed the offending fingerprints.

Ben Douglas crouched down and looked underneath the vehicle. "You'll need more than that hanky – the road's all over your wheels and axles," he added, starting to wonder what was so important as to necessitate a visit which had resulted in the desecration of the new vehicle.

Kent Lawrence ignored him. "Can we talk?"

"Talk all you like," said Ben Douglas.

"Inside? Out of the sun?" almost pleaded Lawrence whose face was as pale as the whitewashed rendered walls of the lighthouse.

"Out here will be fine." Ben Douglas had no respect for Thurrough Council and even less for its General Manager.

"Fine," responded Lawrence. "Thurrough lighthouse has been selected as a strategic position for the war."

Ben Douglas raised his large arms as if embracing the vista. "Of course it has! For the love of all that's good and decent, can't you see the place is just crawling with Germans?"

Lawrence ignored him. "The lighthouse is to be manned by a soldier from the Australian army. He's being posted to watch the coastline for enemy vessels." He handed Ben Douglas the envelope. "And Thurrough Council has granted its permission."

Best's father scanned the contents. "Since when does Thurrough Council have any jurisdiction over this lighthouse?"

Kent Lawrence hopped back into his Buick. "As you know, Council owns this land and it's leased back to the New South Wales Maritime

Association of which you are an employee. The request from the army was made to them, and as the landowners, they have quite rightly deferred the matter back to us. We, in turn, have agreed to the army's request." He then proceeded to don white-stitched black leather gloves. "We must all do our bit to aid the war effort!"

Ben Douglas motioned his hand in a farewell gesture that he wanted Best to interpret as a wave, but his real intention was something less polite. "I'd give my left lung to know how a council man can afford to fork out four hundred and twenty-five pounds for a two-seater. Like the blessed Trinity, it's a bloody mystery to me!" And as the vehicle snorted its way out of the grounds, Best's father read in detail the official request sent to the Maritime Association by a General Robert Zuma confirming the claims made by Thurrough Council. "Of all things," he muttered as he handed Best the letter.

CHAPTER THREE

DANIEL Finbar hobbled around his room as best he could, given that his body was supported by two legs made of wood. He rubbed his forehead furiously and cursed the fluorescent tubes, which always gave him a headache. The lighting was necessary even in the daylight hours due to the monstrous apartment block that leered outside his window keeping the room in perpetual shade. He tapped hard on the scratched glass of his seventeen jewel Girard-Perregaux wristwatch, almost trying to stall the minute hand that, with every tick, was picking away at his sanity.

The paperboy sprinted in. He didn't look up. He knew he was running late.

Finbar raised his hand and tried to clip the boy over the ear, but the boy was far too nimble and he missed by at least a foot. He threw seven coins into the paper barrow. The paperboy forced a weak smile on noticing the five cent tip.

"You should've been here ages ago!" barked Finbar.

The paperboy glanced at the bedside table clock. "It's close to three," he offered feebly.

"Close to three ain't three," Finbar replied gruffly as he lunged forward to take the meagre tip back out of the barrow.

The boy was used to Finbar's tactics, and he quickly shunted the barrow out of the old man's reach. Ever so slowly, Daniel Finbar tumbled down like a felled oak tree.

The paperboy resisted the urge to utter *"timber"* before clasping Finbar's arm to prevent him crashing to the unforgiving linoleum. He helped him to his feet with the kind of dexterity that only repetition could hone.

Finbar blushed slightly; his position of authority undermined yet again. "I can get up by myself!" he spat out indignantly after the paperboy had shown remarkable strength in dragging him up to the edge of his cot. "And it's only close to three when it's before three – not after!"

The paperboy was already half-way out the door, content to escape with his tiny tip. "See you tomorrow, Mr Finbar."

Finbar took a long deep breath. "Maybe," he mouthed in that silent void where conversations are shared only with one's self.

In a shire where high-rise developments seemed to sprout indiscriminately like weeds with no set pattern or reason, it was just good fortune that Saint Bede's north-facing sunroom was positioned between two apartment blocks that flanked the Home, allowing for a four hour window from mid-morning to mid-afternoon in which to enjoy the sun. In the chill of winter, when cool westerlies blew off the snow-capped mountains hundreds of kilometres inland, the sun's rays paraded under the eaves, showering the room with natural light and rendering the fluorescent fixtures superfluous. To further brighten up the space, one of the more conscientious nurses would often bring in water-filled vases of floating white frangipani flowers harvested from the front lawn. It seemed to work, as most of the residents, even the sickest, made regular pilgrimages to the sunroom. It was considered a kind of oasis where nature could be felt and touched even within the double-brick walls.

Daniel Finbar swung himself in and plonked down in one of the two soft recliners parked strategically by the window. The chair gave out a high shrill sound due to the heavy duty vinyl that had been applied to the chairs to protect them from the incontinent amongst the residents. Finbar always read the newspaper in the sunroom. His anxiety for its delivery was born out of his desire to capture some of the afternoon sun before the concrete and mortar of the building next door swallowed it, returning the room to its state of artificial light, which mirrored his own clinical quarters.

Charley Pelegranetti, whose fast talking days had not ended after his retirement from real estate, popped his head out from behind his copy of the *Daily Chronicle* and tapped Finbar on his right wooden leg with the pen he would soon use for the crossword. "Did you read that stuff about the Northern Territory?" he asked.

Finbar looked up annoyed, but decidedly more at ease now that his skin was absorbing the therapeutic rays of the sun. "If I could reach my arse, I'd be wiping it with this paper!" he shot back after the vibrations of Charley Pelegranetti's engraved Parker had finally migrated up the grain of his leg to reach flesh and blood. "Just what crap are you referring to?" he asked shaking his own copy. "This paper's littered with it! And what's with the mug shots of all these journalists? Do we have to be subjected to their ugly skulls when we read the articles? It should be like the old days. There was only one shot we were interested in seeing. And you could get the bikini girl with the big melons out of the way after the third page – then you could concentrate on reading the news proper."

Charley Pelegranetti nodded his head somewhat nostalgically before shaking the paper officiously. "The Northern Territory has the dubious distinction of being the first place in the world to legalise euthanasia – the mercy killing of the terminally ill." He whistled. "Boy, that's something."

"Yeah, that's something to be proud of – killing people. That's quite the bloody first. At least in war, you had other countries trying to snuff us out. Now, our own countrymen are going to do it for us! And who gives a rat's arse about the Northern Territory anyway? Does anyone actually live there?"

"You don't have to worry," assured Pelegranetti. "It's all voluntary."

"Yeah, so was the War," responded Finbar. "And that was over fifty bloody years and two legs ago!"

THE glass frothed with antiseptic as Best plunged his fingers in to grab his false teeth. This reaction to a pending visit was not motivated by vanity, but rather a desire not to frighten visitors, especially young ones, whose appearances were rare. He quickly shoved the dentures in as the yellow barrow turned into the room. He fumbled to close his dressing gown after checking that the fly of his pyjama pants was suitably shut. On occasion, he had witnessed the unexpected appearance of an old bloke's twog, its lifeless state testifying to the complete innocence of the occurrence. He had seen Lucy Pemberton stumble across one such sighting, and she had never seemed the same since.

The paperboy took a couple of steps backwards on realizing he had startled Best. "I'm the new paperboy," he said, holding up the evening edition of the *Chronicle*.

Best raised his hand, surprised. As he never read the papers, he couldn't remember the last time he had seen a paperboy. "I don't..." he stammered. "I... lost my glasses..." Best thought more about it. It had been well over two years since he'd last seen them. "Really haven't missed them."

Not having read a single newspaper in some years, Best had become totally ignorant regarding "current affairs." The lack of such knowledge didn't prove a hindrance. He had advanced all he was going to in this life. In fact, having obtained an ocean-front room, he had risen to the pinnacle of nursing home existence. Also, in some strange way, he became liberated by his ignorance. Being blissfully unaware of all the injustices committed every day, he was seldom bitter or depressed, unlike those who did know but were rendered powerless by their age and incarceration to do anything about them – people like Daniel Finbar who, Best thought, was always angry about something, and generally it was something that had appeared in the newspaper.

Best and the paperboy looked out the window at exactly the same time, almost as if the move had been rehearsed. The southerly wind was decreasing in knots. The ocean was beginning to calm. It was as if the clouds had lost their hold on the sky. The tentative sun started to reflect off the water, causing the surface to shimmer like a foil streamer fishtailing in the wind.

"You sure have a good view from here," said the paperboy, taking in the expansive aspect from Best's window.

"Thanks," answered Best.

Best's room jutted out over the esplanade like a Juliet balcony. It gave him uninterrupted views for 180 degrees, marked by Thurrough Lighthouse to the north, which stood on the tip of the headland like a Paschal candle, and the tips of the gum trees to the south, whose leaves adorned the ridge of the Royal National Park like dishevelled hair.

"The surf's starting to settle down," remarked the paperboy.

"The Southerly's losing steam," added Best.

As Best looked closer at the boy, now that his pupils had adjusted to the light, he saw in him something vaguely familiar. He shrugged off the feeling. At his age, nothing was concrete anymore; nearly everything was vaguely familiar. And the cataracts which had formed in his eyes over the years made everything appear less acute, like he was looking at the world through a soft-angled lens.

"Think the surf'll be good this afternoon?" asked the paperboy.

Best was slightly taken back. To be asked his opinion was something he had not experienced in some time. Most people just seemed to talk at him, like they were delivering a monologue rather than conversing with him. Best eventually concluded that most "conversations" he had been involved in could have taken place whether he was present or not. He was far more used to hearing Daniel Finbar's and Charley Pelegranetti's impassioned views, and when they ever asked Best for his, he got the feeling that their questions were mainly rhetorical. As he considered them friends, he would just nod politely and say very little.

"Well," said Best thoughtfully, "it's starting to settle down and find some shape." Like the moods of life-long friends, Best had witnessed all the changing temperaments of the ocean, and was adept at predicting them, something that was impossible with his curmudgeonly friends.

"I might go in after I finish my paper run," said the boy, as he swivelled his barrow around to move out of the room.

"What kind of board do you have?" asked Best. It had been a long time since he had talked about the sea, which seemed to exist only to be taken for granted by most of the residents with ocean-front rooms. And those without, like Daniel Finbar, who never saw it anyway, were not able to bring themselves to visit the "premium" rooms, as they were called, for fear of the jealousy it might ignite within them.

"A single fin," answered the paperboy, stopping.

"Not much of them around anymore," responded Best.

The paperboy giggled. "That's for sure! It's a real relic. It was lying around my home. Nobody knows whose it was so I just started using it. I'm saving to buy a Thruster. A Thruster's got..."

"... Three fins," chimed in Best.

"Yeah... that's right!" The paperboy was impressed. "Did you used to surf?"

Best gave out a laugh; a deep laugh. He felt his chest. He had dislodged some phlegm. He hadn't laughed like that in some time. "No," he eventually replied, after discretely coughing into a tissue. "But I would've liked to."

The paperboy took his hands off the handle of the barrow and came to stand by Best at the window. Best was able to see him more clearly, the natural light of day accentuating the boy's features. Although Best found guessing someone's age a completely subjective exercise, like when Lucy Pemberton arrived and Daniel Finbar emphatically pegged her age at seventy-five whereas Charley Pelegranetti wistfully assessed it at fifty-five, he reckoned that the paperboy was no more than twelve years old. What Best found unusual was that although the boy's skin was decidedly fair, almost translucent in the light, it wasn't marked by the usual freckles and moles that regular exposure to the Australian sun would produce. And as the boy's face was devoid of any blemishes, its round form was dominated by large curious hazel eyes and remarkably well-set teeth, which seemed an anomaly given the boy's age. Best assumed that children must be getting braces earlier these days, as they were the kind of teeth that only the brute force of wire could arrange so perfectly. The only aspect of the boy's appearance that was haphazard was the salad-bowl shape of his haircut, which was obviously inflicted by someone with no hairdressing or barber qualifications whatsoever. Best noticed that the boy was continually flicking the fringe from covering his eyes as it hung down like a shredded plastic-strip door curtain over his forehead.

The paperboy looked out at the ocean for some time in silence, intently analysing each break of waves along the beach for their afternoon mid-tide potential. Best witnessed this behaviour all the time. Countless young men would pull up in their cars or bikes and just stare out to sea until they quickly took off either to go and get their surfboards or to be seen another day. Best raised his bony finger and pointed up towards the northern end of Thurrough Beach. "Looks like Greensands might be all right," he said.

Greensands was a section of Thurrough Beach so named because of the tufts of wild grass that grew on small mounds left over from what once were giant sand dunes.

The paperboy nodded enthusiastically. "Yeah, you're right! That's what I'm thinking."

"What colour's your stick?" Best knew all the terminology. On oppressive, hot days, when the Home's air conditioning was labouring, he'd open up his window to gratefully receive the north-easterly. During those times, the language of the beach would waft past his window much like the sea breeze.

"It's red on the bottom and yellow on the deck."

They both looked out at the ocean again in perfect sync. "I'll look for you at Greensands," said Best.

The paperboy jolted back to the reality of his paper run, having forgotten for a time that he was in the middle of his round and had yet to deliver to Oak Legs Finbar. He shuffled the newspapers in the barrow so the transaction with Finbar would be a quicker, and hopefully less painful one. "I'll wave to you from Greensands this arvo," he said as he adjusted his money belt.

Best smiled. That would be nice, he thought. He never even contemplated waving to people on the beach as he didn't know them, and they would just think him a silly old bloke.

The paperboy looked at his watch. It was five past three. He was in for it now with Finbar. "My board's twice as big as me," he added quickly. "You can't miss it."

As Best watched the paperboy depart, the reality of their exchange began to dawn on him. The paperboy wouldn't wave. It was a polite offering, but the boy would soon forget. That's what these nursing homes were for – congregating old folk together so that they could be forgotten collectively. And as most of them were physically unable to leave the Home, their presence was not felt anywhere, which made the process even easier. Besides, thought Best, the paperboy was a nice boy, but he was young. He shouldn't do anything in his life thinking of an old man. The paperboy wouldn't wave, thought Best. The paperboy shouldn't wave.

"What do you think of the Northern Territory Government's euthanasia?" Charley Pelegranetti asked Best when he had positioned his wheelchair beside him in the sunroom.

"I think youth anywhere's a good thing," innocently replied Best, still thinking of the paperboy.

Charley Pelegranetti knew better than to mistake Best's response for sarcasm. He understood that Best wasn't being insightful nor sarcastic.

Charley Pelegranetti never confused Best's naivety with senility. Over the ten years they had spent together in the Home, Charley had come to recognize that Best's contentment was linked to a distinct lack of interest in the world. It held little appeal for him. He had lived through nine decades. It was all the same only twice repeated – like the war – as Best would often say to Daniel Finbar when conversations centred on more morbid subjects, as was often the case with the elderly.

Best glanced around trying to locate the frail form of Old Lady Lucy Pemberton who the nurses would often tuck in the corner so that she could enjoy the warmth of the sun and who could often be found listening to the impassioned ranting of her visiting nephew as he bemoaned the environmental decline of Thurrough.

Charley followed Best's eyes. "She's gone," he said gravely.

"Gone?" asked Best, surprised.

"Gone," Charley repeated. "Gone to Garrawarra."

"Gone to Garrawarra?" echoed Best softly.

Charley nodded soberly. "Gone to Garrawarra."

CHAPTER FOUR

BEN Douglas lifted the iron block off the plate of the woodstove and began to quickly press Best's white shirt in order to avoid scorching it. Two shirts with brown-fringed diamond holes burnt right through them had taught him that speed was of the essence when using the contraption. He noticed a button was missing. Then he remembered: Best had told him about it over a month ago. Every Sunday since, he was reminded of it when he ironed the only decent shirt Best had left. Still, he kept forgetting to sew one back on. She would have done that. The Davenport stone china plates with their distinctive anchor mark (given to them by a sailor they had once rescued from the reefs) which she had arranged decoratively on the hutch, were now stacked pragmatically in the pine cupboard. The crystal vases on the east-facing kitchen windowsill remained barren, no longer home to the tulips and sunflowers she tended, which had lined the vegetable garden that was now home to clover and paspalum. They were just little things, but they spoke intimately about her. He missed her more than he could ever tell

Best.

"Porridge's ready!" he yelled to Best who was just rousing from sleep.

Best dragged himself into the kitchen. His father handed him his shirt. Best noticed the missing button. He didn't say anything.

His father looked sheepish. "We'd better hurry or we'll be late."

THE timber bench was strategically positioned in the shade of an ailing old gum tree, which shed its branches in strong winds. Granite walls protected the church from these wayward limbs that would assault its structure. Bark mixed with sulphur-crested cockatoo feathers was strewn over the patchy lawn as the birds often battled to strip the tree of its skin, only to be dispersed by Father Cruickshank's thirteen-year-old Labrador whose age had turned her gallop into a waddle. There was just enough of a breeze to scatter the blowflies that had gathered to nibble at the meat.

Ben Douglas carved the leg with all the prowess of a butcher, skills learned from years of filleting fish. "Looks good," he said.

"He usually gives me the choice cuts after confession," whispered Bill Cruickshank so as to not be heard by the donor sitting two seats up, who had taken his place amongst the twenty or so regular parishioners that met for lunch every second Sunday after Church in order to combine their food resources. "He thinks somehow it absolves him." He took a deep whiff of the neat slice that Ben Douglas had placed on his plate. "And with prime lamb like this, maybe it does? Who am I to argue against his conscience?" Father Cruickshank grasped two wine glasses in his callused hand and filled them generously with red wine.

"Used this in Communion today," he remarked casually as he offered a glass to Ben Douglas.

Ben Douglas baulked.

"Don't worry," Father Bill interjected quietly. "I'm not altogether convinced about transubstantiation." And he took a long sip as if he was testing his claim.

Father and son looked at each other. They privately joked that

Bill Cruickshank tasted the ceremonial wine with a good deal more enthusiasm than he did the bread. The War had put a limit on many resources and the Priest's only contact with any type of alcohol came via the Catholic Church's supply of sacramental wine.

Father Bill smacked his lips. "It's not a bad drop for church wine though." He passed Best a plate full of potatoes and carrots. "Consider yourself fortunate, Best. Young men are returning from the war with a good deal missing from their bodies and what can't be seen from their minds."

Best nodded. He'd seen the limbless loitering around Thurrough with no prospects of employment, and not enough money for decent accommodation.

"The problems is," Cruickshank continued, "they have no refuge – no shelter. I've asked the diocese if they'd consider starting a hostel here that could house them – perhaps offer medical care." He topped up Ben Douglas' glass.

Cruickshank's Labrador, who had been sitting patiently under Best's feet, was rewarded with a stray piece of lamb Best snuck into her waiting mouth.

Father Bill witnessed the act out of the corner of his eye. Best looked ashamed, worried he might be chastised for wasting such a precious resource.

Cruickshank put his arm around Best and smiled. "Even dogs get to eat the scraps that fall from their Master's table." He turned back to Ben Douglas. "I've located some land owned by the Telfords… I might need a good builder?"

"Know one?" asked Ben Douglas.

The Priest laughed. He then sat back in the warmth of the noonday sun, reinvigorated by the knowledge that he had parishioners around him who were givers amongst the many takers. They were represented by citizens like Ben Douglas, whose pact with Cruickshank had resulted in a new church for the Parish and a new lighthouse for Thurrough.

*

TIPODY was meticulous. He knew that his selection was crucial to his cause. He had spent years forming the ideal profile of the prospective VAE candidate. The matrix of required behavioural characteristics intersected a desire for solitude with simple-mindedness (but not bordering on dementia). He had spent weeks holed up in his city office pouring over the resident manifest of Saint Bede's. He was able to eliminate most of them on paper alone. He tucked the documentation under his arm and strode down the corridor where the lunch trolleys clattered in front of him like noisy schoolchildren. His visits were methodically timed. He had learned over the years that hospital and nursing home residents lived their lives more by the clock than those on the outside. They were always waiting for something: meals, injections, blood-pressure tests, doctors, visitors – all subject to the clock. Consequently, many of the residents spent their time in a state of perpetual anxiety as they did little else but wait... for something. Tipody was acutely aware of this phenomenon, which was why he always timed his visits after meals – when anxiety had been partially quelled by some fulfilment before it welled up all over again like a perpetual geyser.

At age eighty-six, Charley Pelegranetti stood all of about 5'4" tall. Old age had conveniently provided him with an excuse. "Of course, I've shrunk," he'd exclaim to those who dared to question his height. But the reality was that he'd only ever been one inch taller. From an early age he'd made up for his lack of stature by talking incessantly. He was a new breed of post-World War Two youths who'd been too young to fight but remained unsettled by the upheaval of war, and who longed for a more peaceful place that might preserve its heritage rather than let it crumble like the centuries-old buildings ravaged in the crossfire of battle. When Charley arrived in Australia at age twenty-two, four years after the end of World War Two, in answer to the country's call for migrant labour to work the Snowy River Mountain's Power Scheme, he wasn't just involved in preserving a young country's heritage, but considered himself a part in creating it. He spent a total of ten years in the harshness of the Snowy Mountains before moving to Sydney, where he applied himself to just about everything. In between sponsoring his widowed father to come to Australia, he ran a fruit shop, sold vacuum-sealed packaged assorted nuts to grocery stores, managed two Italian restaurants, and for the last thirty years of his working life, ran his own boutique real estate agency where he specialised in selling old weatherboard houses to Italian and Greek families who took great delight in demolishing them in order to build their own Parthenons and Colosseums set within concrete jungles.

Richard Tipody was welcomed into Charley Pelegranetti's room like a long lost son.

"Come in! Come in!" Charley proclaimed, ecstatic to have a visitor. "Sit down. Put your feet up."

Tipody found the familiarity distasteful. As he glanced around, he noticed a stack of Realtors piled on the floor at the foot of the bed and several bleached timber plaques hanging lopsided on the wall. "Local business awards," Charley said proudly, as he pushed his plate of unfinished leather lamb and rubber carrots to one side.

Tipody raised his eyebrows in recognition as he moved to the aluminium dresser. There were several photos stuck to the wall above it with blue tack – all unframed, all faded with age, much like memories. Charley Pelegranetti didn't get many visitors. Tipody had been in enough old-age homes to know that regular visitors ensured photos were safely contained within new, protective, lovingly-embracing frames that hugged the photos like a grandfather would his grandchildren.

"Who are the children?" Tipody asked as he fingered the stamp-sized photo of two young boys.

Charley came to stand behind him. "My boys... my son's boys... when they were kids... all grown up now... They moved to Queensland when Sydney got too expensive... Timmy works for the Fisheries Department and –"

Tipody raised his folder, interrupting. "I just wanted to ask you a few questions in order to update your medical file." He was distracted by the sight of a lone picture of a striking woman taken against the backdrop of Thurrough Beach. She was half-laughing at her photographer, her almond eyes creased at the corners ever so slightly.

Charley noticed where Tipody's attention had been diverted. He had seen that expression all his life, and it made him proud.

"She was quite the woman," said Charley.

"Your wife?" Tipody enquired, surprised and almost with a hint of envy.

Charley nodded. "She passed away... ten years ago now." With the elderly, time could be a blessing or a curse, depending on how they looked at it. Time could heal wounds, but it also inflicted others.

Unkind people said that Charley had talked her to death, but the truth was that she stopped listening after he convinced her to marry him fifty years before. He had profusely promised that he'd be a good provider, and as they lowered her ornate coffin into its resting place, he took great comfort in the knowledge that he'd lived up to that promise. In spite of all that he had achieved as a materially successful immigrant, he considered her his greatest triumph. Of mixed Egyptian and Greek background, most compared her to Cleopatra, which was essentially the same as comparing her to the young Elizabeth Taylor. As a couple, they were quite the contrast: Charley, with his moon-shaped face and two chins, with the rim of his head rising above its hairline like a mountain peak above the treeline, looked more like Danny Devito.

Charley had been completely reliant on her since having both his hips replaced. After her death, he decided that the support infrastructure of the Thurrough Nursing Home was the best place for him. Besides, loneliness had begun bearing down on him like a blanket of thick fog that he could not seem to see out of, and it was getting denser by the day. He needed to be surrounded by people. For one who liked to talk, he had soon discovered that conversations with himself were severely limiting and extremely one-sided.

Tipody enjoyed Charley's wistful demeanour as he recalled his past.

This was a good quality and had been an important personality trait of Tipody's VAE profile. As Charley began to disgorge details of his life and loss, Tipody listened impassively, as if he was just another one of the pieces of furniture that had been thrown into the room with no thought as to appearance, only functionality. This was Tipody's greatest skill: to remain completely detached emotionally during the most emotional of times.

Early on in Charley's virtually uninterruptible half-hour discourse on his life, however, Tipody dismissed him as a possibility. Charley's Italian background not only made him too animated, but Tipody also came to realise that Charley Pelegranetti was living to remember; living to remember all that had happened to him, both good and bad. His life consisted now of weighing them both up as if he was placing them on a giant scale to see which way it would tip. As Charley was still in the throes of evaluating his life – a process that could take minutes, hours, or even years – his desire to live was far too strong. As Tipody left the room, he forcefully plucked Charley Pelegranetti's name from his list as though he was removing a splinter and never spoke with him again.

CHAPTER FIVE

T HEY had just climbed the last of the sandstone stairs that led up
over the rocky headland from the beach below, when they spied
a body lying lifeless on the north-facing porch of the cottage, its head
resting beneath a slouch hat on what looked to be a canvas duffle bag.
As they got closer, loud snores confirmed the body was that of a soldier
fast asleep.

"Whoa there!" said Ben Douglas, hoping not to frighten him.

The snores continued to vibrate through the humid air.

Ben Douglas kneeled near the soldier's head, which was nestled into
his duffle pillow like a dog in its master's lap. "Hey!" he said again, this
time much louder.

There was no response.

Ben Douglas put his large paw-like hand on the soldier's chest, like a
lioness on her cub, and began to shake him gently.

The soldier threw off his hat and jumped to his feet. "Struth!" he
cried.

Best moved in and helped to steady him. This was difficult, due to the fact that his uniform was two sizes too big for him and draped off his gangly form the way the raincoats hung from the hooks on the cottage hallstand.

"I came up from Thurrough Station early the s'morning. Geez, it's a long way," the stranger explained as he bent down and rolled up his pants to reveal bootless feet. "I got blisters all over me toes. I took off me boots and laid back just for a sec... I must've nodded off." He gently poked his arms. "Think I might've got burnt."

Best nodded on noticing the red blotchy marks appearing on the soldier's skin, which looked like he'd been tagged with red paint.

"Who are you?" asked Ben Douglas.

The soldier instantly stood to attention. "Private Dirk Crenshaw – Australian Army. I'm 'ere to watch the ocean."

"Ah..." Ben Douglas remembered the letter sent four weeks ago.

Dirk pointed to the Thurrough Lighthouse. "What's that?"

Ben Douglas looked up proudly at the glimmering white of the Thurrough Lighthouse. He pointed to the ornate crown that surrounded the lamp room. "That's your post."

Dirk shook his head almost manically. "I can't go up there!"

"Why not?" asked Best.

Dirk began biting the nail of his middle finger but his teeth could find nothing but residual skin left tattered from previous assaults. "I'm scared of heights."

"Kind of defeats the purpose, doesn't it?" Best's father whispered to his son.

"Where am I s'posed to sleep?" Dirk asked as he swung his duffle bag over his shoulder. "Up there as well?" he added, his voice almost trembling.

"We've got a bedroom in the cottage. You'll be sharing with Best," his father added.

Dirk whistled then exhaled loudly. "That's a relief. No way could I sleep on that thing... What'd you call it?"

"A lighthouse," said Best.

"Nothing light 'bout that," remarked Dirk as his neck craned skyward.

Best was about to explain its function, but his father shook his head. "Come on, Private," he said picking up Dirk Crenshaw's boots. "We'll show you to your quarters."

"Anything to eat?" Dirk asked. "I'm starvin'… I could eat the crotch out of a low-flying duck."

"No ducks on this side of the Peninsula," remarked Best. "Only seagulls."

"SO," Dirk began, as he dipped his damper in the pumpkin soup that Best's father had stewed the night before, "why do they call it a lighthouse?"

Ben Douglas nearly choked on his soupspoon. "What did you say?" he uttered disbelievingly.

"The tall thingy," Dirk continued. "Why do they call it a lighthouse?"

"It has a light that warns ships," interjected Best, as his father looked too flabbergasted to elaborate.

"If you ask me," Dirk added thoughtfully, "it'd be easier if the ships 'ad their own lights. Now, that'd make sense."

Ben Douglas gently placed down his soupspoon. As Dirk Crenshaw was now living with them, he felt a sense of obligation to educate and enlighten him as if he were a son. "What if the moon didn't glow?" he began by asking. "If you had a lantern, do you think you'd see it in the sky by holding up the lantern?"

Dirk slowly nodded his head in an attempt to pretend he understood what he was being asked. "What kind of lantern?" he finally enquired.

"It doesn't matter – any kind of lantern. Do you think you'd find a dark moon with your lantern?"

"If the moon was lit up I could," answered Dirk, gaining confidence.

Ben Douglas tried to force his eyes down as they rolled upwards. "But then you wouldn't need the lantern, and that's the whole point –

the moon glows so you can see it. In the same way, a lighthouse glows so you can see it."

Just when Best's father thought he had made headway with Dirk Crenshaw, the Private replied, "I've got it!" as if suddenly struck by a revelation. "What if you stuck lighthouses on ships?"

As Best dried the dishes while his father washed, Ben Douglas leaned over and whispered in his ear, "God help us all if the Germans do make it down here!"

Growing up in the town of Yass, about two hundred miles inland south-west of Thurrough, Dirk Crenshaw had never seen a lighthouse, let alone lived on the site of one. All through his junior years at school he stood out because he was so innocuously untalented. His mediocrity made him popular. His parents, recognising that their son wouldn't survive in the real world of employment, enlisted him in the army after lying about his age. They hoped that the army could play guardian better than they were able to do, a role that had drained them both over Dirk's short but demanding life of eighteen years.

To be fair, Dirk Crenshaw's character wasn't without merit. He didn't have enough intelligence to recognise that he didn't have enough intelligence, but he was always willing to accept the advice and instructions of others. He was a giant lump of clay ready to be moulded by whoever had the biggest set of hands. Consequently, the army was a perfect match. After the outbreak of war, he was inducted into the "Coastal Watchdog Program" and posted to the coastal town of Thurrough because the army hierarchy were virtually certain that no enemy ships would be found within two oceans of the area. There, they could forget about Dirk Crenshaw getting himself into any real trouble. The army dealt with him in much the same way as his parents had – they sent him away and forgot about him.

*

FINBAR's eyelids flickered like a faulty fluorescent tube. If he felt discontent and irritated when awake, he often got no respite while sleeping. His fingers twitched by his sides as if they were typing letters on the sheet. In his dream, he was pumping his feet madly. Of course they were now missing, but he could still feel them. For some reason, which doctors couldn't explain, the phantom pain of his lost limbs had never left him, and was a constant reminder of what wasn't there.

The Lancaster groaned as she was finessed over the drop zone. After thirty-five missions, the pilot was almost a mechanical extension of the aircraft. When he moved, so did the wings. It was an intuitive union. Still, there was always fear. It was a healthy fear; the kind that warded off complacency and sat in the pit of his stomach like the morning's baked beans. No resistance expected. "Drop your bombs at eight thousand feet and get the hell outta there – the ground forces will move in behind your bombs – easy as shepherd's pie," said the briefing Sergeant.

The rear gunner whistled through the radio as flak started pelting the air around them like a meteor shower of shimmering metal that briefly came to life by the glow of the moon before twisting into the dark, only to fall back to earth lifeless.

"Scheisse!" suddenly cried the rear gunner, embracing one of the words he'd learned from their adversaries. "Something just fell from the wing!"

Finbar felt the plane shudder violently before it listed markedly to the left. He craned his head back and looked over his left shoulder only to see that the port wing had a massive hole in it where the ailerons and half the fuel tank used to be. By the time he had determined that the shell had ripped through the second Rolls Royce engine and taken out twelve feet of the leading edge, smoke was billowing into the main cabin from the fire that was consuming what remained of the wing. The death knell of hacking coughs started to splutter over the radio.

The plane began to dive. In an instant, the relationship between Finbar and the plane was over. "All crew bail out!" was his irrefutable order.

The Engineer sitting next to him showed no signs of leaving.

"That means you too, old chap," Finbar said smiling.

"I'm not leaving the cockpit till you do," he replied.

The Wireless Operator, Bomber, Navigator, Mid Upper and Rear Gunners made for the stern door as Finbar struggled to control the yawing aircraft, which was losing height rapidly.

"What about you, Captain?" yelled the Wireless Operator.

Finbar could barely talk, his teeth clenched as he attempted to control the plane, which had lost four thousand feet in less than three minutes and would be ploughing into the ground in just another three. "Just go!" he shouted above the struggling droning of the Merlin engines as he jammed his right foot hard against the rudder to prevent the bomber spinning into a steeper dive.

As his crew donned their chutes and prepared to open the hatch, he quickly adjusted the aircraft's controls. It was all done by reflex: outer port engine fully open to compensate for the huge hole in the port wing; starboard engines half-throttled; full aileron and rudder bias.

"It's jammed!" cried the Wireless Operator into the radio as he and the rest of the crew prepared to jump to safety.

"Get to the front!" Finbar yelled back as he wrestled with the rudder pedal, which was pushing back hard against his foot. He turned to the Engineer. "They're going to need you to open that hatch."

The Engineer realised where his contribution now lay. He pushed himself out of his seat and laid a comforting hand on his Captain's shoulder. "See you at dinner," he offered reassuringly before making his way to meet the other crew.

They fumbled through the thick smoke to the front hatch, struggling against the weight of their chutes coupled with the gyrating movement of the aircraft that was now at two thousand feet and showing no signs of slowing up, in spite of the fact that Finbar had the control column to his chest.

The forward hatch was positioned under the bomb turret. It was awkward for one crew member to get through, let alone six. The Engineer knew the delayed exit had chewed up valuable time. His crackled voice came over the radio, "Dan!"

The controls wouldn't stop fighting against him. Now, it was as if the plane was the enemy. So quickly had their union become corrupt. "Don't worry about me," said Finbar. He looked out to witness four of the crew jumping clear. He breathed a short-lived sigh of relief as their respective chutes opened. "Just get out!"

He looked at the instruments. The altimeter read eight hundred feet. Time to go. But as he unclipped from the seat, the plane went into an uncontrollable dive. Without him at the controls, the ailing Lancaster was too erratic for him to bail, and in less than a minute, the height was too low for him to jump. The crew's exit had robbed him of time. Four hundred feet. He fell back into his seat and attempted to regain control of the bucking aircraft. He ran his hand over his mouth and licked his lips. "Well, Liz," he said, "we're going in." And in an instant their relationship was restored. Finbar was now caring for an ailing friend – one who had saved their lives on many occasions by limping home in spite of having shreds torn off by jagged metal. He was no different to wounded soldiers who carried out their injured mates at the risk of their own lives.

It was just the law of averages, thought Finbar. They'd had a good run. As he looked out the window at the pock-ridden fields of France rushing up to meet them, part of him was glad he was still with her.

The Engineer quickly gathered in his chute and shoved it in his pack before scurrying into the nearby forest. He watched in awe as the flaming Lancaster continued to fly towards the ground, its left wing barely clinging to the fuselage. The plane was now at fifty feet and was hopping like a rabbit towards the deck. The moon lit the scene like a stage spotlight, and the Engineer could clearly see Finbar sitting steadfast in the cockpit, his gaze fixed intently ahead. Underneath him on the fuselage, the image of the plane's mascot sparkled in her bright red dress – a flaxen-haired Australian gal with her hand touching her cherry lips, which had been painted on by an artistic member of the ground crew. The mascot blew the Engineer her last kiss before the plane disappeared behind a treed ridge.

TIPODY wandered into the room just as the damp air created by the algae on the wall of the building next door wafted in the half-opened window. He found Daniel Finbar snoring loudly, his flight now over and his body laid up in a French army hospital.

Tipody approached the bed. The pages of the newspaper strewn on Finbar's chest crackled like flames, rising and falling as he breathed.

Something aside from the noise of the papers woke Finbar. This *something* he put down to his utter distrust for most of humanity. He was immediately alert. "What do you want?" he demanded. He had never seen the doctor before. He was gruff with those he did know, let alone those he didn't.

Finbar's abrupt tone almost unsettled Tipody. He briefly stuttered an answer: "I... just wanted to pop in to introduce myself."

"Who the hell are you then?" asked Finbar, gathering the newspaper pages together defensively as if they offered some kind of shield.

"Dr Richard Tipody." He reached out to take hold of the newspaper, thinking it was distracting the old man.

"What do you want?" Finbar asked again, refusing to give up the paper.

Tipody noticed a pile of newspapers tucked under the bed along with a fruit box filled with old books. "I see you're a reader," he commented stiffly. Tipody's efforts to be familiar were always stilted and laced with insincerity.

Finbar propped himself up. "When I'm not being bothered," he answered.

Tipody was hitting a brick wall. This consultation was not going well. Intellectual pursuits and fierceness of spirit were definitely not consistent with the VAE profile. He read from Daniel Finbar's file. "Your legs... you've lost both of them?" he asked, thinking that there might by a typo on the medical profile.

Finbar whipped back the starched white sheet to reveal his stumps.

He pointed to the other side of the bed.

Tipody nodded on seeing the two wooden prosthetics leaning against the frame of the cot. "How did you lose them?" he asked.

Finbar leant past the doctor to grab them both. "I didn't lose them. They lost me." He took hold of the leather straps and pulled the left one over his stump.

"It says they were blown off in the war," Tipody went on to say.

"Well if it says that, then it must be true," replied Finbar before taking hold of the right prosthetic to slide it over the second object of Tipody's curiosity.

Pelegranetti had no relatives that visited the Home, and the nurses confirmed that Finbar didn't either. That was a good sign. But Finbar was far too spirited. Even after the passing of years, he was like a caged animal. He would make hard work of it. There was enough resentment, noted Tipody. That was always a workable tool. But there was also too much unbridled aggression, which would never allow him to trust. Finbar certainly qualified as a loner, with marked anti-social behaviour. But such anger would make him impossible to break. Tipody left Daniel Finbar alone to his dreams.

CHAPTER SIX

IN the afternoon heat of summer, Best often walked along the beach on his way home from school where he would take off his shoes and socks and skim his feet along the shoreline, letting the waves scurry over his toes. It wasn't unusual for him to run into Dirk Crenshaw, especially on sunny days. Dirk had decided that his task of observing the ocean for enemy ships was best done lying on the sand at sea level, far away from the woozy height of the Thurrough Lighthouse lamp room.

"Hey, Best. How was ya day?" Dirk would ask him.

"Pretty good," Best would answer. "What about yours?"

Dirk always looked down at his tanned forearms admiringly. "Not too shabby. Not too shabby."

After conversations with Father Cruickshank about men who came back from the war much diminished both physically and mentally, Best concluded that Dirk was the luckiest man in the whole war. He was certainly the laziest. And that was what began it. Dirk was too idle.

It was a spring day in late September. Best remembered it by the change in the weather. He recalled all time by the weather. The early morning chill, which accompanied winter and made the sand cold under his feet, had all but gone. The cooler westerly winds, which blew off the mountains, had weakened and turned more north-west, to be warmed on their journey to the coast by the inland plains. By the afternoon, the north-east sea breezes were tugging at land, and had all but put a stop to the westerly. Summer could not only be seen coming; it could be felt and touched.

Best struggled to keep his balance, his hands stuffed inside his shoes. He leaned in towards the sand mountain, not wanting to fall backwards which would see him topple down the steep dune and wind up in a ball of sand at the bottom. He took a deep breath then pumped his legs furiously to combat the sliding terrain and the forces of gravity. Sand spilled from his feet as he sprinted towards the top. He collapsed at the summit, still holding his school shoes. Hunched on all fours, he breathed long and hard. His calf muscles cried out. He lowered his head, careful not to inhale the sand.

After a minute of recovery, he stood up. The onshore breeze collided with the sheer walls of the massive dune. It was compressed upwards, ruffling Best's mop of sun-bleached hair as he stood on the pinnacle. Aside from the top of the Lighthouse, he considered this view the best in Thurrough. From the peak of the one hundred and twenty-foot high dune he could see Botany Bay to the north, and still further, the budding city of Sydney. To the south, he could see the treed rim of the Royal National Park – one of the world's oldest. To the east was the expanse of the Pacific Ocean. He could make out the swirling water and twirling eddies created by the barely submerged jagged outer Thurrough reefs, which stretched in broken sections the entire length of the beach only a few miles offshore.

He stood alone, isolated in this almost desert-like environment, surrounded by majestic sand dunes on either side as they trailed off along Thurrough Peninsula. He spied Dirk Crenshaw in the distance, his back set against the rocky wall of the northern headland on which the Thurrough Lighthouse was perched like a statue. Best jumped up and skimmed down the surface of the dune, almost surfing the wave of sand created by his movement. He repeated the same manoeuvres as he negotiated two smaller dunes before reaching the beach and the sunning soldier.

Dirk was sitting up, rubbing his chin with his hand in much the same way as Best had seen his father do if he had to solve a problem. In fact, Dirk had seen Ben Douglas do this and had decided to adopt the gesture. Best's father stroked his beard; Dirk stroked three lonely hairs that had struggled to sprout amongst several festered pimples.

It looked to Best as if Dirk was thinking. It made an impression on him. Best's father told him that Dirk was as thick as two short pier-planks and that thinking was an exercise that Dirk did little of.

Best glanced around nervously on noticing that Dirk wasn't wearing a shirt. "You're not supposed to do that."

Dirk stood up. "Do what?"

Best pointed to Dirk's crumpled brown shirt strewn amongst the sand. "Be out here... without a shirt on."

"Why not?" asked Dirk.

"It's not allowed," answered Best as he retrieved the offending clothing and handed it to him.

Dirk looked back on the township of Thurrough, which could be seen three miles down the banana bend of Thurrough Beach. "No one comes up this far."

"It's against the law," said Best.

"What law?"

"The law that says you can't take your clothes off."

"I didn't know there was a law against that. How're ya s'posed get changed then? Like at night... into ya pyjamas?"

"It's only on the beach. You need to be dressed on the beach." Best looked down at Dirk's towel, which had been folded up into a makeshift pillow.

"Not much going on out there," Dirk remarked pointing out to sea, trying to play down the fact that he had been sleeping most of the afternoon.

"See anything?" asked Best.

"Nope," Dirk answered as he began stroking his chin again. "But I've been thinking."

Best was happy for him. "Great."

"Yeah," replied Dirk, thinking how great it was that he *was* thinking.

"What about?" asked Best.

Dirk picked up a handful of sand. "This."

"Sand?"

"Not really sand. Not sand."

Best was confused. The feeling didn't surprise him. He was often confused when talking to Dirk Crenshaw.

Dirk carved a wide circle in the sand with his finger. "What's 'ere without sand?"

"What do you mean?" asked Best.

"If I was to take out all the sand, what'd be left?"

"I don't know…." Best considered the infinite grains of sand. He'd never really thought about it. The beach was a constant, and unlike the ocean, never changed, never became angry.

Dirk shook his head. "Neither do I, but I'm gunna find out."

"How?" asked Best, curious as to how Dirk could find the answer to this question by sleeping most of the day.

The lengthening shadow of the lighthouse began to bear down on them. It stretched further out over the beach as the sun descended to the horizon. "I'm gunna build a hole," said Dirk as he buttoned up his shirt.

"What kind of hole?" asked Best.

Dirk formed a circle with his arms. "A big one. A really big one."

It sounded exciting to Best. "How?"

"With a shovel." Dirk began imitating the motion of digging. "I'm gunna dig down as deep as I can. Who knows – I might end up in China?"

Best was sceptical. "You think so?"

"It's on the other side of the world ain't it?"

"It'd be a pretty long way though," added Best so that Dirk wouldn't be too discouraged when he just reached seawater, which had always been Best's experience.

Dirk's enthusiasm was not to be curbed. "It might take some time."

"Lucky you don't have much to do," Best remarked, trying to be positive.

Dirk's eyes lit up. "That's right! I need to keep an eye on the ocean – but I could do that and build the hole at the same time. Couldn't I, Best?"

"Sure you could... How do you build a hole?"

"By taking what's in the hole out of it."

"Is it still a hole when there's stuff in it?" Best asked, needing clarification on this strange concept.

"Yeah, it's just a full hole," Dirk answered assuredly.

"Wow. There must be holes everywhere?"

"Are you kiddin'? They're all over the place. You just can't see 'em because most of 'em are full."

Over the next few days Dirk began his task. The new job of digging a hole didn't much alter his daily schedule. He'd get up at ten o'clock, heat up the leftover porridge which Best had cooked for himself and his father three hours earlier, and if the sun was out, grab his towel and go to the beach. Sometimes he walked the three mile shoreline down to Thurrough where he'd gawk at girls wearing neck-to-knee bathers, swim, sunbake, gawk at girls wearing neck-to-knee bathers, and then go for a swim again. It was relatively easy for him to insert digging a hole into such a flexible program, and once he started he found that he actually enjoyed the exercise. He enjoyed feeling useful.

AS Best approached the Hole sand flew out and stung him in the face. "Hey?" he shouted.

Dirk looked up. "That you, Best?"

Best spat the grains from his mouth and nodded.

"Sorry about that. Didn't see you."

"How's the Hole?" asked Best.

"Getting bigger."

"Can I come in?"

"Sure. Jump down."

Best flung off his shoes and socks and hopped in. As he stood on the bottom, his feet were covered in water. He ran his hand up the sandy wall. His fingers could barely reach the rim. As he and Dirk stood toe-to-toe, he noticed that it was surprisingly dark; neither sun nor sound were able to poke themselves into the recesses of the ditch.

"This is a great hole," remarked Best.

"I was lucky to find it," responded an elated Dirk Crenshaw. "I might've dug in another place and not found a hole this big."

At age twelve, Best couldn't fault Dirk's logic.

Four days later, Best came home from school to find Dirk sitting at the top of the Hole staring despondently inside while running grains of sand through his fingers as if through an hourglass.

Best looked over his shoulder and peered into the Hole. He couldn't see the bottom. "What's the matter?" he asked.

"I'll show you." Dirk sounded disillusioned. He leapt into the Hole. "Now go down to the water's edge and look back this way."

Best sprinted to the shoreline. The water crept over his feet and licked his toes like Bill Cruickshank's Labrador. He looked back.

"See anything?" came Dirk's muffled yell.

"What did you say?" answered Best.

"Can you see anything?!" Dirk shouted louder.

Best studied the sand heaped up around the rim of the Hole. "Like what?"

"Like me?"

Best looked harder. "Nope."

"Just what I thought!" echoed Dirk in distress.

Best ran back to the Hole and looked down. Dirk had strategically carved footholds into the sand walls, which he had lined with seaweed to provide traction to make climbing out easier. He bounded out like a monkey scaling a coconut tree.

Dirk sighed. "This's as far as it goes."

"The Hole stops?"

"Nope, it can get much bigger."

"Then why does it stop?"

"Could you see my head from the water?"

"I couldn't see anything."

Dirk collapsed to his knees and punched the sand with clenched fists. "And I couldn't see the ocean! And if I can't see the ocean how am I s'posed to see if there's enemy ships out there?"

Best sat down alongside Dirk. Neither of them spoke for over five minutes; both just gazed transfixed into the blackness of the Hole.

"Dirk," began Best, breaking the long silence. "Have you watched the Council blokes building that tower down the beach?"

"What about it?" Dirk asked.

After the drowning of several swimmers weighed down by onerous swimming costumes, Thurrough Council had been forced to build lifeguard towers. This was to be the first of a series of seven that would eventually line the length of the beach.

"Have you seen how many fellas are doing it?" asked Best.

"How many?" asked Dirk.

"I don't know exactly, but it seems like an awful lot."

"You don't say?"

"And there always seems to be at least two walking around not doing anything telling the others what to do. Maybe you should get someone to help you?" The truth was, Best's summer holidays were coming up and he wanted to be a part of Dirk's exciting quest.

Dirk sprang to his feet. "Maybe I could get someone to watch the ocean for me?"

"Or get someone to dig the Hole and you watch the ocean because you know how to watch it properly, all army-like," Best added.

Dirk nodded knowingly as he reflected back on his brief training, which consisted of a Sergeant sticking a forty gallon barrel in the middle of a football field and asking Dirk if he could see it from his position on the sideline. When Dirk said that he could, the Sergeant shook his hand and said, "Good luck in Thurrough!"

Dirk frowned. He had second thoughts. "I kinda like diggin' the Hole though."

"Maybe you could teach someone else to watch the ocean?" hinted Best. "Would that take long?"

Dirk glanced at his watch. "The only thing is, I'd need a forty gallon barrel and a footy field."

Best was going to say that he didn't think those items would be entirely necessary, but he did not want to diminish the importance of Dirk's obviously intense training. Beside, Dirk was having a hard enough time taking the hint that Best wanted to do the job.

"Maybe I could do it?" Best finally suggested.

Dirk's face lit up. "And I could keep digging!"

Best looked out across the ocean. "I can see right out there."

"The other thing is," added Dirk sheepishly, "the army needs me to send monthly reports to 'em about what's 'appening."

"What kind of reports?" asked Best.

"Well, if I've seen any suspicious looking ships."

"Have you?"

"I don't think so." Dirk acted like he had just came up with a great idea. "Maybe you could write the reports – especially if you're taking me job as the lookout?"

Best couldn't see the harm in it. "Do I need to write anything special?"

"Nah… you can write though?"

"Yeah, I am twelve," answered Best, offended.

"So can I," Dirk hit back somewhat emphatically.

Best never doubted he could.

"I just wanted to let you know," Dirk went on to elaborate, "just 'n case you thought I was gettin' you to write me monthly reports 'cause I couldn't write 'em me self."

"I didn't think that."

"As long as we've got that clear."

"Got what clear?" Best thought nothing was ever clear when talking to Dirk Crenshaw.

"What I said."

"About what?"

"About not being able to write."

"Who? Me?" asked Best, becoming increasingly confused by what should have been a simple conversation.

"No – me," elaborated Dirk.

"I never said you couldn't write."

"Nah," Dirk responded. "You didn't… Sorry."

CHAPTER SEVEN

BEST wriggled uncomfortably in his wheelchair. Although dull soreness had replaced the knife-jabbing pain that was constant in the days when he still walked, it sometimes revisited him like an unwanted guest when he shuffled into certain positions to relieve the numb pain. That was his dilemma: put up with mild, prolonged pain, or experience it quickly and abruptly like a searing poker iron. Best never complained about his aches. He never complained about anything. Like most things in his life, he had learned to get used to them. Best hadn't been able to walk since his ninetieth birthday, which was about the same time he missed the two-inch step down from the bathroom, resulting in the catastrophic collapse of the entire bottom half of his body. When the bones eventually collected themselves into some semblance of order, the agony he experienced when walking sentenced Best to a wheelchair for the term of his natural life. His left hip was broken beyond repair. More specifically, the doctors said the knob on the end of his left femur had all but disintegrated. The doctors also told Best that he was too old to have a hip replacement operation. Best agreed. He didn't want to be operated on. The idea of being put to sleep didn't sit well with Best. He'd seen dogs put to sleep, then buried in backyard rose gardens.

At ninety-four Best had spent the last thirteen years living in the Thurrough Nursing Home. His room was by no means grandiose: it was the view that made it. Location, location, location, Charley Pelegranetti would mutter. Charley had obtained a room with a similar vantage point by offering its occupier a stack of unused bingo cards. He had first tried to extend this invitation to Best. "Best," spruiked Charley, "for this week only – twenty cards. That's right. Twenty cards." And although with the passing years Charley had lost none of his auctioneer banter, it was lost on Best. He never played bingo. The only pastime that Best dabbled in was solitaire. It was an easy choice, a game that didn't rely on another's input, and an accurate metaphor for the extent of his social interaction.

The magnificent ocean view notwithstanding, Best's room was small. It had space enough for an iron bed, whose lead-based white paint would flake off during periods of high humidity; a beige plastic injection-moulded chair from Sebel; and a cheap chipboard pine dresser that was slowly disintegrating back into the wood chips from which it was formed. These were the few possessions that Best was allowed. He didn't mind. Any more furniture and there wouldn't have been enough room for him. There were no paintings on the walls. What need did he have for paintings that fell far short of the views they were trying to represent? He had all that outside his window. There were also no photographs on the dresser. They had long since faded with the sun, and eventually disintegrated; nothing to give any clues into his past, nothing of the lives that had once been intertwined with his. That's what made him such a tantalising choice.

Best's favourite pastime was watching the waves rolling into Thurrough Beach. They didn't have to be all that big, although it was more exciting when they were. But Best didn't really care. It wasn't as if he had anything better to do. He would watch any time the surfers were out. He got to know the local surfers from afar, just by observing the colours and patterns of their surfboards; like Lucy Pemberton's nephew, who would often roll up in his orange Kombi van stuffed with his quiver of surfboards. Best tracked the progress of these lives by the frequency of their surfing. They usually started around ten years old, surfed furiously up until they left university or got a trade, and when jobs and family began to take over in their late twenties, slowly drifted off the beach into dry dock. Some surfed into their thirties, but not many. Best had seen a lot of that.

Forty years ago, surfers used to ride huge heavy boards that looked like planks. In the seventies, they went to smaller ones, and then in the nineties some of the older surfers went back to big ones again. Best witnessed the surfboard wheel come full circle. He had never tried surfing. He would have liked to, but when he was a boy there was no such thing. When Best was a boy most of the world's future surfboards were still growing in forests somewhere.

By mid-morning, just after Best's second cup of tea, the beach started to get busy. The apartment blocks lining the beach had sprouted where dandelions and clover once had. On a hot summer's day, Best could hardly see the sand for the swarms of people. It was different in the nineties: women went topless, and men wore genital-hugging Speedos. Best hadn't been disgusted, though. He had been amazed. And it made him laugh. He thought the beach was one big circus, which he could view for no admission.

On long hot summer days when the Home's air-conditioning was gasping, like half its residents, for breath, Best's eyes often strayed up towards the northern end of the three-mile beach. If he craned his neck slightly out the window in order to escape the edge of the red brick apartment block next door, he could just see the old Thurrough Lighthouse still standing proud on the tip of Thurrough Peninsula. Thurrough Council had condemned it somewhere back in the late seventies and the Heritage Trust had promptly stepped in and rated it an "A" level sight, signifying that under no circumstances could it be torn down: it had to fall down naturally or be restored. A local group of heritage lighthouse-loving folk formed an organization called, "The Friends of Thurrough Lighthouse," with their number one mandate being the rejuvenation of the lighthouse to its former glory. But as their friendship stopped short of donating the large sums of money sorely needed for its restoration, it sat in a state of disrepair.

Thurrough's new lighthouse, which had almost been made redundant by the on-board GPS systems now on most ocean-going vessels, was situated on the roof of the Telford Towers' twenty-storey hotel. It was unmanned: all done by computers. Best didn't know much about computers, but he knew enough to understand that they couldn't change light bulbs.

RICHARD Tipody took a faint interest in Best as soon as he saw him staring what Tipody perceived to be vacantly out of his window, and a more pressing interest as soon as he spoke with him.

"So, Mr Best," began Tipody while noticing the complete absence of framed photos. That was a good sign. No immediate close family.

"It's just Best," clarified Best.

"That's what I said," Tipody replied frowning. He hated to be corrected by senile old prunes.

"No – you said Mr Best. It's Best. Just Best."

"I was being courteous, Mr Best," Tipody added, attempting to take the upper hand in the conversation.

"If I called you Mr Richard, would that be being courteous?" asked Best, genuinely confused, thinking that he may not be up-to-date with the latest social conventions.

"Your first name is Best?" Tipody asked incredulously.

Best nodded and smiled a gummy smile. He hadn't put his false teeth in since waking from his afternoon nap. In his haste to locate them, he had accidentally knocked over the glass that housed the dentures, sending both them and the antiseptic concoction all over the linoleum.

Tipody laughed boorishly. "What kind of a name is that?"

"Mine, I guess," said Best, taking no offence. "It's short," he added.

"Short for what?"

"Best," replied Best, thinking it was obvious. "It's a short name."

Although Tipody had often reminded himself that this process would most likely be a long and protracted one, he couldn't help feeling slightly exasperated. "What's your second name?" he asked.

"Second name?" asked Best.

"Your surname?" added Tipody. "Everyone's got one."

"I did have one of those... but that was a long time ago."

Tipody read from the sparse details contained within Best's resident file. "It says here it's Douglas?"

"If it's in there, that must be it then... What is it?"

"Douglas," Tipody repeated.

"Has a nice ring to it," Best responded. "Might start using it again... What was it?"

"Douglas!" Tipody answered irritably, not sure if Best was having a lend of him.

Best hadn't heard that name in years, and was enjoying hearing it for the third time in as many seconds.

Tipody glanced down at the file. "It also says your date of birth was January 18th 1904. That would make you ninety-four years old?"

"I guess so."

"Does your hip cause you pain?"

Tipody approached Best and clumsily pressed his hand against Best's left side.

Best jerked. "Only when you do that."

It was of constant amusement to the elderly how their bodies became public property as they grew older and more infirm.

Tipody commenced writing notes.

Best looked out the window. "Three fins give stability and manoeuvrability. And two fins give manoeuvrability but not much stability. And one fin gives stability without much manoeuvrability."

Tipody looked up. "What are you talking about?"

Best raised his withered hand and pointed to the beach. "Surfboards."

Dr Richard Tipody smiled sinisterly. Best Douglas was perfect.

"What was that name again?" asked Best.

"What name?"

"That name. My surname?"

"Douglas!"

"And yours, Richard?"

"Tipody. Doctor Tipody."

Best turned to look outside. "Four fins... I don't understand four-fin surfboards."

"Do you get many visitors?" asked Tipody.

"Well... this week there's been the new paperboy, and... you."

"Would you mind if I dropped in on you again?"

"What for?"

"To talk."

"What about?"

"Just about things."

Best yawned. "If you like." He stared out the window. "Wouldn't like to think you'd be going lonely on my account."

AFTER the doctor had gone, Best noted the lull in the weather pattern. The Southerly had just about petered out. By tomorrow, the north-easterlies would be sucked in from the sea in the vacuum caused by the hot air rising inland. But now, the sea was revelling in the wind's absence. The swell had been whipped up by the southerly change to a relaxing four feet. By the late afternoon there were banks all along the beach where waves were breaking consistently, offering an attractive face for surfers to rip, shred, or carve – depending on their style.

The surfers who religiously followed the weather patterns started arriving one by one. When the surf was good, Best would watch them for hours. He'd watch until the last one hopped out of the sea when there was almost no light left; sometimes an hour after sunset. That's why Best often had dinner in his room, so he could watch the surfers.

Best had no trouble locating the paperboy. His board was tucked uncomfortably under his arm, dwarfing him, almost twice his size. The gap between the boy and his board could be measured in generations – the board was from the early seventies, the boy a product of the nineties. But Best admired the paperboy's attitude as he placed the board gently on the sand to carefully apply a coat of wax to its yellow deck. Once the ritual of applying wax was completed, the paperboy took the weathered black leg rope and attached it to his left ankle. Best realised that this meant that the paperboy surfed with his right foot forward. Best raised his eyebrows. The paperboy was a "goofy" footer. Best hadn't seen many of them around.

The paperboy carried the board to the shore and pressed it into the white water so that the cascading foam around the deck would cool the soft wax in order to harden it. He then waded in the ocean until up to his waist, hopped onto the board and began to paddle furiously out past the breaking waves. Even though the water temperature was a mild twenty-two degrees, the remnant breeze from the southerly front was cool on the surface. The paperboy had worn a springsuit to protect his trunk from the cold. It was a good decision, thought Best.

The paperboy soon found himself amongst the other surfers in the line-up. The break wasn't too crowded. Tomorrow it would be crowded. That's when the remaining three-quarters of the surfing population would discover that conditions were prime, having been informed by the quarter that had already had one liberating surf without telling them how good it was.

It took about ten minutes for the paperboy to feel comfortable amongst the other surfers who had already been surfing the break and had established their rank. Best had studied how surfers interacted in the ocean. Time at a break bred feelings of superiority over those who had put in less time. The new boys out had to catch a few good waves in order to earn the respect of those already in the line-up.

The paperboy took off on a wave. It was a nice gentle wave with a forgiving face that peeled off smoothly. Despite his clumsy board, he rode the wave halfway to shore. Best caught himself cheering inwardly, almost raising himself out of his wheelchair in the process.

Just when the paperboy was about to paddle back out into the line-up to battle the increasing gaggle of surfers for his next wave, he looked behind towards the windows of the Home. He stuck up his hand and waved. Best had almost forgotten about their pact. For a brief moment, Best thought the paperboy was waving to a group who happened to be walking along the shore at the time. But they didn't wave back. Best quickly undid the latch on his window and flung it open. He waved his right arm madly. The paperboy returned the distant signal then paddled back out to the break. He caught twelve more waves that afternoon. Best saw every one of them, and after each ride the paperboy never missed the opportunity to wave up at Best. Following the last wave, as the paperboy was making his way out of the surf, Best felt an overwhelming feeling of joy. He didn't quite know why.

CHAPTER EIGHT

DIRK Crenshaw stood there grinning like the idiot that Ben Douglas thought he was. Best did his utmost to explain the situation. His father looked puzzled, mainly because he was puzzled. He had just spent all day taking apart and lubricating the revolving apparatus that rotated the lighthouse lens in preparation for an approaching southerly storm. He was in no mood for ambiguity. He eyed his son sceptically. "Let me get this straight. You're asking me if I can let you watch the ocean during your school holidays so he," he pointed accusingly at Dirk Crenshaw, "can dig a hole on the beach?"

Best nodded enthusiastically.

"You see, Mr Douglas," Dirk interjected, "I can't dig the Hole and watch the ocean at the same time. It was easy enough when the Hole was small. But now it's getting bigger."

Best's father gave Dirk a strained look. "What's with this Hole anyway?" he asked. "Why for the love of Saint Peter do you need to dig a hole?"

"I dunno..." Dirk's face brightened. "Maybe 'cause it's there?" he answered, thinking the reply was remarkably profound.

Best's father sighed heavily. He was going to explain that before a hole is dug, it is in fact not there, but what was the point?

"It would give me something to do during the school holidays," added Best.

Best's father folded his arms. He always tried to keep his son busy. He had a Protestant Work Ethic in spite of being blindly Catholic. Maybe a bit of responsibility would do Best good, he thought. "All right," he finally said, thinking that Dirk would get sick of digging after only a couple of hours of hard toil. "Does he need any special training to watch the ocean?" he asked.

"Nah," Dirk bleated.

Ben Douglas sighed. "That's what I thought."

Dirk set up a chair on the beach next to the Hole. He told Best to sit there and yell out if he saw any enemy ships. Dirk then jumped into the Hole and began shovelling sand. As the discarded sand mounted up along the rim, Best would spread it out with a rake while keeping one eye on the ocean. After a few weeks, when Dirk was too far down the Hole to hurl the sand out, they devised a system whereby Dirk placed it in buckets, and when full, Best would haul them out of the Hole using a rope and pulley. After emptying the buckets, he'd then lower them back down and the whole process would begin again. They spent hours each day working in this fashion, with Dirk taking an hour off for lunch and to sunbathe, something that the shade of the Hole prevented him from doing.

LATE Thursday afternoon in the third week of their venture, as Best was helping his father refill the lamp kerosene before sunset, there was a thunderous knock on the lighthouse door. As his father was testing the clockwork mechanism that powered the rotating apparatus, Best hurtled down the fifty-three stairs to greet the unexpected visitor. Although he was hardly puffing when he reached the bottom, being well used to the descent, he had to summon considerable energy to budge the large oak door. It groaned deeply as it laboriously levered off its heavy rusting hinges. Suddenly, a giant hand clasped the edge of the door and swung it open as if it was made of cardboard. As the door hit the outside wall of the lighthouse, Best was instantly eclipsed by a large man wearing a grey flannel suit that was at least one size too small for him, and holding a notepad while beads of sweat dripped from his huge brow, blotting the paper.

The man stuck out a huge mitten-like hand. "Harry Heath's the name. I'm a reporter with *Daily Chronicle*." He tried deciphering his own handwriting smudged on the notepad. "Is Tirk Brenshaw here?"

"Dirk Crenshaw?" clarified Best.

Harry Heath strained to read. "Yeah – that must be the bloke."

"He's not here. But my dad's upstairs."

"Can I go up and see him?"

"Sure. Follow me."

By the time they reached the lamp room, Harry Heath's suit looked like he had been swimming in it. It clung to him like a wet bandage, while his red bloated face seemed ready to explode. Best's father grabbed one of the collapsible pine chairs and quickly thrust it under Harry Heath's backside. Harry, who was breathing too hard to mouth an audible response, nodded appreciatively.

Best's father reeled back in surprise. "For all that is good and decent! If it ain't Harry Heath!"

Heath kept nodding.

Best's father dragged Best over to gaze on the shattered form of the reporter. "Harry Heath was one of Australia's toughest forwards," he elaborated excitedly. "He could ram his way through an opposing team's pack like a Mallee Bull."

Harry Heath had been one of the country's most uncompromising Rugby forwards. It was said that he didn't feel like he had played a game unless someone had broken a nose – and it didn't have to be someone on the opposite team. In one famous incident, his own

Captain gave instructions to Harry Heath's fellow forwards to crack him one on the beak when they packed down in the scrum; a tactic designed to fire him up against the opposing team, whom he assumed were the perpetrators. He had the dubious distinction of having broken his nose a record fourteen times. Needless to say his proboscis was a shell of its former self. The tip of it pointed straight at his left ear, while both nostrils hadn't filtered oxygen since his first test match. After his illustrious football career was over, he was offered a job as a reporter, even though all he had written for years had been his autograph. With time, his reputation and star appeal soon faded and he ended up with a small column right next to the daily crossword, although he did learn to become a decent writer and had more intelligence than he was ever given credit for.

Best's father remembered Harry Heath's games as if they had been played yesterday. "I saw you crash tackle that pommy Faraday in the deciding test of 1909!"

Heath smiled. Most of his teeth were gold.

"Faraday still has one of me teeth embedded in his skull," chuckled Heath, who had just started to feel like he might pull through after his torturous climb up the lighthouse stairs. "He tells me it's the only tooth he's got that aches!"

Ben Douglas got Harry Heath to scratch his autograph into the brass of the rotating apparatus right next to the manufacturer's stamp. Heath did so magnanimously, if a little shakily. Best's father stared at the name proudly. It didn't look like Harry Heath's name, and others would never be able to recognize it. But Best's father didn't care. He knew Harry Heath had written it, and that was good enough for him. Every time that lighthouse lamp rotated, one of Australia's toughest forwards would go round with it.

Harry Heath went onto explain that he had come to see the Hole. He might not be able to smell much, he joked, but he did get a whiff of the unusual every now and again.

"What hole?" asked Best's father.

"There's this giant hole down on the beach," Heath wheezed. "Your son has been helping dig it."

"Oh, that hole." Best's father couldn't understand the fuss. Best had talked little about it. "I don't know if it's anything to write about."

When they got down to the beach, Best's father saw how mistaken he was. In just under a month the Hole had grown to over forty feet deep with an opening the size of a small bedroom.

Harry Heath whistled.

"Sweet virgin mother of the living God!" exclaimed Best's father.

Suddenly they heard a voice from deep inside the abyss. "'Ello up there!"

Best leant over the Hole. Forty-foot down, Dirk Crenshaw's grinning face could barely be seen.

"Winch me up," Dirk's voice echoed up to them.

Best began the arduous task of helping Dirk to the surface. The task consisted of turning a circular drum that wound up a rope on the end of which Dirk appeared, four minutes later. Dirk rubbed the sand off his body.

"This is Harry Heath," Best announced triumphantly.

But the introduction was wasted. Dirk didn't know who Harry Heath was. He looked to Best's father for an explanation. Best's father didn't notice. He was glaring at the Hole, speechless.

"He was once a famous footy player," added Best, who could see that his father was in no shape to articulate a reply. "Now, he's a reporter. He's come to see the Hole."

"A Hole?" Best's father finally uttered. "A Hole? This thing's a bloody chasm!"

"What's a chasm?" Dirk asked, beaming like a proud parent.

Harry Heath pointed to the Hole. "This thing."

Harry Heath's article was nothing out of the ordinary, but it did reveal that he still had many loyal followers who had been waiting for him to write about something interesting, and if not interesting, something unusual. And the story of Dirk Crenshaw's Hole was certainly that. The day after the article was published, several simple-minded Thurrough locals walked up the beach to check out the Hole. They were suitably impressed. As far as they were concerned, it was much bigger than the Blue Mountains. Dirk was surprised. The Blue Mountains mustn't be as impressive as he'd always thought. It didn't seem to matter that not one of those locals had ever been anywhere near the Blue Mountains, one of New South Wales' more spectacular natural wonders.

The third day after Harry Heath's article had appeared, over one hundred people gathered by the monster Hole. There were so many that Best could hardly see past them to watch the ocean. They all jostled around the circumference, and some came perilously close to tumbling in, just so they could see Dirk hard at work digging. By the time they had all drifted off, Best was exhausted from having to explain the origins of the Hole countless times. Not that it was a long and complex tale. It basically consisted of Best saying, "He decided to build a Hole." It was just that he had had to say it so many times to every new passing observer.

"Dirk," began Best as they both sat with their legs dangling over the edge of the Hole sipping lemonade. "You know when you go to the circus and you pay to watch the trapeze and the lions and stuff?"

"Yeah?"

"What if we charged people to see the Hole?"

Dirk's eyes widened. "You mean money?"

"Let's say we charged everyone who came today a penny."

"We'd have a hundred pennies!"

"About nine shillings."

"Struth!"

"We could have a ticket booth. Maybe a high one so I can sell tickets and watch the ocean at the same time?"

"And I can keep digging the Hole."

"But you need to have a better story about your Hole."

"Whatdoyamean?"

"When people ask why you're digging it, they seem to lose interest when I tell them you don't know."

"But I don't know. It's like those guys who climb big mountains. Why do they climb them?"

"They usually say because the mountains are there."

"Then how 'bout we say what I told your dad," Dirk announced triumphantly, as if he'd cracked a complex mathematical formula. "That I'm digging it because it's there!"

Best was going to explain that technically a hole isn't there before it is dug, but he didn't want to confuse Dirk Crenshaw anymore than he was already. "And people will always want to come back because the Hole will always be getting deeper," added Best, changing the subject. "How long do you think you could dig for?"

"Let's see – I'm nineteen now. I reckon another sixty years."

"Just think how big the Hole'd be then!" interjected Best excitedly.

"And how much money we'd make!" added Dirk, equally as enthusiastic. "If a hundred people come by every day – times that by one penny, then times that by three hundred and sixty five, then times that by sixty... What's that come to?"

Best was good at maths, but this sum was beyond him. "A lot."

The next day Best and Dirk had cordoned off the top of the Hole. Best was situated in a crudely constructed ticket booth made from two wooden ladders and a plank, on which he perched. As Best sold tickets and watched the ocean, Dirk dug happily in the Hole at his usual pace. Three hundred people later, Best and Dirk had made over a pound.

"Do you think we can charge more?" asked Dirk.

"I think so," answered Best.

And so the price went up to thruppence; a margin that allowed Best and Dirk to print a brochure, giving visitors some background information on the Hole, which Dirk insisted contain a biography of himself and his achievements. It was a very small brochure.

By the end of the second month of digging, Dirk was earning twice as much from the Hole as he was from his army pay, and Best was making more than in his wildest dreams. As Harry Heath had stumbled upon a riveting curiosity, his editor allowed him to expand on the original story. He made the next article a human interest one. He gave some background material on Dirk's unimpressive life before the Hole, comparing it with his growing post-Hole popularity. He also interviewed Thurrough Council's General Manager, Kent Lawrence, who described the Hole as the "best thing to happen to Thurrough!" Harry Heath's story was given second page status, and as news of the Hole spread, people began coming from over three hundred miles away just to see it. Within six months, families were planning holidays around taking in the Thurrough Hole as a major sightseeing attraction.

CHAPTER NINE

JAMES Perry stood hunched over the waters of Botany Bay and sucked in frigid air between dry heaves. The dusk chill of winter lay over the bay like a wet blanket. The howling of the bloodhounds grew closer. As he looked into the still water, he didn't recognize his emaciated reflection. He thought he had been hungry when he was apprehended for stealing loaves of bread in order to help feed his family after his father's death from tuberculosis. Within eighteen months, however, he had found himself on a distant continent twelve thousand miles away. Now, he was starving. As supplies had not yet reached the New Land, conditions were dire six months after the arrival of the First Fleet. Failed crops, and those too young to reap, had further exacerbated the situation. Most of the convicts were well undernourished. What little sustenance remained was distributed by priority, meaning that free settlers got in first. But even they were not immune. Most were afflicted with a general malaise brought on by lack of nutrition, which hung over the future of the colony like a veil of uncertainty. James Perry didn't care much about the settlement, nor the settlers for that matter. All he knew was that he was going to die if he stayed in bonds much longer.

He nodded to the desperate wretch beside him. They had no need for talk or debate, though they had once been full of words. There was only one thing left to do – swim for it. Both plunged into the winter waters of Botany Bay in states of near deliriousness and began the arduous task of making for the other side, three miles across.

The thrashing sound came first, then the blood-curdling screaming. He couldn't stop. He had to keep going. But somewhere buried inside him, the once soft heart, which the penal colony had hardened and hollowed like pumice stone, skipped a beat. He turned and began treading water as the blood slick spread out towards him. The air returned to a deathly quiet. As he saw the pallid face bobbing up and down in the water like a cork, he realised there was nothing he could do. His fellow escapee's legs had already been gnarled from his body leaving just a floating torso. Perry kicked with all his might and hoped that, if he was also to be attacked, it would happen quickly, painlessly.

It was one thing to think of death approaching in the distance like a tall ship on the horizon which never seemed to get any closer. But it was another to have it shoot up from the depths suddenly and with ferocity. Now, in the middle of the Bay, he would have preferred starvation. He continued to propel himself through the water madly, angrily, and bitter at having wound up in this horrific predicament.

The shore was tantalizingly near. His clothes, although too flimsy to protect him from the cold of winter, were now waterlogged and tugging at him like a begging child. He knew he was going too slow, and represented an easy prey for such a skilled predator. Then, in just a few strokes, the shore was looming. It was within reach: just another couple of hundred feet. Surely, he wouldn't be denied now? But his lot in life had been cruel up to this point. He wouldn't let himself expect it to be otherwise now. His teeth clenched, waiting for that lethal lunge.

After what seemed an age, he dragged himself out up onto the southern shores of Botany Bay, known only as the "other side" by the chained members of the colony, and collapsed, too exhausted to consider his good fortune. As his spent body lay spread-eagle on the sand of Thurrough Beach, his eyes squinted up at the orange sun, which had just about dipped below the western horizon.

He heard them approaching but was too depleted to move. The group circled him gingerly as if they were performing some kind of ritualistic dance. They were being cautious. They had seen the damage that the *firesticks* could do and weren't about to take any chances. After several minutes, one moved closer and aimed his spear at the middle of Perry's forehead, blocking out what light remained.

"I'm not armed," Perry gasped while attempting to lift his hands to reinforce the point.

His gesture only served to make them more agitated and several more spears bore down on him. He spied the Elder standing back from the group staring at him while running his bony fingers through a long, greying beard that shot from his face in all directions, lacking the discipline that comes from grooming and mirrors.

After several minutes, the nimble old man danced over to Perry and waved the spears away. He looked down on him thoughtfully. He yelled something out, and two young women appeared with water and herbs. The Elder pointed to Perry and the women hesitated. He pointed again, this time more insistent. "Noranigibah!" he yelled, startling Perry.

At the Elder's cry, one of the girls quickly knelt beside Perry and began wiping the sand from his face with the soft back of a rubber plant leaf, which she folded and used as a funnel to run fresh water into his mouth and through his hair. As she cupped his head in her hand, he studied her kind face – unblemished black skin with pink healthy lips and teeth as white as seashells, lacking the pasty, gaunt appearance of the settlers. He was also struck by the fact that she was topless. She smiled nervously. Satisfied that she was doing what was expected of her, the Elder moved away leaving her to finish ministering to Perry.

She quickly ran her fingers lightly over Perry's body, and after determining that he was uninjured, motioned for two males to come forward and help lift him under each armpit, raising him to his feet. They guided him back to their camp, which was nestled well within the forest of eucalyptus trees that, in the late 1700s, covered Thurrough Peninsula like plush carpet. Unbeknown to Perry, he had stumbled upon the Gweagal Aborigines who formed part of the Dharawal tribe that inhabited the coastal regions south of Port Jackson, or as it much later became known, Sydney Harbour.

INTERNED inside the penal colony at Port Jackson, Perry had never awoken to the sound of waves breaking on the sand. Each wave created its own crescendo, and the noise, coupled with the rising sun poking its rays through the slits between the bark striations of his hut, woke him much more gently than the watch-soldier's dawn bugle. He sat up only to notice that he was wearing nothing but a hair-woven girdle around his waist. He was about to search for his convict clothing when the girl who tended to him on the shores of Botany Bay suddenly appeared at the entrance carrying a wooden bowl laden with berries and fish. His face went bright red when he saw that her breasts were exposed. She sensed his discomfort, but didn't understand it. In summer months, the tribe barely wore clothes at all, and only used possum-fur coats in the winter or when nights got colder. She motioned for him to come outside and they sat cross-legged facing each other, while Perry tried to look everywhere else but at her chest. She became self-conscious. She was at the age where tribal women usually married, and being the Elder's daughter, had many suitors. She misinterpreted his lack of focus on her as indifference.

She offered him the red berries. "Lilly Pilly," she said.

"Lilly Pilly?" he repeated, and looked her in the eyes for the first time.

She smiled broadly, happy to have gained his attention. She nodded furiously. "Lilly Pilly."

He laughed, and forgot about her nakedness.

She broke off a piece of fish and offered it to him. He knew it by the colour. It was a luxury food within the colony.

"Salmon," he said.

"Salmon?" she repeated.

He suddenly felt hungry and took the morsel eagerly. As he chewed, she raised her hand towards his mouth and surprised him by plucking a small bone out from between his lips. She held it up to show him and frowned as she clenched her throat with her hand. She coughed incessantly to enforce her point.

"Thank you," Perry said. "Choking... yes, I understand that."

She craned her head closer to him and gently touched his cheek beneath the right eye. She then pointed to the sky. She then touched her own cheek and pointed to the bark of the hut.

Perry looked up. The sky was a rich shade of azure. He touched his own cheek. "Blue," he said. He then reached out and touched hers. She gave a short whelp of joy. "Brown," he remarked.

She touched his cheek again. "Blue," she responded, extracting pleasure from feeling his soft skin.

Having finished feeding him, she left quickly to show the other tribal members that associating with the white man was a mere chore instead of an enjoyment. But the truth was she was already in love with him.

Over the course of the next few weeks, she appeared at the same time every day to feed Perry either fish and figs, or a viscous concoction that Perry could only describe as "mashed grubs." During these meals, he began to talk about his life. She would laugh as he gestured with his hands, attempting to explain how he had ended up thousands of miles away from where he was born. As crazy as it seemed, Perry could have sworn that she understood him, as if she possessed some sense that enabled her to interpret his language. His emaciated state prevented him from exerting himself too much and he began to look forward to her visits, as she was his only contact with anyone from the tribe. And as the winter temperatures began to manifest and the cooler south-westerlies blew across Botany Bay, she donned a possum-fur coat to keep warm. Now she was clothed, Perry could relax. When he thought about it, he realised that he had not been with a woman in some time.

He had decided against bartering with some of the female convicts in the colony, who were hungry enough to trade their virtue for scraps of food. But the constant sight of her brown breasts had become more than he could bear. For a time, the sexual tension between the two of them was diluted.

As his strength improved, he was permitted to move around as he wished, but was never invited to eat with the tribe. At odd times, a male, or several, would appear with their spears and stare at him. Then, content that he was suitably tame, they would leave again. Each day when he awoke, he expected the tribe to go on the move, leaving him behind. But it never happened. The common perception amongst the colonists was that the black people moved around freely and somewhat aimlessly. The pastoralists who set up farms inland, where the soil was richer and better for sowing, constantly complained about the Aboriginals, who not only trespassed on their land, but would also help themselves to growing crops. How dare they graze on land that had been granted to the settlers by the authority of the Empire!

But the Gweagal never left. Perry came to realise that there was nothing nomadic about them. When she took him into the gorge of the upper reaches of the Port Hacking River and he saw the elaborate tidal pool that the Gweagal had constructed out of sandstone in order to trap fish on the out-going tide, he began to understand. There was no reason for them to move on when they had access to an abundance of fish and other foodstuffs in the heavily timbered waterways of Botany Bay and the Port Hacking River. Perry came to realise that the Gweagal people were quite unlike their inland relatives, who were forced to roam by a lack of food resources. The Gweagal's roaming was to come much later, and only from force and necessity.

After several weeks, the girl extended her hand to Perry one day and led him to the more salubrious shelter of the Elder, which was situated on higher ground and adjoined a cave whose walls were adorned with scenes of tribal life depicted in clay paint.

The Elder motioned for Perry to sit and gestured that he should cross his legs like himself. He smiled and pointed to the girl. "Noranigibah!" he said.

Perry looked at her.

"Noranigibah," she mouthed softly.

Perry pointed to her and smiled. "Noranigibah?" he asked.

She nodded her head enthusiastically. She had never been so presumptuous as to introduce herself without the consent of the Elder, her father.

The Elder laughed. Perry laughed. He then stuck out his hand to shake the Elder's hand, startling him. "James Perry," he said. "That's my name."

"Jamesperri," repeated the Elder, then motioned for Noranigibah to do the same.

"Jamesperri," she echoed.

"Yes," Perry affirmed. "Jamesperri!"

The Elder asked Noranigibah to serve Perry some moth grubs, which the tribe considered a delicacy. He spoke animatedly and waved his hands about as if trying to impress upon Perry the importance of their meeting.

Two days later, Perry was again brought to the Elder's dwelling. The Elder handed Perry his convict garments and gestured for him to leave. The rest of the tribe formed a kind of receiving line and directed their spears to indicate the direction that Perry should take. He glanced across at Noranigibah. She had tears streaming down her cheeks. Perry did not want to leave. He took his convict clothing and threw it in the nearby fire. He then dropped to the ground, crossed his legs, folded his arms, and lowered his head in a gesture of supplication. Out of the corner of his eye, he saw a faint smile on Noranigibah's face. She spoke excitedly to the Elder. The Elder danced over to the other tribal men and gestured for them to surround Perry. As the Elder took hold of a boomerang, the other men pinned Perry to the ground. The Elder forced Perry's mouth open, and with one swift blow, knocked out one of Perry's front teeth. The Elder then picked up the tooth from the dirt and yelled out in jubilation. In unison the other male members also joined in the cries. It was at that moment that Perry noticed they were all missing a front tooth. As blood spilled down his chin, Perry realised he had just been initiated. He was now a fully-fledged member of the tribe.

Attracted by their simplistic lifestyle and kindness, Perry became one of them, and since there were no mirrors here, which were vainly positioned throughout the households of the wealthier settlers, he soon forgot that he was different. In time, he even began to pick up on the nuances of the language, much to the surprise but delight of the Elder and Noranigibah.

Once a week, Perry was summoned to the Elder's cave to share food. When Perry started fishing with the tribe, he would even bring his own offering to the Elder, usually small bream. The Elder would politely accept the gesture, but would shunt the fish away to the children in order to enjoy more prestigious fish, such as salmon. Perry didn't mind. He would become a better fisherman in time.

The Elder pointed to the wall of the cave. Perry noticed the new drawing depicting a tribe fleeing from colonists with rifles.

"They soon approach?" asked the Elder.

"I'm afraid so," responded Perry.

The Elder rubbed his hand through his beard. This was a totally new predicament for him. He had always looked after the tribe, settled them in an area rich in food resources, created harmony by making sure all members had a role; some were fishermen, some were weavers, some were painters, and others built canoes and shelters. But this encroachment was like nothing they had ever experienced before, even from other tribes.

"I will do what I can," offered Perry.

The Elder grabbed Perry by both arms. "Son," was all he replied.

The Elder was acutely aware of the proximity of the settlers, and saw in Perry an ally, one that might help protect them due to the colour of his skin. He wasn't to know that Perry himself was an outcast, and knew firsthand just how cruel some of the settlers could be.

Initially, Perry kept his distance from Noranigibah out of respect to the Elder. But he couldn't help staring at her, and she always returned his gaze. The time they spent together when she nursed him back to health had created a special bond between them, and he couldn't shake off those feelings, which were almost the kind that develop between nurse and patient. At first, Perry thought that those emotions might dissipate when he joined the tribe and was not reliant on her company alone. But they didn't.

One late afternoon in November when the temperatures were beginning to rise again, Perry took a dip in the ocean. Noranigibah was bathing near the shore further along the beach. He waved to her and she began to wade towards him. Wanting to lessen the distance of her swim, he began to walk towards her in the knee-deep water. As he approached, he noticed that her black skin was glistening in the setting sun, and as the water trickled down her body, its fresh touch caused her nipples to become erect. Perry gulped. He looked around. They were totally alone. The other members of the tribe were preparing for a corroboree to celebrate the beginning of the summer. He felt compelled to reach out and wring the seawater from her hair. As he delicately pulled it back behind her head, it revealed the absolute splendour of her face. He gazed into her brown eyes; he had never seen anything quite so beautiful. She moved closer to him, her chest just kissing the hairs of his. He could no longer contain himself. He pulled her forcefully into his embrace and they collapsed together onto the seashore.

The Elder was not ignorant of the blooming relationship between his daughter and Perry. He detected the awkwardness of their affection any time they were together. He summoned Perry and Noranigibah to the cave. They both stood embarrassed, wondering if their secret encounters had been exposed. The Elder pointed to the wall. In rich red was the mural of two people holding hands. One of the subjects was portrayed in a brown pigment, the other white. "Noranigibah!" said the Elder. He grabbed her hand and placed it in Perry's. "Jamesperri!"

Ten days later, Jamesperri and Noranigibah were united in a tribal ceremony. Soon, their union had produced twins: Joseph a boy, and Taranna, a girl.

Oftentimes around the tribe's campfire, Noranigibah shared with Perry and their young children stories of the Dreamtime whilst Perry, in turn, recounted stories that enthralled them about characters called Noah, Moses, and Jonah. Noranigibah always smiled at how animated Perry became when telling of Jonah being swallowed by a fish. The tribe had seen fish that big. But the children's favourite stories were those of celestial beings like the angel Gabriel who, like giant seagulls, would swoop down to Earth from time to time to intervene in the affairs of mankind.

Noranigibah took hold of the children and quietly stole away one January morning while Perry was still sleeping. They trekked over the giant sand dunes and followed the shoreline until they found the clay pits. Due to its moon-white colour, this natural deposit was one of the Gweagal's sacred sites, and was unique to the region. They would use this clay for a variety of applications ranging from canoe-bottom weatherproof liners through to ceremonial paint, tinted with berries.

Inspired by Perry's tales, Noranigibah sat Taranna and Joseph down and together they formed their father's birthday present. As the sun pushed its way off the horizon, they smuggled the clay back to their home, and when the morning of his birthday dawned, presented him with a painstakingly-fashioned angel figurine made out of the brilliant white clay with the letters, "JP" crudely inscribed in the bottom. Perry looked lovingly at his family and held the statue tight against his chest. To Perry, the angel sculpture came to represent hope, and the belief that, no matter how desperate circumstances appeared to be, he should never give up. It was this attitude that had forced him across the shark-infested waters of Botany Bay, into the tender hands of his Aboriginal wife; a tale he often recounted to his children with a good deal more amusement than when he had actually lived through it.

CHAPTER TEN

THE vines crept up the outside of the sandstone facade and fluttered against the windowpane, casting shadows into the room that slithered on the dull sheen of the walls like the hair of the Medusa. Dr Fiona Chalice's nose balked at the dust that clung to the sombre curtains like algae. She examined the old timber panelling. It had been painstakingly fixed below the picture rails that ran along every wall, only interrupted by the window that looked out into the University Quadrangle. The timber, she thought, would have crackled nicely inside the woodstove back on the farm. The dank stench of age seemed to permeate through the entire room, and even the ornate cornice and skirting board could not redeem the space. This office was in drastic need of a woman's touch, she concluded. She was briefly amused by this example of what happens when something is left entirely up to males.

Richard Tipody could barely contain his excitement. He pulled out an enlarged photo of Best, hastily snapped without his false teeth, and displayed it proudly as if he were holding aloft a trophy. He passed the image to her. "The subject's perfect," he began. "Physically restricted… mental state questionable. No history of dementia… No immediate family… No visitors."

Fiona Chalice frowned. She glared at the photo that, to her, represented Tipody's ridiculous presumptuousness. She was astute enough to recognize that her appointment to the Geriatric Advisory Committee was a politically motivated one. She was the token female. "What do you mean his *mental state questionable?*" she asked.

"His general knowledge is abysmal," Tipody replied. "Doesn't even know what day it is. Doesn't even know his last name!"

Fiona Chalice leaned back on her chair. She studied him closely, finding his oily hair repulsive, and something vaguely familiar about his leering manner. "Dr Tipody, have you ever taken, as medical researchers are wont to do, extended leave for a period of time – maybe for six months – maybe even for a year?"

Tipody slowly nodded his head. He wasn't sure what she was getting at.

"Weren't there ever any times during those sabbaticals," she continued, "where you wondered what day it was? I know I've had such moments of not being bound by the constraints of time… Moments of freedom where time no longer has any demands."

Tipody thought Fiona Chalice was way out of her league. A medical practitioner who set up her practice in an aging country town before specialising in Gerontology was not qualified to make objective decisions with regards to the elderly. She was far too attached to them. Besides, he thought – ogling her long cherry hair, tied back and highlighting a strong jawline and plum-like cheekbones, a hint of gloss accentuating wind-blown lips – with such childbearing hips, she should be at home having babies. A fleeting feeling of lust came over him. The years had been kind to her.

"What are you getting at?" asked an increasingly curious Dr Mangos, who was a lecturer in Social Medicine at the University of New South Wales, where the subject was a kind way of letting impressionable medical students know that, after they graduated, they would become highly paid public servants relying on the Government to support them.

Fiona Chalice adjusted her glasses, which made her brown eyes appear even larger than they were. "I'm merely pointing out that just because somebody doesn't know what day it is, doesn't mean their life should be cut short for lacking such knowledge."

Dr Mangos nodded and she interpreted this as his acceptance of her explanation, although he was more enamoured with her than her reply. He had been recommended to the GAC based on the fact that he didn't want to be recommended, and was certain that the VAE Bill would never be passed, which would result in a waste of all their time and efforts. However, in Fiona Chalice's presence, he was beginning to think that it had been worthwhile after all.

Dr Flavian Broad faked a smile, and his numerous collagen lip injections made him look like a groper. Having established himself as a relatively well-known geneticist who was manipulating horse DNA in order to clone the ultimate racehorse, he was on Tipody's side, and didn't disguise it. "Let's try not to get emotional now, my dear," he remarked condescendingly.

She glared at him. "There was nothing emotional about the statement. It was one of fact. Unless, perhaps, Dr Broad, you've always known what day it's been?"

"As a matter of fact," he answered, turning to Tipody and grinning like a hyena, exposing PVC-like teeth. "Unlike you, I don't remember a time when I didn't know what day it was."

Fiona Chalice narrowed her eyes. She was smarter than the three of them combined, a fact that Tipody was starting to suspect. Now in her early forties, she had long since overcome the male medical bastion that once judged her on her looks rather than her ability. She wasn't about to let Broad, who she thought had become a pompous caricature of himself through his numerous cosmetic procedures, escape from such a foolish admission. She went after him with all the restraint of her cattle dog. "Interesting… When's your birthday?"

"My what?" asked Broad, not all that confidently, having detected a hardening in her voice.

"Your birthday? When were you born?" she continued.

"Second of July," he replied slowly, deliberately, almost warily.

Tipody feigned a yawn. "I fail to see how this possibly has any relevance."

"Me neither, but I'm sure it does," echoed an amused Mangos, who was starting to enjoy his position on the GAC.

She ignored Tipody, but was encouraged to get some support from Dr Mangos. She wasn't concerned as to Mangos' motivation. She smiled blithely at him, and knew by his goofy expression that she had at least won him as an ally.

"What year?" she asked, pressing on.

"I'm older than I look, my dear," responded Broad quickly, letting down his guard, his ego nearly inflating to the size of his lips.

She stifled an involuntary chuckle. She had worked on cadavers that looked more alive.

"Nineteen forty-two," announced Broad triumphantly as his face cracked into a million lines created by years of fake tanning.

"And I suppose you remember that day perfectly?" she suggested, smiling genuinely for the first time, which caused the dimple in her chin to become more pronounced, and for Dr Mangos, made her natural beauty even more unique and increased his infatuation. "I suppose as soon as you were expelled from your mother's womb you knew precisely what day it was?"

Mangos gave out a hearty laugh. Dr Broad did not find things quite so amusing. His grin vanished involuntarily, although he tried hard to fight the process, which resulted in a nervous twitching at the left side of his mouth. "Of course I didn't," he spat back frowning, his forehead remaining wooden due to his regular schedule of botox injections.

She sat back and delicately crossed her legs, now extracting an unexpected enjoyment from their exchange. The claustrophobic timber panelled walls and grey ceilings now gave way to the breathtaking architecture of the University Quadrangle, which she suddenly noticed beyond the heavy curtains. She turned back for the sting. "Then perhaps your life should've been terminated right then for lacking such knowledge."

There was a brief silence as the welt appeared.

"What point are you trying to make?" interjected an annoyed Tipody, who was suddenly confronted with the awful reality that she *was* smarter than the three of them combined.

"My point is," she concluded, now leaning forward and staring at Tipody intently, "don't cheapen your stance with abstract theories using lack of knowledge as a basis for assisted death. If we approved that then we'd have to eliminate half the world's population."

"Maybe we should," Tipody suggested.

Fiona Chalice smiled. "Then, Dr Tipody, we may not have the pleasure of listening to the rest of your discourse."

Tipody paused, fighting back the derogatory remark on the tip of his tongue.

"I'm not suggesting this subject as an actual candidate," he explained, attempting to backtrack. "I'm merely trying to help formulate our understanding of what a suitable candidate might be."

The rest of the presentation was decidedly less heated. Dr Richard Tipody revealed why he considered the Best Douglas profile fit for assisted death. At the forefront was Best's lack of observable productivity. Tipody pushed the productivity line, for therein lay the Government's justification: how could they continue to support a percentage of the population who were no longer productive? Fiona Chalice was quick to remark that those very people had been taxed all their working lives in the belief it would eventually be returned to them in the form of pensions.

"I can concede that many aged aren't economically productive members of society," she added. "But is that the measure of one's right to life? There are millions of unemployed in exactly the same position, much younger."

"Unemployment isn't a permanent state," responded Tipody. "Age is… The point is this subject has no living relatives. He has virtually no social interaction with his peers at the nursing home. His Voluntary Assisted Expatiation," Tipody relished using the term that he had coined, "would have little effect on life around him. His absence would barely be felt."

Fiona Chalice ran her delicate hand over the bound document as though she was dressing a wound. "The Northern Territory enacted the Euthanasia Bill to deal with medically terminal conditions. What you're proposing is indiscriminate extermination. Any VAE bill must be limited by application… After all, we're talking voluntary here. Not selected termination. Perhaps you should remember that."

Tipody looked the other way. Voluntary only got rid of those who wanted to go. What of all those senile shrivelled vegetables that should be the first to go but lacked the state of mind to volunteer? That was where he was going. He wanted to drop the voluntary, and Fiona Chalice was astute enough to perceive it.

CHAPTER ELEVEN

FOR the first time in two weeks, Best had Nurse Selby shower him in place of the self-inflicted sponge bath he often awkwardly performed on himself. The indignant feeling of sitting in a plastic chair with the wrinkled flab of his bare bum pushing through the slots in the seat like potato through a masher had long since left Best. Even so, he attempted to make mundane conversation to somehow distract her from comparing his ninety-four year old body with that of her twenty-four year old boyfriend.

"The water's refreshing today," commented Best as she lifted his left arm to run the wet sponge under his armpit.

"Ah huh," she responded kindly, knowing that Best could not remain silent during such an intimate exercise. "The water restrictions have been lifted," she explained. "You can stay under as long as you like."

Best smiled. "Not too long... don't want to be more wrinkled than I am already!"

Nurse Selby laughed freely and Best felt pleased he could still elicit that type of reaction from someone. She helped him put on his favourite pair of chocolate-brown trousers and his antique suspenders, even though his pants were not about to fall anywhere due to his confinement to the wheelchair. She left him sitting by the window glancing frequently at his old Seiko, even though his arthritic left hand hadn't subjected the automatic timepiece to enough movement to keep it operative. He thought it was three o'clock, but it was actually two. Time seemed to be slipping by; he tempered his excitement. The paperboy was just being nice, humouring an old man.

Right on three, the paperboy stood by Best's door. "Can I come in?" he asked.

Best smiled – a huge smile. "You don't have to ask. Nobody ever asks. They just come on in."

"That's why I asked. I've seen that lanky doctor barge into your room."

Thinking about Richard Tipody was tiresome. "You got some great waves yesterday," remarked Best, changing the subject. "You ride that old stick of yours pretty well."

The paperboy's face almost went as red as the bottom of his board. It was a proud, deep red; the kind of reaction that a father's praise would evoke.

"So you're a goofy footer, eh?" said Best.

"You sure are observant."

All visitors to the Home were required to wear an identification badge. "Let's check out the surf," suggested Best as he squinted in an attempt to read the paperboy's ID.

The paperboy ironed out the creases in his shirt to make his name easier to see.

But it was no use. Best could not decipher the small italic print. He rubbed his brow. "I did have glasses... I'm not sure where they got to," he explained, looking half-heartedly around the room.

The paperboy smiled. "That's okay. Nobody calls me by my real name anyway. Orie's what they call me."

"Orie?"

"That's my nickname. Short for Orion."

"Like the constellation?"

"I guess so." Orie laughed. "Maybe I'll be a star one day!"

"Get your skinny backside in here, boy!" abruptly came the shout from the room across the corridor.

Orion grimaced. "Oak Legs Finbar... I'd better get going."

"Going surfing today?" asked Best.

"Too much homework." Orion grabbed his newspapers. "See you tomorrow."

And Best did see Orion tomorrow, and the day after that. In fact, Orion began to stop and chat with Best every weekday, spending as much time with him as Oak Legs Finbar would tolerate. It usually cost Orion a smack on the ear from Finbar, but he put up with it. Best appreciated his surfing. A gentle cuff on the noggin was a small price to pay. It didn't matter that Best never bought a newspaper.

One Saturday, Best's phone rang. He was so startled he almost jumped up out of the wheelchair. His phone never rang. He looked at it in bewilderment. Who could it be? Best had only heard about unsolicited calls from other residents. He'd never had the pleasure of experiencing one himself. Even salesmen didn't call him. He reluctantly picked up the phone. "Best here," he announced officially.

"It's Orie."

"Orie? What's the matter?" asked Best, still disorientated to be answering the phone.

"Nothing much. Just going surfing. Thought I'd let you know."

Best felt an instant wave of relief and calm pass over him. Courtesy of his conversations with Richard Tipody, he'd recently experienced the return of constant feelings of anxiety. "Great!" he responded enthusiastically. "I'll look out for you."

"And I'll wave," added Orion, thinking that it was an important detail.

So began the ritual. Before Orion went surfing, he would phone Best.

And when Orion stopped by on his paper route, they'd talk about all the waves that he had caught. Orion loved the way Best's face lit up whenever he spoke about one of his waves, and how his good right arm would make all kinds of gestures showing how Orion rode up and down the wave's face.

One afternoon, when Orion was on the way out of Best's room, just about to do battle with Oak Legs Finbar, Best took him gently by the hand. "Do you remember when I told you I'd never surfed?" he said softly.

Orion nodded.

"Well… I've started."

Orion smiled. He understood completely. Best had become as much a part of his surfing as his old red and yellow board. He put his arm around Best. "We're good surfers."

"Yes, we are, Orie. Yes, we are."

CHAPTER TWELVE

AS the sand dunes swallowed the late afternoon sun, towering over the northern end of the Thurrough Peninsula like the Ancient Pyramids, Galbraith Telford remained at the lip of the Hole. The fading light was dispersing the mass of curious onlookers. He shook his head as he stared down into the void. It never ceased to amaze him how chance seemed to favour the dimwitted. Dirk Crenshaw was becoming a minor celebrity. Young women who once frowned upon him now surrounded the Hole to watch him dig through fluttering eyelashes. And, as those tourists who came to view the Hole had begun spending money at local businesses, Dirk Crenshaw was also being lauded as an economic genius. At a time when the War was acting as a sedative to the country's economy, Thurrough Shire, in complete contrast, was booming, and the Hole, for all its pure silliness, was the stimulant. The price of land in Thurrough was climbing at a time when the fervour of War was pushing the values of real estate in all other areas down. As major landholders, the Telford family had reaped rich rewards, and for that Galbraith Telford felt a strange affection for the Hole. But he needed more. The Telfords had always craved control. Complete control.

As Galbraith Telford flicked the sand from underneath his spats, he heard the approaching sniffling. Kent Lawrence let out a forced cough, as if needing to announce his presence even further. He need not have bothered. Galbraith Telford knew exactly where he was. To him, life was a game of chess, and success came from knowing on which squares all the other pieces had positioned themselves.

"Who would've thought this ridiculous venture by that imbecile Crenshaw would've resulted in this," said Lawrence, forced by the pressure of silence to say something. "The best thing to happen to Thurrough," he added without thinking.

Galbraith Telford struck out like a viper to clench Lawrence's wrist. "The Telford family's the best thing to happen to Thurrough! You'd do well to remember that before you go spruiking to fat, has-been reporters or you'll be walking to work!"

Lawrence winced. "I was only making press," he offered defensively as the vice-like grip on his arm slowly relaxed.

Telford plucked his handkerchief from his breast pocket and rubbed his hands with it so vigorously it was as if he was sanding wood. He detested touching others, and rarely shook hands, considering it a grossly unhygienic practice. "This Hole's getting out of control. It's about time Thurrough Council stepped in," he remarked as he neatly folded the handkerchief and returned it to its pocket.

"But the Mayor's content to let it alone to run its course," answered Lawrence, still not in tune with Telford's manic personality.

"The Mayor? The Mayor!" Telford berated him, getting steadily louder with each utterance. "I own the bloody Mayor!" he screamed, attracting the attention of those onlookers who were leaving the beach.

Kent Lawrence glanced around nervously. "I'll make the recommendation."

Galbraith Telford nodded contentedly as the hot blood of aggression slowly drained from his face. "Oh, and Lawrence?" he added.

Kent Lawrence leaned towards him, hoping to contain their conversation to their ears alone.

"I've come across some vintage bottles of French Shiraz that were smuggled out of Paris just before the War," he said, narrowing in on just one of the many vices in which he held Lawrence's ethics. "Shall I arrange for them to be delivered to Chambers?"

Lawrence nodded like an obedient puppy. He loved lapping up such luxuries, knowing that they never seemed to make his benefactor happy. The truth was that none of the baubles of success satisfied Galbraith Telford. He was only close to contentment when he had achieved control over his environment. And the Telford family had always controlled the destiny of the Thurrough Shire. They virtually owned Thurrough Council and had done so for decades. The two institutions were synonymous, and to the residents of Thurrough, it was sometimes hard to tell the difference.

*

WHEN Curtis Telford stepped off the gangplank inside Port Jackson he bore none of the scars of confinement. His hands remained smooth and supple, and free of the chains that had bound his convict shipmates. His voyage to the New Land was entirely voluntary. Adventure had been the motivation, and the idea of building a dynasty in a colony whose youth would welcome such an attitude. The Telford family had been established in Yorkshire for over two hundred years, during which time they had built their fortune from sheep grazing. The middle of three sons, Curtis could have lived off the wealth created by his forefathers whose landholdings were amongst the largest in Britain. However, not content to wallow in the idleness of his class, which he was embarrassed to read disparagingly portrayed by the Bronte sisters, who were also raised in Yorkshire, he was determined to duplicate the labours of his ancestors and create the same legacy on a foreign land.

He left England with enough funds to secure some property and the rest of his possessions condensed into a leather duffle bag, which his mother had tearfully presented to him as a parting gift.

The British possession of the New Land under the Latin motto, "terra nullius" – a rhythmical and euphemistic way of disguising the much plainer, and harsher English interpretation, "land belonging to nobody" – was causing massive conflicts with the nobodies: the Aboriginals. And the Gweagal were feeling the brutal sting of this policy as the Crown granted white settlers ever increasing portions of the land on which the Gweagal had always relied to sustain themselves.

Jamesperri became the Elder that Noranigibah's father dreamed he would. He often served as a mediator between the tribe and encroaching settlers. Recognizing that his skills in handling these peaceful negotiations were far more valuable than his incarceration would be, the colony had granted him his freedom. His reputation for solving disputes without the use of violence grew to the status of legend amongst the settlers. But even he could not protect his tribe from a new, stealthier form of onslaught.

When Curtis Telford arrived in Australia, he was granted a sizable allotment of Crown land, due to the standing of the Telford name, as well as funding to procure non-grant land. These were both offered in return for his pledge to convert all his land into sheep grazing territory. This would not only provide wool for the growing colony, but also for export back to England. The Crown land, and the additional parcels that Telford acquired, happened to take in most of what would later be known as Thurrough Shire: a vast oasis punctuated by towering sand dunes, majestic eucalyptus trees, and a labyrinth of waterways.

Although Telford's primary objective was to farm sheep, he soon discovered another use for the land. As the thick forests needed to be culled in order to open the land up for sheep, he quickly saw an opportunity to supply timber as building material for the growing colony. With the proceeds gained from selling this lumber, he was able to purchase even more land, and so his landholdings increased.

As a result of this large-scale logging, the Gweagal were forced to migrate further south. Jamesperri took his tribe as far as the Port Hacking River, but was reluctant to cross the river into what would later be known as the Royal National Park for fear of causing conflicts with tribes already ensconced there.

As Curtis Telford acquired more land, the time required to survey its area increased significantly. Curtis Telford's land spanned south from the tip of the Thurrough Peninsula to the northern opening of the Port Hacking River, then five miles west along the Port river before heading north again to meet the Botany River five miles west of its mouth: a land mass of fifteen thousand acres.

Curtis Telford accompanied the Crown's surveyor as he set off to map Telford's land. Telford had slowed his mount to a trot when he spied a long funnel of smoke emanating from a clump of Sheoaks. As he got closer, he saw that the smoke was rising from a crudely constructed chimney propped on top of a shanty dwelling near the riverbank. He hopped down from his horse and took his rifle from its saddled casing, raising it to his shoulder. He moved cautiously towards the hut, which was made from a mixture of clay and eucalyptus leaves; the type of housing only Aboriginals possessed the expertise to construct. He stuck his rifle through the opening and moved slowly inside. As his eyes adjusted to the dark, he saw Taranna Perry hunched over the cot of her father with her brother Joseph tending to a broth nearby. They swung around, startled at first, but then seemed disinterested, as if sapped of vigour and any urge to mount a protest. They knew they were beaten. Smallpox had annihilated their tribe. By 1820, the Gweagal were backed up against the southern waterway with nowhere else to go as the culling of trees extended southwards. Jamesperri's decision to cross the Port Hacking River came too late. The Gweagal were soon decimated along with the trees. By the time most of Thurrough's oldest trees had been converted into new housing for settlers, almost three-quarters of the Gweagal had died from smallpox.

Curtis Telford lowered his rifle. "Do you speak English?" he asked.

Joseph moved slowly across in front of his sister as if to protect her. He was not ignorant of the way white men looked at her. He held up his hand, armed with nothing but a wooden ladle. "No further," he simply said.

Telford thought about raising the rifle again, but didn't. "I mean you no harm. I was riding and saw smoke." He pointed to the contained fire encircled by sandstone that had been set into the dirt floor. "This is my land."

Joseph went back to the pot and scooped a shallow serving into a clay bowl then handed it to his sister. She tried to bring it to her father's lips but he seemed unable to drink it. As she pinned her long, brown hair back over her ears so that strands would not find their way into the soup, Curtis Telford was struck by how beautiful she was.

"Our father," she finally said, surprising Curtis with the clarity and tone of her English, "is sick."

"Our mother, our family, our tribe," interjected Joseph, "is gone… most left at Skeleton Cave. The sickness has taken them." Skeleton Cave was at the tip of Thurrough Peninsula. It was one of the locations where the local Aboriginals left victims of smallpox who could not be saved. Noranigibah had died in her husband's arms.

"Smallpox," Curtis Telford quietly remarked to one of his wranglers as he entered the hut. The man was quick to retreat on hearing the word. As Curtis studied their complexions, he recognized the drawn face of the man lying on the cot. "Your father's Jamesperri?"

Taranna nodded vacantly.

"He needs more attention than you can give. I will send for a cart. You can come to my house. Gather your things."

He watched as Taranna Perry delicately embraced the angel that she and her brother had made for their father on his birthday. She expressed no interest in anything else.

"Is that all you wish to bring?" he asked in astonishment.

"There is nothing else," she replied.

Taranna Perry nursed her father for another three days in the decidedly more comfortable surroundings of Curtis Telford's guest quarters. Between bouts of extreme deliriousness, James Perry hummed Aboriginal chants interspersed with old English hymns. Late one night, he grabbed her tightly by the arm, and craned his neck towards her.

"It won't be easy for you, my daughter," he said. "I'm sorry to leave you... Carry the clay with you. It was my hope."

In the early hours of the morning, the disease finally claimed James Perry's life, at the age of fifty-three, as it had countless Aboriginals whose immune systems had not been conditioned to prepare for this foreign attack.

Taranna bent down and scooped the paste from the clay bowl and applied it to her face along with red ochre. She handed the burnt wood to Joseph who applied the charcoal to his face and body. As Taranna sat by the body of her father, wailing, Joseph held the knife-like slate he had fashioned for the ceremony and made three slits along his chest, which quickly seeped blood.

Thinking that Joseph was about to do himself mortal harm, Telford approached him.

Taranna waved him away. "Please leave him. When his wounds heal, his mourning will be over."

Curtis Telford retreated and watched on curiously as incoherent shouts of mourning gave way to broken stanzas of the Lord's Prayer.

Curtis Telford insisted that James Perry's body be burned, and that their bungalow home be consumed by fire in order to aid in eradicating the disease. "You may stay and work here," he invited Taranna. "You can perform house duties and live in the servant's quarters." He turned to Joseph. "How well do you know this land?"

"We are this land," he responded.

Telford nodded his head, pleased with such a seemingly arrogant answer. "Good," he replied. "Good."

Joseph Perry had little choice but to be absorbed into Curtis Telford's work force. Telford was intent on using Perry's intricate knowledge of the region rather than set him loose in a harsh colony where he would be persecuted for being of "mixed blood."

When he mentioned to Joseph that he wanted to graze sheep on the land, Joseph laughed.

"What are you laughing at?" asked Telford.

"This coastal land is not for your sheep."

"How do you know?"

Joseph bent down and dug his fingernails into the ground. He pulled out a clump of dry grass. "What do you see?"

"Grass," replied Telford.

"What kind of grass?"

"By no means Yorkshire grass, that's for certain."

"What do you see where the grass was?" continued Joseph digging his nails further into the ground like a soldier crab.

"Is it sand?"

Joseph Perry nodded his head. "All sand as far as the eye can see. Sand on clay."

Curtis Telford let out a huge sigh.

Instead of importing the large head of sheep he had intended, he brought in only twenty head. Within six months all of them had died either of foot rot or insufficient water. The coastal land was no good for sheep. Joseph Perry had saved Curtis Telford, not only from a huge embarrassment, but also the cost of many head of sheep that would all eventually have perished. Following this much less costly experiment, Joseph Perry became one of Curtis Telford's most trusted advisors.

Although timber proved to be by far the most apt use for the land, Telford tried just about everything, much to Joseph Perry's amusement. Curtis wrote to his brothers and managed to convince his youngest brother, Benton Telford, to make the journey to Australia in order to bring a French oyster spawn with him in an attempt to establish an oyster culture. Six months after his brother's arrival, the muddy waters and the summer heat killed off the spawn. Lack of sufficient water and suitable grasses also made the area unsuited for cattle grazing. Curtis and Benton Telford took out coal mining rights in order to take advantage of the rich Illawarra seam which ran under Thurrough through to the north. They utilised Joseph Perry's knowledge of the area, giving him the role of seeking out potential test drilling sites in order to try to locate coal. However, after several test drillings, they were unable to locate the seam.

Whereas Curtis Telford was always scheming and never static, Benton Telford was in complete contrast, content to watch the region grow around him, never exerting himself to contribute to the effort. He would sit on the front porch of the main house, as he often did in Yorkshire, and muse on his brother's energy. Benton Telford was the idle rich; a dangerous breed with too little to do and too much time to think. To him, Australia was the land of opportunity, just as long as others created that opportunity for him. In this regard his brother was the perfect foil: Curtis Telford was only too willing to drag his lazy brother up with him as a dingo drags its pup by the scruff of the neck.

One of the earmarks of Curtis Telford's dynasty was his drive to try and create new uses for the land, a quality that endured long after he stepped off the boat from England. By 1850, after most of Thurrough had been surveyed, title was officially given to the Telford family for most of the land in and around the small coastal village of Thurrough.

For his services to the Telford family, Curtis Telford granted Joseph Perry his own seven acre plot at the tip of the Thurrough Peninsula. As tensions between the few remaining Aborigines and the settlers escalated in some parts to full-scale hostility, the colour of Joseph's skin was never fully accepted, and except for the times when Curtis Telford summoned him for help, Joseph was a virtual recluse on his land, which he made self-sufficient by growing fruit and vegetables as well as holding poultry.

It was glaringly obvious to her fellow servants that Curtis Telford cared deeply for Taranna Perry. He favoured her with the gentlest tasks in the homestead, and she was often called upon to serve meals just so that he could interact with her. If he found her startlingly attractive caked in dirt while tending to her dying father in a damp, dark hut by the river, it was nothing compared to her visage once she had a chance to groom herself and wore the clothes with which he adorned her. But it was her humble spirit that finally snared him. He found himself drawn to her with a desire that he was finding increasingly difficult to quench. When his brother Benton went to Sydney for a week of rum and rollicking, Curtis arranged for Taranna to serve him a late dinner. Due to the hour, he insisted that the other servants retire to their quarters, leaving him alone with her.

As she was about to return to the kitchen, he gently took hold of her hand.

"Won't you sit down and join me?" he asked, without releasing his soft but persuasive grasp.

She blushed. Although she was not ignorant of the way he looked at her, she had never entertained the idea that these were anything more than furtive glances with no objective.

"I shouldn't. You must eat." She often marvelled at how hard he worked himself, taking on manual tasks that he refused to delegate to his workers. "You need your strength."

He pulled a chair closer and motioned for her to sit. "I need... you."

Taranna Perry did not require the sanction of a white man's ceremony to validate the relationship that developed. In any case, she was totally unfamiliar with the procedure of white man's matrimony so she did not miss it. For her, their relationship was like the Aboriginal tradition of a pact between two people, which is sometimes declared in front of the tribe, but sometimes not. Whereas Curtis Telford had far less honourable reasons for concealing their union – what would be said if others found out that he had formed a relationship with an Aboriginal girl? – to Taranna, it didn't matter. She was blissfully ignorant of any need to tell others. To her, it was an intensely private matter between two people, whereas any white woman would have been grotesquely offended by the clandestine nature of their union. And so they stole intimate moments whenever they could. She would never spend entire nights in his chambers, and although such pretences never fooled anyone, nothing was ever said.

Increasingly, Curtis Telford gave Taranna tasks that limited her almost exclusively to inside the homestead. He recognised that she required a buffer from the prying eyes of the outside world. However, he was unable to protect her from the less than honourable forces inside his own home. On one cold winter's night, Taranna's living quarters were invaded by Benton Telford, who had been drinking while Curtis Telford was away on business. He threw her forcefully down onto the bed and told her that her job was to service the entire Telford family, not just his brother. Then he snuffed out the light.

The next morning, Joseph Perry found her sobbing outside his hut clutching her father's angel doll to her chest. When he asked her what was wrong, she couldn't tell him. She was never able to speak of what happened that night. Intuitively, she knew that things could never be the same. The violation had altered her mentally – and physically. She was pregnant.

CHAPTER THIRTEEN

DIRK Crenshaw loved the clanking sound the coins made as they rebounded against the sides of the Campbell's Soup tin can. Best would count the money then hand it to him. Best never complained about the way Dirk enthusiastically hurled the money inside the can. He knew Dirk got a kick out of the noise, even if it was distracting and he sometimes lost count. Once, Dirk picked a penny up and asked Best whose head was on the back. When Best told him it was George, Dirk thought that he must have been a special bloke, and that it would be great to have his head on the back of a coin one day. But it wasn't the noisy money that was important. It was the silent money. It was all about the paper, said Best.

Just as Dirk was stuffing the remaining notes away, Best heard the unmistakable echo of an approaching vehicle chugging across the Thurrough Peninsula, the sound getting louder as it wound its way to the lighthouse. He stood guardedly as Kent Lawrence descended gingerly down the sandstone stairs to the beach and through the sand towards them in his Italian leather shoes. He carried a briefcase, occasionally putting it down so he could wipe his face with his sleeve, jumping when he scratched the tip of his nose with a cufflink.

He stopped and peered down the Hole. Aside from the red welt near his left nostril, Dirk immediately noted that the man's face was pale-white with no semblance of a suntan. To Dirk, anyone who didn't have a suntan wasn't spending their time productively.

"The attraction's closed," said Best, copying a line he'd heard from the travelling circus, which came through Thurrough every January.

Lawrence took off his shoes to shake out the sand. "I'm not here to see the attraction. I'm here to see Dirk Crenshaw."

Dirk stuck up his hand. "That's me."

Lawrence moved over to shake Dirk's hand. "And I'm Kent Lawrence."

"From Thurrough Council," added Best warily.

Whenever Best's dad talked about Thurrough Council, he used words that he said he'd wash Best's mouth out with soap if he ever heard him repeat.

Best was guarded. He tugged on Dirk's shirt. "We should be going."

Kent Lawrence recognized that he had to gain Dirk Crenshaw's attention quickly. "Do you realise you're operating this business on public land without a permit?"

Dirk shrugged his shoulders. The revelation didn't faze him. He'd just add it to the massive list of things he didn't realise.

"Maybe I should go and get my dad?" suggested Best.

Lawrence ignored him. "We're going to have to shut this operation down... unless...?"

The "unless" Kent Lawrence was referring to was a joint partnership between Dirk Crenshaw and the Thurrough Shire Council whereby the Council would advertise the Hole in major publications, set up a ticketing and operational infrastructure, and take three-quarters of the profits. Due to the fact that Harry Heath had elevated Dirk's profile status to one of semi-celebrity, the Council had prudently decided to appoint Dirk the Thurrough Hole Manager and figurehead. In addition, the Hole would open every day of the week, not just weekends as had been the case ever since Best had gone back to school.

"You're obviously a brilliant entrepreneur, Mr Crenshaw," Lawrence stated with all the inflexion of a sycophant. "Council just wants to make sure the attraction is handled correctly to ensure its longevity."

"What's that mean?" asked Dirk.

Lawrence smiled. "A man who cuts to the chase. I like that. It means that Council sees you're on to something and wants in. You may well ask, 'what's in it for me?'"

"What's in it for me?" Dirk asked obediently.

"I wondered when you'd get to that. The Council has the wherewithal to make this," he looked down into the Hole, "pit a major attraction. You've taken it this far and you should be congratulated. But Council can take it to the next level – the next profit level. We're offering you the potential to make ten times the money you're making now."

And with that, Kent Lawrence reached inside his briefcase and pulled out a single piece of paper. He handed it to Dirk along with a pen. "Just sign at the bottom and we'll take care of everything."

Best came to stand between them. "We should show this to my dad."

But Dirk ignored him and quickly scribbled a hieroglyphic that looked quite unlike anybody's signature.

BEN Douglas came in from the lamp room to find a plate half-full of mashed potato and carrots on the table. Best was lying down when Ben Douglas went to his room to check on him. "There's no use getting upset," he began as he sat on the edge of Best's bed, rubbing his son's head affectionately with his large knuckles. "It's just a stupid hole in the sand."

"Dirk and I were partners."

"But you have to go to school during the week."

"He didn't even mention me to the Council. He just stood there and made all these plans without me."

"What plans?"

"Dirk's going to be the Hole's Manager."

"He couldn't manage his way out of his mother's womb... Who's going to keep digging?"

"The Council's bringing in their workers to do it. They said it'll be quicker."

"Doesn't Dirk still need you to watch the ocean?"

"The Council's getting someone to do that as well. They're going to set up ticket booths and serve food and stuff... and they're going to let visitors with cars park up here near the lighthouse."

Ben Douglas sighed. He rued the day his wife's father had to sell the land. He glanced out the window to see Dirk packing Kent Lawrence's Buick with his army-issued duffle bag. "Where's he going?"

"He's moving into a room in the Telford Towers. He says it's better for his new image."

"Who's going to write his reports for him?"

Best shrugged his shoulders. For the last six months, on the last day of every month, Best had penned Dirk Crenshaw's Coastal Watchdog Surveillance Reports, and dutifully mailed them for him.

Best's dad hopped up. "Come on. Let's get our clothes on the line before this southerly change hits or we'll have no undies left."

Dirk Crenshaw was just about to hop into the car when Best appeared to hang out the laundry. Dirk went over and leaned against one of the clothesline poles.

Best ignored him.

Dirk lit up a cigarette; a habit he had agreed to take up just that afternoon. He inhaled deeply then coughed uncontrollably. "Best?" he eventually wheezed.

Best continued to ignore him, despite the lung-pounding cough.

"You gotta understand. It's business." Dirk pulled out a one-pound note and shoved it into Best's hand. "Here you go, kid. Go and buy yourself some lollies."

Best looked down at the bill in disgust. "I don't want it."

"Go on. Take it."

"I don't want it!" Best threw the bill on the ground. "And I'm not writing any more of your stupid reports."

"Doesn't matter. Army's over for me. I'm now in business."

Best grabbed the laundry basket and ran back inside the cottage.

Dirk bent down and put the bill back inside his pocket. He stuck the cigarette awkwardly into his mouth, burning his bottom lip in the process. "Ow!" he yelled. "Damn ungrateful kids. You take 'em under your wing and they turn around and kick you right in the guts." He fingered inside his breast pocket to clumsily retrieve his recently acquired fob watch. He gazed at it thoughtfully for several seconds. He was going to have to learn to tell the time. If anybody had witnessed the scene they may have discovered one of Dirk's closely held secrets: he was completely illiterate.

IT was the middle of a typical summer weather pattern. The north-easterly winds would blow for four or five days, then out of the south would come the "Southerly buster" – a cold front that often brought moisture with it. People flocked to the beach during the nor'easterly when the warm weather and refreshing ocean made an irresistible combination.

As Best peered out the lighthouse window, he had a view of the coastline for miles in each direction. To the south across the Port Hacking River was the thirty-three thousand acre Royal National Park. Distinguished by clumps of wattle bushes and eucalyptus trees, it was the second oldest National Park in the world. Behind the lighthouse to the northwest, he could just make out the entrance to Botany Bay, which the First Fleet had sailed into in 1788. And to the northeast, he could almost touch the tip of Thurrough Beach, which met the sea less than half a mile away. Behind the beach stood huge sand dunes that rose up out of the sand like volcanoes. Best would live to see the Thurrough Peninsula turn into the home of a massive oil refinery. He would also live to see the erosion of the giant sand dunes, not, as nature intended, by the steady breath of offshore winds that blew the sand into the sea, but by the insatiable appetite of the sand-mining industry.

He looked down at the beach below him. The area of sand surrounding the Hole had been transformed into a kind of grotesque carnival. The Council had erected several obtrusive billboards along the beach path advertising the ever-increasing pit. They had also attracted the interest of "Big Smoke," a cigarette company that had insisted not only on naming rights to the Hole, but that the figurehead, Dirk Crenshaw be seen puffing on at least twenty cigarettes a day. The Council came to a compromise, however: they retained the naming rights, but said they would get Dirk Crenshaw to smoke forty cigarettes a day. Big Smoke accepted the deal, and Dirk was left with a cigarette protruding from his mouth for the term of his tenure. The Hole fast became a money pit into which the Council and its vested interests dipped their hands to pull out profit in much the same way as the workers excavated the sand. It had become a bizarre business that fed off curiosity. Big Smoke's sponsorship, the concession stands, and tacky tourist posters and pens were making three times as much as the Hole's admission fees. Clowns and other buskers surrounded the outside perimeters while scantily clad females from the sponsoring cigarette company frolicked their way through the onlookers. It was a circus.

Dirk Crenshaw had traded his military uniform for a three-piece suit. At over thirty degrees Celsius, he was sweating profusely. But he didn't seem to mind. Large breasted women with glistening suntans now followed his every move, ready to force upon him cigarette after cigarette. He was a smoking star.

The top of the Hole had been fenced off, with the only entry point being a small gate, which allowed the diggers access to the area. Below the gate, sticking out from the Hole, was a wide, wooden ladder, which the workers used to climb in and out of the Hole. Best craned his head. He couldn't tell how many workers were down there, but judging by the rate at which the Hole was growing, it must have been a substantial number. Thurrough Council now had a team of men doing a job Dirk

Crenshaw had once done single-handedly.

When Best saw the kinds of people who turned up to view the Hole, and who left their rubbish strewn all over the beach, he felt that a group of mindless idiots had invaded Thurrough. And those patrons whose vehicles spared them the fifteen minute walk along Thurrough Beach parked their precious automobiles haphazardly around the lighthouse as though they were mounting an attack on a fort. Oftentimes, at dusk, he had to dance through the papers that had been thrown and left scattered on the beach to be consumed by the incoming tide, polluting the ocean. Best began to hate the Hole and all it stood for.

Ben Douglas glanced at the sky. The Southerly was due around midnight. Often, when ships at sea were unaware of predicted changes in weather, the results could be disastrous. Before the advent of the lighthouse, many a Southerly had blown distressed vessels onto the treacherous outer reefs that formed a horseshoe gateway into Thurrough Beach to be pulverised against the sharp, jagged submerged crags. The Southerly could blow up in a matter of seconds, although signs of its impending arrival were visible to the discerning eye. During most anticipated southerly weather fronts, Best and his father would bunk down in the lamp room. A lighthouse's effective operation was always important, but if there was a time when it was crucial, it was when the Southerly was due at night.

The two makeshift bunks barely fitted inside the lamp room. Best's father refilled the kerosene, and after checking that the bearings of the revolving apparatus were operating freely, he climbed inside his bunk and promptly went to sleep.

Surrounded by three hundred and sixty degrees of viewing glass, Best could see the eastern sky in all its speckled glory. He looked skywards to the south and located the Southern Cross. Like its distant cousin Polaris, the Northern Star, the Southern Cross was the Southern Hemisphere's index finger in the guiding hand of constellations. When Best shut his eyes to sleep, he closed them on a sky littered with stars that had helped navigators to chart ocean courses for centuries.

The crash of thunder woke Best instantly. He turned to his father, who was still fast asleep, used to sleeping through such storms. Best checked the lamp. It was glowing brilliantly. The approaching storm front with its low cumulous clouds of moisture had shut out the Southern Cross like a window blind. Within the troposphere, the cool air of the front was forcing the more tepid air over its bold face like a wave over sand, creating thunder and lightning in the process. Then came the rain. Minutes later, the sky had all but hidden its starry hosts and blankets of clouds were spilling their tears over the entire coast. The Southerly hit. In an instant, the sea became a mess of white water with its choppy peaks and troughs. A Southerly could change the size of the swell in the twinkling of an eye, and when Best leaned out of his bunk, he saw that the waves had almost doubled in height.

Best never would have noticed the brilliant glow if he hadn't been transfixed, watching the Southerly's pageant unfold. At first, he thought it was a flash of lightning. But there was no accompanying thunder. Then he saw it again. It was coming from the beach. Perhaps it was a reflection of the lighthouse lamp in the sea slowly crawling up the sand? Best strained his eyes. No: the water hadn't made it that far. And the tide was at its lowest ebb. It was some storm all right. The waves were cascading over the coastal headland rock-shelves. But Best had seen much worse. The water wouldn't make it that far up the beach, even at high tide. There would have to be a huge swell for that to happen.

The glow pulsated from the beach once again. Best was now almost certain of its position. It was coming from inside the Hole. Someone must be down there. If the rain continued, or the sea did manage to reach all the way to the Hole, whoever was in there would surely drown.

"Dad! Wake up!" urged Best.

Ben Douglas rolled over and checked the lamp. It was burning to his satisfaction. He rolled back on his stomach. "All's well," he mumbled. "Go back to sleep."

Best nudged him. "But dad!"

"The lamp's fine. Go back to sleep."

Best nudged him again. "I think there's someone trapped down the Hole."

Best's father sat up groggily. "What are you talking about?"

Suddenly, a bolt of lightning crashed through the glass of the lighthouse and struck the object of its attraction – the clockwork mechanism that governed the rotation of the lamp. As glass rained down on Best and his father, the lighthouse lamp slowly grinded to a stop.

Best's father hurtled out of bed. "Quick! Get the bunks out. I need room."

Best began dragging the bunks into the stairwell. "What are you going to do?"

"I've got to move the lamp!"

Ben Douglas positioned himself behind the lamp. He grasped the handles on both sides of the brass rotating apparatus, which were fixed in place for just such an emergency. It wasn't heavy to rotate; it moved smoothly along its round, well-greased bearings, but it was tedious, especially in the middle of the night. He settled himself as comfortably as he could manage, given that large droplets of rain were pouring in where the glass had shattered. He gripped the handles to begin the laborious task, made a little easier by the fact that he was facing Harry Heath's autograph. He'd just think on all those great Rugby games.

"Best!" he shouted, as rain spilled down his forehead. "Go get the raincoats from the cottage."

Best had no choice. With his dad engaged with the lamp, he would have to check the Hole by himself. "On my way back."

"Back? From where?" his dad asked, half in shock.

"The Hole."

"The Hole? For the love of the holy apostolic church – forget the bloody Hole!"

"I think there's someone down there!" Best's voice echoed back as he started his descent down the cavernous stairwell.

"Be careful! For the love of all the dearly departed saints, be careful!"

The rain was still pelting down when Best stepped outside, and within seconds he was completely drenched. He trudged his way through the wet sand. Best hadn't returned to the Hole since Kent Lawrence's first visit, and when he came to the perimeter of the area he found it virtually impenetrable due to the six-foot high fence surrounding Thurrough's most popular tourist attraction.

A burst of light shot out from the depths of the Hole.

"Is anybody down there?" shouted Best.

The steady beat of rain was the only reply.

Best groped his way along the fence until he reached the gate. It had been padlocked. There was no other option. He had to climb the fence. He took hold of the wire and hauled himself up and over the barricade. Once on the other side, he saw that there was a five-foot gap from the bottom of the fence to the rim of the Hole. He danced around the base of the fence, careful not to step too close to the Hole in case the shoulder of sand gave way. The ladder the workmen used to enter the Hole should have been right under the gate. It wasn't. They must have yanked it out. Best had no way to get down inside the Hole. That must be the problem, he thought. Somebody had fallen down there and was unable to climb out.

The rain was soaking the ground and clumping the sand. Best circumnavigated the Hole. He couldn't see any other way to get down. He was about to climb back over the fence with the aim of returning to the cottage to get some rope, when a blinding flash shot out from the Hole paralysing his vision. He screamed as his pupils contracted in pain. Disorientated and temporarily blinded, he stumbled too close to the edge. The wet sand shifted and gave way. Best's left foot slipped down with the flowing sand. He reached out and tried to claw the bank with the tip of his fingers. But it was to no avail. The sand he lunged at also gave way. With his arms flaying about, grasping nothing but air, he plummeted helplessly into the bowels of the Hole.

CHAPTER FOURTEEN

THE rain trickled down the windowpane. There was nobody on the beach. The Southerly had transformed the ocean into a swarm of whitecaps. Only the most ardent surfers were out battling the confused, choppy waves.

Richard Tipody winged into Best's room and perched himself behind Best like a seagull waiting for a chip to be thrown his way.

Best turned as much as his degenerated vertebrae would allow. "Oh," he remarked, sounding disappointed. "It's just you."

"A day that pities neither wise men nor fools," Tipody quoted inaccurately as he clumsily slapped Best on the back, causing Best's false teeth to vibrate against his palate and the three real teeth he had left.

Best pivoted his wheelchair around to face him. "What's that, Richard?"

"Shakespeare."

Tipody placed a miniature tape recorder discreetly on the window ledge.

Best picked it up to examine it. "What's this?"

"I've enjoyed our little talks so much over the past three months that I've decided to start recording them."

Best was surprised. These same little talks had bored him to tears. There seemed to be no point to them. "You should get yourself a hobby, Richard."

"I've got a hobby." He half-snatched the dictaphone from Best and placed it back on the sill. "Talking with you… That's my hobby."

Poor wretch, Best thought.

Tipody clicked on the recorder. "What do you think about death?" he asked boldly.

Best raised his right shoulder. Arthritis in his left shoulder prevented him from shrugging it in unison. "I don't think much about it at all, but I must be getting closer."

"Do you like living here?"

"I've lived in Thurrough all my life."

"I mean here – in the Home?"

"It's home now."

Tipody slid the recorder closer to Best. "And tell me about where you used to live?"

Tipody had spent the last three months researching Best's life to such an extent that he knew more about Best than Best could remember about himself. He had become so obsessed with Best that he could not even pretend to take a vested medical interest in any of the other residents. This preoccupation did not go unnoticed by the nurses who had dubbed him "Doctor Do-Little".

"You used to live in the lighthouse cottage?" Tipody asked almost rhetorically.

"That was a long time ago," answered Best.

"Still," Tipody probed. "It was also your home for a long time. It must've been hard for you to leave, having been there since you were a boy?"

Best looked detachedly up the beach towards the old Thurrough Lighthouse. "My grandfather built the original lighthouse."

Tipody raised his eyebrows in order to look impressed. "He did a good job. It's still standing."

"My father virtually rebuilt it. That's why it's still standing." A fleeting look of longing passed across Best's face. "After my mother… went, that's what he did. Day and night he worked on the lighthouse. It'll stand forever. It has his blood running through its walls."

Tipody perked up. He got up and leaned out into the corridor. The orderlies were preparing to serve dinner. He told them not to come into Best's room. He said that Best was undergoing treatment. He closed the door and dragged his chair over to Best, positioning it so close their knees were almost touching.

"Tell me about your mother," Tipody asked softly.

Best looked at his Seiko. It was an old watch, an automatic, but it still worked whenever Best generated enough energy to keep the mechanism wound. And although he hadn't been able to read it in quite some time, having mislaid his spectacles, that didn't seem to matter. He looked at it by force of habit. It was dinnertime; he knew it by the gurgles in his stomach rather than the hands of the old wristwatch. The orderlies were late. He looked towards the door, hoping his dinner would shortly arrive.

Best felt an ache in the pit of his stomach. "I'm hungry."

"Forget food," interjected Tipody abruptly.

Best looked away. "I want to eat dinner."

Tipody jumped up, defeated again. "We'll talk again tomorrow."

"I'm hungry," Best said for the third time.

RICHARD Tipody and Flavian Broad had both studied medicine and graduated from the University of Sydney the same year. They were not the best of friends, but circumstances had thrust them together on a number of occasions, the last of which was the Geriatric Advisory Committee. Due to their unhealthy devotion to their respective careers, and Broad's desire to spend less time with his wife, they often met to discuss their mutual interest. Both lacked the imagination that healthy social interaction with others usually fosters, so the venues for their rendezvous were normally pale, lifeless and completely without character; qualities they shared in common with their patrons. On this particular day, Tipody wanted to talk over some elements with Broad that he felt were best discussed outside their regular Committee meetings, where they could both talk freely without the prejudice they were forced to endure from Fiona Chalice.

Broad had selected a place just outside Sydney City Hospital where the café was as sterile and tasteless as the hospital itself, with the only distinguishing difference being the level of hygiene. A young bohemian-looking girl, her face pierced with earrings in every place but her ear lobes, placed a cup of black coffee as thick as soup on the table where Richard Tipody waited.

As Tipody pored over his notes on Best Douglas, Flavian Broad rushed through the door, and after ordering a café latte with skim milk, occupied the seat across from Tipody.

Broad nodded his head. "Doctor."

"Doctor," Tipody responded.

Although the two addressed each other courteously, Tipody's politeness did not extend to rising to greet Broad. Social etiquette was not one of Tipody's strong points.

Broad opened his attaché case and stuffed inside the copy of the Daily Chronicle that was lying lifeless on the table. "For the form guide," he replied in response to Tipody's enquiring look.

Tipody raised his eyebrows. "I didn't peg you for a gambling man."

Broad smiled. "It's my new medical journal."

Richard Tipody was familiar with Broad's DNA research on behalf of a well-know horse owner. "Created any winners yet?"

"It's only a matter of time."

"And money?"

"Particularly money. Yet all the money in the world can't buy complete sanction."

Tipody simultaneously ripped open two sachets of sugar and poured them into his cup. "Stem cell research in humans is touchy, but I would've thought nobody would care too much about horses?"

"Ah, but you see, animals are always the stepping stones. Any forward-thinking person knows that what's done today with animals is done tomorrow with humans."

The waitress plonked Broad's latte on the table, spilling some of the contents into the saucer. She walked away quickly as Broad lifted the saucer to pour the coffee back into the cup.

"Still, I can't see too many humans having the speed to run in the Melbourne Cup," quipped Tipody.

They both laughed, relieved to find humour in an issue that neither of them was morally attached to.

Broad took a sip from his latte. "So how's your old man doing?"

Tipody shoved his notes aside and took off his glasses. He rubbed his brow furiously. "Just can't seem to crack his veneer."

"He's old. Is there anything to crack?"

"Oh, he's surprisingly lucid. And he can be perceptive on some occasions… but remarkably simple on others."

"What makes you think he's your candidate?"

"He's perfect," Tipody exclaimed as his face lit up. "For his age, he's quite healthy aside from some arthritis."

"Not bad for ninety-odd years."

Tipody nodded fervently in agreement. "And he shows absolutely no signs of dementia. For all intents and purposes, he will represent a robust, sane, aged individual who merely wants to end it all."

"So where's the stumbling block?"

"I cannot possibly fathom why he would want to keep on living, after all that's happened to him."

Broad asked the waitress for another latte, complaining about the tepid nature of the first. He ignored her expression as she rolled her eyes. He turned back to Tipody. "Maybe he's just too simple."

"I thought that at first. But he's no simpleton… he could be smart enough to use simple-mindedness as a defence though."

"You're not giving him too much credit are you?"

"Never underestimate your enemy."

There was a brief pause as they both pondered Tipody's description of Best.

"Then you must find a way through his defences," Broad commented as his microwaved latte found its way back to the table. "I've watched them with the racehorses. It's vastly different to when they break a horse. When they break a horse, they deny it food, comfort, and dignity until the horse has to finally submit to survive. With a racehorse, they give it everything – the best food, the best lodgings – the best of country comfort. Even the slow nags that are financially supported by gullible idiots are treated like kings because their owners believe they'll go from rags to riches in just the next race. The question you have to ask yourself is, is your man a racehorse?"

Tipody shook his head. "Not sure. I usually visit after meal times so at least one physical need has been met."

"Nursing home food is hardly pampering him," responded Broad.

"Because you'll get nowhere if you treat him like an old mule if he is, in fact, a champion."

CHAPTER FIFTEEN

WHEN Curtis Telford returned from Sydney four days later, Taranna Perry was gone. His brother, Benton explained away James Perry's half-cast daughter's departure as the wandering way of her race. Crazy blacks, he said. But Curtis Telford thought otherwise. He believed his reluctance to reveal their relationship had finally shamed her. He never discovered the real reason. And pride in his reputation stopped him from chasing after her, as this would have dispelled all doubt about their secret union. So he mourned her loss quietly and alone. And while he attracted many suitable prospects due to his wealth and standing, he never married. He remained too affected by the memory of Taranna, and was later content with the fact that his brother's wife bore children who, in time, would continue the Telford family's legacy. So, whilst he suspected that she had fled to her brother's hut a mere two miles away, he never went near it.

As is often the case, Benton Telford's offspring were far less generous with the wealth their uncle had created than he had been himself.

When Baine Telford, Benton's eldest son, hopped on his horse one day to survey the extent of Joseph Perry's land, he was shocked to find that it took in several dunes and ran out to the tip of Thurrough Peninsula. Although most of the soil had steadily blown away over the years, Baine Telford found it deplorable that his uncle had granted an independent free-holding of seven acres within their vast estate to a half-cast, even though it represented a mere dot on the landscape of the Telfords' land in Thurrough Shire. Those most concerned with the Telford family's landholdings had done little to acquire them.

When Curtis Telford was on his deathbed, Baine Telford pleaded with him to revoke Joseph Perry's free-hold, evict him, and absorb the land back into the Telford fold. But Curtis Telford's memory was long even though his time was short. He remembered James Perry's honourable feats of conciliation, and he could not dismiss the immeasurable help he had received from the hands of his son, Joseph Perry. Far more than either of these considerations, he had never let Taranna Perry out of his heart. His dying request was that Joseph Perry's land be granted to him unconditionally.

Taranna Perry wasn't the only Aboriginal woman to fall into the clutches of less than honourable white men. So much so that Joseph Perry's hut, perched near the tip of Thurrough Peninsula, became a halfway house for desperate women who were more often than not accompanied by their illegitimate children. By the time Taranna gave birth to James Joseph Perry in 1835, he joined seven other children and their mothers. To cater for this increasing social need, Joseph erected crude tin shelters to house these outcasts. In the course of the next hundred years, some seventy people resided within tin sheds nestled between the sand dunes, hidden from the view of the general Thurrough populace who may have wandered down the beach, but seldom ventured amongst the dunes. This community, which became commonly known as "Tin Town", was an eclectic mix of Aboriginals, ex-convicts who struggled to make ends meet after their release, distressed women, and later, returned servicemen, who in many instances were either physically or mentally incapacitated.

By 1860, Tin Town had become its own a tribe, much like the Gweagal, and order was maintained by Joseph Perry, who acted as a type of Elder. Young children would gather at the feet of Taranna Perry as she regaled them with stories of the splendour of the Telford household, which she told partly to entertain but mostly to inspire them to aspire to lives beyond Tin Town. And as Taranna's own son grew, she experienced considerable joy in recognizing that he had an uncanny resemblance to the taller Curtis Telford, rather than his much shorter, pugnacious brother. She was thankful that his father was a man of principle and not dishonour.

Little John Selby stared up at Taranna Perry with eyes as wide as saucers. The eight-year-old orphan loved hearing about tales of treasure. He would always sit at Taranna's feet by the beach fire and take in every word she uttered about the Telford fortune and the gold contained in the cellar of the main house. He longed for a life beyond Tin Town. He always listened enviously as Taranna spoke glowingly about her father, the famous Jamesperri, while affectionately stroking the clay angel she had made for him. John had never known his father, and his mother had died of pneumonia when he was just four. He knew, from an early age, that he would have to carve his own way out of Tin Town. No one was going to do it for him.

In 1865, when the New South Wales Maritime Association was looking for potential lighthouse sites in Thurrough in order to reduce the numerous shipwrecks on the outer Thurrough Reefs, Joseph Perry and his nephew stepped forward. Their barren land on the tip of the Peninsula would be perfect. But there was one catch: the Maritime Association would not build a lighthouse on private land. Despite the protestations of Baine Telford, Joseph Perry offered the land back to Thurrough Shire for a nominal amount, only insisting that his nephew be trained and paid to tend the lighthouse so as to provide an occupation and source of income for James Joseph and subsequent Perry generations. Thurrough Shire Council agreed. Work on the lighthouse was to be undertaken by the well-known convict architect, Francis Greenway. In what was perceived to be a gesture of reconciliation, the Telford family offered to supply the sandstone for the lighthouse, in spite of Greenway's warning that the poor quality of the sandstone would result in the premature aging of the structure. Wishing to placate the well-connected Telford Dynasty, however, the Government accepted the Telfords' tender. Greenway, who had been emancipated by Governor Macquarie after his work on the Macquarie Lighthouse, walked away from the project, considering it doomed to failure. By the turn of the century, Greenway was proven right. The lighthouse was virtually inoperable and crumbling into the sea. A widower at age sixty-five, with one daughter and without a functional lighthouse – and, as a result, without employment – James Joseph Perry was on his knees. Sensing that his prey was vulnerable, the old, decrepit Baine Telford offered to buy the land back from Thurrough Shire for half its value. Since the Telford family had such influence, no private bidder dared counter the offer, and so James Joseph Perry was left a vulnerable sitting duck, with Thurrough Council about to sell the land right out from underneath him.

The son of Scottish immigrants, Ben Douglas was a young local builder who used to fish in a small dinghy off Thurrough Beach when the swells were small and the fish were biting. Being young, cocky and full of bravado, he would often dance perilously close to the Thurrough coastline in order to navigate through schools of snapper. He had met James Joseph's daughter, Norah, while dragging his dinghy up the beach one day, and struck up an immediate friendship with her as they both shared a love of the sea. Being the lighthouse keeper's daughter, she would often look out for him, making sure that his small vessel was safe from harm. On hot, summer days, she would even swim out past the breakers to meet him on his return to the shore. When the lighthouse was condemned, and had become inoperable, Ben Douglas was furious. He argued that the lighthouse should be restored. He had not only grown fond of Norah, but also of her father. He took it upon himself to champion their cause. He and Norah worked tirelessly until they had convinced the NSW Government that the lighthouse was crucial and that the Government, with the help of Ben Douglas, should rebuild it. The long fight only brought Ben Douglas and Norah Perry even closer, and by the time the NSW Maritime Association finally agreed to renew the land lease, they were well and truly in love. But there was one snag: although the Government would partly fund the new lighthouse, the difference would have to be provided by the Thurrough Shire community. Baine Telford and his son, Galbraith, exerted all the influence they could muster to stop anyone, including the Council, from dipping into their coffers to support the new project. By stalemating the venture, the Telfords hoped to watch the old lighthouse fall down. Then, they would buy back the land, eradicate the last remnants of Tin Town and evict the residents.

Following the death of Norah's father, James Joseph, Ben Douglas spent the next couple of years using the old lighthouse's sandstone to build a new cottage much closer to the lighthouse, and had begun repairing the aging lighthouse. In 1904, while Ben Douglas was desperately trying to secure community funding to continue the restoration, Norah gave birth to a boy she named Best, because he was the *best* thing that had ever happened to her.

CHAPTER SIXTEEN

THE Hole was forty feet deep and ten feet wide the last time Best had been inside it. Since then, it had grown close to sixty feet deep, and its width had almost doubled. Best braced himself for the impact, knowing from experience that packed sand could feel like concrete when dropped on from a considerable height. Suddenly, unexpectedly, he plunged into deep water. He continued to sink, slowing down and finally making gentle contact with the bottom of the Hole. He quickly found his feet and sprang off the sand to make for the surface. His lungs were bursting for air. When he broke through the surface, he spat out a mouthful of water. It tasted salty, and he realized that it wasn't rainwater but seawater, which must have somehow seeped into the Hole, filling it up like a tidal pool.

He tried to tread water, but he was sinking. He couldn't swim. He was afraid of water. As he gasped to regain his breath, he could feel the light touch of the rain on his face as it floated inside the cavern. He began to panic and only his need for air suppressed his urge to scream.

A bright glow lit up the bottom of the Hole, the rays striating the water. Best looked down. The light was coming from underneath him. He felt something tugging at his feet, then the water began to swirl, gradually increasing in intensity until it was rotating like a tornado. The water was being forcefully sucked towards the bottom of the Hole, drawing Best with it. He tried to dig his fingers into the side of the Hole. But it was no use. The swirling torrent just swept him along in its frenzy to escape.

He felt like he was being sucked down a funnel, when suddenly, he found the seawater had disappeared, leaving him behind, sprawled out on the sandy bottom. He was shivering. He looked around for the opening through which the water had madly escaped. In the dark he saw the faint outline of what seemed to be a small hole dug in the side of the wall bordering the floor. He crawled over and glanced in. Without warning, the mysterious beacon shot out once more from the opening, knocking him backwards.

Best thought he was screaming. He numbly fingered his mouth. It was open, but it wasn't making any sound.

A voice thundered.

The bellow shocked Best to his feet. Without thinking, he scrambled to the side of the Hole and tried to clamber up the flimsy wall. But it was in vain. The sand just broke away. He was trapped.

The voice boomed again.

"Who's there?" Best asked, quivering.

The voice resonated, and for a split second, Best thought it was the thunder of the storm. Tears welled in his eyes as he shut them tight and collapsed on the wet sand.

There was silence. Best didn't dare look.

"What do you want?" said the voice, more constrained.

"I thought someone was down here and needed help," answered Best.

"There's no one here that needs your help."

"I saw a light."

"Where?"

Best refused his curiosity's desire to lift his head. "Coming out of the Hole."

"Why don't you look up?"

Best buried his head into his hands, like an emu in the sand. "I'm scared."

"Of me?"

Best nodded quickly.

The voice laughed.

Best opened one eye.

"Curiosity getting the better of you?"

Best was quick to shake his head again.

"Then look, boy. Look!"

Best counted to three then opened his eyes and stared in the direction from which the voice was coming. It took his pupils some seconds to adjust to the lack of light. He spied a figure merged with the darkness. Suddenly, a bright flash emanated from the form. Best averted his eyes and tilted his head upwards. The glow seemed to rise up out of the Hole and hover in the night air like a wisp of fog.

"Is that what you saw?" the voice asked.

Best nodded.

"An illusion."

The form came towards Best and stood in front of him. Best saw it clearly now. The defined features of the face made it almost visible in the darkness. It had a countenance not unlike a strong man's, not unlike his father's. Best looked closer. The face seemed deeply worn, not so much due to wrinkles or lines, but due to its expression. The eyes, although big, were dark and sullen, almost lifeless. It was too dark to see what colour they were. The mouth opened, exposing teeth that were perfectly set but stained a dull shade of yellow. As the figure lifted up its arms, Best studied the shapes of the outstretched limbs. Hanging flimsily from the arms were what looked to be the sleeves of a long, tattered gown. The shadows they formed on the surrounding walls of sand didn't seem quite natural. Best's imagination started to run wild.

All he could think was that this man had wings, broken wings.

Best's eyes opened wider in amazement. "Who are you?" he asked in a soft, trembling voice.

The figure stepped closer. It lowered itself to look directly at Best. "A Keeper."

Best looked up. The rain had stopped. He saw the flicker of some stars in the sky. He could hear nothing but the sound of the wind funnelling down through the Hole.

The Keeper smiled; his teeth straight as a picket fence. "And who are you?"

Best couldn't help staring. "Best," he answered. "Are you one of the workers?" he asked.

"You're already insulting me and we just met!"

"I didn't mean to... I meant..." Best was afraid of upsetting him, so remained quiet. He sat on his haunches and wrapped his arms around his knees in an attempt to warm up.

"You must have more questions?" The Keeper asked incredulously after a minute of Best's self-imposed silence.

Best's teeth were chattering. He slowly nodded his head.

"Then ask them, boy. Ask them."

"Are you a Keeper for the Hole for the Council?" Best asked, thinking that they must have stationed a guard.

"I am a Keeper, but not of this Hole."

"What are you doing down here then?" asked Best.

As the Keeper came and ran his large palm over Best's back, Best sprang forward as if jolted by electricity. He soon relaxed, however, when he felt the heat radiate through his skin. His shivering stopped instantly.

"The question is," the Keeper began, "what are you doing here?"

Best recoiled away, suddenly afraid of the unusual effect of the Keeper's touch. "I fell."

"Ah... well I was before the Hole." The Keeper looked around almost contemptuously. "But it has exposed me."

"Why don't you get out of here?"

"A good question."

Best's mind was now saturated with confused thoughts. "How did you get here?"

The Keeper lifted up his eyebrows, and for the first time seemed at a loss for words. "I don't know," he simply said. "Maybe I did something wrong," he added absently, as if unable to come up with any definitive answer. He waved his hand away. "In any case, some warped fellow-men of yours have got it in their thick skulls to excavate this dungeon and expose me for the rest of the world to see, which is what they'll do once they discover me – or is that what you'll do?"

"What about the light?"

"I told you, the light is an illusion. It represents former glory. It cannot help me. It torments me."

"But you got rid of the water. You rescued me."

"I can neither confirm nor deny that observation, young man. Part of the Hole gave way. The water drained through the opening."

"Can't you get yourself out?"

The Keeper frowned. "All I can do is sit here until I'm discovered by that idiotic species collectively called mankind of which you, my boy, it seems are a naive member!"

The angered tone of the Keeper's voice rattled Best and he reeled back towards the wall of the Hole.

"Are you the devil?" Best asked tentatively, thinking that the Council had been stupid enough to dig too deep.

The Keeper turned from anger to amusement and laughed a deep, hard laugh. "No," he said finally. "Although I've had the misfortune to be acquainted with him on occasion… but he prefers the company of weak-minded humans."

Best slumped back against the wall of the Hole. He couldn't think of any more questions. It was better if he didn't think at all. He rubbed the back of his head. He felt dizzy.

The Keeper came forward and gently wiped Best's forehead with the sleeve of his gown. He showed the red blotch to Best. "You have a graze."

Best moved his fingers beneath his hairline and felt the sticky residue of seawater and coagulated blood.

"So," began the Keeper after a few seconds of stalemated silence. "When are you going to tell them I'm down here? Just think how popular you'll be. Does that interest you – being popular? It interests most humans, especially that numbskull Crenshaw up there. He must've gone back to the appendix line when the brains were being handed out!"

Best craned his head to look out of the Hole. "I can't get out."

"Once your mummy discovers you're not tucked safely in your bed she'll come looking for you... Won't she?"

Best shuffled his feet in the sand.

"Doesn't your mother love you? Won't she come looking for you?"

"I... don't know."

"What do you mean you don't know?"

"She's..."

The Keeper glanced away. "Well... I'm sure someone will come looking for you," he said, not pressing the issue any further.

"Best!" suddenly came a cry from the top of the Hole.

The Keeper backed away out of what little light there was coming down into the Hole from the now star-lit sky.

"Best?" cried his father. "Are you down there?"

Best was on his back. He turned his head to the side. The Keeper was gone. "I'm at the bottom!" he answered.

Best heard the rope drop by his feet. Soon, the large footprints of his father's feet thudded into the bottom. He moved over to Best and cupped his head in his large hand.

"What happened?" he asked, relieved to find Best conscious.

"There was something down here. I slipped," replied Best.

"Hop on my shoulders."

Ben Douglas scaled effortlessly up the Hole, and when they reached the top, he wrapped Best in the warm patchwork quilt that Best's mother had made. "What were you doing in there?" he asked, half relieved, half annoyed.

"I fell." Best glanced back down the Hole and rubbed his head. "I was bleeding." He ran his small fingers along where the wound had been.

Ben Douglas examined Best's forehead. "Can't see anything."

Best's fingers fumbled around for the dry blood, but it was gone.

"Come on," said his father, hoisting Best over his shoulders. "I've got to get back to the lamp room."

Best looked up at the lighthouse and saw that the beam was still, shinning out in a north-easterly direction, representing hope only for those vessels that happened to be sailing in that particular area of the sea.

*

THE day after his eighteenth birthday, John Selby, along with six Tin Town accomplices, infused with Taranna Perry's tales of gold, crept silently inside the Telford compound. Under the cloak of a moonless sky and the din of a recent Southerly, which was shaking the Lilly Pilly trees back and forth like maracas, the group made towards the meat cellar. John wasn't disappointed. Taranna's story had been true. Like a relay, the seven-man team formed a line running out of the cellar and loaded Telford's carriage with as much gold as it could handle without the wheel rims buckling under the weight. They quickly bridled two of the horses, and then made the four mile journey to the dock at Botany Bay where a schooner was waiting. The gold was not the only item Selby stole that night. He had often looked, enchanted, upon Taranna Perry's angel doll. Before making off for the Telford Estate, he crept into her room and snatched her most valued possession while she lay sleeping.

Over forty years later, Captain John Selby had come up from his cabin as soon as the Southerly hit. His crew addressed him as Captain only because he was their commander. He had never undertaken any formal training or been given any formal rank. He was self-taught, and his classroom had been the sea. Born into Tin Town, he was too impatient to serve twenty years in the navy to gain his own command. Besides, the pay wasn't attractive enough. So he had ascended a much quicker ladder to reach his objective. He had become a pirate. He didn't have the traditional parrot or eye-patch, nor did he lack any part of his anatomy. But he was a pirate in every sense of the word. His ship, the *Black Swan,* which he had acquired with the ill-gotten gains obtained from the Telfords, had been terrorizing the South Pacific for nearly half a decade. Selby had done well for himself. He was smart. He never carried stolen cargo around for too long. Once a job was done, he'd slip into the nearest port and off-load the bounty. He had contacts onshore who would transfer the goods into untraceable currency. Bills would be transferred into gold. Bullion would be transferred into bills. And other high priced commodities such as jewels would be quickly sifted through a network that would see them end up on the other side of the world.

The war had been good for just about every industry except piracy. The ratio of military ships to merchant crafts was not stacked in the pirates' favour. But the South Pacific was better than some places. Pirates operating in seas such as the Mediterranean were feeling the pinch as their plundering grounds were too often intertwined with major naval routes.

The past week, Selby had gotten lucky. He had stumbled upon an eccentric New Zealand landowner who was sailing a forty-foot schooner with his young bride from Auckland, New Zealand to Sydney, Australia. Selby hadn't killed them. That wasn't his style. He was a thief and a scoundrel, but he was not a murderer. He liked to perform his duty with a minimum of fuss. One of his crew made a move on the man's bride and Selby promptly felled him to the deck with the back of his hand and demanded he return to the *Black Swan.* Selby was a professional, and liked to think he was all class. Such antics from his crew did nothing for his reputation. The New Zealander managed to pull a revolver. Selby overpowered him, using no more than reasonable force, and locked the couple inside his own private chamber on the *Black Swan* so that he and his crew could plunder the couple's vessel away from their prying eyes.

The New Zealand man had sailed extensively. Only one form of currency transcended international boundaries – gold. And he had a hull full of it. He had told Selby that there was nothing on board. But Selby knew better. Wealthy individuals couldn't help but travel with some of their loot, especially during times of uncertainty, like times of war. The gold was quite a haul – worth about one hundred and fifty thousand pounds. Not bad for an afternoon's work. It would join some of Selby's own loot, which was painted black and disguised as ballast hidden deep inside the *Black Swan's* hull.

Selby and his crew had just about finished loading all of the gold onto the *Black Swan*. In his prison in Selby's cabin, the New Zealand man was listening to their movements impatiently when a strange clay figurine perched on top of Selby's night table caught his eye. He picked it up. There was a crude imprint on the bottom. He didn't recognize it. He brought the figurine into the light to examine it better. He was about to put it aside again, however, when Selby walked in.

"What are you doing?" Selby asked.

"It's an angel doll," the man said.

Selby snatched the figurine from the man and fingered the delicate craftwork of the wings. "I know that. But do you know where it's from? Where does it originate?" he asked, testing the man.

The New Zealander shrugged his shoulders. "I don't know. But based on the crude imprint it's over a hundred years old. These Aboriginal pieces attract quite a premium at British art houses," the man offered, thinking this information might placate Selby.

Selby had often heard tales of pirates stumbling across priceless pieces of art, but had doubted it would ever happen to him. He had no trouble admitting that he lacked the discerning eye and knowledge to recognize such pieces. He never suspected that the clay figurine, which he had taken on a whim, and which had been his good luck charm, would turn into something well beyond that. Now he decided he would sell it when he got the chance. He was not sentimental. It was always about the money. Besides, he'd heard from his contacts inside Tin Town that Taranna Perry had died many years ago. There was nothing linking him to her prized possession any longer.

The *Black Swan* was travelling slowly north when the Southerly hit. Selby had expected its arrival. He tried to get closer to the coastline for some protection. He'd performed the same manoeuvre many times. He would hug the coast by following the lighthouses until he found the opening to Botany Bay, where he would slip quietly inside to unload his precious cargo, safe from authorities, and the blistering swells the Southerly sometimes incited.

All was proceeding according to plan. Although wind and rough seas were buffeting the ship, Selby was following the protection of the coastline obediently. The *Black Swan* had just rounded the southern headland of Thurrough Beach when something unexpected happened: the Thurrough lighthouse went out. Selby blinked as the northern tip of the Thurrough Peninsula plunged into eerie darkness.

"Head due east!" Selby quickly barked to his crew. He was well aware that the northern headland of Thurrough Beach extended further than that of its southern headland, dropping off to form a submerged outcrop. Disguised by the seemingly undisturbed ocean, it ran further out barely twenty feet under the surface of the sea to form part of the calamitous Thurrough Outer Reefs. The lighthouse was situated near the tip of the northern headland and represented the eastern most point of the coastline for over two hundred miles in either direction.

Selby glanced up at the sky. It was overcast. No Southern Cross. Sometimes, in darkness, the senses couldn't be trusted. They had been sailing north when the Southerly hit them from behind, accelerating their boat's speed by some knots. By the time they had made the course correction, the boat was within three hundred feet of the northern headland. The *Black Swan* had shaved the Peninsula by less than fifty feet. But the Southerly had pushed her slightly to port, and as she crashed out through the increased swell, she hit the jagged northern reef located a hundred feet east off the headland. It was the last obstacle between the *Black Swan* and open sea. She snapped in two like a toothpick.

The irony was, that of the crew of six, only four could swim. And three of those drowned as they attempted to swim to shore. Captain John Selby never chose to go down with the *Black Swan:* he was far too pragmatic to adopt such a high-minded philosophy. His gesture was eventually glorified, but the reality was he was locked in his cabin by two of his crew, who thought a mutiny was best accomplished by the drowning of the Captain.

The ship's descent was made all the more rapid due to the weight of the gold contained in her belly. As the ship gasped for its last breath of air, through the tiny porthole Selby suddenly spotted the unmistakable glow of the Thurrough lighthouse shining out like a huge spotlight onto a stage of disaster on which he was playing front-and-centre.

CHAPTER SEVENTEEN

A FTER changing into dry clothes, Best went back to the lighthouse to keep his father company, and to relieve him, for short periods, from the arduous task of manually rotating the lamp. He said nothing to his father about the Keeper. He wasn't sure if it had been real, anyway. He had hit his head against the sand. He could've imagined the whole episode. Ever since his mother's death, he often had vivid dreams. He had a headache. Besides, even if someone was down there, words like pride, popularity and fame didn't mean anything to Best. He was a mere boy, still shrouded in innocence, who hadn't yet been tempted with such desires.

After manually rotating the lamp all night, Ben Douglas was exhausted. As the sun peeked over the ocean's horizon, he slowly made the fifty-three-stair descent from the lamp room, barely able to lift his legs. He went into the cottage and plopped down on his unmade bed without even taking off his shoes. When Best came in and removed them for him, he mumbled a thank you and began to snore an entire opera. Best shut his door and left his father to enjoy his well-deserved rest.

The sun was up and burning off what remained of the low cloud brought in by the Southerly. By nine, a crowd of tourists had already gathered in front of the ticket office in order to view the Thurrough oddity. There was also another unexpected attraction: bits of a ship, which had struck the reef during the night, were washing up on the shore, providing further items of curiosity for those whose curiousness had brought them to the Hole in the first place.

As the workers began to mill outside the gate, awaiting their boss, Manager Dirk Crenshaw, who would arrive shortly in his shiny new automobile to unlock the gate and let them in, the carnival started into full swing. The Big Smoke girls, with their bright red lipstick, paraded through the throngs, encouraging the gullible to begin a lifelong addiction to cigarettes. And, with such perfect white teeth, their sales pitch was hard to resist. Clowns selling fairy floss had suddenly sprouted and were also plying their trade. Concession stands opened, catering to the hysteria of the moment, selling shirts, postcards, pens, and anything else on which could be written, *I've been to Thurrough's Big Hole!*

Best was sick of the people who were now invading what he considered his front yard. The Hole had grown into a perverse spectacle well beyond the exercise that he and Dirk had originally embarked on. It had to stop. He had to stop it. He wanted the digging to stop, and he wanted the cars to go away.

It was only when Best saw Dirk getting out of his bright red car wearing his sixth three-piece suit in as many days that he got the idea. He quickly ran over to where the workers awaited their imbecilic boss.

"Hi Mister," he said to one of the workers.

"G'day kid. You won't have long to wait. The Hole'll be open soon."

Best pointed over to the twenty-deep line of people in front of the ticket booth. "A lot here already."

"There always is," the worker responded in a tired croaky voice as he lit a cigarette. "And they don't stop coming 'til the day's done."

"That's a lot of people."

"Yesiree."

"How much does it cost to see inside the Hole?"

"A shilling."

"That's a lot of money."

"Yesiree."

Best spied Dirk making his way down to the beach, only stopping to admire some of the females that had come to the Hole just to see him.

Best knew he had to act fast. "How many people come here a day do you reckon?"

The worker sucked back long and hard on his cigarette. "Heaps."

"And the Council charges a shilling a person?"

"That they do."

"And you make the Hole bigger?"

"Sure as night follows day."

"And how much an hour do you get paid?"

The worker chuckled gruffly. He signalled to his fellow workers around him. "Hey fellas, the boy wants to know how much we get paid!"

They all howled in laughter.

Best laughed too. "You must make a stack of money with all these people coming to see your work every day?"

The workers hushed. Within a matter of milliseconds not one of them was laughing. Within a matter of seconds not one of them was smiling. Best had hit a nerve. The workers gathered around their Foreman like bees around their queen.

"After all," added Best. "That's all Dirk Crenshaw did. He dug a hole. But you're like actors – important people. The crowd come to watch you guys. You're performers."

The worker tossed down his cigarette and kicked sand over it. "It's the same old story," he said to the Foreman. "Even the kid can see it."

"Yeah," chipped in another worker, "we do all the digging and

Crenshaw and the Council make all the money. Something's wrong with the system. Everybody's thinking it – the kid's just got the guts to say something about it!"

Another worker swore. Best had tapped into a vein seething with discontent.

'We're slaving our bum cracks off in that sweat pit and for what?" said another.

"For a lousy, stinking bundle of a big bunch of Jack Squat!" interjected another.

"And his brother, Didley!" yelled another.

Dirk Crenshaw took in the tourists lining up at the ticket office and smiled. Another day, another suit, another bevy of sweethearts. He boldly approached the workers like the General that he thought he could have been.

"Ready for the day ahead, men?" he asked as he pumped the air with a clenched fist.

The question was supposed to fire the men up, but as they'd heard the same old line for months, they found it particularly grating, especially in their agitated state. The Foreman jabbed Dirk in the chest with his thick index finger. "Listen Crenshaw, me and the boys have been doing some serious thinking. We're being screwed over here – royally screwed over. Look at you. You're wearing another bloody suit. You've got a bloody new car. And we're doing all the bloody work!"

The workers shouted calls of solidarity.

Dirk loosened his collar. "I am the Hole's Manager."

"You couldn't manage a chook raffle in a hen house!" a worker shouted.

The Foreman threw his shovel down at Dirk's feet. "You dig the bloody Hole then. And when you step one foot into that pit, we'll pull every Council worker in the Shire out on strike for using scab labour."

"And we're not coming back unless we get more money you greedy bugger," one of the workers yelled over his shoulder as he joined his co-workers and Foreman, who were indignantly marching off the beach.

Best slipped away inconspicuously amongst the workers. One of them patted him affectionately on the head. "Thanks for being man enough to put it in perspective, kid."

"I just hope I haven't caused any trouble," Best replied innocently.

Ten minutes later, Thurrough Council's General Manager, Kent Lawrence arrived.

"What's going on, Crenshaw?"

"The workers are on strike."

Lawrence picked up a shovel and handed it to him. "You know what to do. Get in there and start digging."

"But I'm wearing a suit."

"You'll be the best-dressed digger around. Get in."

"But the workers said they'd go on strike everywhere if we get someone else to dig the Hole… The garbage men, the sewer men, the gardeners – everyone."

Lawrence knocked the shovel out of Dirk's hands. "Why didn't you say so?"

"You never asked."

"Keep the gate locked. Under no circumstances let anyone down there or we'll have one gigantic Shire-wide dispute on our hands."

"What about all the tourists?"

"They can still see the Hole can't they? Nobody's digging that's all. Charge them half-price."

Kent Lawrence rushed up the beach and drove back to Council in order to negotiate a new wage deal with the workers. While Dirk Crenshaw took steps to slash the ticket prices in half, Best looked on in amusement from the sanctuary of the lighthouse.

CHAPTER EIGHTEEN

FOLLOWING Flavian Broad's advice, Richard Tipody made sure he always brought Best some kind of small offering when he visited the Home. On several occasions, he even brought additional morsels so that Best would associate feelings of contentment with the doctor's visits, treating Best like one of Pavlov's dogs. And, although Best rarely ate these enticements as the appetites of the elderly were bird-like – the result of their sedentary lives – he started to consider that perhaps Dr Richard Tipody was a more generous spirit than he'd originally given him credit for.

Having discovered Best's friendship with the paperboy, Tipody had also started bringing Best surfing magazines so that he could pass them on to the paperboy. This gesture endeared Tipody to Best even more. And, as Tipody had observed that Best was more distracted when the surf was good, and infinitely more whenever the paperboy was surfing, he began to call only when the miserable state of the waves provoked feelings of boredom in Best. A social metamorphosis occurred: Best started to look forward to Tipody's visits.

Tipody leaned towards the window as he placed a ham and cheese croissant on Best's bedside table. "Not many out today," he remarked, feigning interest in Best's favourite pastime.

"Not yet, but there will be. The Southerly's weakening. The ocean will be as smooth as glass by dusk."

"What are the biggest waves you've seen?" Tipody asked, although his extensive research had already furnished him with the answer.

"Big."

"How big?" Tipody probed.

"Big," Best repeated, as he picked away at the croissant like a mouse.

Tipody was going for it. He had sought Flavian Broad's counsel and treated Best like the winner of the Melbourne Cup, but now it was time to prepare him for the dog food factory. "Cyclone Enid?" he enquired delicately.

Enid. Best was surprised to hear that name. The Bureau of Meteorology never used the same name twice when christening a cyclone. Best had not heard that cyclone mentioned in many years. He slowly nodded his head.

Tipody hurried to capture the moment. "How big were those waves?"

Best looked vacant, as if watching a film in which he himself was featured. "Cyclone Enid was a massive low-pressure system… category five. The swell came from the north out of nothing. That's where the cyclone swells come from… the north… where cyclones are formed out of warmer sea temperatures. We didn't have the weather equipment they have today. It was all done by word of mouth. But the waves of Cyclone Enid were too quick and too silent. They came up without as much as a whisper."

Tipody lowered his voice to make it sound as soothing as possible, which almost produced a quivering in his words. "What happened that day? The day of the Enid swells?"

Tipody's theatrical act of verbal intimacy prompted Best to continue. "My mother and father fished on the rocks. They would stand on the rock shelves and cast their lines out for hours at a time. They always took me with them. It was safe enough. They made sure the swells were small and never went on the king tides… not because it was better for fishing but because it was safer. No chance of getting washed off the rocks." Best subconsciously rubbed his left shoulder. "My mother used to tie me to her waist with a boat rope."

Tipody reached inside his pocket and pulled out the miniature recorder, which he placed on the edge of the bed. This time it went unnoticed by Best who, instead, never took his eyes off the sea outside his window. "The odd bigger wave often came out of nowhere. It was almost a pattern. These waves would splash over the rocks and spray our faces. But they weren't dangerous. My father said they were just messages from the sea telling us we were near its territory and to be alert." Best spoke in a monotone, almost like a scripted narration, as if his age was too advanced and his memory too distant to conjure up any emotions. "My father never saw the wave coming. There was no warning. It just came up at us. It took her from the rocks and tossed her into the sea like a rag doll. It was so quick… so quick."

Tipody was leaning so far forward that both his knees were touching Best's. Such intimacy would not have looked out of place between a son and father, but it was incongruous between two individuals when one was intent on killing the other.

"He had been standing in front of her," Best continued. "He'd been closer. But somehow it had spared him. Almost as if it had selected her."

Tipody was riveted. He craned his neck to sneak a peek at the dictaphone to check that it was still recording. He smiled inwardly to himself. The GAC would never get to hear this account. No, Tipody would never be so careless as to shatter the illusion he had created – the picture of Best as a simple old man. But it might be found in a future hardcover book that Tipody planned to write on the first subject to be expatriated. He quickly checked himself. He must not get too carried away with the idea of fame. A book was a long way down the track. Still, he had to plan ahead. He didn't want to be unprepared when publishers and agents came knocking.

Best spoke as if he wasn't aware of Tipody's presence at all. He was in that trance-like state that such intense memories induce. "She always tied the rope between us tightly." A rope which, to Best, represented the umbilical cord that had bound them once, and had symbolically bound them ever since. "I was dragged along the rocks. My father lunged for me and caught my left arm and leg just when I thought I was going into the sea. Between the pull of the rope and my father's grip, it felt like every joint was being yanked apart." Best suddenly looked up. "You know something, Richard?"

The question hit Tipody unexpectedly, snapping him out of his captivated coma.

"I only have arthritis down one side of my body – the left side."

"Is that a fact?"

"His first instinct was to save me," continued Best.

"A natural reaction I would assume," added Tipody.

Best nodded, but he wasn't listening. "When he saw the rope from my body running into the sea he saw hope – the hope that he could save her. I saw it in his eyes. He tried to hold me tight. But as she was being cast further away, I was being drawn towards the sea. He lunged for the rope. He took hold of it and began pulling madly. For a moment, this took some pressure off me. I was able to grab the nearest rock. I just hung on tight. I watched him working with all his strength and just hung on tight. By then, walls of water created by the cyclone twelve hundred miles away were crashing down on us. Still, I managed to cling to the rock and he managed to hold on to the rope, but I still don't know how. It was cutting into his hands, even though they were as tough as leather."

Best stared out at the ocean through his salt-stained window. The sea was beginning to calm. The initial impact of the Southerly change was dissipating just as he had predicted. This front had been weak; its effect was already being forgotten as the sun shoved away the remaining cloud.

Tomorrow the sea breeze would be back, and so would the people. Best eyed the sea suspiciously, as if he considered it a sleeping menace. "Suddenly," he continued, "he went flying back. He got to his knees and pulled on the rope. It came to him easy – much too easy. When he saw the frayed end of the rope he cried out." Best paused thoughtfully before continuing. "He pushed himself to his feet. He tried to capture some glimpse of her. But he just couldn't see her. He looked at me."

Tipody had read and re-read the account of the drowning of Norah Douglas in the Thurrough Shire's Public Library's archives of the Daily Chronicle. Now, he gorged himself on the details as if he was having his last meal. "Did your father try to go in after her?" he asked, trying to push more of Best's memory's buttons.

Best briefly rubbed his forehead. "I yelled at him to help her... to try and rescue her. But the seas were just too rough." Best coughed to hide the slight inflection in his voice. "As I was clinging to the rock, I saw him readying himself to dive in. But then he stepped back..." Best's voice trailed off as if he was still trying to make sense of the vision – a scene that was still so vividly clear to him in spite of all the years that had gone by. If he had been aware enough, he would have heard the steady droning and occasional squeaking of Tipody's recorder as the tape wound its way around the spool.

Tipody let out an involuntary sigh. Best Douglas was certainly an enigma. He possessed more insight and more intelligence than Tipody had ever given him credit for. In that instant, he couldn't help but admire Best. Tipody quickly regained his composure and placed a sympathetic hand onto Best's withered one, causing Best to jump unexpectedly. Tipody soothed him down with gentle but firm pressure on his arthritic shoulder. Tipody had finally manoeuvred Best to where he wanted him. It had taken six laborious months, but he had opened up a passage into Best's past through his memories. Having struck a gold mine in Best's consciousness, which contained a wealth of recollections, he would now use this against Best.

"I'm sure," Tipody began manipulatively, "you must have felt like dying yourself?"

Best was slowly coming out of his memory-induced stupor. "That was a long time ago. I've forgotten how I felt."

"It must have been difficult for you – a little boy without his mother?"

Best didn't respond.

"And how do you feel now?"

"About what?" Best asked, not entirely sure where the conversation was heading.

"About life? Do you want to live?"

"Live? That's what I'm doing now," Best replied, still not sure what Tipody was getting at.

"I know you want to live," Tipody went on, "but there comes a time when we have to shed our mortal bodies in order to move on to the next realm – the spiritual." Tipody was almost making himself sick. He was an avowed atheist who believed the final destination of man was the grave, where the body was greedily received by the earth as sustenance.

Best rubbed his tired eyes. "It soon could be time for me to move on. I'm getting old."

Tipody grabbed the arms of Best's wheelchair and swung it around to face him. "If I gave you a choice between whether you could live or die, what would you choose?"

Best smiled knowingly, becoming more animated but made a little uncomfortable by the doctor's proximity. He could now see a tiny strand of lettuce that was caught between Tipody's teeth. "You couldn't give me that choice, Richard."

"But what if I could?"

"It's out of your hands, Richard."

"Of course it is. I'm not God."

"No. You're not," Best added sternly, just in case his companion was under the mistaken notion that he was.

"But what if I could give you that choice? What if I could offer you that option? What would you do?"

Best turned to look out the window towards the old Thurrough

Lighthouse. "I'd live."

Tipody frowned. "Why, Best? Why?"

"That's all I know."

Tipody became angry. "What if God gave you that option?" He pointed outside at the light rain, which was the Southerly's last gasping breath before petering out. "What if God gave you that choice?"

Best tracked a solitary raindrop as it ran down the glass. "I'd leave it in his hands."

"And what if I was God?"

Best shot him a look of pity. "But you're not. You're Richard Tipody."

Tipody stood up and ran his hand through his oily hair in frustration. "But what if I was? What if I was God?"

"I'd leave it up to you then. I'd leave it up to you."

Tipody snatched the recorder from the windowsill. "Thank you, Best! Thank you!" He then marched triumphantly towards the door, brushing past Orion on the way out, who had to pull his barrow out of the way to prevent the doctor tumbling over it.

CHAPTER NINETEEN

BEN Douglas confined himself to the lamp room for the night. He had managed to repair the brass rotating apparatus, but wanted to make sure it was operating correctly. This presented Best with a prime opportunity. He told his father he would come up later to sleep with him in the lamp room just to keep him company. His father said he appreciated Best's thoughtfulness, but knew Best was too scared to stay in the cottage by himself. He always had been, particularly since Dirk Crenshaw had left. He went along with Best's pretence, however. He saw no reason to make the boy feel embarrassed.

Best grabbed one of his father's sturdy boat ropes and made for the Hole. He was anxiously excited, and after the other night, didn't know what to expect. He wasn't sure if he had dreamed the entire episode. But, just in case the mysterious Keeper was real, he stuffed some pudding into a paper bag and shoved it inside his shirt, taking it as a gift for the stranger. He climbed over the fence and tied the rope to one of the fence poles. He gave it a tug. The pole wasn't going anywhere. He made his descent cautiously.

His bare feet hit the sand with a gentle thud. He glanced around. "Keeper?" he called. The Hole looked deserted. He shook his head. Maybe he had dreamt the whole thing? Maybe the fall had knocked him out and he had imagined the entire episode? He felt a little foolish even saying the name "Keeper". What kind of a name was that? Surely it was a name that could only be invented by the imagination? He located the rope, and feeling silly, began the arduous task of scaling the sixty feet back to the top, squashing the pudding against his stomach as he climbed against the sand wall.

"Best?" a voice resonated from beneath him.

Best peered back down. He could see a faint glow. "Keeper?"

"Yes!" the voice answered.

Best quickly slid back down the rope. On reaching the bottom, not knowing quite what to do, he pulled the soggy pudding from inside his shirt. "Here – take this."

The Keeper stepped towards him. "What is it?"

"It's pudding. I cooked it for dessert. It's pretty good."

The Keeper smiled. "I don't need..." it, he was about to say, but stopped himself mid-sentence. He took the mashed pudding gratefully. "Thank you," he added, but by the clinical way he consumed it, Best got the impression that the Keeper lacked any physical inclination to eat.

"Good?" asked Best hopefully, proud of his cooking ability.

"I would say... good." He looked affectionately at Best. "Why did you do that today?" he asked.

"Do what?" asked Best, feigning ignorance.

"Stop the diggers from coming down?"

"I didn't. They went on strike."

"I heard you."

Best glanced away.

"You've caused me to think a great deal." The Keeper paced away from Best, his dishevelled gown dragging along the sand. "I can't quite remember when, but I roamed the earth a long time ago... before it was covered by water."

"What was it like back then?"

"Much like it is today I suspect. Men fighting against each other. Committing atrocities. I haven't seen it. But I can hear it. I can hear the diggers talk. I can hear what they talk about. They talk about a war they know nothing about. They talk about a war fought on battlefields and oceans when the real battle is being raged in the hearts of men. I hear them more clearly each day. I know they are getting closer to my chamber." The Keeper smiled tenderly and pointed to the right hand wall. "Behind there, waiting to be discovered. No point showing it to you yet – it's empty."

"How long have you been down here?"

The Keeper cocked his head to one side. "I have existed for a long time – if time is indeed the measurement. But I'm not sure it is."

The Keeper sat down and crossed his long legs and, extending his hand, invited Best to do the same. "What about you?"

"I live in the lighthouse," Best answered.

"With your mother and father?" the Keeper asked, but in such a way that implied he already knew the answer.

Best began doodling in the sand with his finger. "Just my dad."

The Keeper nodded knowingly. "I may not know what I'm doing down here," he began. "But I do know that life is sometimes mysterious and beyond our comprehension."

Best nodded fervently. "Yes, I know!" he blurted out unrestrainedly. "I don't know why God allowed my mum to die!"

There was a stagnant silence. Best felt awkward. He had never spoken of his mother's death in such abrupt terms. He had never questioned God out loud before, even to Father Cruickshank, but something about the Keeper's manner drew it out of him.

The Keeper shuffled closer to Best. "Ah... yes... your beautiful mother."

Best looked up expectantly. "Did you know her?"

The Keeper looked away, almost sheepishly, as if he had revealed too much. "I know her through you."

The Keeper rose to his feet. As he towered over Best, he was an imposing figure, with angular features, and a captivating smile that instantly put Best at ease.

"I have many questions for God," the Keeper said. "Not the least of which is just what I'm doing down here."

"So you need answers too?" asked Best.

"Yes, but a human's concept of time makes him believe he must have the answers immediately. This is not the case. Perhaps the answers may come in the course of time, but they may come outside time. Let's not let the questions tie us up in knots in the meantime."

Best nodded slowly as he began to understand. "Are you saying that I should stop questioning Him about my mum?"

The Keeper shook his head. "Not at all. I'm just suggesting that you be patient for the answers. Very patient – like me. It may take hundreds of years. Let us just trust that the Creator of the Universe knows what he's doing... even if you happen to be down a hole!"

Best suddenly felt the rope that tugged at his heart and bound him to his mother unwinding.

"I don't know how long they'll be on strike for," said Best, feeling increasingly calmed by the Keeper's words.

"Maybe I'm meant to be discovered. You can't stop them from digging."

Best stared back at the Keeper with a kind of affection that he didn't understand. "I can try."

The Keeper raised his eyebrows. "That's true! And maybe you're meant to try?"

Before Best climbed back up the rope, he turned to the Keeper. "I have one more thing to ask you...?"

The Keeper held the rope so that Best could steady himself. "Anything... but I can't promise I'll be able to answer it."

"Your name," Best began almost reluctantly, "it's kind of strange."

The Keeper frowned, then laughed. "Perhaps it's strange to you, but it has a very specific meaning. It was given to me for a reason as, I'm sure, was yours. To this day, I have not discovered that reason. But when I find out, I'll tell you… OK?"

Best nodded. "OK."

TWO hours after Best had bunked down in the lamp room with his father, he had a dream. In it, the tide crept up Thurrough Beach; the first of the abnormally high Christmas Tides, so named because the highest and lowest watermarks were reached around December–January due to the celestial positions of the sun and the moon. But even on the highest Christmas tide, the sea would stop several feet from Crenshaw's Hole. In Best's dream, however, it inched further, as if influenced by another invisible force aside from gravity.

He could see a clay figurine bobbing up and down with the gentle motion of the sea. The water cajoled and pushed the fragile piece further up the beach, as if the fickle sea had tasted it and decided to spit it out. The tide crept closer to the rim of the Hole, nudging the clay angel like a seal pushing a ball with its nose. When the water finally reached its destination, the figurine balanced precariously over the edge of the Hole. Then the sea began to withdraw, as if changing its mind; it vainly attempted to drag the clay doll back with it. But the lure of the Hole was too strong, and as the Pacific Ocean released its clutches, the figurine toppled into the Hole.

The Keeper was waiting; his head craned up, looking out of the Hole at the star-filled sky whose lights were diminished only by the brilliant shine of the midnight moon. He was holding his arms out as if embracing something. Best heard a swishing sound, which seemed to instantly get louder. He looked up and noticed that the clay figurine was falling towards them. A fraction of a second later, it landed softly in the cushion of the Keeper's hands. He examined it and smiled at Best. He carefully took it into his chamber and placed it on a pedestal made entirely of sand. When Best awoke the next morning, the dream was forgotten.

*

BEST Douglas was six years old when his mother was swept off the Thurrough rocks. Although Best's father combed the ocean every day for three months looking for her body, his search proved fruitless. Racked with the grief of loss and the unbearable remorse that came with the decision to cut the link between mother and son, he threw himself into the task of lobbying for the restoration of the Thurrough lighthouse once more. The Government's decision to only partially fund the project was proving to be a massive obstacle. After the death of Baine Telford, his son, Galbraith, seemed even more vitriolic. His influence over Thurrough Council and other key Shire stakeholders was more than enough to scuttle any initiatives Ben Douglas proposed to raise money for the costs of construction. Telford wanted the land back, and over the years, the closest emotion he experienced to pleasure was seeing the old lighthouse crumbling away like an arrowroot biscuit. He also suspected that some of the residents of Tin Town had stolen from the Telford family's gold reserves years before, and was adamant that the vagabonds and their crude dwellings be eradicated once and for all.

BILL Cruickshank had no problem taking the vows of chastity or poverty. Being of portly appearance, although more stocky than overweight, with a face that bloated and puckered like a puffer fish whenever he was deep in thought, he did not attract the attention of those women in the parish who might have lusted after a man of the pulpit. He had known colleagues who had succumbed to that particular weakness of the flesh. After all, they were only human. "For Christ's sake," one of them had told him during confession, "Peter denied Our Lord three times and he was his best mate! Nobody's perfect!" Cruickshank also lacked the desire to collect anything substantial materially, spending his first eight years out of seminary living amongst the downtrodden in Tin Town where his accommodation consisted of five sheets of tin held together by pieces of 4 x 2's. He had experienced temptation – just in a different form. He enjoyed a cold beer or three, and the odd bottle of red wine. Some of his parishioners secretly murmured that he was an alcoholic, but these rumours were never substantiated. He may have bred some resentment, as he was always hard on his flock, hounding them weekly to help in the construction of the new church. But this was his strength. He was a builder, and a doer. His knees would eventually give out on him, not so much from praying, but from nailing floorboards. He and Ben Douglas were kindred spirits in many ways, not the least of which was their predisposition to work. Neither could sit still.

Ben Douglas stood next to the vacant block, which was located between the main Thurrough beach and the proposed site of the new railway station. He instinctively kicked the dirt with his boot – sand and clay. The foundations would have to be deep enough to reach rock. Cruickshank looked at him expectantly while his Labrador, Sheba, lovingly licked his hand.

Ben Douglas reached over and shook the Priest's hand despite knowing it was laced with dog slobber. "I'll do it," he said.

Bill Cruickshank smiled. "There's more than one way to skin a cat!" he exclaimed.

The arrangement with Ben Douglas meant that Thurrough Parish would make up the shortfall in the funding of the new Thurrough Lighthouse in return for receiving a share of the new brick that was to replace the old sandstone, and Ben Douglas's building expertise. Bill Cruickshank would have his new church in the centre of Thurrough constructed of brick rendered with cement and plastered on the inside, just like the new lighthouse, as well as a small adjoining cottage to house himself and visiting clergy. The fact that he was diverting parish funds to aid in the construction of a lighthouse was a minute detail that he need not bother the Sydney Archdiocese with, which was also contributing to the funding of the church. After all, he was in the business of saving souls, and a lighthouse certainly did that! With funding secured, the Government green-lighted the development much to the disgust of Galbraith Telford who added the Catholic Church to the list of institutions he despised.

*

VERY few parishioners participated in the rite of confession. Father Cruickshank would light all the candles in the half-finished church at three o'clock every Saturday afternoon, and as there was not yet glass in the windows, a breeze would funnel in and cause the flames to dance. He would then proceed to don his ceremonial garb and take his place within the confessional chamber. It was a small space no bigger than a wardrobe. The two halves of the chamber were separated by a timber-panelled wall in which a fine wire mesh window was inserted, which could be closed by way of another sliding wooden panel.

Aside from Best's father, who would come in for confession the first Sunday of every month, and a few other ditherers, the afternoon became a time for the Priest to consider his own weaknesses. With his head buried in his hands, he brought to mind his personal shortcomings: his love of alcohol, his short temper with lazy parishioners, his liberal use of profanities, and his nagging doubts about his next project – a respite house for the residents of Tin Town who Galbraith Telford wanted evicted. He heard the confessional door open and shut ever so softly. There was a small cough from the other side of the panel, followed by a gentle tap.

The Priest slowly slid back the timber panel. The wire mesh was supposed to hide the confessor's identity so that they felt free to confess their sins in relative anonymity. But Bill Cruickshank could see quite clearly through the device, unbeknownst to his parishioners, who never seemed to ask themselves why, since they could see the Priest so plainly, couldn't he see them?

"Father Bill?" asked Best tentatively, not used to seeing the Priest draped in such a costume.

Bill Cruickshank had to quickly check himself from saying Best's name. "Yes, how are you, umm, young man?"

Best deepened his voice to further disguise his identity. "I'm fine, Father. I just thought that I'd come and talk to you... to confess... to try and talk about my sins."

Father Bill smiled but then quickly covered his mouth, not wanting Best to think that he was making light of the boy's confession. "I sense you're a young man. What sins could you possibly have?"

Best knelt down by the window. "Sometimes I have bad feelings towards my dad."

Father Bill sighed. Poor Best, he thought. The Priest had already heard the confession of Ben Douglas and was obliged by the ordinance of the sacrament not to reveal confessional details to other parties, even if those parties could benefit by the information. But Cruickshank knew that true healing couldn't happen with the Priest as a conduit.

When Ben Douglas came to make sure the foundations were deep enough for the Priest's cottage, Bill Cruickshank steered him away from the labourers who were busy digging. The Priest put his arm around Ben Douglas's shoulders. It was an unusual gesture as Bill Cruickshank rarely touched others. He wasn't that type of person.

"I'm worried about this bloody lighthouse lens of yours," the Priest said.

"Lepante are the best. Their craftsmanship is unequalled."

"It's not the construction – it's the voyage back here."

Ben leaned over one of the foundation holes and assured himself that they had reached rock. "I'm sure they'll pack it and ship it without too much fuss."

"You're more trusting than I am. Once it gets on that ship, who do you think's going to watch over it? The bloody French? No, they'll be too busy guarding their national treasures – their bloody wines – not that I take exception to that." It was close to five in the early evening and Cruickshank smacked his lips at the thought of a glass of red or cleansing ale. "There's only one solution," he continued, getting back to his objective.

"And what's that?" Ben Douglas asked in mild amusement.

"You and Best need to go over there and show those bloody Frenchies that you won't be trifled with!"

WHEN Ben and Best Douglas stepped on their vessel bound for London, there was a divide between them. Best could barely look at his father since his mother's drowning. And, as for words between them, there were very little. Whereas the loss should have brought them together, it had torn them apart, and Ben Douglas felt powerless to do anything about it. His only answer was to take Bill Cruickshank's advice and remove Best from the place of his mother's passing – to try and remove the pain.

As the sun set over the Indian Ocean, it spread orange rays across the sea like an octopus's tentacles which gyrated and slithered with the movement of the water, creating a kaleidoscope of colours. Many of the passengers gathered by the port-stern railing to witness this show of nature, and Ben Douglas found Best, hunched over the guard rails, resting his chin on the top rung. He was a determined man, and was adamant that he and his son would not continue to exist in this way. He came to where Best was standing and put his arm around him. As he squeezed him tighter, six-year-old Best Douglas started to cry.

"Why... why didn't you go in after her?" he asked, his young voice trembling.

Ben Douglas felt tears welling in his own eyes. "I couldn't. I just couldn't."

"But why?" pleaded Best.

"I thought about it. I've thought it ever since. But I swear sure as God made little green apples, I was going to drown. Your mother wouldn't have wanted that. She wouldn't have wanted to leave you alone to fend for yourself."

"But you might have saved her?"

"Even if there was a slight chance, she wouldn't have wanted me to take it."

Best began to cry uncontrollably, clinging to his father even tighter.

"When I saw the rope dangling from your waist, I knew part of who she was was still with me on the rocks."

But the core of the confession of Ben Douglas remained unsaid. And, as parents often do, Ben Douglas kept his secret from Best, and his guilt followed him to his deathbed.

FOLLOWING the NSW Government's approval, Ben Douglas lobbied the maritime association to provide the services of the high profile architect, James Barnet, whose lighthouse designs were normally typified by an ornate crown that capped a lighthouse tower much like the regal head of a Queen. Ben Douglas wanted his lighthouse's monumental crown to be a permanent memorial to his wife, and even requested that her name be inscribed within the delicate craftsmanship. Following its completion, it wasn't long before the new Thurrough Lighthouse became known by just one word – *Norah*.

While Barnet toiled on the design of the lighthouse, Best and his father were well on the way to France via London on the passenger liner, *SS Osterley*, for a round trip that was scheduled to take over six months to complete. Ben Douglas maintained that the lighthouse lens needed to be upgraded from a Fourth order lens to a First order, which would extend the light reach of the lamp further out to sea. The official reason for the journey was that Ben Douglas would take personal possession of the lighthouse's new optical lens and escort it back to Australia. Containing seven hundred and sixty pieces of polished prismatic glass, and weighing eight tonnes, after his passionate discussion with Bill Cruickshank, Best's father would not trust its passage back to Australia with anyone else.

Although the French company, Societe des Establishment, Henry Lepante, Paris, had been commissioned to produce the Thurrough

Lighthouse Fresnel lens well in advance, by the time Best and his father arrived in France, the lens was still not completed, and wouldn't be for another three months. Having arrived in the middle of an unusually hot European summer with barely enough funds to see out a month let alone three, the company suggested that Ben Douglas make for the sea port town of Saint Nazaire where they would arrange work for him in the shipyard, building what would become one of the world's best known liners, *France 1912*.

Being a builder and a lighthouse keeper, Ben Douglas had no trouble selling his services to Chantiers de Penhoet, and was put to work in the welding department whose primary task was to join the huge plates of steel which together formed the hull of the project ship. Chantiers put Best and his father up at a local boarding house run by a widow and her eleven-year-old daughter. Charlotte Sommer was a young woman whose life had been forever altered when her husband was tragically killed at the shipyards just after their daughter was born. In her, Best's father found an empathic soul whose personal tragedy mirrored his own. Her daughter, Marie, took on the role of Best's surrogate sister, and quickly educated him on the finer nuances of French life. Through Marie, Best came to appreciate the passion of the French people, and the devotion they had to creative pursuits. Even though the construction of *France* was such a precise exercise, the French still allowed for creativity in aspects of the aesthetics, which was precisely the reason that Ben Douglas had insisted on the Henry Lepante-made lens for the lighthouse.

While Marie hauled Best everywhere on her daily errands, Ben Douglas contributed his considerable handyman talents to the upkeep of Charlotte Sommer's boarding house. Instead of resting on his days off – a concept totally foreign to him as he believed there was always something to do – he fixed plumbing, built retaining walls in the courtyard, replaced roof shingles, and generally mended anything broken, so much so that Charlotte felt guilty when Chantiers de Penhoet reimbursed her for Ben Douglas's accommodation.

Ben Douglas was sensitive enough to keep his relationship with Charlotte Sommer a secret from Best. He had not wanted to fall in love with her. In fact, they both resisted the attraction for some time, each assessing their motives. Were they merely compensating for the void left behind by their respective partners? Or did they have genuine feelings of love for each other? In the final analysis, it didn't really matter. Oceans away from people and places that evoked memories of Norah, and deeply wounded, Ben Douglas found love in a kindred spirit. He could not resist her affectionate nature, and she in turn loved him for what he essentially was – a decent, but wounded man.

As Best was whisked around the seaside town by Marie, his father would often stroll down by the seaside with Charlotte. They would bring their own wine and cheese to enjoy sitting side by side on one of the seaside jetties, where they could hover their legs above the water and dip their feet to feel the cool touch of the Atlantic.

Ben Douglas' love of the sea began to return on these nightly walks, when the glorious setting sun cast its orange hue over the deep blue tones of the Atlantic, and along with the shimmering surface, acted to create an ocean alive with millions of flickering lights. They spoke openly and freely about their losses, each of them hungry to hear of the other's partner, and the qualities that drew them to one another.

Ben Douglas was normally one for stoic manly pride, not wanting to talk of feelings buried deep within. But Charlotte's soft, feminine touch, coupled with her overwhelming desire to heal his pain, was a panacea for all that was ailing him.

One night after they had shared a bottle of French Sauternes, which Ben had bartered for in exchange for his Akubra hat, and which mixed beautifully with the salty tang of the seaside air, he broke down as the words became too much to bear.

Charlotte quickly embraced him as a mother would a son.

"He would never forgive me. He would never understand," he fumbled out, trying to prevent the sobbing that was overtaking his composure. "When he was being dragged into the sea..." But he couldn't finish the words. They were too painful to articulate. He dropped his head into her lap: the destructive demon had partially been exorcised.

Charlotte stroked his hair affectionately then tenderly kissed his forehead. "You're his father. It is not easy sometimes. But we must make these decisions, even though they drive a stake through our hearts. You must not condemn yourself for these decisions."

Ben Douglas took her in his arms. Her sympathetic English words, cloaked in a soothing French accent, seemed to wash over his entire being and cleanse him. She never judged him, even though she guessed what it was that he found too painful to reveal. He loved her for that. He kissed her tenderly, then passionately. Ben Douglas had intentionally broken the bond between mother and son to save the son. This was the pain he had to live with. And that was the gaping wound that Charlotte Sommer treated like a tender nurse.

By the time Ben Douglas had to leave for Paris to take possession of the prized lens, he and Charlotte Sommer had enjoyed a profound relationship, which was tempered only by his need to return to Thurrough, and Charlotte's need to remain in France. When Best and his father leaned out the train window, waving goodbye, Ben Douglas knew that he would never see Charlotte Sommer again. It was a sacrifice that both of them made for what they perceived were the best interests of their children. It was another of those decisions that Charlotte Sommer spoke of – the kind that drove a stake through the heart. The day after they left, she went and bought back Ben Douglas' Akubra hat. It was the only thing she had to remember him by. What Charlotte Sommer could not possibly foretell was that Ben Douglas had left her with a much more enduring legacy, one that would kiss the feet of Best Douglas many, many years later.

CHAPTER TWENTY

RICHARD Tipody's grin was a cross between superciliousness and nervous apprehension. He hit the stop button on the cassette recorder. The last words heard from the recording were poignant: "Could be time for me to move on.... I'll leave it up to you, Richard." Tipody had planned it that way. That's why he had selectively edited the conversation with Best. When he saw the solemn expression on their faces, he began to congratulate himself. With such an extraordinary talent for manipulating the truth, he should have been a journalist.

Fiona Chalice tried not to appear too affected, although the words had hit their mark. She removed her glasses and almost threw onto the desk the manila folder that contained copious amounts of Richard Tipody's notes on Best Douglas. "His statement is somewhat vague," she responded.

"I think it's clear as crystal," Tipody replied. "Don't you, gentlemen?"

Dr Broad nodded. Dr Mangos nodded too, but only because he'd seen Broad nod. He hadn't been completely listening. Mangos thought they were all wasting their time. The VAE Law would never see the light of day. Any sane government would see to that.

Tipody stood up self-righteously. "There's no point delaying our work any longer. If the VAE Law is passed then we have a protocol and a test subject to proceed with a Voluntary Assisted Expatriation."

"Yes, we have agreed on the protocol but I beg to differ on your subject," interjected Fiona Chalice, not making any attempt to get out of her seat.

"You can beg all you like, but the fact is a candidate has been sought out, screened, interviewed over six painstaking months, and proved suitable." He held up his notes. "It's all in here. Black and white. Totally transparent."

"He fits the profile we've all discussed," Broad commented.

"No family," added Tipody.

"Limited social interaction," supported Broad. "And he's of sound mind, quite able to make his own decision regarding his destiny."

"Will the subject be available for us all to interview?" she asked.

"That's a good point," offered an undecided Dr Mangos. "Perhaps we should interview him as a combined panel?"

"That's not part of the protocol," interjected Broad. "The process must be as unobtrusive as possible. Dr Tipody has acted alone in this regard due to the fact that the secretive nature of the work has leant itself to such delicacy."

Dr Tipody offered an appreciative nod in Broad's direction. "I've painstakingly recorded all of my encounters with the subject. I've laboriously profiled his psychological state. I'm now ready to make a recommendation, and then seek a determination from this Committee. Whatever feelings we may personally hold, we're not here to debate the morality nor the ethics of Voluntary Assisted Expatriation. Our role has been to humanely construct a medical procedure to enable a VAE, then profile just what a suitable candidate may be, and then systematically select that subject. I vigorously maintain we have that individual. In accordance with this Committee's mandate, I would now like to proceed to the vote."

A democratic vote was taken. It was three to one. Best Douglas was deemed a suitable candidate for euthanasia should the VAE Law be passed, which would pave the way for the first test. As torn as Fiona Chalice was about VAE, she remained convinced that a democratic government would not reach such an outcome. But there was that word again – democracy – and that one word was beginning to worry her. As she left the meeting, Fiona Chalice felt a sinking sensation in the pit of her stomach; exactly the same feeling she had experienced fifteen years earlier when her doctor told her that she was unable to bear children.

*

BEST'S father was staring wistfully out into space. Although it was ten years since he had left France, his feelings of guilt over his relationship with Charlotte Sommer often re-emerged in the cottage that he and Norah had sweated over and built together. But, more often, his memories of Norah and Charlotte became jumbled so that the two women sometimes merged into one. It made dealing with it that much easier. But Ben Douglas never sat still thinking for long. He was always willing to throw himself into the next project, and having completed Bill Cruickshank's new cottage and the lighthouse, he was keen to embark on something else that could now consume his waking thoughts. It was better that way. Best didn't need a father that moped around all day feeling sorry for himself, shaking his fist at the world in anger.

He called Best for breakfast, and while cooking their porridge, set his mind to the task ahead.

"Best," he began thoughtfully, "what would you say if I told you that I've been reading a lot about electricity?"

"You read a lot about a lot of things."

Ben Douglas smiled. "That I do. Nevertheless, by all the names of the blessed saints, I think I might be onto something."

Just when Ben Douglas had succeeded in adapting the Thurrough

Lighthouse from whale oil to kerosene, he was looking into electricity. The more he read about it, the more he got excited about it, almost as if he himself was charged with it.

Ben Douglas pushed all the information that he had been studying in front of Best. "You'd better learn all about this stuff. It's going to power God's living Earth!"

Best's father was an immensely pragmatic man, which is why he never understood Dirk Crenshaw's unusual desire to dig a hole on Thurrough Beach. The Hole had no functional value. It didn't produce anything, and yet the mere spectre of it was odd enough to make it a huge attraction, and line the pockets of everyone associated with it. Yet, in all the time that Ben Douglas lived next to the Hole, he rarely went near it. Up until Dirk Crenshaw's Hole had come along, the Thurrough Lighthouse was the main attraction of Thurrough. And Ben Douglas, although at times inconvenienced by people milling around, could understand that *Norah* was a glorious attraction: a glistening white column that reached into the sky. But it was also, importantly, functional. And it was its functionality that justified its existence, not its architectural distinctiveness. Ben Douglas could never appreciate an object unless it had a practical application. This same attitude was apparent in his occupational choice for his son. He knew that Dirk Crenshaw's parents had turned a simpleton into an idiot. He would not make the same mistake with Best. He would steer Best where he felt Best should go. And Best, who didn't know where to go, decided to trust his father to do the steering.

Best was directed away from nebulous pursuits that lacked concrete results. There were certain professions that Ben Douglas would not tolerate: law produced nothing except legal complexity designed to create more work for lawyers; accounting created nothing more than mathematical systems, which justified the need for accountants to interpret them. The arts were also not exempt from his scrutiny: a landscape painter just duplicated, on a much lesser and imperfect scale, a scene that had already been made stunningly real and perfect in nature; a writer of fiction invented stories when real life was richer, more painful, and more complex than any made-up account could possibly be. If Best had any inclinations towards such pursuits, they were discouraged. As far as his father was concerned, Best's school grades weren't the springboards to his professional life, although the three Rs were not neglected. Rather, the odd fix-up jobs around the lighthouse and cottage, which were assigned to Best regularly, were the tools of his apprenticeship – an apprenticeship of practicality. These were the tasks designed to instil working pragmatism into his son.

Ben Douglas often called Best up to the lamp room at night to point out the change in course of a ship that had been warned off the Thurrough Reefs by the shining beacon. "Best, my boy," he would say as he directed Best's attention to the distant vessel, "if the Captain of that ship was close to the unforgiving shoreline in the middle of a ferocious storm, and then suddenly the lamp went out, who would he most want to be in that lamp room – an uneducated handyman who could go to work and fix the problem, or a Nobel Prize winning grey beard who could expound how the lamp operated, but could do nothing to fix it?"

Best would chime in on cue with the appropriate response, having soon realized that his father's question was not rhetorical.

"That's right!" his father would reply proudly. "In a crisis, talk's cheap."

And Best saw enough crises in the lighthouse to experience first-hand just how cheap talk was.

Perhaps it was the frequency with which his father related this "Captain at sea when the lamp goes out" story that prompted Best's interest in working with the light, or perhaps it was the exciting emergence of electricity at a time when very few people actually understood how it worked. Whatever the case, becoming an electrician was a natural progression for a lighthouse keeper's son. And when the lighthouse became powered by electricity in 1920, Best was well under way to understanding how it all worked.

*

ORION would often notice Best looking towards the tip of the Thurrough Peninsula where the faint form of the lighthouse could be seen in the distance amongst the mist of the sea spray. It wasn't long before Orion started arriving at the Home half an hour earlier, just so that he could spend some more time talking with Best. Best told Orion many stories from his youth. Orion particularly liked the story about Dirk Crenshaw and the Thurrough Hole and couldn't help laughing when Best recalled how Dirk had broken his nose. Orion soon knew all about where Best used to live, and his days at the lighthouse.

"Electricity, my dear dad used to tell me," Best recalled energetically, "electricity. He worked like a madman to make it happen. In three years, *Norah* was the most efficient lighthouse in the entire world."

Orion whistled with intense interest.

"Her power was produced by two De Meritens magnetos weighing two and a half tonnes each," expounded Best.

Richard Tipody was about to barge in, but on hearing this snippet of the conversation, he balked at the entrance.

"They were driven by an eight horsepower Crossley otto cycle silent horizontal coal gas engine at eight hundred and thirty revs per minute," continued Best. "We only ever used the electric apparatus in bad weather. When the weather was really bad, the second magneto was brought into operation, making the lighthouse one of the most powerful in the world at the time."

Tipody was stunned. He was amazed at the level of detail that Best could recall. From their conversations, he had become increasingly aware of Best's mental acuity, but this dialogue was making Best sound like a Harvard Professor. Tipody was going to have to act quickly.

"Anyway," said Best, turning his attention back to the waves of Thurrough Beach, "how much have you got saved for your new surfboard?"

Orion placed a bundle of surfing magazines on the bedside table beside the glass of antiseptic that normally housed Best's teeth. "I reckon I'm looking at sometime next year."

"How much do you have saved?" asked Best again.

"About a hundred," reluctantly offered Orion.

"What'll it cost?"

"About four."

Best gave out a hoot that startled Richard Tipody by the door. "That's quite the amount. Will your folks give you some money to put towards it?"

Orion looked down and began shuffling his feet. He quickly grabbed hold of his barrow. "I think I can hear Oak Legs Finbar calling for me," he responded sheepishly.

Best couldn't hear anything.

Orion quickly glanced at his watch. It was ten to three. He was early for Finbar. "I'd better get going."

"Okay," said Best, surprised at Orion's hasty exit. "See you tomorrow then?"

Orion nodded then rushed out, but not before taking note of the loitering form of Dr Tipody. Orion shot him a suspicious look as he entered Oak Legs Finbar's room across the corridor, who was taken back to see him arriving early.

Nurse Selby stood nearby with the dinner trays. As Tipody glanced at her, he saw her shoving several packets of condiments into her pockets to take back to her tiny apartment. She was a caring nurse who was always willing to devote time to the residents, but she did possess light fingers – a trait that she found hard to control, as if it was a disease, almost like a hereditary condition. Tipody caught her look of embarrassment but really didn't care. He told her to hold off on serving Best's dinner. He didn't need Best primed by food now. It was time to treat the racehorse like an untamed Brumby that needed to be broken. Contentment was counterproductive to Tipody's preparation.

Best was doodling on a paper napkin when Tipody took the liberty of snatching it out of his hands. Best felt indignant, but stopped short of protesting. The elderly got used to being physically imposed upon. It was just the way things were. The wheel turned full circle and they were treated like children again with people clutching at them, except now people did so with some revulsion rather than affection.

Tipody fingered through the collection of surfing magazines that was neatly stacked on Best's bedside table. He considered the drawing on the napkin. "It looks like a surfboard."

Best nodded.

"What on earth are you doing drawing a surfboard?" Tipody asked, as if charged with overseeing Best's every action.

"It's for Orion," Best answered simply.

Tipody was alarmed by Best's new sense of purpose, which seemed to have been ignited by the paperboy. It was not what he had come to expect from him. He was prepared to support Best's friendship as long as contentment made Best easier to manipulate. But it seemed that it was now making Best stronger, more independent. Best had been so easy-going. He had always responded to most subjects with calm indifference. That's why Tipody had decided on Best. He was apathetic. He didn't seem to care about a whole lot. Now it looked like he did care about some things. That would have to be discouraged.

"Best," Tipody began, wanting to dismantle Best's defences, "I really want you to get in touch with your feelings about your wife." Tipody now wished to shatter Best – to make him despise life, to regret it, to reject it – and he believed that talking about Best's wife was the key.

"Feelings?" Best numbly repeated. "What feelings? I loved her. If you had a wife, you'd love her too."

"Of course," Tipody answered, although he wasn't so sure about that. He knew plenty of men who hated their wives. He could imagine being married and despising his wife. "How did you feel when you first met her? Was it love at first sight? I bet it was... she was quite a beauty I believe?"

Best thought for a moment. That was a long time ago. He had never tried to remember that moment when he opened the cottage door to find her radiant, sunburnt face smiling at him – challenging him.

"It felt like I was looking at the morning sun," he replied, poetically.

Tipody took a long pause in order to give the impression he was in deep thought, but the reality was he was just following a thoroughly concocted plan. "I think that's the reason you still seek the morning sun. Perhaps to feel her touch? To relive that first moment at the cottage?"

Tipody didn't think anything. He had read the *Chronicle's* account, written by Harry Heath, and was intimate with every word from the archives.

Best turned away and stared blankly at the ocean. "I don't swim," he said as if remembering another time.

Tipody laughed inappropriately. "I figured as much. I don't know many men your age who do."

"You don't understand. I don't swim. I've never swum."

Up until this point, Tipody was slouched in his chair as though he was watching late night TV. He began to straighten up. He leant forward. "You've lived beside the ocean all your life. What do you mean you've never swum?"

"The ocean… my mother… the sea… it frightened me."

Tipody was spellbound. He had the same feelings towards Best that a microbiologist would have towards a virus like Eboli – feelings of utter astonishment and incredible respect along with a certainty that it had to be annihilated for the survival of mankind.

But Best had no desire to continue. Summoning such memories did not accomplish anything. There was nothing to be gained by them. They had once made life excruciating. He had no wish to return to them, content to live with the physical pain of being old.

Best suddenly looked at Tipody as if he suspected him of being the reason he had missed dinner. "I wonder where my meal is?" asked Best.

Tipody glanced guiltily towards the door. "I'll go and check for you."

Best nodded appreciatively, his accusing stare gone. "I'm a little hungry."

THROUGH the open window, Best could hear the high tide lapping against the shore, much like the sound a dog makes drinking from a water bowl. Nurse Selby sat in front of him, her legs crossed in order to support the notepad she'd taken from the Superintendent's office. She often came and spoke to Best, telling him about her boyfriend's unhealthy obsession with surfing and how he preferred to live on the dole so he could surf his days away. Actually, to Best, it sounded like a pretty good life. Best kept his hand steady as he completed his work before handing it to her.

"It has to be a rounded pin tail," Best said emphatically.

She nodded knowingly.

He asked for the notepad and quickly wrote something. "Five-foot nine," he added.

"Have you thought about those new four-fin surfboards?" Nurse Selby volunteered, trying to be helpful.

Best was not to be influenced. "He wants three fins. It has to be a Thruster."

"What about the design?" Nurse Selby asked. "Have you thought about that?"

Best had thought long and hard about that. He craned his head out the window and looked up towards the northern end of the beach. His old eyes found the lighthouse and the cottage. "I want a lighthouse on the bottom of the board."

"A lighthouse?" she repeated in surprise.

Best smiled. "Yes... a lighthouse." His smile became broader. His false teeth shimmied in his mouth. "A lighthouse overlooking a beach with perfect waves."

Having sent Nurse Selby off on her mission, Best called the local newsagent for whom Orion distributed the *Daily Chronicle* to ask for Orion's phone number. They told Best that they didn't give out personal information. But Best was persistent. He explained that he wanted to send Orion a tip for the splendid service that he always provided.

Best didn't normally lie. Lies often confused things. In this instance, he could justify it. The truth would have been more confusing. The newsagent withheld the phone number but did give Best a name and address: Barclay House, 1403 Pacific Road.

There were plenty of apartment blocks in Thurrough. The local council seemed to have the ear of property developers, although Charley Pelegranetti said that well-intentioned individuals ran for council from time to time with the aim of curbing the prolific nature of these developments. They had had mixed results: apartment blocks continued to rise and flourish. Best assumed Barclay House was just one more of them.

Best had long since parted company with the Thurrough Shire telephone book. Aside from having no one to call, arthritis in his left hand prevented him from handling the expanding volume, and his eyesight prevented him from reading nearly all except the first few pages of instructions. He called Directory Assistance. They gave him a phone number for Barclay House saying it was most likely the Building Manager's number. Best dialled the number awkwardly on his black push-button phone.

"Barclay House," a soft woman's voice answered.

Best turned up the volume on the phone. "I wonder if you could tell me what apartment a boy called Orion lives in please?"

There was a slight pause – a puzzled pause. "Apartment?"

"Yes."

"I'm sorry, sir. We don't have apartments at Barclay House – only dormitories and rooms. The boys live in twenty-bed dorms until they're given a share room on their thirteenth birthday."

"Barclay House isn't an apartment building?" asked Best.

"No… It's an orphanage."

The phone went limp in Best's hand.

"Sir, are you there…?"

Best put the phone tightly to his ear so that he did not miss a single word. "Yes… I'm sorry. I'm still here."

"Did you want to speak to anyone in particular?"

"No... If you could just tell me what room Orion's in please."

"What's his surname?" she enquired, keen to dismiss any threat to Orion's safety, which often came in the form of irate, alienated parents.

"I don't know his last name... He does a paper run along the Esplanade. I live in the Thurrough nursing home and he visits me," Best elaborated. "I wanted to send him something."

"Oh that Orion," and she slowly pronounced a surname that Best neither heard nor thought an important enough detail to get her to repeat. "He's in room 302."

"Thank you," said Best. "You've been most helpful."

ORION and his roommate, Justin, were rolling around on their bunks laughing. Orion was trying to convince Justin that he looked like he was from the town of Geeksville when he combed his hair with the top sticking up like a peacock's feathers. Justin remained unconvinced. He got up and looked in the mirror. He had gotten his hair cut short at the sides but left it longer on top. He tried smoothing down the disobedient hair. Justin respected Orion's opinion. He had known Orion all his life. They had grown up like brothers. Justin's mother was fifteen when she fell pregnant to her high school sweetheart, who stopped being sweet when he found out. After being sent down the coast to live with her aunt to have the baby, she put him up for adoption. She had her whole life ahead of her, and didn't find the prospect of spending the next twenty years of it raising a son all that attractive. Unfortunately for Justin, he was born with a cleft palate. Nobody wanted to adopt him. The only person in his young life who had not judged him by his looks was his natural mother. She did not discriminate: he was up for adoption no matter what he looked like. To seal the deal, they took him away right after he was expelled from her womb so feelings of maternal association would not be ignited by her seeing him. Sadly for Justin, prospective parents wanted a perfect baby – a cute, adorable one that friends could fawn over. Justin ended up in Barclay House. He was seven years old before he had an operation to correct his abnormality. The surgeon, who donated to the House on a regular basis, having once been a resident, volunteered his time to perform the corrective surgery. This same doctor was one of the country's most highly regarded plastic surgeons. He had operated on Australia's social elite, sculpting their faces to make them look even more elite. For him, Justin's operation was therapeutic. He had to do it. Not for Justin's sake, but for his own. A life-altering heart attack had made him reflect on his life, and he wanted to repay the kindness he had experienced at Barclay House, and forget the grinning hyena-like faces he had created for socialite money. The surgery was brilliant. All that was left of the abnormality that had been Justin's infant scorn was a pencil-thin scar that ran from the top of his lip to the bridge of his nose.

Orion had never once mentioned Justin's disfigurement. All through their years growing up together, Orion never said a word. While others teased him, Justin started to wonder if Orion actually saw his handicap at all, as if Orion had somehow been miraculously blinded to it. The truth was, Orion didn't see it. And when Justin returned to Barclay House after his operation, Orion never acknowledged the change.

Unlike Justin, Orion had no history whatsoever. He was what Barclay House referred to as a "Basket Baby," meaning someone had dropped him off at Barclay House's gates when he was but a few weeks old. In most cases, Barclay House was able to trace the mothers of Basket Babies, and provide them with the necessary counselling to help them overcome their post-natal depression. In the majority of cases, these mothers welcomed the return of their newborns. In some cases, though, Barclay House would determine that it was in the best interests of all concerned if they continued to care for the offspring of these vulnerable women. In Orion's case, his mother was never discovered, nor anybody else who could offer any enlightenment as to his heritage.

Justin was smoothing out the tufts of hair jutting from the top of his head when there was a knock on their door. Mrs Packer, the House's kindly Matron, a woman of big heart with a body to match, shuffled into the room straining to carry an object taller than her, which was shrouded by various sheets of cardboard.

"This is for you, Orion," she said puffing. "I don't know what it is but it sure looks interesting."

Orion's mouth opened in surprise. He recognized the shape instantly, as did his roommate.

"It's a stick!" Justin cried. "You bought a new stick! Why didn't you tell me, you troglodyte? I didn't think you had enough funds?"

Orion jumped off his bunk to study the cardboard for some signs as to its origins. "But I didn't," he responded, bewildered.

Mrs Packer's rosy face lit up. She loved to see her charges receive unexpected gifts; it didn't happen often. "Just make sure you put the cardboard in the recycling bin," she said to Orion before leaving the two of them to debate the most likely perpetrator of the package.

Justin punched Orion affectionately on the shoulder. "Come on. You bought a stick."

"I'm telling you, I didn't. I don't have enough money saved up yet."

"Then who did?"

Orion raised his arms. "I dunno. There must be some mistake."

Justin read Orion's details on the delivery tag. "There's no mistake. This is Barclay House, and you're Orion, and this is room 302."

"What about Ryan in Jupiter Dorm?"

"He's three years old!"

When Orion finally acknowledged that the large parcel was indeed intended for him, he could hardly contain his excitement. He stripped the prize of its cardboard facade with the enthusiasm that, until now, he had almost exclusively reserved for Mrs Packer's regular, thoughtful Christmas present.

When Orion saw the bright resin of the new surfboard shining like a beacon, he collapsed on Justin's bed, taking the board down with him in a loving embrace.

Justin had to pry the surfboard away from him to get a look at it. "Well? What do you reckon?" he asked as he studied the sleek surfboard.

Orion's mouth was agape. He mumbled something incoherent.

"Orie?"

"It's incredible!" Orion whispered, as he took in the detailed portrait of a lighthouse overlooking a sea bulging with perfect waves. Orion steadied himself. He felt weak. He slowly got up and began to study the board.

"This is some radical design," said Justin. "Look at this lighthouse."

Orion ran his finger along the smooth glossy finish of resin over the fibreglass. "The lighthouse... it's the old Thurrough Lighthouse. It's *Norah*."

Justin took a closer look. "Cool."

Orion was dumbfounded. His mind went back to another place, another time.

CHAPTER TWENTY-ONE

FIONA Chalice rose slowly from her haunches and clutched her lower back. It had been sore for a few days now and she put the pain down to her time spent in the garden. Flowers that were once strangers to her in the city were now like fighting siblings, shoving each other out of the way to reach her, pleading to be clipped and caressed.

She bent back down and carefully deadheaded the pink rosebush that was a magnet for bees and whose suckers jutted out across the letterbox. The bush often pricked the postman, and if the thorns didn't get him, the bees sometimes did. It was a great deterrent to those delivering the unsolicited catalogues hawking the wares of the town's shops.

The Chalices had located from Sydney to Moss Vale after Fiona's husband's frenetic surgical schedule caused him to have a silent heart attack. Ignoring the symptoms he could have easily identified in his patients, he put his overwhelming lethargy down to simply feeling flat. Within weeks, other vital organs began shutting down as the ailing heart acted to protect itself. One Sunday afternoon, on his only day off, he was rushed into emergency surgery where his peers performed a quadruple bypass. Both husband and wife recognised that he needed to drastically alter his breakneck lifestyle, and, not constrained by the roots that having children often puts down in a community's soil, they happily opted for the much slower pace of Moss Vale. Situated about two hours from Sydney, it was far enough to be in the country, but close enough to allow them to frequent the city.

Tom Chalice had met his wife at Sydney University where they were both studying medicine, and where he and just about everybody else was captivated by her. Not only was she understatedly intelligent, she was also uncommonly beautiful. With long auburn hair, large brown eyes, and a soft dimple in her chin, her fellow male students whiled away many fruitless hours studying her instead of their notes. Tom soon realised that he had a lecture room full of competition for her affection so he immediately... did nothing. Patience was the key, he contended, and for the first year he almost totally ignored her at a time when every other male was throwing himself at her. It took some time, but after several months her eyes began to wander over to the boy who seemed so aloof. Didn't he find her attractive? Did he already have a girlfriend? It was during these almost subconscious musings that she started to find him rather good-looking. Blessed with broad shoulders and high cheekbones set under sleepy hazel eyes, he didn't possess any distinguishable feature that made his face handsome – but it was anyway, as if the arrangement of ordinary features had produced something extraordinary. His eyes were small, and his nose was on the bigger side, but he was undeniably handsome, and she found herself staring at him. When he noticed her gaze, he knew all his patience had been rewarded. They began innocently flirting while shuffling out of lecture theatres. He would tease her about the neatness of her notes and she in turn would make fun of the untidiness of his. Soon, they each began saving vacant seats, hoping that the other would take the hint, which they usually did. When their Anatomy Professor had his back turned towards the board, drawing a rudimentary picture of the male reproductive system, Tom leant across and finally asked her in a whisper if she wanted to come with him to the University's production of the depressing Sam Shepard play, *A Lie of the Mind*, in which one of his friends had a minor part. She didn't have to give the request much thought, and quickly opted out of the game of volleyball she had previously committed to. As the characters in the play spoke of the utter helplessness of their wretched existences, Tom and Fiona laughed and laughed until the final act, when they were asked to leave by Tom's friend who'd exited his scene prematurely with the express intention of pointing out that the play was not a comedy. The fact that they laughed so easily with one another was part of the glue that bound them. From that night on, they were virtually inseparable.

Tom had been obsessed with becoming a doctor since his father died of a heart attack at the age of thirty-nine, when Tom was just ten years old. Later, he could not identify the moment when he had decided to opt for cosmetic surgery, but he ashamedly admitted to Fiona that it might have been for the money.

After spending close to eighteen years treating others, he could not deny the genes he had inherited. Perhaps children might have slowed them both down, but their efforts to conceive had proven fruitless so their work had become their child. In view of Tom's onerous workload, coupled with a heart that was predisposed to disease, it was really only a matter of waiting for the attack. After Tom was given a second chance, a gift not extended to his own father, Fiona realised they had to relocate. So, after Tom had performed a surgical favour for one of the boys from Barclay House orphanage, they set up a dual practice in Moss Vale. There, the aging population lent itself to her specialisation of Gerontology and the prevalence of melanomas and mastectomies meant there was always a need for a cosmetic surgeon. In time, they recruited younger doctors to share in their practice so as to reduce their own involvement, which freed up time for Tom to play golf, and for Fiona to increase her knowledge of her own field. Several of her papers on the lifestyles of the elderly and the need for social interaction and low impact physical activity appeared in major medical journals, so she was invited to apply for a position on the Geriatric Advisory Committee. As an academic who regularly gained hands-on experience in her own practice, she was considered an excellent choice.

Fiona collected the shrivelled roses and placed them carefully in an old tin cookie can. She would dry them out and grant them another life inside an ornamental vase. She didn't like severing their ties with the rose bush when in full bloom. She felt there was something not quite right about that dismemberment. Tom came out with a tray containing a jug of iced tea and two long glasses. He placed the tray on top of the wrought iron table on the front porch, and after pouring them both a glass, brought the tea over to Fiona. Located in the Southern Highlands, Moss Vale could be bitterly cold in the winter, but its summers were often dry and relatively hot, as it missed out on the sea breeze that kept coastal towns cooler.

She sipped the drink gratefully, and nodded appreciatively to her husband. He noticed that she had slight beads of sweat forming on her forehead under the wide brim of her straw umbrella hat. He smiled. He had fallen in love with that face. Aside from some subtle wrinkles fanning out from the corner crease of her eyes, and some darkening of the skin beneath them, she essentially looked the same – maybe a little heavier, but nothing noticeable. And, although the heart attack had weakened him considerably, aside from a thinning and receding hairline, she thought that he also looked unchanged.

When Tom returned to sit under the shade of the porch, she followed him. He clinked her glass. "Cheers," he said light-heartedly as she sat down.

She returned the toast then became pensive. Gardening always provoked thoughtfulness; she considered it a poultice that could draw out inner feelings, which she could then arrange in a rational sequence – much like the letters in a game of scrabble – so that they could be understood and articulated. She was a thinker, and never said anything rash without first giving it due consideration.

Tom knew her moods intimately. "You're thinking about the GAC aren't you?" he asked with some accuracy.

She nodded. "The Geriatric Advisory Committee is supposed to profile just what an acceptable candidate might be for voluntary euthanasia. But, so far, I just can't seem to agree on what might constitute an acceptable candidate."

Tom poured them both another iced tea. "A difficult impasse."

"Increasingly so," she replied. "Yet Dr Tipody seems adamant."

"Is he a little premature?" asked Tom.

"Yes, and no," Fiona answered. "If the NSW Government pass the VAE Bill, which, given the Northern Territory's Euthanasia Bill, they just might, then we are supposed to offer as a sacrifice the first victim to test the process."

Tom shrugged his shoulders. His recent heart attack had made him a lot more pragmatic when it came to the frailty of human life. He'd almost adopted a Jobian philosophy of resignation – *The Lord giveth and the Lord taketh away.* "Someone's got to make the call, and I have every faith in your judgement."

A frown formed wrinkles in her forehead. "Yes, but I'm only one of four, and the more we meet, one thing is becoming clearer and clearer – I'm not sure we possess the wisdom to support an individual's decision to end their own life."

Tom rose from the table and collected the empty jug and glasses and returned them to the tray. He kissed his wife on the cheek. "Like I said, I have every confidence in you, Fi."

As she returned to the roses, she gained little satisfaction from her husband's encouragement. Unfortunately, she didn't possess that same level of confidence. And not only that, what little self-assurance she had was being eroded away by every GAC meeting. After all her studies, and all her work with the elderly, one undeniable doubt was growing, much like the noxious weeds that often crept up amongst her elegant roses – a doubt as to whether she, or anyone else, was capable of judging such an issue.

CHAPTER TWENTY-TWO

BEST felt like he had crossed his fingers for days. So much so that the knuckle of his right index finger began to swell. But it seemed to work. On the second day, the workers began to picket the site. They didn't exactly stop tourists from crossing the picket line, but they didn't make it easy for them either. Their occasional threatening remarks and hostile presence alone was enough to intimidate even the most curious. As a result of the labour dispute, Dirk Crenshaw and Thurrough Council experienced a drastic decrease in revenue. Kent Lawrence was concerned and even more concerned when summoned to meet with Galbraith Telford.

Telford signalled for the waiter to top up his glass of port, but stopped short of offering Lawrence any. "What the hell's going on down there?" he began. "Can't you get those deadbeats back to work? Are you that incompetent that a bunch of arse-sweating Neanderthals are able to close down Thurrough's major tourist site?"

"Money's the issue," Lawrence lamented.

"Of course it is," half-shouted Telford. "It's always the issue… whether you have none or got plenty."

"We're trying to solve it quickly and quietly."

"You're not having any success on either front. Harry Heath's having a field day with this conflict, and he's cast the Council in the part of the capitalist swine."

Lawrence was parched. He gulped. He was dehydrated since having to supervise the Hole out in the unforgiving summer sun. "I've tried to present to him our side of the story."

"There is no *our* side. Heath's painting Thurrough Council out to be blood-sucking slave-drivers who are treating the diggers like yesterday's mistress."

Not ever having had a mistress, Lawrence failed to understand the metaphor.

"Bad word of mouth's a deathblow to a tourist attraction. You need to solve this problem quickly, or I will be forced to step in and solve it for you."

The Telford family's numerous landholdings had increased significantly in value ever since the snowballing popularity of the Hole. But they were never ones to play front-bench politics, desiring to work their influence in the back rooms of government or gentlemen's clubs and brothels. History had shown that whenever their interests were threatened, they would strike hard and with little regard as to how public that blow might be. Galbraith Telford was prepared to expose the corruption of the entire Council if need be since the Telfords' vast fortune kept him and his family immune from any unpalatable fallout.

Kent Lawrence could not help but air his frustrations. "Then what do you suggest we do?"

"What do the workers want?"

"More money."

"Then give it to them!"

"That will impact on the profits of the Hole!" Lawrence cried, increasingly frustrated by the fact that, in this game of poker, he was holding nothing.

Galbraith Telford spent his life irritated. Wealth had not brought nor bought him contentment. Now, he felt even more annoyed than usual. The hairs on his back began rising. "Have I ever, through this whole affair, ever, ever, intimated that Thurrough Council need reimburse me in any fashion whatsoever for my part in advising how best to conduct yourselves during this enterprise?"

Kent Lawrence was unsure of what he was getting at. "No..." he replied uncertainly.

"Just so we understand each other, I don't give a goddamn how it impacts on your profits. I'm not a greedy man. We're lucky to be living in a free enterprise society. The Hole's success has been all of Thurrough's success. But you're killing the fatted calf, just when the rest of the herd are sticking their heads in the trough to feed off the surplus!"

Kent Lawrence looked even more confused that he had been before the meeting.

Galbraith Telford sighed. "Give the workers more money, you idiot!"

Council would meet the workers' demands, which were not entirely unreasonable considering the profit being made from the Hole. After an hour of intense arbitration early Tuesday morning, the workers agreed to go back to work the following day.

Harry Heath had always kept one eye on the Hole and one eye on anything else of interest. But his prime focus always came back to the Hole. He felt that he owed the Hole. He was indebted to the Hole. The Hole had been his life preserver. The Hole had lifted his rugby player-come-journalist life out of the obscurity into which it had sunk. He followed the strike with interest and was devoting part of his second page column to the "Showdown at Thurrough Hole."

Kent Lawrence, who recognized that Harry Heath was one of their most important sources of free advertising, wasted no time in letting Heath know that the strike had been resolved to the mutual satisfaction of both parties. He gave Heath a few relevant quotes from himself and the Foreman, plus an innocuous statement from Thurrough Hole's

Manager, Dirk Crenshaw, who was always miffed if an article appeared about the Hole and his name wasn't mentioned. In return, Harry Heath promised an article detailing the events of the strike's resolution in the Tuesday afternoon edition of the Daily Chronicle.

Best blamed himself. He should have kept his fingers crossed in spite of the swelling, in spite of the pain. He knew that trouble was afoot when he noticed the workers packing up the demountable toilets, which they had been frequenting while picketing (beer and sun were a lethal combination for the bladder).

Best sprinted down and caught the last of them just before they carted the toilets off on a Council truck. The stench was overwhelming. "Where are you going?" he asked as he screwed up his nose.

"Home," one of the workers replied, scratching his backside.

"Why?"

"It's all over."

"But what about your money?" Best asked in desperation.

"Hey," another worker chipped in, "that's the kid who told us to go on strike."

The Foreman leaned out of the truck's cabin. He extended his hand and shook Best's furiously. "Thanks kid. Don't know what we would've done without ya."

Best nodded his head vacantly.

Just as the truck was pulling away, the Foreman added, "See you on the morrow, kid. We're gonna dig that sucker dry!"

The truck chugged off down the street with the toilets clinking in the back and the workers singing songs of solidarity despite the repugnant odour.

GENERAL Robert "Punch" Zuma was not in the best of moods to begin with. It was seven-thirty in the morning, and his secretary hadn't yet arrived with his "bacon and eggs sunny-side-up breakfast" and newspaper. On top of that, he hated his secretary. It wasn't that his secretary did a bad job. In fact, he was remarkably efficient, and wasn't normally late. It's just that he *was a he*. Punch Zuma was a ladies' man. At least he believed he was. He must be, he thought; he danced with all the women at the officers' parties. Of course, he was not to know that his lower ranked officers always bribed their wives and partners to ask the General to dance, hoping to gain his favour. As Major Robin Simpkins was heard to whisper to a newly posted officer, "nothing endears you more to the Punch than letting him believe he could woo your wife if he chose to pursue the option. That belief has a remarkable, sedating effect on him, and he'll want to keep you near him just so your presence reminds him of that belief."

When the army issued the General with a male secretary (actually it was Major Robin Simpkins who performed the transfer as a practical joke designed to boost the morale of all the men who were forced to grovel to the General), the General went and complained bitterly to Simpkins, pleading why in the name of the King's Army was he assigned a secretary who was a man? The Major listened patiently, while his face artificially manufactured a look of apathetic understanding, before his brilliantly rehearsed reply.

"General, you may as well ask yourself why you were born so dashing and debonair."

The General did a double take. He quickly twirled his handlebar moustache... more as a nervous reaction than anything else.

"If," Simpkins went onto explain, "we made the mistake of issuing you with a civilian female, she would have fallen so helplessly," he paused to disguise a chuckle as a cough, "in love with you that she'd have been no good to you nor the war effort. No good whatsoever."

"I suppose you're right," the General begrudgingly agreed. He snapped his fingers. He suddenly had an idea. "What if you gave me an ugly female? Insidiously ugly?"

"You'd have to look at her every day. Could you do that every morning?"

The General shuddered. He already had to perform that gruelling task. His wife's nickname, known only amongst the men, was "the whale that walks."

So General "Punch" Zuma was forced to put up with Arthur Chellows, a timid, quietly-spoken man who served an important function which far outweighed any clerical duties that he had. He was, to the men, the practical joke that endured.

If Dirk Crenshaw had one of the easiest tasks of the war, it ran a close second to the responsibility of General "Punch" Zuma. The General headed the administration directly responsible for the coastal lookouts manned by the army, which were fragmented all along the Australian coastline. It was the General's responsibility to keep tabs on the men assigned to the lookouts, process the monthly reports sent by these men, and to pass on any urgent reports which may arise in the event of an unusual ship being spotted in their zones. The whole idea of the "Coastal Watchdog Program" actually came from Robin Simpkins, but he required the rank of the General to pass it off as a respectable military program.

Most other Generals thought that the idea of watching the Australian coastline from lighthouses was absolutely preposterous: how in the world would a German ship ever make it down to Australia, and furthermore, why in the world would it? General "Punch" Zuma, however, begged to differ. "Why should we take that chance?" he lobbied the powers that be, "when we have perfectly able men, who can be redirected to minimise this country's risk?"

The General's case was rather compelling, and when he boldly, forcefully presented the scheme he met with little opposition from those politicians who were all about minimising risk to damaging their careers. His plan was well and truly accepted when, after the declaration of war, the gunners of Fort Nepean, which were situated at the entrance of Port Phillip Bay in Victoria, fired upon the German freighter *Pfalz* in order to prevent it escaping to open sea.

Since the beginning of the "Coastal Watchdog Program," the General had only received one so-called "urgent report": a bewildered soldier who thought he'd seen a giant sea monster, and thought, as in the story of the Trojan horse, that the Germans were hiding inside ready to mount an attack. It was then discovered that this man, who was assigned to northern New South Wales, was smoking some of the strange plants that grew in abundance in the region.

If, by some slight chance, the General ever received a legitimate report of a sighting of an enemy ship, he was to send the details to the defence forces immediately, and they would then be despatched to the site in question. Over the entire period of the war that never happened once. In essence, the General's administration of thirty men became a kind of military library that collected and methodically filed coastal lookout reports. The army had been good to the General. And most of the men under him recognized that their part in the General's function was infinitely better than being sent overseas with two legs and coming back with one. The truth was, every soldier who cared more about his life than the thrill of adventure wanted to be near the General. Proximity meant safety. Bribing their partners to dance with the Punch was a small price to pay for escaping the ultimate price that sixty thousand Australian soldiers paid with their lives.

Arthur Chellows walked gingerly into the General's office with a large silver breakfast tray balanced precariously in one hand and the previous afternoon's *Daily Chronicle* in the other.

"Where have you been, my lad?" bellowed the General.

Chellows lifted a dome cover off a dish, which contained seven strips of bacon and four sunny-side-up eggs. "The cook was sick today. I had to make your breakfast."

The General frowned. He took a fork and gently pricked the membrane surrounding one of the bright yellow yokes. "They seem a little hard, soldier."

Arthur Chellows winced. "I should have taken them out earlier... but the bacon had yet to crisp... and I know how you like your bacon crispy."

The General snapped a strip of bacon in two. "A little too crispy... Dismissed."

Arthur Chellows shuffled out with his head cast down. Being General Zuma's secretary was turning him into a miserable wreck. Carrying the burden of the practical joke wasn't easy in spite of the many pep talks Major Robin Simpkins had given him on "doing it for the morale of the men."

General "Punch" Zuma didn't like the morning paper. It was far too big and clumsy. There was no way he could handle that beast and eat a hearty breakfast at the same time. That being the case, he always read the previous afternoon's paper, as it was much more manageable and lent itself to the meal reader. But to say that he read the paper is a misnomer. He didn't read it as such; he merely browsed and would stop only if the headline of an article caught his eye. The front page and first couple of pages of every newspaper were always almost exclusively devoted to the war so he never read those. As far he was concerned, his war was confined to that section of ocean fifty nautical miles off the Australian coastline, and nothing ever happened there. His war was a good war and it made him feel content.

There was really no reason for him to read Harry Heath's column. He thought that Heath had been overrated as a footballer, let alone a journalist. And the headline was not that appealing: "Council Digs Themselves out of Hole Heap of Trouble." If the truth be known, a glob of egg yoke dripped from his fork onto the paper. It was only when he quickly attempted to dilute the offending stain with a napkin dipped in tea that he noticed the name Dirk Crenshaw. He slowly picked up the paper and scanned Harry Heath's article.

He stopped chewing. "Chellows!" he cried. "Get in here!"

Arthur Chellows wasted no time in answering the call. He stood in front of the General's desk in a matter of seconds. He had performed the same mad dash many times. Just when he thought he couldn't possibly improve on his best time, he'd complete the distance even faster. His life had been reduced to such trivial, meaningless challenges.

The General never noticed such details. "Be a good lad and fetch Major Simpkins for me."

Since Major Simpkins actually ran the administration on the General's behalf, he saw no urgency in the request. In fact, at the time, he was playing tennis with a soldier who he had personally conscripted into the Regiment because the young man was an up-and-coming tennis star and Simpkins wanted to improve his own backhand.

"The General wants you now, Sir," Arthur Chellows repeated for the second time after seeing the Major readying to serve yet another game.

"Yes, I heard you the first time," Simpkins casually replied.

Chellows bit his lip nervously. "I think the General meant right now, Sir."

Simpkins was clearly not happy about being interrupted on his second serve, as it resulted in a double-fault. Still, he was always remarkably composed, no matter how straining the circumstances. He strolled to the sideline while attempting several practise swings of his backhand. "My good man," Simpkins began, as if talking to his dearest friend. He put a comforting arm around the disconsolate Arthur Chellows' sunken shoulders. Such gestures were unusual in the army, but did act to create a special bond between Officer and Soldier. "You have delivered your message in good faith and now your duties have been discharged. You're better to leave right now without turning back and without the knowledge that I will tarry here until this set is finished."

"But what shall I tell the General?"

"Tell him that you delivered his message as ordered."

Chellows nodded obediently before taking his leave.

"And Chellows?" Major Simpkins called after him. "You're doing a fine job for the men."

Chellows smiled weakly before averting his eyes so as to not witness the Major serving yet again. He also began humming *The Battle Hymn of the Republic* in order to block out the sound of the ball meeting the Major's racquet.

The set took over forty-five minutes to complete and only then did Major Simpkins respond to the call.

"What took you?" the annoyed General asked in frustration as

Simpkins sat down, crossed his legs, and requested a cup of tea from Chellows.

"The war," Simpkins replied simply.

A look of respect made a shadow pass across the General's face. "Of course."

"Punch" Zuma shoved the article in front of Simpkins, who scanned it in a half-interested fashion before handing it back.

"Something's got to be done," the General felt the need to comment after not getting much of a reaction from the Major.

Robin Simpkins was impressed. He had obviously misjudged Dirk Crenshaw when he'd labelled him an imbecile of the highest order. "Such as?"

The General's face went beet red. "What do you mean 'such as'? We can't have men going off and running all kinds of moneymaking schemes when they're supposed to be in the bloody army! Good heavens man, the army's not an aid to self-employment!"

Simpkins couldn't see what all the fuss was about. As far as he was concerned, it was just another example of a local numbskull making good. "What do you suggest then?"

"A court-martial! A court-martial for abandoning his post!"

Simpkins raised his eyebrows. "Could be considered a little extreme," he commented, beginning to devote more thought to the situation.

"Crenshaw's supposed to be watching the bloody coastline. How can he possibly be doing that when he's running a bloody tourist attraction?"

Simpkins had to concede on that point. He bent over and picked up a folder the General had been studying, labelled with Dirk Crenshaw's name and location. "These reports are obviously written by a man with the vocabulary of a ten-year-old," he said on flicking through one such report. "'No Bad Ships,' it simply reads." He quickly scanned some others. "It looks like it's the same report each month – 'No Bad Ships'. Still, he's submitting them on time... I guess that counts for something."

"Let's hear it for Crenshaw – the deserting swine can write on time!"

A devious smirk appeared on Simpkins's face. The General recognized it instantly. In fact, he welcomed it. Whenever it appeared, he had to do less work. That was why Simpkins was his right hand man; that and his certainty that he could easily seduce Simpkins' pretty blonde wife if ever he wanted to.

"Technically," Simpkins began as he sipped the tea, which had discreetly been served to him by the ever-humble Chellows. "Dirk Crenshaw's operating under the authority of the military."

"Why do you think I'm so bloody concerned?" the General interrupted.

"Yes, but if he's under our authority," Simpkins went on to say, ignoring the General's outburst, "or, should I say, under the military's authority, then technically speaking that Hole's being dug with the expressed consent of the military."

The General often found it hard to predict where Simpkins was taking him. "But that's just the point – it bloody-well hasn't been!"

Simpkins again ignored him. He was used to treating the General like a petulant child. "Which would mean that the military – or that division of the military responsible for Crenshaw – is fully entitled to the profits of this," Simpkins formed quotation marks with his fingers, "'Military Exercise.'"

With one loud exhale General Robert "Punch" Zuma signalled that the Major had lanced all the tension from his worried mind. He was pleasantly surprised. "Surely Crenshaw wouldn't agree to that?"

"Then we will court-martial the spleen for being lax in his duties."

"And the Hole?"

"We just say that Crenshaw was digging the Hole as a secret military exercise because we received intelligence that there was something under the sand that had implications for the war effort."

"Such as?"

"Such as... a German submarine perhaps?"

The General smiled and turned to Chellows. "Be a good lad and fetch us a vehicle. Major Simpkins and I are heading for the coast."

CHAPTER TWENTY-THREE

THERE seemed to be more heated discussion in the public gallery than in the Upper House. Heads of churches, charities, and other lobby organisations were all in attendance along with Dr Richard Tipody. The VAE Bill had been accepted by the House of Representatives. It was now up to the Senate to do the same. The House passed the recommendation rather painlessly, more so than most had expected, including Richard Tipody. Those familiar with the hidden agenda of the reigning NSW Government weren't surprised, however. The Northern Territory Government had blazed a trail, and other like-minded State Governments were keen to keep forging it.

The Senate was proving to be stubborn, and it was the independents, who had the balance of power, who were causing the most problems. With a vote of YES from two of the three independents, the motion would pass. The Accountable Australia Senator, the Reverend Jack Mackey, dug in his heels. He wouldn't agree to any such proposal. He was quite emphatic. He wasn't changing his mind. Mackey was out.

But the other independent was in. That left Alice Crompton from the Green Environment Party who was undecided.

Tipody sat back, bemused by an argument that had broken out amongst those in the gallery.

"I will concede," an Anglican Minister whispered to those around him, "that the lives of some of the elderly are considered not only unproductive by society's standards, but unproductive by their own standards."

"A great majority of these aged people simply don't want to live any longer," Tipody interjected heartily. "Some consider themselves too old or ill to live."

"Should we prolong their lives against their wishes?" asked Right-To-Die who happened to be sitting to the left of Tipody.

"Perhaps not," answered the Head of the Uniting Church who found herself behind a Catholic Bishop.

"However," began Pro-Life who was sitting just to the right of Uniting Church. "What will be the implications – the sociological implications – if government steps in to perform a task that, up to now, has been nature's prerogative?"

A Professor of Sociology's face lit up. "That's exactly what I'd like to find out. If we could get a test subject and expatriate him, then we could study the effects it has on those around him."

Tipody turned enthusiastically to the Professor. "Let's face it – if euthanasia becomes government policy, nursing homes will feel the brunt of it. That's where we should study the ramifications of expatriation. The general community won't even be affected by it."

"That remains to be seen," remarked the Minister, who found Tipody's and the Professor's observations a little insensitive and distasteful. "It may be that life will be considered even more dispensable than it is already."

Religion caused more problems than it solved, thought Tipody. He liked being an atheist.

"Next we'll be knocking off the unemployed!" someone else joked.

"We kill babies, why not their grandparents?" commented Pro-Life caustically, bringing a hint of emotional spite to what had been a relatively unemotional, almost inhuman discussion.

"Foetuses," said Pro-Choice. "The correct term is foetuses."

"Just a question of semantics," responded Pro-Life.

Tipody recognized that he needed to guide the discussion back onto the cold hard rails of logic. "It may well be that VAE is not a humane alternative, but how can we assess its implications if we never implement a test? Surely one individual, who is consenting anyway, is expendable in order to dismiss or validate the process?"

The gallery came to an abrupt hush as the Senate's arguments were tabled.

The Green's Senator Alice Crompton listened attentively to both sides of the debate. It wasn't right to play God, said Rev. Jack Mackey. It wasn't right to prolong a life of pain and suffering if that person wanted relief from the agonies that life had bestowed upon them, said the opposing view. In the end, Alice Crompton sided with the YES vote. The Bill passed. Outside in the corridors, after the session was over, Rev. Mackey approached Alice Crompton and asked her why.

"I saw my mother waste away to the grave with cancer," she told him.

"It's a terrible disease," the Reverend replied sympathetically. "Do you think your mother would have ended her own life given the chance?"

Alice Crompton thought about her answer for some time before responding. "No. She was too strong-willed."

"Then what makes you think you can speak for her?"

"I saw the pain she was in."

"Whose pain are you trying to end – hers or yours?"

"I don't know," Alice Crompton answered vacantly, now weighed down with the realisation that it had been her decision that would make VAE a reality.

"By agreeing to someone's decision to die, you're acknowledging they have no hope," the Reverend added.

"Without hope, we are less than nothing," she mouthed softly, absently, as if remembering a long forgotten phrase.

"Excuse me?"

She smiled sadly. "That's what my mother used to say."

The Reverend Jack Mackey left Alice Crompton alone with her thoughts in the corridors of power.

After the VAE Bill was ratified, the Geriatric Advisory Committee had to complete their mandate by constructing and compiling a manual that would detail the entire methodology of the VAE. The medical practitioners were to focus on the means by which the subject would be expatriated. Religious ministers were to collaborate on what contact the subject should have with the clergy before his or her death. Professors of Sociology were to concentrate on the ways in which the sociological and psychological impact of the death could be limited on those around the subject. And lawyers were to draw up a step-by-step checklist, which the subject, or next of kin, would use to make sure that their affairs and estate (if there was one) were in order. All these facets were combined into one large manual, which was to serve as the guide in the expatriation of the test subject. The manual, simply titled, *Voluntary Assisted Expatriation – the Application,* was the means by which the process of expatriation would be implemented.

*

BEST was up at five o'clock in the morning. The sun hadn't yet crept above the horizon. The ocean was smooth and calm. Gentle three-foot breaks were lining up uniformly all along Thurrough Beach. He stuck in his teeth and wheeled himself over to the window. The tip of the sun seemed like it was poking its head out of the water, as if checking whether it was safe to come out. It made its ascent warily. It was in no hurry. It had more than twelve hours to get to the other side. No reason to rush.

It was when the sun cast its first light of the day that Best spotted the giant letters. Best fumbled for his glasses on the bedside table even though they had not resided there for over two years. Each letter was over thirty feet in length, four feet wide, and dug two feet deep into the sand. In the early light, Best couldn't quite make out the words. It was only when the sun made its full appearance over the horizon that he was able to read the huge message:

"THANKS BEST!"

Then, to the left of the words, just by the shore, he spotted Orion waving madly and holding up his surfboard. Best flung open the window and waved back. Orion ran into the surf and paddled his new board out to the virgin break.

"Let's go surfing, Orie," whispered Best. "Let's go surfing."

*

THERE was an exit meeting of the Geriatric Advisory Committee before it was to be disbanded. Fiona Chalice felt a queasiness in her stomach as Richard Tipody placed the one hundred and forty page manual in front of her and the other members of the panel.

He stroked the document affectionately. "The VAE manual has been rubber stamped by the Department of Health and is now recognized as the official protocol of the VAE in accordance with the VAE Law." Tipody paused for effect. "We are proceeding with a test," he continued, caressing the manual as one would a child, "and this is how it's all going to happen."

Fiona Chalice was speechless for one of the rare times in her life. She wasn't sure what she had done. She was no more certain about VAE than she had been, though those in government seemed to be. Still, she had dutifully made her contributions to the document, which centred primarily on gradually withdrawing the subject from those around them prior to the VAE in order to minimise the social impact following the procedure, but she was still uneasy with the whole outcome. It was all too quick.

"This manual," Tipody went on to state, "has been formulated to outline the various steps that will be taken before and after the subject's expatriation." Tipody loved this speech. His life's work was coming to fruition. His dream of having a society that made decisions about mortality on behalf of its senior citizens was surely one step towards Utopia. The world would be burdened with less people; less people to provide drinking water for, less people to feed, less people to clothe, less people to support and pay pensions to. This was an important step in preserving the planet. Tipody was going to be one of the great names of history – right up there with Ghandi, Buddha, and Hitler.

Tipody looked over at Fiona Chalice. Her head was cast down. It didn't even seem as if she was listening. She was missing a pivotal moment in history; the selfish bitch, Tipody thought.

Tipody held up the manual. "As we all know this has been created with the help of medical, religious, and sociological experts in order to ensure that the process runs as smoothly as possible with as little impact on the subject and those around him, and I thank you for your efforts in its compilation."

Flavian Broad nodded his head. "Can't have the VAE scaring other residents. Might be spooked into thinking they're next!" he joked.

"It's not a game show," coolly commented Mangos, who was still stunned that the Law had passed, and thought that levity was inappropriate.

Not yet, anyway, thought Tipody.

Fiona Chalice was not angry with Richard Tipody. He didn't deserve to have any emotions expended on him. In some crazy way, she admired him. He had been so sure of his stance on VAE. But then she realized that his zeal didn't mean he was right. She was angry at herself. Yes, she had voted against the test subject, but she should have done more. She should have turned her doubt into action. She should have trusted her instincts when they were telling her to push back against the VAE. Her sense of uncertainty could have been her argument. It was all right not to be sure, she could have said. More research and time with the elderly was what was needed. But butting heads with Tipody had been like going up against a stag's horn. After realising that protesting was too hard, she, like Mangos, had been content to sit back in the belief that the VAE Bill would never pass. But it had, and now she was powerless to do anything about it.

Tipody flicked the manual to page forty-three. He knew the document backwards. "The manual also states that the subject will have no contact with any one else except a religious minister of his choice and his personal physician once he has made the decision he wants to be expatriated." He looked across at Fiona Chalice. "That includes anyone from this panel."

Dr Flavian Broad nodded in agreement. He could see the sense in that: can't have a subject open to influences that might change his mind. That would cost the taxpayers money.

"The test on Best Douglas is due to commence in three months," Tipody added in conclusion, which gave him enough time, he hoped, to prepare Best properly.

Fiona Chalice stood up. She felt sick, almost faint. "I need to leave. I'm sorry."

All three men rose to their feet in a rare gesture of chivalry. Tipody smiled sinisterly. "I do hope you feel better," he offered insincerely as she turned to leave.

Before Fiona Chalice walked out on the meeting, she turned and asked Tipody, "What date is Best Douglas's procedure?" She still could not bring herself to use the term that Tipody had coined.

"He's due to be expatriated on the eleventh of November."

She nodded silently. That was the date of remembrance for lives lost in war. Richard Tipody smirked. The irony was not lost on him.

THE rain trickled down the windowpane. Best's short breath was fogging up the inside of the glass. He rubbed it with the sleeve of his grey woollen cardigan; the one his wife had knitted for him. It was now ill-fitting and hung on him as on a clothes hoist. It had holes in the wool where silverfish once feasted, but it still kept him warm. The memory of she who made it comforted him, rather than the wool from which it was made.

The ocean was small and choppy. There were no surfers out; no one for Best to watch. Orion rushed in excitedly carrying his normal load of papers, plus a shoebox wrapped crudely in second-hand Christmas paper.

He went over and hugged Best.

Best wasn't sure how to respond. Nobody had embraced him like that for a long time. People didn't like to touch him in that way.

"You sure are something!" exclaimed Orion.

"How does it go?" asked Best, his colour returning to normal after having blushed with embarrassment.

Orion gestured with his hands. "Like a beauty."

"Doesn't slide out at the critical sections?"

Orion smiled. Best really knew the surfing lingo. "Nope. It's solid. Real solid. I love it."

Orion handed Best the shoebox.

"What's this?" asked Best.

"I bought you something."

"You shouldn't be doing that."

"Sure I should. I had eighty bucks saved up."

"You should've kept the money for yourself… For a new wetsuit… or something."

"Open it."

Best's arthritic hand struggled with the wrapper. He handed it back to Orion. "You do it."

Orion took hold of the box and systematically shredded the paper to bits. He handed the box back to Best.

Best opened the lid. His eyes lit up.

"Now you can really watch the ocean."

Best took out the shiny new binoculars and looked through them out the window. He directed them down to the northern end of the beach.

Norah looked so clear. He felt as if he could touch her.

"I don't know what to say."

"You don't have to say anything."

There was a loud hacking cough from Oak Legs Finbar.

Orion looked at his watch. It was one minute to three. "I'd better be going."

"No surfing today."

"Nah. It's blowing hard onshore. Might whip up the swell though."

"You shouldn't worry about Oak Legs Finbar," said Best, a little annoyed that his own time with Orion was being cut short yet again. "He's got all afternoon to wait for the paper."

"Ah, he's all right," Orion replied as he turned his barrow to leave. "Bit of an old codger, but he's all right.

BEST had never been presumptuous enough to enter Oak Legs Finbar's room, and he had never been invited. He was reluctant to visit any of the other residents unsolicited for fear of rejection, and Oak Legs Finbar's scowl did not exactly lay out the welcome mat.

"What do you want?" Oak Legs growled on seeing Best stationed apprehensively by his door, not long after Orion's exit.

"I wanted to talk to you about Orion."

"What's to talk about? He's a paperboy. What else's there to say?"

"You need to go easy on him."

The lines on Oak Legs' forehead created by his frown deepened further, carving out gorges in his pale skin. "Go easy on him? I am easy on him."

"He's a special boy."

"He's special all right. The three o'clock special. I just want him to turn up when he should. That's all. That's all I want. Is that too much to ask?!" Oak Legs chanted, the tone of his voice becoming more and more crazed.

Best swivelled his wheelchair one hundred and eighty degrees, ready to retreat back to the safety of his room. This had been a bad idea. His attempt to discuss Orion rationally had failed miserably. He rubbed his eyes. The fluorescent lighting was starting to make them sore. "Just give the boy a break. That's all I'm saying," said Best attempting to be stern.

Oak Legs hopped madly over to Best. "I'll give you the break, Douglas!"

Best was so stunned that Oak Legs Finbar actually knew his last name that it never entered his mind to move out of the way. As Oak Legs was about to launch at Best, in a token attempt to shove the wheelchair out the door, the toe of his slipper caught on a divot in the doormat. His left leg was yanked out from underneath him, and as he collapsed to the vinyl floor, the leg fell off leaving him stranded.

"I s'pose you think this is funny?" spat out Oak Legs, feeling humiliated, lying spread-eagle on the floor.

Best wheeled over and picked up the missing leg. He handed it to Oak Legs who snatched it back and began the difficult task of re-attaching it to his body.

"Not really," answered Best, even though he did find the situation amusing, and would later laugh about it. "Do you want me to get a nurse?"

"No!" Oak Legs yelled desperately, not wanting to lose all dignity.

So Best let Oak Legs prop himself up against his wheelchair while he struggled to put the leg back on – a process that took at least fifteen minutes.

"Miserable day outside," said Best, hoping to crack the tension as Oak Legs jerked against his wheelchair.

Oak Legs growled.

"Southerly's blowing," continued Best.

Oak Legs growled.

"Might get some moisture with it?" he persevered.

Oak Legs growled.

After Oak Legs had inserted his stump into the artificial limb, he picked himself up and hobbled backwards breathlessly to the edge of his bed where he could lift and extend the offending prosthetic along his mattress in order to strap the limb to his torso. After he had completed the laborious task, he glanced over at Best and was suddenly struck with the realisation that Best was in a wheelchair. He realised that he had never seen Best walk. "I s'pose I should be grateful," he admitted begrudgingly. "At least I can still walk of sorts."

Best slowly edged back into the room on recognising Oak Legs' statement was one of empathy, not cynicism. "Doctors wanted to stick a foot-long rod with a great big ball-bearing on the end of it into my left leg to give me a new hip," said Best.

Oak Legs grinned. It was the first time Best had ever seen him smile. "Needless to say, you didn't like the sound of it and now your arse's as numb as my stumps."

The reminder of Best's deadened backside made him shift in his wheelchair. "Something like that."

Oak Legs Finbar got up gingerly and shuffled towards the bedside table. He motioned for Best to come further into his personal space, and as if reinforcing the gesture, plugged in the kettle to reheat the water. He then opened the first drawer of the dresser. He stared indecisively at the tattered, yellowed newspaper that barely had enough substance to stay together. He pushed it down inside the drawer as if to suppress it, and yanked two teabags from their strewn moorings at the back of the draw. "My legs were blown away in France," he said.

Best wanted to say something, but didn't quite know what. He'd been in this situation many times before. It was easier to say nothing. People preferred it when he said nothing. What could he possibly say? Many had found comfort in his silence, as if the sound of their own voices was therapeutic.

"Some French soldiers found me, otherwise I reckon I would've bled to death." Oak Legs tapped affectionately on his left leg with the butt of the tea-cup. "Anyway, that's how I come to have these… Oak Legs."

"Oak Legs Finbar," Best mouthed softly, before realising he had said it out loud.

Oak Legs laughed. He glanced knowingly at Best. "It's all right. I know what they call me. It's okay by me. Oak is fine, sturdy wood." He picked up the crisp newspaper that Orion had delivered. Its stiff pages were in total contrast to the flaking old French wartime newspaper that he had stuffed back inside the dresser drawer, and which had aged like himself and Best. "When I was hospitalized in France, I was visited every day by a French Private who used to bring me in the French papers and read them to me even though he knew I couldn't understand the bloody language. Laying there feeling sorry for myself, that poor blighter would sit with me for what seemed to be hours every day and just read those papers to me from cover to cover. I never understood a single word. But the language sounded just so beautiful… so bloody beautiful. I was sent home after two months and never saw him again… Never had the chance to thank him. When Orion started doing the paper run here, something about him made me think of that French Private, and I suddenly realized that the young bugger had saved my life. I finally had someone to be grateful to."

Best patted his wheels. "I wish my story was half as exciting as yours. I fell down a two-inch ledge."

Oak Legs nodded. "I know you did." He focused his gaze on Best, displaying uncharacteristic sensitivity. Although fifty year had gone by, the lingering unexplainable presence of phantom pain was a permanent reminder of what he had lost, unbeknown to most of the Home's residents who were constantly confronted with his cantankerous veneer. "I read all about your family growing up," he went on to say, and was not sure whether to finish the sentence. He paused before continuing, "I knew Elizabeth."

"Oh," was all Best could manage to say.

"She was one of a kind. My old man did work for her father. He was one of the few mechanics in Thurrough back in those days. He worked on all her father's cars."

The mere fact that Oak Legs knew her fanned a tiny flame inside Best – like the pilot light on the old gas stove in the Lighthouse.

"I actually got to know her pretty well," Oak Legs continued. "I used to help out my dad out on the odd occasion. When she started bringing in her old Ford to the garage those odd occasions got less odd. She was headstrong, but a real gem. When I told her I was going to be a pilot, she thought that was great. She said that flying like a seagull looked so free... free from the shackles of earth is what she said. I didn't know what shackles were back then. She was way too smart for me."

"That makes two of us," chimed in Best.

"I never would've thought that my love for flying would turn into something I could barely recognise."

Best nodded, and in that moment they were both comforted by the fact that Best could never begin to understand what Oak Legs Finbar had been through, and would never be so bold as to pretend. Best had seen enough return servicemen to understand that a gulf existed between them and those who remained at home untouched by the absolute horror of war.

Best noticed that the bookshelf by the bed was overflowing with books.

Oak Legs tapped the spine of one of the collection tenderly. "Stories... Poetry mainly. I never had the nous to fully express how I felt back then... that was part of the bloody problem. But these guys did it for me...

"Will they never fade or pass!
The mud, and the misty figures endlessly coming
In file through the foul morass,
And the grey flood-water lipping the reeds and grass,
And the steel wings drumming.

"The hills are bright in the sun:
There's nothing changed or marred in the well-known places;
When work for the day is done
There's talk, and quiet laughter, and gleams of fun
On the old folks' faces.

"I have returned to these:
The farm, and the kindly Bush, and the young calves lowing;
But all that my mind sees
Is a quaking bog in a mist – stark, snapped trees,
And the dark Somme flowing.

"Vance Palmer's poem's about World War One – but wars... they're really all the same, ain't they Best?"

Best nodded, not because he knew but because he understood that Oak Legs Finbar knew.

But today, to Oak Legs Finbar, the war was a long time ago. He had tried with limited success to lay those demons to rest along with the marrow and bone from his legs. He wanted to dwell on his life before the war. "To tell you the truth, I had the fanciful notion of marrying Elizabeth. But I was too young and stupid for her. Rest assured, those feelings weren't reciprocated, much to my bloody disappointment!"

"She would've had many suitors," remarked Best.

"I was too crude for her anyway... too much of a lad. She needed someone sensitive... someone special. Someone to take her away from the life she hated... Someone like you."

*

BEST and Elizabeth Douglas were married by Bill Cruickshank in the Thurrough Catholic Church on the 25th of February 1936. They stood facing each other on the tip of the dune, overlooking the pristine sea as it sent waves of congratulations which seemed to break into a chorus as they rolled gently onto the sand of Thurrough Beach. Behind them stood about thirty close friends and relatives who, after sitting through the ceremony in Saint Bede's Catholic Church, were thankful to feel the refreshing touch of the afternoon's north-easterly sea breeze.

Elizabeth took Best by the hand and led him down onto the beach to escape the prying eyes always keen to scrutinize the actions of the bride and groom. She pointed out the northern headland. "Remember when you came down to rescue us?"

Best nodded his head. "I thought you were in trouble."

Elizabeth laughed easily. "With the company I was keeping, I was in trouble… But then you came and rescued me, didn't you?"

She pulled him closer; her head pressed gently against his chest, and then, as if suddenly struck by an idea, pushed him away, and began taking off her shoes.

"What are you doing?" asked Best when she motioned for him to undo the back of her dress.

"I'm going for a swim," she replied as she handed Best her veil.

"You can't swim now. They'll be expecting us back."

"They can wait," she yelled as she ran down to the shoreline after heaping her dress over Best as if he was a clothes hanger.

Best sat on his haunches and smiled as he watched her wade out into the sea wearing only her undergarments. He had no objections. It was exactly this carefree spirit that had brought her to him. How could he expect to tame it now?

She swam out lazily past the breakers. She knew better than to wave him in after her.

Best had met Elizabeth in the same place he had most of the people in his life – on the beach. She was out sailing with some friends who had positioned their vessel perilously close to the north Thurrough headland. Thinking they were in trouble, Best wandered down from the lighthouse to the rocky foreshore to warn them away. Her friends interpreted Best's actions as hostile and began heckling and hooting at him from the sleek schooner, but Elizabeth watched on wistfully as the lighthouse keeper with the mop of sun-bleached hair bothered to hike all the way to the headland in order to save the lives of some rich snobs. Three days later, she was brave enough to knock on the door of his cottage.

"I wanted to meet you," she said as Best's rugged form appeared in front of her in a singlet and pants.

"Why?" asked Best.

"I wanted to know where a poor lighthouse keeper gets the courage to brutally warn off one of the wealthiest men in Thurrough."

"Poor?" responded Best in amusement. "You haven't seen my view!" he added as his sinewy arms embraced the magnitude of the vista.

Elizabeth laughed. "Well, you'd better show me then."

Best signalled for her to proceed to the lighthouse with him. "If you think you're up to it?"

She rolled up the long sleeves of her blouse. "Oh, I'm up to it."

He gave her taut figure a brief look up and down. "We'll see about that!"

But, fifty-three stairs later, as she made the ascent barely puffing or raising a sweat, Best saw that there was more to Elizabeth than he had expected. As they sat high above the ground below, Best gave her the three hundred and sixty degree tour, taking in the Royal National Park to the south beyond the main township of Thurrough, Botany Bay and Sydney to the north and, to the west, the faint outline of the Blue Mountains. Elizabeth, for her part, knew in her heart that Best was exactly what she had expected, what she had hoped for: a rugged, charming man with no thought for the game of social etiquette. When Best looked at her fair, almost translucent skin and flushed rosy cheeks, he thought she almost looked like English royalty.

Coming from money, Elizabeth longed for a simpler life, where the expectations were not nearly as onerous as they were when your family was so well off and high profiled. She soon drifted away from her social set, preferring to spend her days with Best at the beach, and her nights with him, gazing at the stars from their tower to the sky. There, at the tip of Thurrough Peninsula, she felt disconnected from all the things she had grown to despise – the pomp and ceremony of wealth and status. Best was able to take her away from all of that. And, much more importantly, she loved him for who he was, and who he had made her become – a free spirit bound only by the love she had for the simple lighthouse keeper.

When they were married, only some of Elizabeth's family attended the wedding. Her widowed father refused to come. He thought that the whole affair was beneath him and the dignity of his family name. Baine Telford's son, Galbraith, was a stubborn old snob who had been almost solely devoted to preserving his daughter for one who deserved to replace her last name. The public servant, Best Douglas, was an affront to all the Telford family had achieved.

Despite Best's attempts to placate his father-in-law, Galbraith Telford made it painfully clear that he didn't consider Best worthy to marry his only daughter. One windy evening about two months before the wedding, just after the Southerly had blown through, Galbraith Telford knocked on the cottage door.

Ben Douglas tried to mask his surprise upon opening it. He had never spoken to Galbraith Telford.

"I've come to speak to your son," Galbraith said sternly, without any form of greeting.

"He's in the lighthouse… Come in. It's cold out."

For the moment, Galbraith Telford's self-interest outweighed his stubbornness, and he accepted the invitation to sit out of the weather. Ben Douglas boiled a cup of tea, which Galbraith took without uttering a word. "This marriage cannot go ahead," he eventually uttered.

Ben Douglas sat down opposite him. "I don't think I'm the person you should be talking to. Your daughter would have her own views on the matter I'm sure."

"She doesn't know her own mind. She's far too headstrong to know what's good for her."

"She seems a sensible lass to me."

"She's too infatuated with all this," he flung his arms about, "poverty to know her own mind."

Ben Douglas ignored the insult. "I think you're underestimating her."

Galbraith Telford rose quickly up from the table, inadvertently spilling the remaining tea from his mug in his haste. "She can't spot gold diggers... that much is clear!"

Ben Douglas pushed his own chair behind him and also stood up so that both men were standing within inches of each other.

"You obviously don't know your own daughter," shot back Ben Douglas. "And in the name of all that is good and decent, you certainly don't know my son."

Galbraith clenched his fist in a reflex action. "You have meddled in the affairs of my family far too long." He flung open the door and stormed out. "Mark my words, as long as there's breath in my body, I will destroy you and this blight on my land!" he called behind him before disappearing into the night.

"Thanks for the visit!" Ben Douglas yelled out after him. "Come back anytime, you stubborn old bastard!" He then slammed the door shut, determined not to let Best know of the visit.

But he was not to know that his son had looked down on the scene and saw Galbraith Telford leaving abruptly. Once Elizabeth discovered what her father had done, she confronted him, but their differences were irreconcilable, and from that time on, they barely spoke to each other.

AS the newly-weds sat atop the lighthouse tower with Elizabeth draped in her wedding gown, she whispered something into Best's ear.

"Do you think so?" asked Best.

"I know so!" she replied with unbridled certainty before they came together in a tender kiss that they had kept for themselves and reserved just for this moment.

*

OAK Legs realized he had inadvertently lulled Best into an air of melancholy by talking about Elizabeth. He changed the subject. "Do you play cards?" he asked.

"Sometimes," replied Best. "Solitaire."

"I'll bring some over tomorrow," announced Oak Legs, as if they were occupying two houses next door to each other. "We'll have a game of rummy. Besides," he said, pointing to the grotesquely grey building which loomed outside his window, "your view's better than mine."

CHAPTER TWENTY-FOUR

BEST had hardly slept a wink all night. And when he did, his boyhood dreams were a maze of confused nightmares. In one, the workers discovered the Keeper, who shrivelled up in front of them like a frangipani flower fallen from its branch, crying, "Help me, Best! Help me!"

Best jumped out of bed at five-thirty. It was early, but he couldn't stand the thought of having another dream. He stole away to the Hole before his father awoke. He tied the rope to the gate and made the descent.

The Keeper helped steady the rope until Best's feet touched the sandy bottom.

"The workers are coming back today," said Best.

"I know."

Best's head was cast down. "There's nothing more I can do."

The Keeper laid his large hand on Best's small shoulder. "You've done all you could."

"What will they do when they find you?"

"I'm not sure. Humans are unpredictable."

Best began to cry. He tried unsuccessfully to wipe away the tears with his woollen sleeve before the Keeper noticed.

The Keeper bent down and gave Best a reassuring hug before helping him erase the traces of tears from his cheeks. "If, for some reason, they don't discover me today..." he began.

Best glanced up hopefully. "Are you allowed to leave now?"

The Keeper shook his head. "That I don't know... but if something happens and they don't find me, a long, long time from now you may need my help, just as I've needed yours – and when that day comes," he said as he drifted across to where Best's rope was dangling, "I want you to come down here. I want you to come down and visit my chamber. I'll be here with you. I promise you, Best. I'll be here if you ever need me."

The Keeper took hold of Best's young hands and placed them on the rope. "It's time for you to go now."

"I'll do anything to make sure they don't find you."

"I know you will."

Best sniffed. He took out his handkerchief and blew his nose loudly. He looked at the Keeper and was surprised to see droplets falling from his strong face.

Best found the climb out difficult, as if weighed down by all the emotions he was feeling. The Keeper had enlightened Best. Through the Keeper, he had come to realise that the constant questions he had about his mother's death did not have to be silenced, but could be buried in sand, much like the Keeper, where they could be dug out and dealt with at the appropriate time. When Best reached the top, he stopped to rest. There, he fell into a deep, uneventful sleep.

Sometime later, the sounds of the workers arriving at the Hole woke him.

"What are you doin' inside the fence?" one of the workers shouted.

"I wanted to see the Hole," Best answered groggily.

Two of the workers climbed in and lifted him out. "Be careful next time, kid," one of them said. "It's a long way to the bottom."

The workers swore and smoked as they waited for their boss to arrive. At precisely nine o'clock, Dirk Crenshaw came happily strolling towards the Hole.

"Hello men!" he said excitedly.

Murmurs were the only replies.

"Let's get to work then shall we?" asked Dirk almost hopefully.

He unlocked the gate and the workers carted in the ladder needed to take them to the bottom. Many of the public had read about the resolution of the strike in Harry Heath's article the previous day, and some of them had already gathered near the ticket booths waiting for them to open while munching on concession food that never should have seen the light of morning, let alone the rest of the day.

Best stepped forward and shut the gate.

"Best?" Dirk said, surprised. "What are you doing here?"

"You can't dig the Hole anymore."

The workers laughed.

Dirk smiled condescendingly. "Why not?"

Best folded his arms. "Because."

"Because why?"

"Just because."

"Look, kid," said the Foreman, whispering into Best's ear. "You did your bit. Thanks to you, we're getting more cash from these tightwads. Now be on you way." He gave Best a gentle shove.

But Best wouldn't budge. He grabbed hold of the gate with both his hands. "You can't go in."

"This little guy's a real agitator," remarked one of the workers.

Dirk Crenshaw's smile disappeared. "Get out of the way."

Best shook his head.

Dirk signalled to his workers. "Grab him."

One picked Best up, and the other pried his grip from the gate. Before apologising to their young advocate, they dragged him off kicking and screaming.

"You can't! You can't!" Best yelled as they hauled him outside the parameters of the attraction, dropping him softy to the sand. Best spat the gritty beach from his mouth as he watched the first of the workers make his descent into the Hole. He began beating the sand with his fists. "No! No! No!" he screamed.

"What seems to be the trouble, boy?" a deep, booming voice asked him.

Best looked up as an imposing form eclipsed him. He pointed to the Hole.

"Ah, the Hole," responded General Robert "Punch" Zuma. "We will see to that. Won't we, Major Simpkins?"

Best turned to see another soldier bending over, methodically wiping the sand from his glistening black boots. "Indeed we will, General," answered the Major. "Indeed we will."

All the authority of the military was evident in the upright personas of General Robert "Punch" Zuma and Major Robin Simpkins as they marched in unison towards the Hole.

General Zuma barged through the waiting tourists as if he was playing Rugby and stood at the entrance to the gate, his broad frame preventing the rest of the workers from entering. "I," he thunderously declared, ignoring in his anger their previously hatched plan, "am commandeering this Hole on behalf of the Australian Army!"

The first of the workers, who had already stepped halfway down the ladder, scrambled up and poked his head out in order to see what all the fuss was about.

"Get out of that Hole," ordered Major Simpkins, who was quite happy to now let "Punch" play the aggressor upon realizing that there were no journalists present. "This is no longer civilian property."

Dirk Crenshaw adjusted his necktie. He'd seen the soldiers approaching from his position near the ticket office. At first, he'd thought they just wanted to purchase tickets. But he soon dismissed that notion when they charged right on by.

He boldly approached the two officers. "How dare you interrupt this enterprise!" he chastised them, mustering uncharacteristic bravado. "Who do you think you are?"

General "Punch" Zuma tried to constrain himself, but it wasn't easy. His nickname had been born out of a preference for solving disputes with his fists rather than his tongue.

"I, you deserting, treacherous swine, am your Commanding Officer! And I expect to be treated as such or I'll haul your puny arse straight off to a court-martial, you poor excuse for a soldier!"

Dirk gulped. "But I'm not in the army any more," he replied uncertainly.

"Oh?" remarked an amused Major Simpkins. "And how did you arrive at that conclusion?"

"I thought I could quit any time I liked."

Major Simpkins stifled a laugh as he shook his head. "You simple, simple man."

General "Punch" Zuma didn't find things quite so amusing. He rolled up his left sleeve, being a southpaw, drew back his fist, and then proceeded to land it right on the bridge of Dirk Crenshaw's nose, breaking it in the process.

Dirk collapsed to the ground in agony as the blood from his nose spilled profusely onto the sand.

"You make me sick!" snarled the General.

"Who, pray tell," asked Major Simpkins, as he stood over the crumpled form of Dirk Crenshaw, "has been watching the coastline?"

"The Council," replied Dirk painfully as his lips began to swell, making him sound like he had a speech impediment. "They were getting someone to do it, but they stopped."

"Why?"

"Because they didn't," he swallowed hard, "think it was necessary."

"And what about your ridiculously brief infantile reports?"

"What reports?"

"The 'No Bad Ships' reports?"

"I... haven't written any."

Major Simpkins raised his eyebrows. "Well then, that begs the question… just who has been writing them?"

Dirk pointed a shaking finger to Best lying prone on the sand.

"The boy?" asked General "Punch" Zuma incredulously.

Dirk nodded his head, and in the process increased the flow of blood from his shattered nose.

"And this is how you treat him?" interjected Major Simpkins, shaking his head in what looked to be disgust, but was actually amusement.

Unfortunately for Kent Lawrence, he chose that exact moment to make his appearance.

"What the hell's going on?" he berated everyone, on observing that not one man was working. "You got more money, you lazy bums. Now, get to work!"

"Who, may I ask, are you?" enquired Major Simpkins.

"Kent Lawrence – Thurrough Council. We own half the Hole."

"Then enlighten me, Lawrence," said the fuming General, "since when does Thurrough Council make decisions regarding the country's war effort?"

"What do you mean?"

"For instance," expanded Major Simpkins, "when did you decide, in your esteemed wisdom, that Thurrough Shire didn't require a coastal lookout?"

"The war's thousands of miles away," scoffed Kent Lawrence. "Only an idiot would think we need a lookout here."

"I'll have you know," said Simpkins, as he delicately stepped aside just so General Zuma could position himself opposite Kent Lawrence, "there's a lot of fine men involved in the Coastal Watchdog Program."

"Yes," replied Lawrence cynically as he looked upon the sprawled body of Dirk Crenshaw. "I'm sure there are."

The General's face went bright red. "Why you pompous ass!" He then rammed his fist so hard into Kent Lawrence's nose that he left nothing intact but sagging skin.

As Dirk Crenshaw and Kent Lawrence clutched their bleeding beaks, the blood from which was staining the yellow sand of Thurrough Beach a brilliant red, Major Simpkins detailed the manner in which the Hole would be handed over to the army, not forgetting for one moment that the army was entitled to all of the income the Hole had earned since its inception.

Best was watching in awe as Major Simpkins effectively shut down the Hole when Ben Douglas, who had heard the commotion, came down to stand beside him.

"What in name of Nebuchadnezzar's going on?" he asked.

"The army's shutting down the Hole," Best uttered in amazement.

"Dirk finally got caught shirking his duties, eh?"

Best was speechless. He nodded. It had all been so sudden.

After Dirk Crenshaw was carted away by the military police, and after Major Simpkins made arrangements for the army (via the hands of General Zuma) to be reimbursed, Simpkins took the General aside.

"I've been giving the matter serious thought," he said.

The General was all ears whenever Major Simpkins gave anything serious thought. Major Simpkins glanced around distastefully at the parade of cheap pageantry that had surrounded the Hole since the Council's involvement. "This Hole's a tacky scam. It's like a freak show at a circus. Frankly, it doesn't befit your impeccable reputation and isn't something I feel the military should be associated with."

"Do I have an impeccable reputation?" the General asked, impressed, but surprised.

"Yes, and you've earned it by being above," Simpkins looked disdainfully at the clown who had just approached the General with a stick of fairy floss, "cheap shams like this."

General Zuma stuck out his chest. "What about the money?" he whispered.

"We've – you've – already done well out of the venture for little effort. The accountants are doing the numbers as we speak. They say it's quite a windfall."

"What are you suggesting?"

"Let's fill it in. That way we can close the book on Dirk Crenshaw and this whole sordid affair."

Major Simpkins was shrewd enough to avoid schemes that were not beneath the radar of the popular press. There was no way that he was going to expose himself to an enterprise that had the attention of Harry Heath, who would have loved to have reported the army's involvement in the Hole at a time when men were losing their lives on foreign lands in the belief that they were fighting for beaches like Thurrough.

The General thought long and hard, more for effect than anything else. He never contravened the recommendations of his Major. "The damn Hole would be more trouble than it's worth?"

"And its popularity is beginning to wane," reinforced the Major.

"Then fill it in! In the name of His Majesty, fill it in!"

So Major Simpkins called in a regiment of soldiers to fill the Hole until there was nothing left but a twenty-foot diameter circle in the sand. It took the military forty-eight hours to fill in a hole that had taken Dirk Crenshaw and seven council workers just over a year to dig.

After the military had pulled out, Best shuffled through the sand in the late afternoon sun and stood on top of where the Hole used to be. "I hope you're all right down there," he whispered.

The crash of the waves was the only reply.

CHAPTER TWENTY-FIVE

T HE sun was setting behind the south-western wall of the Home, bestowing an almost luminous green hue to the algae that had made its residence on the red brick. Oak Legs' eyes fluttered with the dreams of a fitful sleep as he sat slumped in the rocking chair by his window in order to take advantage of what little light his room's aspect afforded him.

His right arm jerked against the arm of the chair.

To his right, in the distance, he could make out a 16th century church steeple on a hill, guarding the town below. Ahead were scattered fields of various shades of green, arranged like a patchwork quilt separated only by the seams of stone hedges. This part of France had been spared the vicious assault of war that turned fertile paddocks into cratered landscapes littered with trenches cut into the land like deep wounds.

He yanked back the control column and rabbit-hopped the ailing Lancaster over the pines that lined the ridge. The canopy of the trees clipped the nose wheel, causing the plane to tip downwards. He pulled back harder but the plane was no longer flying; just toppling towards the earth. As the nose struck, it tore apart from the rest of the fuselage, and he was catapulted from his seat through the jagged metal gap that had opened up like the jaws of a giant shark. He felt a faint sensation of pain down his right leg as he shot through bits of metal, which hung like flesh from a shark's teeth, until he cleared the debris and was flung forty feet before his body thudded against the forgiving French turf. Both sections of the Lancaster tore across the ground together, ploughing ditches in the soft soil, following him as an injured dog would its master, the mortally wounded plane coming to rest only inches away from him. He regained consciousness just in time to see flames spewing from the ruptured fuel tank. Knowing that an inferno was only seconds away, he attempted to rise but couldn't get to his feet. He frantically crawled along the ground, using his elbows as levers to propel his body forward. When he thought he was at a safe distance, he raised his head to see Elizabeth smiling at him through her cherry lips. Then, the plane exploded and engulfed the nose section, setting the mascot's hair on fire. Soon, her pretty face was blackened against the dark smoke and flames.

He awoke suddenly in a cold sweat. He heard a flurry of French – a doctor was having an animated discussion with one of the nurses. He felt surprisingly euphoric, one of the side effects of morphine. He looked down at his body and was reassured to see both arms bandaged by his sides. He tapped the fingers of his hands against the crisp sheet and breathed a sigh of relief. He was just about to do the same with his toes when the doctor approached him.

The doctor spoke English, and knew from experience that, more often than not, it was best to confront a soldier with the state of their injuries as soon as they regained consciousness. The first awareness was never easy, and in the haze of painkillers, the acceptance of life-altering injuries was a process that needed time.

"Your legs are gone," the doctor said quickly and without emotion. "I'm sorry," he added, because he was sorry – for the entire war. He'd seen men in much worse shape, some coming in as mere torsos with all their limbs blown off, but with their hearts still beating, keeping them alive for lives of ridicule and hardship.

Oak Legs looked down. The white bandages at his knees blended in with the sheet. Beyond, was just a grey woollen blanket, which had been peeled back to allow air to circulate around the stumps. He couldn't process what he saw. At first, he thought the bed was far too short. Maybe French people were not as tall as Australians? But as he looked closer, he realised the bed ran its normal length – it was just that his body, somehow, didn't. It took a few moments before it sank in. There was nothing: no knees, no shins, no feet, no toes, no socks, no warm slippers. They were all gone.

While the doctor inspected his wounds, Oak Legs said nothing. There was nothing he could possibly say. He didn't even know what to think. He tilted his head back against the pillow and peered up at the ceiling. He noticed the chandelier and the ornate cornice. Such trivial observations were now a welcome distraction. He later learned that the building was a Château belonging to a wealthy landowner, turned into a hospital three years previous.

The doctor stood over him and proceeded to lift his eyelids in order to inspect the colour of his pupils. "You had flak in your left leg that ruptured your femoral artery."

Oak Legs looked out vacantly. He must have been shot in the cockpit and hadn't realised. It was remarkable how adrenalin could mask some senses and heighten others when necessary. He had seen turret gunners still shooting, missing half their faces.

"You were found some distance from the wreckage," the doctor went on to say. "Your right leg must have been shorn off at the top of the tibia when you were thrown from the aircraft."

Oak Legs had a vague recollection of his right leg being tugged at, but had no memory of how he happened to be out of the bomber. He remembered seeing Elizabeth's face appearing, coming closer, and then vanishing in smoke.

"It is important that you get as much rest as possible," the doctor added.

"Well," Oak Legs finally uttered, "I'm not about to go anywhere."

The doctor smiled weakly. "Infection is now the enemy." He pointed to the nurses. "That's what the penicillin's for," he added before moving off to the next patient whose entire charred body was shrouded in bandages like an ancient mummy.

Oak Legs turned away. He clenched his eyes shut and went back to sleep. The morphine helped. It made sleep easier, and it was better than being awake. Dreams disguised his pain and tricked him into thinking he was still intact. It also drowned out the sound of the mummy man's constant groaning. During the moments when he was awake, Oak Legs began wishing that the mummy man would just die already. The anguished moaning from the burnt soldier was excruciating. Oak Legs would never know that the poor blighter was wishing for the same release. A week later, they both got their wish, and the mummy man was buried, still encased in his bandages, in an unidentified grave.

For over three weeks, Oak Legs spent both days and night sleeping, waking just long enough to pick at food like a bird. One month after his accident, he awoke in the late afternoon to the almost musical sound of somebody reading aloud in French. He turned his head to one side to see a soldier sitting beside his bed holding up a French Newspaper. The soldier smiled. Oak Legs was struck by his gleaming teeth. The soldier turned back to the paper and kept reading. The language was so rhythmical and soothing that Oak Legs didn't mind that he couldn't understand a single word. After what seemed like hours, the soldier tucked the newspaper under his arm, saluted Oak Legs, and took his leave. This ritual continued for weeks. When Oak Legs became more alert, as the morphine dosages were throttled back, he observed that the soldier only ever came to read by his bed. Even more fascinating was the fact that the medical staff went about their duties ignoring the soldier, almost as if he was a chaplain administering sacred rites.

Only once did Oak Legs attempt to talk to the soldier, but the soldier just shrugged his shoulders and kept on reading. To Oak Legs, it didn't matter. There was nothing to talk about anyway. He'd lost his legs, and didn't want to go home a cripple. He just wanted to stay in that bed forever and listen to that French Private. To him, that was all there was in the world.

OAK Legs heaved himself out of the rocking chair and shuffled into his bathroom where he hunched over the small sink and splashed water on his bristled face. He looked at his watch. Much time had gone by. He was now an old man. He had spent more of his life without his legs than with them. He hobbled back into the room and looked at his bookshelf. That French Private had given him a gift. Words had somehow saved his life, and he hadn't even understood them.

THERE were surfers in the water but, as the sky was overcast, Best could hardly make them out; his failing eyesight relied heavily on the revealing light of the sun.

Orion looked away from the waves and glanced down at his watch. "He never talks about it," he added as he related the story with all the intricate details, almost as if he'd been there. "He was snoozing one day in his rocking chair, which he likes to do in the afternoon. He'd left the old French newspaper out on his bedside table so I read it."

"Your French sure must be good to pick up all that," Best commented.

"We learn it at school," Orion answered quickly.

"So he was a hero?"

"Yep – a war hero."

Orion's eyes glazed over as if viewing another time and place. "He was piloting a Lancaster on a bombing run over Cologne in France. After his bombs were gone, the plane was hit by heavy flak. It ripped a hole in the port wing. The ailerons were shot to bits."

The chart of Best Douglas' life did not include war. His birth year of 1904 meant that he was too young for World War One, and too old for World War Two. Having lived through both, he saw enough of the tragedy surrounding the soldiers that didn't return, and those that did, to know that he was one of the fortunate ones.

"As the plane went into an uncontrolled dive," continued Orion, his hands gesturing the path of the doomed plane, "he ordered all the crew out but it was too late for him. He crashed and lost his legs."

Best whistled.

Orion methodically organised the bundle of newspapers in his barrow so that Oak Legs Finbar's was at the top. "The Flight Navigator reckoned he saved all their lives. The aircraft was impossible to fly. How he got them out was a miracle. Yep, he was a hero all right."

"You seem to know an awful lot about it," remarked Best.

"I… did a school project on it for modern history. Oak Legs was embarrassed when I told him I'd read the old paper. Getting him to fill in the missing bits was like extracting teeth – doesn't like to blow his own trumpet."

"I thought he only yelled at you?"

"He likes me to think he's a cranky old man." It was ten minutes past three. Orion paused to listen for the familiar yell from Oak Legs' room. It was conspicuously absent. "I think it's more for your benefit than mine."

Oak Legs Finbar limped into Best's room.

"I was just about to come!" Orion yelped in surprise.

Oak Legs' contorted scowl turned into a glowing smile. "It's all right, me boy. I'm just checking in with Douglas over there," he replied as he lumbered over to the window and guided himself down into the chair opposite Best.

Best pointed to the cards scattered over the table. "We've been playing the odd game of cards."

"What's odd is I haven't won a bloody game yet!" added Oak Legs laughing.

Orion smiled as he considered the frail forms of both men. He placed Oak Legs' *Daily Chronicle* by his side. "You can pay me tomorrow, Mr Finbar."

Oak Legs raised his hand as if he was going to clip Orion over the ear, but instead touched him affectionately on the back of the head. "Call me Oak Legs. Oak Legs's who I am."

CHAPTER TWENTY-SIX

RUMOURS of a vast treasure of gold beneath the shallow waters of Thurrough Beach had been circulating around the town for years. Some said it was a myth. Others swore to the truth of it, but didn't know the exact location. It was believed that, around the time of World War One, a pirate ship had sunk with all its stolen bounty, with none of the crew surviving to reveal its whereabouts.

Valentino Pelegranetti meticulously studied the history of the pirates of the South Pacific. He had learned all about Captain John Selby and his plundering vessel, the *Black Swan*. He had even tracked pieces of the ship that had washed up onto the beach and subsequently found their way to the local maritime museum where they charted part of the history of the carnage caused by the treacherous outer reefs of Thurrough. Valentino had infected his son with grand tales of pirate treasure and misadventure, so much so that, eventually, they were both determined to find the lost gold bullion from the perished *Black Swan*.

Under the pretext of fishing, they spent hours floating about the waters that danced over the jagged reefs below, searching for signs of the ship's resting place. On their fifth outing, just when they began to feel discouraged, Charley Pelegranetti surfaced from the water, his mouth agape, yelling something incoherently to his father.

"Whata ya taking about, boy?" shouted his father in his strong Italian accent above the wind-chop of the sea, which was lapping hard against their small dinghy.

"I saw something down there!" yelled Charley as he swam closer.

"Lika what?" his father asked.

"I could just see it. It's covered by a bunch of barnacles. It looks like part of the reef but I don't think it is."

His father began to get increasingly excited as he dragged Charley back into the boat and wrapped a towel around his shivering body.

"It… looks… like wood… rotting wood," Charley stuttered.

"Wood'sa good. What else?" his father asked as he tried to decipher whether his son's stammer was a function of the cold or excitement.

"I'm not sure."

"Surea what?"

"Sure of what I saw."

"What didya saw?"

"I'm not sure."

"Of what?"

"Of what I saw… but…"

"Buta what?" His father's limited English was becoming even more limited with his mounting agitation.

"There's something down there."

Valentino Pelegranetti lunged forward in the dinghy, almost capsizing it in the process, and covered his son's mouth with his hand. "Don't speaka. Don'ta saya anotha word!" He grabbed both the oars, and after taking bearings from the point of the northern headland, frantically rowed back to the obscurity of the beach. The plan was that, after procuring a diving suit, they would make their way back to their marked spot under the cloak of night.

By the light of a solitary lantern, Valentino lowered his son over the side of the dinghy. However, he had grossly misjudged the weight of the suit that Charley was wearing, and as the small vessel listed dramatically to one side, he quickly and involuntarily proceeded overboard with Charley. With no anchor to fix it, the dinghy began floating away. With a moderate swell moving into Thurrough Beach, riptides created by the reefs below pulled Valentino further out to sea, still gripping the rope, whilst the weight of the suit not only sank Charley, but also fixed his position in the ocean like a maritime marker.

Ben Douglas would often spot ambitious fishermen off the coast chancing their hands by night in order to reel in that illusive catch. He knew something was wrong when the lantern moved violently from port to starboard, which to him represented a small craft toppled by the swell. He ran down and grabbed one of the many ropes he always kept at their disposal. He instinctively yelled for Best, but Best and Elizabeth had decided to take a rare outing to the township of Thurrough. He would have to go out alone. He made his way to the tip of Thurrough's northern headland and tied the rope to a mooring ring that he had set into the rock after Norah's disappearance. He shivered as he stripped to his undergarments and secured the rope around his waist. Swimming at night in the middle of winter was not something he looked forward to. He made the sign of the cross as he approached the edge, then plunged in.

He aimed for the light of the lantern. After ten minutes of swimming and ducking under the increasing swell, he managed to haul himself up into the dinghy, only to find it empty save for the air tube that was running down to Charley's suit and a rope secured to the bow which ran back out into the sea. He pulled on the rope furiously. First to be caught was Valentino, who had been hanging on for dear life.

"My son'sa down there!" he yelled.

Ben kept pulling on the dinghy rope until the boat was dragged directly over the weight. As he struggled to bring Charley to the surface, Valentino held up the lantern to illuminate the scene, and just as he did,

Ben Douglas had a clear view of a brief, almost blinking, gold shimmer in the light of the lantern. He was unsure of what he'd seen, but after he managed to drag Charley and his heavy suit into the boat, Charley muttering something about finding no gold, it became increasingly clear just exactly what the nature of their expedition was, especially as they were also minus their fishing rods. Valentino was sheepishly silent as Charley sprawled out on the bottom of the boat, attempting to rid himself of the millstone-like suit. He repeated to his father that there was nothing down there. Regrettably for the Pelegranettis, this assumption was brought on by Charley's oxygen deprivation. Profusely apologetic to Ben Douglas, and thankful to escape with their lives, the father and son wrongly concluded that they were just being fanciful and never attempted to locate the bounty again. But Ben Douglas knew what he'd seen. He just wasn't sure what to do about it.

Seven days later, Ben Douglas was bedridden with a severe flu that developed into full-blown pneumonia. Years of exposure to the weather on harsh nights like the one he had spent rescuing the Pelegranettis had left him with failing health. It became apparent that he was not going to recover. With Best tending to the lighthouse, Elizabeth became his nurse. Just as the sun was setting on an early spring day in 1942, she appeared in the lamp room. Her expression said it all. Best quickly made his way to his father's bedside and asked Elizabeth to call for Bill Cruickshank.

Best took his father's hand, into which the sun, sea, and years of hard work had carved deep lines that formed valleys between mountains of calluses. Best noticed the faint scar that ran down the palm.

Ben Douglas coughed violently when he tried to sit up. "On my weary soul, you've always been a good lad."

Best took hold of his pillows and lowered him back down. "You need to rest."

"I might not've done everything right," continued his father, "but you turned out fine… Do you know why your mother called you Best?"

Best shook his head.

"Because she said you were the best thing that'd ever happened to her."

A lone tear ran down Best's sunburnt cheek, which he quickly wiped away.

"She was right, son. You've been the Best she'd always thought you'd be."

Suddenly, Ben Douglas gripped Best's arm, showing remarkable vigour for his weakened state. He then began to tell Best about what he had seen the night he rescued the Pelegranettis.

"What should I do about it?" asked Best.

"It has been my experience that wealth doesn't mean contentment… just look at the Telfords. But you should know it's there, that's all." Ben Douglas chuckled hoarsely. "Remember before we converted the lamp to kerosene how we used to haul whale oil up to the lamp room?"

Best nodded nostalgically, and gave a deep sigh. Even the thought of those heavy wooden barrels made him tired.

"Do you remember how much they weighed?" his father continued.

"How could I forget?"

"Do you think you could carry up one last barrel?"

"Of whale oil?" asked Best.

"Of me?"

"It's dark out there. And it's cold – the westerly's blowing."

"I can't die in this bed. I can't see anything. At least in the lamp room, I can look out from the bunk and watch the night sky, and if the good Lord sees fit to give me another couple of days, I can spend those with you in the lamp room… What do you say?"

"Are you a humpback or a blue whale?"

"Does it matter?"

"A humpback would be lighter!"

So Best carted his father up the fifty-three stairs to the lamp room and set up two bunks for them both to sleep in. Elizabeth spent the next three nights in the cottage by herself. She didn't mind. She understood.

The sixty-two-year-old Bill Cruickshank rolled his eyes when

Elizabeth told him where they were. "Fifty-three stairs!" he exclaimed as he stood by the cottage door rubbing his knees. "I'm too old for this!"

Still, he stoically and laboriously made the ascent.

"Perhaps today I might join you in Paradise!" he said as he entered the lamp room and plopped down on a stool Best had shoved under his exhausted body.

"Cruickshank!" replied Ben Douglas, relieved to see the Priest. "You've plenty of years left in you yet."

Bill Cruickshank grimaced as he stretched his legs. "I'm not so sure after those stairs!

Bill Cruickshank went on to tell them that Galbraith Telford was negotiating to buy back the land on which Tin Town was situated. Even though its numbers had dwindled significantly over the years, it was still a refuge for the downtrodden, particularly returned servicemen. "The diocese will fund it, but who am I going to get to build a hostel for these helpless people?" he asked.

"Don't you Priests ever slow down?" whispered Ben Douglas.

"It's really quite inconvenient of you to leave us in the lurch," Cruickshank added.

Ben Douglas smiled. "My building days are over, my friend. Better talk to Best. I taught him everything I know."

Best nodded. "And I'm still learning!"

"Aren't we all?" answered the Priest.

As the mood became more melancholy, Cruickshank eventually draped the sacramental ribbon over his shoulders and proceeded to administer the last rites. When the official part of the ceremony was complete, he bent down and kissed his most supportive parishioner on the forehead. "Godspeed, Ben Douglas!" he said, and then he shook Best's hand before leaving them alone. As the Priest made his weary descent, he thought about how special the relationship was between father and son. His chosen path in life did not allow for such a bond. It made him momentarily sad to think that he might die alone. He snapped out of his self-pity and offered a quick prayer of thanks for the companionship and skills of Ben Douglas.

For three days, Best and his father talked about many things. Ben Douglas smiled as he craned his head to read Harry Heath's autograph on the rotating apparatus. They laughed together as they remembered Dirk Crenshaw and how his nose was broken before he was dragged away by the army.

At night, Best lay down beside his father and they both stared out at the crisp sky. These nights in the lamp room were almost magical – so clear that Best felt he could just reach up and touch the Southern Cross.

Ben Douglas knew his time was close. For two days the lamp room had kept him alive, but his body was losing the light the room had temporarily imparted to him. "Best, there's something I must tell you… that I've always wanted to tell you."

Best leaned over to face his father who was now unable to raise himself off the three pillows Best had propped him up on.

"The day your mother disappeared… I did something."

Best took hold of his father's quivering hand and placed it underneath the warmth of the blankets.

"When the rope was pulling you towards the sea…" continued Ben Douglas.

Best automatically rubbed his left shoulder where the force of the tugging rope had almost ripped it from its socket.

"I swear the ocean was going to claim you too. You were going in sure as night follows day." He took a deep breath as he struggled for air. "I lunged for the rope… there was a sharp crag I used to snap fishing lines on… I took the rope and worked it back and forth…"

Best reached over and tucked his father tenderly under the quilt as, in his agitated state, he had loosened the bed sheets. Best no longer needed to hear this confession. "I know," he said, interrupting.

A look of surprise lit up Ben Douglas' face, bringing back a faint blush of life. "You knew?"

"I couldn't talk to you for months afterwards."

"Because you knew?"

Best shook his head. "Not because I knew, but because I never understood."

"Do you understand now?"

"I understand great men sometimes have to make great decisions, and that those decisions can only ever be judged in the light of time. I've loved my life here with you, and now with Elizabeth."

In that instant, the tension that had gripped Ben Douglas for over thirty years finally left him, almost as if his soul had broken the last crucial chain that bound it to his body. He lay back and nestled his head into the soft comfort of the pillows.

"And dad?"

"Yes?"

"I knew about Charlotte Sommer as well."

"How?"

Best tried to stifle a chuckle. "Her daughter told me. It shocked me at first, but then I just thought you were friends with Charlotte like I was with her daughter. Then, years later, I saw some of her letters."

"Did you understand?"

"I understood. Everybody needs a friend at some point."

"That they do."

"I knew you and mum were friends."

"The best of friends."

In the early hours of the morning, Ben Douglas suddenly awoke startled, bolted near upright, grasped Best by the hand and yelled, "Mains Power Electricity!" It was the last thing he said.

At age seventy, he succumbed to the pneumonia and passed away with Best by his side. He had never intended to weigh Best down with any last minute confessions, and his final words had a therapeutic effect on Best, who took them for what they were – instructions on how to improve the operation of the lighthouse.

So the rope that had once been severed from his mother and reattached to his father – that intangible umbilical cord which could never be seen nor touched, but always felt – had been cut once again. But grief was a great motivator for Best. The profound bond he shared with his father translated into zeal for Thurrough Lighthouse – *Norah*. Almost immediately, Best lobbied the State Government to extend the city's power supply to the Thurrough Peninsula where the lighthouse could be converted to mains electricity. The Government wasn't particularly interested in devoting resources to a lone lighthouse when the keeper had done an adequate job in ensuring its operation without such power: the petrol-fuelled generator that had replaced the coal one seventeen years ago would do just fine. In order to pass the buck, they deferred the matter to Thurrough Council, who had owned the land ever since Joseph Perry gave it to them. They also expressed indifference to the project, pointing out that, although it was their land, they were leasing it back to the State Government and the Maritime Association. As far as the Council was concerned, it was the Government's responsibility.

At the same time, Galbraith Telford was increasingly worried. His family had numerous landholdings in Thurrough, and many of them were along the coast and waterways of both Botany Bay and the Port Hacking River. With the world at war yet again, and with Australia's proximity to the conflict when the Japanese entered the fray, waterfront land began to devalue in light of the impending threat of invasion. When the Japanese attacked Darwin, and sent three midget submarines into Sydney Harbour, land prices plummeted. Galbraith Telford had to do what his Great Uncle, Curtis Telford, had done before him: adapt, and quickly. Just holding land was not going to be good enough.

The city of Sydney was starting to grow with such robustness that increasing amounts of construction material were being insatiably consumed. When the Perrys gave their land back to Thurrough Council, who subsequently leased the land on which *Norah* stood to the State Government, this land parcel included most of the magnificent sand dunes that towered over the northern end of Thurrough Beach. Although Galbraith's father, Baine Telford, had tried desperately to reclaim the land that was once the family's, his son was about to raise the stakes.

ONCE inside the council chambers, Bill Cruickshank was struck by just how much pomp accompanied what was basically a bureaucratic process. By choice, the Mayor was dressed in an ornate purple robe. Hanging from his neck were gold chains, attached to which were medallions that recorded the terms of past mayors. Although previous mayors had done away with such ceremony, upon his election, one thousand taxpayer pounds were spent on cleaning the chains, which contained two coats of arms, fifty monogram links, and sixty Lord Mayor links all in eighteen carat yellow gold. As the weight of the chain collar was over two kilograms, when the Mayor sat down he could barely keep his head up. Spending most of his time on building sites, Cruickshank never dressed like a member of the clergy, and rarely wore the Priest's collar. He was uncomfortable when he witnessed the garb and pageantry associated with the higher church offices such as Bishop and Archbishop. The early apostles got around in sandals, and a basic robe bound by a simple belt. How did the Church become so enamoured with dress? How did the Mayor become so intoxicated with the traditions of the office? Cruickshank was worried. He just hoped that the Mayor was not as silly as he looked.

Galbraith Telford never attended council chamber meetings. They bored him senseless. A group of people sitting around trying to find common ground on which they could agree was the downside of democracy. It was far too time consuming. Telford gave orders that he expected to be followed. It was that simple. There was no room for discussion.

His legal representative stood up in front of the Councillors and frowned. "The Telfords are prepared to offer Council a premium to buy back the land on the Thurrough Peninsula. It's worthless anyway."

The Council was under increasing pressure from Galbraith Telford due to the attractiveness of the price being offered. They were close to agreeing to sell the land. They reasoned that, as the land was useless, why not cash up and direct funds back into the Council coffers?

Cruickshank rose to his feet and cleared his throat. "If the Telford family is allowed to purchase this land, Tin Town would disappear forever."

"Wouldn't that be a shame," Galbraith Telford's lawyer sarcastically commented.

Several of the Councillors nodded their heads in agreement. Cruickshank could see that they were of the same mind. He was up against it.

He quickly appealed to their sense of propriety. "If Tin Town's eradicated then you'll have every vagabond who now lives there begging on the streets of Thurrough and living in flower boxes. Do you want that?"

The Councillors shook their heads furiously. No, they did not want that. It might affect their property values.

Much to Galbraith Telford's chagrin, Bill Cruickshank was the voice of conscience in the transaction. He suggested to the Council that the Telfords should donate land elsewhere in Thurrough, where he could possibly persuade the diocese to build a replacement home of respite.

The Mayor fingered the chains around his neck thoughtfully. His predecessors had lived in the Telford family's pockets. He had earned his election on the back of a promise to end corruption in chambers. He took the office seriously, and believed his traditional ceremonial attire made that plain for all to see. He smiled at the Priest and told him that Council would discuss his proposal and then make their decision.

WHEN the Council handed down their verdict, Galbraith Telford was furious. His father had told him years ago just how the meddling Priest had outwitted the family on a previous occasion when he helped fund the construction of the new Lighthouse. But Cruickshank had the Council by the moral "short and curlies" as Cruickshank himself amusingly told Best. The Council agreed to sell, just as long as the Telfords donated a parcel of land earmarked for a respite home for the displaced residents of Tin Town. Telford's infuriation did not match his overwhelming desire to see the land back under his family's fold, so he begrudgingly agreed.

BILL Cruickshank stood smiling at one end holding the red ribbon. At the other, was a sour-looking Galbraith Telford. When the Mayor's scissors cut the ribbon in two, the first resident to hobble in under the new brass sign, passing by the frangipani tree in full bloom, was a returned soldier with legs made entirely of oak. The lowly Priest, who had twice outwitted his more fancied opponent, decided to call the home Saint Bedes, not after the saint, but after the beads of sweat he had shed in getting the Home built.

BEST was rigging fishing lines when he heard the convoy of trucks roaring towards the lighthouse. As the dust rose violently from the dirt road, the vehicles veered off amongst the dunes before reaching the cottage. During the following months, Best and Elizabeth would wake each morning to the sound of excavators whose grinding whine would send shivers down their spines. Whenever Best looked down from the lamp room, he saw with horror what was taking place less than five hundred metres away. For the next fifty years, trucks would continue to consume virgin Thurrough sand, turning the magnificent sand dunes into decrepit mounds.

Not only did this venture make the Telford family more wealthy, as they were the almost exclusive supplier of sand concrete to Sydney's builders, it also made them immune to the downturn in their land values. And, although they sold some of their holdings, in the years following the end of World War Two, this waterfront land again became prime real estate making the Telford family one of the richest in the country. Unfortunately, as a result of Galbraith Telford's concrete dynasty, the family were also responsible for single-handedly decimating what might have eventually been looked upon as one of Australia's most magnificent natural wonders.

In a strange twist of fate, as Galbraith Telford required mains electricity to power his sand mining operations, it was extended through to the Thurrough Lighthouse. Best quickly converted the lighthouse to mains power and replaced the clockwork mechanism with an electric motor.

GALBRAITH Telford pushed himself up the face of the diminishing dune and perched himself at the top. He rose to his feet when Elizabeth appeared in the distance. From the lamp room, Best often observed the old man's behaviour. Galbraith Telford would sometimes watch the lighthouse for hours at a time just to catch a glimpse of her. This ritual went on for several years, but he never breached the gulf that he had placed between them.

CHAPTER TWENTY-SEVEN

WHEN Dr Richard Tipody began to observe Best's increased interaction with Orion and Oak Legs Finbar, he became agitated. Such socialisation was completely unacceptable, incredibly dangerous, and put the entire VAE in jeopardy. Best Douglas was turning into the Home's social butterfly, in complete contrast to the almost hermit-like character that Tipody had initially unearthed.

Tipody stared disdainfully down at the pack of cards strewn haphazardly over the table, quickly discerning that a game of gin rummy had been played, instead of Best's usual isolated game of solitaire.

He asked the question even though he knew the answer: "Been playing a bit with Finbar?"

Best had no reason to be secretive about it. "Do you play, Richard?"

"He's a bitter, twisted man," remarked Tipody, ignoring Best's question.

"He's not that bad. Has quite the sense of humour actually."

Richard Tipody crouched down, grabbed hold of Best's wheelchair handles, and whipped the chair around to face him, straining Best's frail ninety-four-year-old neck in the process.

"You'd do well to avoid him," Tipody spat out, spraying unwanted spittle in Best's face like a snake.

Best felt uncomfortable with such proximity. He began backing his wheelchair away, almost subconsciously.

"He's a bad influence," Tipody went on to say, becoming more constrained. "Not the kind of gent I would wish for your company."

"He's a war hero, you know."

"He's a cantankerous, bitter old man."

"He saved his whole crew."

"He'll only bring you down, Best."

Best shrugged his shoulders. "He's a hero," he repeated. "Did you know that?"

Tipody stood up and straightened out his suit pants. "I wouldn't spend too much time with him. He'll make you like him… All bitter and twisted… A life despiser."

Richard Tipody's comments were ironic – those feelings were exactly the ones he himself was trying to evoke in Best.

"He's not a bad bloke," added Best, thinking that he should defend Oak Legs. "Lost his legs to save his crew."

Tipody's anger was rising again and he wasn't discreet enough to hide it. This frivolous, wanton developing friendship could ruin everything. He had brought Best so far, and it had taken so long. He wasn't about to see this fraternisation ruin everything.

"You stay away from him. That's my advice," he commented, his remark sounding more like a threat than counsel.

Best shook his head, not wanting to provoke an argument. He was too old for arguments. He quickly changed the subject. "The surf's getting bigger."

Best's response quickly diffused Tipody. He looked out the window, content to let the matter rest for now. "Yes," he replied distractedly, not knowing what signs to look for in the ocean in order to validate Best's observation.

WHEN the Queen knighted Sir Errol Telford in 1994, it was said that his knighthood must have been due to a typing error in the Honours list. After all, there were far more deserving candidates. The rumour ran that this title was supposed to have been bestowed upon Dr Errol Teeford, the famous Australian medical missionary who spent most of his life working with lepers in India, but that the Foreign Office could not very well admit to the mistake – that would undermine the pomp and credibility of the whole process – so they just hoped there was someone called Errol Telford who deserved the award by default.

The rumour was never substantiated, so the fact remained that Errol Telford was now addressed as "Sir". His reputation had been originally confined to his family's dynasty in Thurrough where they had numerous landholdings and had established Telford Concrete, which, since the mid-forties, had stripped the place of its unique sand dunes. In the fifties, they had also leased their remaining coastal peninsula land to an oil company, which turned half of the historic Gweagal grounds into a massive oil refinery. Errol Telford's name, however, became indelibly stamped onto the Australian public's mind when he purchased one of the country's national television networks, followed by most of its daily newspapers. Once he controlled his own press machine, his power and success accelerated dramatically. He soon became even more recognized internationally when he started developing five star hotels, which began sprouting up in every major city in the world.

In spite of his enormous successes, most considered him a surprise choice for a knighthood. He was a controversial figure, having been married four times, twice to the same woman. But it was his blatant support for over-development that caused many people to question his bent for mortar and bricks at a time when natural resources and heritage needed to be protected. Australia was already well on its way to becoming a Republic, and when the Queen's honour roll was released, the Republican movement pointed to Telford's knighthood as just another example of the monarchy being completely out of touch with the modern world. Maybe, they argued, it would have been appropriate sixty or seventy years ago to confer recognition on an individual who contributed significantly to architectural development, but it was quite another matter to bestow a prize on someone who was destroying what was left of the natural landscape in order to build huge monuments to himself. Not knowing that nominations were, in fact, put forward by their own countrymen via the Foreign Office, most thought the Queen was out of her royal mind.

Errol Telford didn't care if the Queen was crazy. He was now Sir Errol, and that for him was the conclusion of the matter. His family had made itself great on the back of Thurrough, first through lumber, then sand mining, then through leasing prime Pacific Ocean-front land to the Bell Oil Company, who subsequently turned most of the Peninsula into a mass of modern industry that spewed flames and distilled fumes into the air. Having been raised beside the Port Hacking River, the seaside municipality held a lot of childhood memories for him. Not only had he completely eradicated the mountainous sand dunes, but his company had also mined the sand eight metres below sea level, creating a huge man-made lake. Having raped the natural landscape of as much sand as ecological watchdogs would allow, Telford wanted to turn his attention to other uses for his family land on the Thurrough Peninsula. Many assumed that since Telford loved Thurrough he would be dedicated to keeping it unspoilt, unlike his wealthy forefathers who had gone before him. But those people didn't know him very well. His thinking was that, since he enjoyed Thurrough, why not let everybody else in the world share in it, even if that altered what he used to enjoy about it in the first place, namely, its unspoilt charm? That was when Geoffery Certi, Telford's main real estate trouble-shooter, presented his boss's glorious plan for a five star beachside resort to Thurrough Council.

At first, Council was sceptical. The oil refinery at the northern end of Thurrough had discouraged other hospitality conglomerates from suggesting development at the Peninsula so Council wasn't accustomed to hearing such grand ideas. Also, their fellow Councillor and environmentalist, Tindall Pemberton, had been berating them for years about the danger of excessive sand-mining. Pemberton maintained that he had geological evidence that proved that the sand excavation now taking place below sea level could potentially cause flooding on the Peninsula in heavy rain and seas. It was half-flooded already, Pemberton argued, alluding to the salt-water lake that had been created.

But the more Certi spoke, the more Sir Errol Telford's plans sounded attractive. What he proposed was a major resort casino and accompanying golf course to be situated where the sand dunes used to be, which could be open twenty-four hours a day, fully illuminated at night by monstrous lighting towers. Certi was smooth. He had done similar presentations in nearly every major city in the world. It was second nature to him. He knew exactly what buttons to push. In his final summation, he pointed out that the resort development would bring in a staggering amount of tourist dollars, employ many locals, whilst at the same time catapulting Thurrough into the hub of the booming Australian tourism industry. He reserved his last comment for a pot-shot at Tindall Pemberton, calling him a drugged-out hippie who was as crazy as his grandmother who resided at the nut-house at Garrawarra. Whilst the Council thought his last comment was a little uncalled for, they didn't necessarily disagree. They had suffered from Pemberton's emotional outbursts for two terms now, but as an elected representative there wasn't much they could do about him.

On the contrary, most of the Councillors were enthusiastic. Many had businesses in Thurrough that would benefit greatly from such a venture. Subject to an Environmental Impact Study, which Certi would arrange, they could envisage no overwhelming obstacles. But there was one catch – the only land suitable for the resort development extended from where the sand dunes used to be right through to where the old Thurrough Lighthouse stood. Certi was matter-of-fact: the century-old lighthouse would have to be demolished along with the old cottage beside it.

Council recoiled. At least at first. Tindall Pemberton screamed in protest and was escorted out of the meeting. There was much discussion. Certi didn't need to say much, however. He merely guided the conversation as a policeman would direct traffic. He eventually steered Council into concluding that they could do without the lighthouse, seeing as it was no longer functional. After all, the resort would bring in fifty (perhaps a hundred, suggested Certi) times as much income as the lighthouse ever had. But it was all speculation. In the final analysis, even if Council was to approve plans, the fate of the lighthouse lay nestled within the maternal, protective hands of the Heritage Trust. It was simply not Council's decision to make. The Heritage Trust had rated Thurrough Lighthouse an "A" level sight. It must not be torn down.

Geoffery Certi politely bowed his head. He was well-accustomed to dealing with such obstacles. That's why he was working for one of the country's most successful developers. If Telford Developments, he asked Council, was able to reach some agreement with the Heritage Trust, would they tentatively endorse plans for a resort development? Most of Council said they would. The others told him that Telford Developments didn't stand a hope in hell. The Heritage Trust was an unbending, formidable opponent dedicated to preserving buildings of historic significance. Certi smiled knowingly. Throughout his twenty-year career he had been to hell several times. He'd always made it back, and only ever with a slight singeing of his jet-black hair.

As it turned out, Certi's meeting with the Heritage Trust proved to be rather sedate. Yes, they were concerned about the fate of Thurrough Lighthouse. Certi too was concerned. And when he produced two "independent" geological reports outlining how the eroding effects of tide and onshore winds were undermining the sandstone foundation on which the lighthouse was built, the Heritage Trust's Executives could see just how concerned he was.

"Sir Errol," Certi began, "... my friend, Sir Errol," he went on, using the familiar term for his boss that always seemed to make an impression, even though Certi had never been friends with his employer, nor would he be, because he simply didn't like him. But he did like the lucrative salary he was paid for his services, and for that he could pretend to be his friend. "... has a special place in his heart for the township of Thurrough. He doesn't want that lighthouse crumbling to the elements any more than any of you good people do."

The Executives of the Heritage Trust smiled. Yes, they were good people.

"What Sir Errol is suggesting is this," Certi paused for effect, "the complete removal of the entire lighthouse from its current site and its relocation to one prepared especially for its unique architecture."

"Incredible," exclaimed one of the Executives.

"Yes," responded Certi, "but not impossible. I've already spoken with Thurrough Council," he lied, "and they have assured me that they could possibly relocate it into the new strip mall that will be constructed in Pacific Street."

"But the cost?" exclaimed the Trust in unison.

"Entirely met by Telford Developments."

Two weeks later, Certi was once again in front of Thurrough Council minus Tindall Pemberton who had just about had a nervous breakdown after having his reputation so publicly dragged through the mud at both the Council meeting and in several columns published in Telford's newspapers. After Certi revealed the plan to relocate the lighthouse, the response was almost overwhelming. What a great idea! Remove the lighthouse to the new mall! There it could become a major attraction designed to pull in shoppers! But what about cost, one of the Councillors asked. Entirely met by Telford Developments, Certi answered as if acting in a matinee performance after receiving a standing ovation on opening night. Then came the applause.

Two months later, Telford Developments architectural plans for the massive resort complex appeared at Council Chambers for approval. Under the development, Telford Developments, after relocating the lighthouse, would begin construction of the resort, which would include half the area of beach below the old lighthouse. As coincidence would have it, Telford Developments also wanted to build a fifty metre saltwater tidal pool precisely over the site of the Hole that used to be Thurrough's biggest tourist attraction over eighty years ago. Council didn't miss the irony: the new attraction was, in some mystical way, building upon the foundations of the old.

*

CAPTAIN Marcus Swanson hung on every word Jese Sommer uttered as they darted and weaved cautiously through the one hundred and twenty-hectare shipyard of Chantiers de L'Atlantique, where the largest ocean liner in maritime history was being constructed for the British-based Winston Line. When Winston's issued the tender for the construction of the massive vessel, most industry pundits believed the contract would logically fall to Belfast. But Winston's surprised them all, much to the shock of the British Government. Winston's was unrepentant. Their rationale for choosing a French-based shipbuilder was summed up in two words: Jese Sommer.

Jese Sommer was one of the world's most prominent architects in modern maritime history. He was lauded for his innovative designs, and his ability to translate those intangible concepts into commercial production. He had a reputation for working hand-in-hand with the builders until that very last victorious moment when the bottle of fine French champagne was cracked against the hull of the ship. He had designed numerous ships out of the shipyards of Saint Nazaire, but the design and construction of the *Queen of the South Pacific* was by far the grandest and most expensive project he had ever been associated with – or that anyone had ever been associated with.

Captain Swanson listened in awe as Jese Sommer pointed out the phases of construction and the enormity of the process. "This ship, Sir," began Sommer, "will represent over eight million working hours by the time it is finished. The hull is made up of ninety-four blocks of steel, some of them weighing over six hundred tonnes and built from three hundred thousand steel pieces involving some fifteen hundred kilometres of welding, and all this in less than two years."

Swanson looked up at the ship being formed in dry dock. "Tell me more. I want to know everything."

As the two men, both infused with a love for the sea, toured the shipyard, Jese Sommer revealed the intricacies and nuances of the ship that he had designed, and that, in the next twelve months, Marcus Swanson would captain on its maiden voyage. He went on to elaborate that the twenty-five hundred French workers devoted to the construction of the *Queen of the South Pacific* were building a ship three hundred and forty-five metres long that weighed some one hundred and fifty thousand tonnes, and would cost the Winston Line approximately one and a half trillion dollars. Some thirteen hundred rooms, five swimming pools, and numerous other facilities would cater for three thousand, six hundred and seventy passengers and twelve hundred and eighty-five crew. But Jese Sommer sensed from the Captain's reaction to this information that these details were of passing interest to him.

"Come," he finally gestured to the Captain, knowing only too well where the man really wanted to go.

Sommer led him up to the most sophisticated, technologically advanced bridge that had ever been built. He pointed to the engine controls. "She's powered by four diesel Wärtsilä engines through two gas turbines."

"And the propulsion?" Swanson asked with a hint of anticipation.

Sommer smiled. "Four twenty megawatt Mermaid pods – two fixed and two rotating."

"Props?"

"Fixed-pitch highly-skewed blades."

There was a period of quiet reverence on the bridge as Swanson absorbed this information.

"Go on, Sir," said Sommer, breaking the silence. "Ask the question."

Marcus Swanson laughed. A large reason for Sommer's design

success was because he was able to empathise with the wishes and desires of both passengers and crew, and this was made manifest in the design of his ships.

"All right then," the Captain happily conceded. "What's her top speed?"

Sommer chuckled. As much as captains of cruise ships had to be restrained by many other parameters, boat speed was still important to them.

"Thirty knots."

Swanson nodded his head in approval. A ship of this magnitude being able to generate that speed was quite the achievement.

"She won't break any records, but it's not bad for one hundred and fifty thousand tonnes, no?"

"Not bad. Not bad at all."

When completed, the *Queen of the South Pacific* would be the latest in cruise ship technology, and the bridge was the point at which most of these advancements intersected. Sommer went on to explain that her operations would be controlled by no less than seven computers, three of which were back-ups. Just as the English-French consortium of Airbus had created airplanes that "flew by wire" as opposed to heavy mechanical interfaces, the most sophisticated ships were now designed and built in much the same fashion. Not only were these new interacting systems much more precise and finely tuned, but vessels could now be engineered without the additional weight of mechanical systems. In both air and sea this resulted in lighter crafts, which as a result, did not consume as much fuel.

"Her navigational positioning and route planning are achieved through the use of orbiting satellites," Sommer outlined. "By receiving signals from just two satellites, the QSP's computers will pinpoint her exact latitudinal and longitudinal position, and then translate that information into the navigational systems. It is the first time a Global Positioning System has been fully integrated to control the navigation of a ship of this magnitude."

The Captain smiled wistfully. "Long gone are the days when we had to rely on stars, compasses, or even lighthouses for that matter."

Captain Marcus Swanson had had an illustrious career. After leaving the British Navy in 1957, he was quickly snapped up by the Winston Line. His maritime experience had literally spanned the oceans of the world. He joked with Jese Sommer that calling him the "Captain" of a ship totally run by computers was a liberty. He felt more like a programmer. But Jese Sommer knew that nobody ever ran to a computer in times of crisis. That's when the four gold bars worn on the Captain's shoulder became twenty-four carat in the eyes of the crew and passengers. Jese Sommer had insisted on these planned orientation sessions with Marcus Swanson as he felt compelled to reveal every possible detail about the ship in order for the Captain to be able to make the most informed decisions in times of uncertainty. And being the Captain that he was, Marcus Swanson responded to these sessions like an eager school student.

Whereas Marcus Swanson had blue blood flowing through his veins – the son of a British Lord and a graduate of Cambridge University – Jese Sommer's blood was as black as the soot on the hands of the Saint Nazaire shipyard workers. His family had served in the French shipyards for as long as he could remember. His father had been a welder. He was told that his grandfather had also worked the yards, but that he had set sail one day before his father was born and never returned: the only sign of his existence a rabbit fur felt hat that his grandmother had placed on a bust of Napoleon, perched on the mantelpiece.

As a young boy, Jese's life had revolved around the shipyard. Throughout his childhood, he observed the construction of all types of vessels first hand as he would often take his father his dinner when he was working back late in order to fulfil an order. His father would tell Jese how the Sommers had worked on such liners as *France* (1912), *Ile De France* (1927), *Normandie* (1935), and the infamous *Dunkerque* (1940). During these exchanges, Jese Sommer became fascinated with the whole process; how something of such magnitude could be designed so precisely so that all the independent parts could come together as a whole, much like a jigsaw puzzle. He loved the earthy humility of the shipyard workers like his father, but he also fed on the intelligence of the architects and engineers who he would often hear in heated debate during the various stages of a ship's construction. His father saw in him the fascination that only passion could ignite and was determined to see his son break the family tradition. His son was not going to build ships for a living; he was going to design them.

Jese Sommer's father spent many hours working additional shifts so that he could provide his son with the opportunity to undertake the necessary studies that would allow him to fulfil both their ambitions. When his father fell from two massive sheets of steel he was welding, injuring his neck, he was transferred to a desk job where he was involved in securing the materials necessary to build the massive ships. In this position, he had the ear of the hierarchy of Chantiers, and when Jese was old enough, applied to have him sponsored by the company. When management recognized how enchanted Jese was with the process of shipbuilding, they awarded him the company educational scholarship in engineering, thus setting the young prodigy on the path his father had hoped for him.

Unlike many of the "white collar" workers within the shipyard, Jese Sommer never forgot where his family came from, nor considered himself to be any more important than the workers who were black and sweaty from the intense flames that shot out of their welders. Years after his father's retirement, he would often spend lunches sitting with the remainder of his father's welding crew. It was during these stints on the factory floor that he gained a much deeper appreciation of the process of shipbuilding, and far greater insight than could ever be gleaned from books. It was this interaction that subconsciously equipped him with a considerable advantage over his colleagues, which in time distinguished him well above his peers. As an ultimate tribute to this informal part of his apprenticeship, served by choice amongst the welders of Saint Nazaire, Jese Sommer was affectionately dubbed by the French workers as, *"l'architecte sale."* He even came to be known by this appellation throughout the English-speaking maritime world, where his peers had no idea how or why he came to have such a title bestowed upon him, one that translated crudely into English as "the dirty architect."

*

DR Richard Tipody towered over the stooped form of the Home's Superintendent. He slapped a folder on the desk. "I've studied the man's demeanour," he began forcefully. "He's becoming delusional and dangerous, not only to himself but other residents as well."

The Superintendent opened the folder and studied the file. He shrugged his shoulders. "He's aggressive at times, but I think his bark is worse than his bite."

"Do you want to take that risk?"

"A recommendation to transfer him to Garrawarra is a big step, Dr Tipody."

"If you're prepared to ignore my recommendation and something happens then I'm afraid I wouldn't be able to defend your actions in any shape nor form, especially in light of the advice I've given, which I've volunteered out of duty."

Due to his previous indiscretion, which had resulted in his being stripped of his license to practise medicine, the Superintendent of the Thurrough Nursing Home liked to be invisible. He avoided any situations that might attract unwanted attention. He reluctantly took a form from the desk drawer.

"My report on Daniel Finbar is conclusive," Tipody added as he turned to leave. "I think you'll concur that Garrawarra is the right option."

The Superintendent nodded, but not at all convincingly. He knew that Garrawarra was a nursing home for mentally ill patients, situated ten kilometres inland from Thurrough, deep in the bush, and represented the last step for the sane mind. If Daniel Finbar wasn't insane before he entered Garrawarra, thought the Superintendent, then he sure as hell would be after he'd spent any length of time there. He also knew that, for some inexplicable reason, Richard Tipody had a direct line to the hierarchy of the Department of Health. Desiring to stay beneath the Department's radar, the Superintendent quickly scribbled his signature before he had a chance to consult with his conscience.

It was ten o'clock at night when the men in white coats appeared outside Daniel Finbar's room. Most of the residents had long fallen asleep. As the sedating needle slid into Oak Leg's arm, he turned and swung a left hook in the direction of the prick, half-connecting with the jaw of the perpetrator.

"What the f–?" He never got a chance to finish his sentence.

BEST felt like he had been shuffling the cards for half an hour. He didn't know what time it was, but he had expected Oak Legs just after lunch. In that time, Best had watched the sun descend from its prominent noon position. There was no doubt about it. Even by nursing home standards, Oak Legs Finbar was running late.

Best's joy at seeing the shadow of someone about to glide through his door was fleetingly short-lived when the shadow manifested itself as Dr Richard Tipody's.

"Shame about Finbar," Tipody began, wanting to confront Best with the awful reality head-on; all part of his grand scheme to diminish Best's grasp on his own worth.

Best slowly and methodically placed the infinitely shuffled deck down on the windowsill.

Tipody barged towards his revelation. "Who'd have thought they'd have him committed?"

"Committed to what?" asked Best, not quite grasping what Tipody was extracting so much pleasure in revealing.

"Gone to Garrawarra."

Best couldn't repeat the name. No sane resident liked to mention that name.

"He suddenly snapped during one of our sessions," lied Tipody; he could see by the expression on Best's face that Best was having a hard time believing him.

Best turned and stared out his window.

Tipody sat down on the edge of Best's bed feeling incredibly pleased with the way events were unfolding. He hopped up to stand directly behind Best, who was looking to the north where his rock of Gibraltar was still rooted steadfast: the only certainty in an uncertain world.

Tipody decided to leave Best with one last morsel of bitter pill. "Did you hear about the resort they're building?"

Best pulled himself away from his thoughts. He shook his head. He rarely heard anything.

"They're building it up where you used to live."

Best perked up. "Up near the lighthouse?"

"They're going to move it."

Best looked horrified. "Move it? They can't move it. It'll collapse."

Tipody shrugged his shoulders. "They're also going to build a big golf course over the dunes."

Best sighed. For the last fifteen years he had watched the Thurrough he once knew being slowly transformed into a confused mass of buildings and over-development.

"And you know where the old Crenshaw Hole used to be?" added Tipody.

Best's eyes darted up at him.

"They're going to build this huge tidal pool. They're going to call it Crenshaw Pool."

Best began to shake uncontrollably.

"Are you all right?"

"Yes," he said quivering as Tipody poured him a glass of water.

Tipody grabbed a blanket from the bed and laid it across Best's lap. He didn't want any harm coming to him when things were panning out so well.

After Tipody left, Best picked up the binoculars. He scanned up the beach to the point just below the lighthouse. With the help of Orion's gift, he could clearly see the excavation equipment. The pool trench was being dug, and now plans were afoot to move the lighthouse. Best winced. He felt helpless. After all these years, *Norah* would be destroyed, and Best was too old, and too powerless to do anything about it.

*

SIR Errol Telford and his right hand man, Geoffery Certi, surveyed the proposed resort construction sight from the lamp room of the old lighthouse. Telford's Development Application was passed rather effortlessly in the end. There had been a minor obstacle: the Council's Environmental Impact Study unearthed a report by Tindall Pemberton. It maintained that years of sand-mining had made the Thurrough Peninsula prone to flooding. In an extreme deluge, it was highly likely that the strip of land, which tapered to only a hundred metres across at the narrowest part, could find itself underwater, thereby cutting the Peninsula off from the rest of Thurrough. Tindall Pemberton had been a lone voice on Council against the prolific amount of development that had taken place over the last twenty years. The rest of Council considered him a radical. To enforce the Council's collective opinion of Pemberton and his hare-brained Environmental Impact Study, Certi mustered together his own team of geologists who quickly discredited his report as that of a weed-smoking crackpot. Unfortunately, Pemberton's recent mental collapse had also acted against him, and after a few well-placed favours to certain Councillors, the DA was stamped "approved".

Telford wiped the dust off the brass revolving mechanism. His eyes squinted as he tried to decipher the engraving etched into the brass. "When are they going to attempt the removal?" he asked.

"Thursday week," replied Certi.

"Should be interesting." He ran his finger along one of the many cracks making inroads in the old brick render. He studied the prismatic lens made dull from years of accumulated dust. He could barely see the lamp tucked behind it. "Think it'll hold together?"

Certi was quick to shake his head. "Not a chance."

Telford located the lamp's control box and flicked the activating switch out of curiosity. He nodded his head smugly when nothing happened. *Norah* was finally dead, soon to be buried. "You sure about that?"

"She'll crumble under pressure, like Tindall Pemberton did, as soon as they try to lift her off the foundations."

Telford was always concerned with image. "Have you got our papers briefed?"

Certi nodded. He always covered all the angles. "The story will go something like, '*Brave attempt to move old lighthouse foiled by Father Time himself – the old girl was just too frail...*' How's that sound?"

"Believable. But will the Heritage Trust go for it?"

"They will when we tell them our geologists and structural engineers said it would've fallen down over the next couple of years anyway. The building's a public nuisance. It could kill someone. We'll be doing the public a favour."

"My father hated this lighthouse... When are they starting on the golf course?"

"Two months."

"And the pool?"

"Next Tuesday."

"Why so soon?"

"They're going to excavate the trench to take advantage of the Christmas low tides."

"Great... I'll be doing laps by February."

Certi smiled as he attempted to disguise his "who cares?" look.

ANYTHING to do with real estate, and Charley Pelegranetti was "all over it like a cheap suit" – so went one of his favourite sayings. He devoured all the articles on the Telford development that were written in the *Daily Chronicle,* which Telford also happened to own. Charley was Best's most reliable source of information on the construction of the new resort, and as Charley loved to talk, he was tickled pink that Best took such an interest in a topic that was so near and dear to his own heart.

Best began taking his dinners in the common room as Charley always had some titbit of information on the development, helping Best understand how the whole process would come together. When Charley started talking about the salt-water pool, Best put down his knife and fork and stopped chewing. Charley loved this willing audience.

"You see, Best," began Charley as if conducting a seminar, "although the tide's going to be the primary means by which the pool will be replenished with new water, residue will still remain at the deeper sections of the pool totally untouched by the tide. It's this residue, which represents one-fifth of the volume of the pool, that's going to need draining every three months. And the drainage tunnel – to be linked to the open sea – is how it'll be accomplished."

Best quickly wheeled himself back to his room and grabbed his binoculars. He strained his eyes, trying to take in every minute detail. He took a deep breath. He was almost certain that this crucial drainage tunnel was being excavated at exactly the same location as Crenshaw's Hole.

"How deep is this drainage tunnel going to be?" Best asked the following night, as he nestled his wheelchair by Charley Pelegranetti.

Charley could barely contain his excitement. He was thrilled that Best was showing such an interest in a project that also fascinated him. He pulled out his reading glasses and took great pains to read verbatim all the details of the proposed construction as they appeared in the *Chronicle.* "The drainage tunnel's going to be excavated to a depth of thirty-three metres in order to reach rock where the water will be naturally filtered as it makes its way back to the sea."

Best's mouth opened. Charley Pelegranetti thought it was in amazement. But it was actually in horror. Over the years, visions of the Keeper had often returned to Best unexpectedly. Sometimes, as the full moon radiated onto the sand below and ran a shimmering stream through the ocean, he would remember. These glimpses were almost like dreams, surreal and far removed from what he had experienced all those years ago. He now bore no resemblance to his younger self, as if he too had become distorted. Was the Keeper real? Had he ever been real? And how much of what Best remembered were merely fanciful visions, conjured up by the mind, parading as memories? Was that one of the barbs of old age? Did reality and fiction become fused? Best was not sure. So many things had happened in his life. Nevertheless, one thing was tragically certain – the drainage tunnel Telford Developments was excavating was deeper than Crenshaw's Hole and was going to eradicate that section of the beach that he had loved as a child. He had to do something. *Norah* would be destroyed when Telford Developments attempted to move her. There was little doubt about that. He needed help.

CHAPTER TWENTY-EIGHT

RICHARD Tipody considered the request out of character. Nurse Selby had told him that Best wanted to see him ASAP. Best had never asked for him before, and as visits were always initiated by Tipody's own agenda, the urgency of the request was out of the ordinary. That bothered him. He wanted to keep everything the same, then just snuff out the light.

Best had come to appreciate the time the doctor spent with him, but it had never reached the stage where he sought out his company. Still, in some ways, Richard Tipody had become like a friend. He seemed interested in Best. And wasn't that the mark of true friendship, Best thought? Concern about another's well-being?

As Tipody sipped his lemon tea, Best began reluctantly. "Can I tell you about something that happened a long time ago?"

Tipody smacked his lips. "Of course you can. I love hearing about your past."

"You might think I am a little crazy."

Tipody laughed insensitively. "Worried I might send you to Garrawarra?"

Best didn't find the joke funny. "No."

"I'm sorry," Tipody said, quickly checking himself. "Go on."

"When I was a boy I helped Dirk Crenshaw dig the Hole."

"Thurrough Hole?" Tipody asked, surprised.

"I used to watch the ocean for him so he could dig."

Over the last few months, Tipody found himself growing increasingly impatient with Best. Up until then, Tipody had steered their conversations, which were guided by his VAE objective. But recently, Best seemed to be more stimulated by the past than deflated by it. This was unacceptable. Tipody wanted Best's memories to suck the life out of him, not breathe life into him. "What about it?" he asked, a hint of irritation in his voice.

Best paused then took a long, deep breath. "One night," he went on to relate, "I went to the Hole during a storm."

Tipody stifled a yawned. This was hardly riveting stuff.

"There was someone down there."

Tipody placed his tea on the windowsill. "What do you mean, there was someone down there?" he asked, his curiosity starting to rise, albeit slightly.

"There was some... one," Best replied.

"Just a kid goofing around, I suppose?"

"No. Someone else."

"Who would be down a hole at that time of night?" asked Tipody, not sure where the conversation was going.

Best rubbed his head. "I don't know."

"You don't know who was down there, or you don't know if anybody was down there?"

"It was a man – of sorts."

Tipody was now experiencing the same feelings of confusion that he had when he first met Best and quizzed him about his surname.

"He was some kind of man... I think."

Tipody attempted to hide the smirk that he could feel forcing its way onto his face. It soon left when a terrible thought struck him. He had profiled Best to the Geriatric Advisory Committee as a sane, simple man who just wanted to call it quits. Now, Best was giving him cause to suspect that he was a fruitcake.

"What did this *man of sorts* say to you?" Tipody enquired, increasingly concerned with Best's mental state, and thinking that maybe he had pushed Best too far, tipping him over the edge of sanity.

"He told me if I ever needed his help one day that I should come to him."

"And how exactly were you to do that?"

"Dig I suppose."

Tipody got up and went to the window. He put his hands behind his back as if in deep thought, although he knew, halfway through this ridiculous conversation, what he was going to say. "Best, sometimes, when great tragedy envelops us, the mind seeks an escape, it seeks an alternative, it seeks an answer."

"What do you mean, Richard?"

"I'm merely suggesting that you were a little, vulnerable boy who had lost his mother in a tragic, awful occurrence. You can't underestimate what that incident would have done to your young, impressionable mind."

Best contemplated the explanation. He supposed that could be true. "It wasn't just that. He told me something that I've never forgotten and it helped me through the years."

"Oh yes," replied Tipody flippantly. "And what was that?"

"He said that it's okay to ask questions of God, just as long as you're patient for the answers."

Hardly a revelation, Tipody thought. "The brain is a wonderful thing," elaborated Tipody. "It will protect you from terrible memories, even if it has to lie to you."

Best looked out the window towards *Norah*.

Tipody bent down on his haunches and laid a comforting hand on

Best's left knee. "You witnessed your mother die. Can you imagine the enormity of the scars that left on your young mind?"

"I never thought I'd been affected in that way."

"This *man of sorts* was really an illusion created by you in order to help overcome this tragedy. Do you understand that?"

"I guess it might have been," replied Best. "Although, I'm not sure I could've come up with that advice."

Tipody could see from Best's expression that his explanation hadn't totally convinced him. Best's questionable mental state was starting to concern him. The VAE's credibility would suffer irreparable damage if the test subject was shown to be mentally unfit. The whole premise for the process was founded on eliminating subjects who were of sound mind. Tipody needed to act quicker. He needed to bring Best's VAE date forward.

Best wasn't in the habit of examining himself. His skin was now full of so many imperfections – liver spots, sun damage and wrinkles – that it was better not to own a mirror. Similarly, he never thought much about his mental acuity. But after the doctor's hasty exit, Best was struck by the clarity of his own mind, and he suddenly felt that his faculties were in no way diminished by age, in stark contrast to other residents in the Home. Through his process of introspection, he firmly believed that his mind had not deteriorated as others' had. It was this revelation that cast a niggling doubt over Tipody's psychoanalysis. At the same time, Best also entertained the notion that perhaps his mind was tricking him into believing that it was unimpaired – a self-defence mechanism to mask the onset of dementia, in which case, Richard Tipody might just be right. And then it came to him: he could no longer trust his own judgement. There was one more ear he needed to confide in: a younger ear not contaminated by the confusion caused by the passing of years.

BEST was quick to close the door behind him. Orion was puzzled. He had never seen Best so jittery, and had never witnessed Best shut the door to the room, no matter how personal their conversations had become.

"Orion," said Best slowly, motioning for him to sit down, "I need to tell you something very important."

Orion looked at his watch. It was a minute to three. He missed the sound of Oak Legs Finbar's hollering.

"Don't worry about Oak Legs," Best reassured him. "If anyone can get out of there, it'll be him."

Orion nodded hopefully. "What's up?" he asked as he parked his barrow by the bed and dragged a chair over to the window, placing it beside Best's.

Best's eyes narrowed, revealing a seriousness Orion had never seen in him before. "You must promise me you won't tell another soul what I'm about to tell you. Even if you think I'm a crazy old man."

"I don't think you're crazy."

Best looked up the beach to the lighthouse. "You might after hearing this."

Best took an energetic breath, and didn't stop talking for the next half an hour.

Orion sat transfixed as he listened to the story of how Best had discovered the Keeper and how he had stopped the diggers of Crenshaw's Hole from unearthing him.

When Best had finally finished, Orion assured Best that he didn't think he was crazy. He told Best that he believed him, that he'd always believed him.

"And you haven't tried to get to him again since the army filled in the Hole?" Orion asked.

"Once," Best replied as he craned his head back to look longingly towards the cottage where he had spent most of his life. "He told me that if I ever needed him, he'd be down there waiting for me. So one day, I dug for him."

Orion's eyes lit up in anticipation. "Did you find him?"

"No." Best stared out the window at the waves rolling into Thurrough Beach. "I stopped digging before I reached him."

Orion seemed disappointed. "Oh."

"I don't swim," added Best unexpectedly.

"You're nearly a hundred years old. That's a pretty good reason."

"No… I've never swum."

"Not even when you were a boy?" Orion asked incredulously.

"Not after…"

Orion was solemnly silent. He didn't want to make Best remember, especially as he knew the answer already. But it was too late. Best's mind was about to liberate itself of one more memory.

"Elizabeth was a good swimmer," began Best. "She loved to swim. And she loved the surf. She liked the waves. She never asked me to swim with her because she understood I couldn't. She used to swim with her father, but when she married me she was on her own. I wished I could swim with her, but I just… It wasn't easy for women in those days. They used to have to wear these big, baggy costumes. Not like today."

"They hardly have to wear anything anymore," remarked Orion, sounding pleased with that aspect of progress.

"It was during the war. The waves weren't that big… but it was rough… a solid easterly swell. You know the type… just crashes down on the sand bars."

Orion nodded knowingly. Such waves caused more accidents for surfers than any others.

"I wasn't happy with her going out by herself. It made me uncomfortable. But that wasn't new. I was always uncomfortable, even if the waves were small. And the sea that day was no different to many other days she'd gone in. I came down to the beach so I could keep an eye on her. Her head was bobbing up and down with the swell beyond the break, then all of a sudden, she disappeared."

Orion's face went white.

"I wanted to go in after her." Best rubbed his eyes. But there were no tears. The memories had gone well beyond tears. "I wanted to with all my heart. But I couldn't swim. I just couldn't. I ran down the beach towards some fisherman. I yelled at them that she was out there, and they went straight in after her. Then the lifeguards arrived. They were out there for hours. No one ever found her."

"What did you do?"

"The only thing I could. I ran to where Crenshaw's Hole used to be and started digging with my bare hands. And as the sand built up under my fingernails, I just kept saying his name. I just kept saying it."

A solitary tear ran down Orion's pale cheek.

"I stopped after a couple of feet. It was totally useless. I was useless."

*

FINBAR's legs always shook before a mission. It wasn't an involuntary twitching. He would sit during the briefing and use his feet to push his legs up and down. It was more like a warm-up, to get the blood flowing.

The telegram was handed to him by one of the Air Force clerks whose expressions were always bland whether they were delivering good news or bad. They were used to dealing out scripts of doom, and the deaths the telegrams recorded meant little to them. After a while, they never even bothered to read more than the name of the person to whom a telegram was to be delivered. It was much easier that way.

As the clerk moved off, Finbar wondered about the content. There had been no recent casualties in his squadron, and he had just received a telegram from home, where all was well. He glanced down. The Briefing Sergeant halted his dissertation on seeing that the Captain was distracted.

Elizabeth Douglas missing, feared drowned

Daniel Finbar had become somewhat immune to the deaths caused by war, but he was unprepared for this news. His face went ashen white.

"I'm sorry," he began, rising to his feet, "I need to check on Lizzy."

Finbar scurried out to the airfield to greet his Lancaster, which was being refuelled by the ground engineers. He gently traced the outline of the mascot. He had always loved Elizabeth Telford, ever since he first saw her strolling brazenly into his father's garage. So headstrong, yet so free spirited – like the sea eagles that soared the sea breeze updrafts created by the sheer faces of the Thurrough sand dunes. That was why he was so attracted to flying – he wanted to be like her.

He touched the mascot's cherry lips tenderly with the tips of his calloused fingers. He'd named his plane after her, and her image went everywhere he did. Now, the only thing that remained of her was the portrait on the skin of the Bomber.

By tomorrow, that too would be gone.

*

WHEN several Japanese midget submarines entered Sydney harbour and attacked the ferry, HMAS *Kuttabul*, killing nineteen Australian and New Zealand sailors, the Coastal Watchdog Program proposed and implemented by General Robert "Punch" Zuma nearly three decades before suddenly seemed sensible. Literally overnight, beaches were lined with barbed-wire barricades that housed bunker-style lookouts. High on the Southern and Northern Heads, which marked the entrance to Sydney Harbour, gun turrets were carved into the sandstone rock. It was a dark time in Australia's history when, for the first time since World War One, the country was forced to face its fear of invasion.

The War, along with the death of his wife, amounted to the darkest period in Best's life. Not only was his Elizabeth gone, but the landscape in which he had always found solace had been obscured by man-made obstacles designed to keep out the invaders from the north. Although far from the battlefields, the bleak face of war could be observed not only on the sand of the beaches, but on the faces of the population left to wonder if the country would remain theirs. And, as the injury toll from the war mounted, so did the residents of Tin Town.

The full fury of the Telfords seemed to come down on Best. Galbraith Telford was determined to ostracise the lighthouse keeper, who he blamed for his daughter's death. He used his influence to help enact regulations that prohibited the keeper from leaving his station under any circumstances. This made Best a virtual hermit. He tried to point out to the New South Wales Maritime Commission that he needed additional help. But since they had only ever granted a stipend for one keeper, which Best and his father shared, they weren't prepared to outlay any additional expense. However, the Commission agreed to offer Best any length of leave with the stipulation that he must vacate the cottage for the relieving keeper. This was of little value to Best. Where would he go? What would he do?

Best began to feel trapped. He was now a contracted lighthouse keeper with no existence outside the space that contained *Norah* and the humble cottage. He had always shared his love of Thurrough with somebody: first his father, then Elizabeth. Now, they were both gone. He felt completely alone.

He waited for a gentle swell coupled with the milder offshore winds of early autumn, when water temperatures were still close to summer levels. Then, just on dawn, he quietly rowed out to the location his father had spoken of on his deathbed. He anchored the boat, and after removing his shirt, slipped a rope around his waist and tied the other end to the bow. He fitted one diving flipper onto his right foot, which had always been the stronger leg. He stared down at the water. It was only sixteen feet deep before it hit this shallow part of the reef. Still, he was nervously, almost manically, apprehensive. He hadn't been in the ocean since his mother's drowning. He began sweating, which was unusual, given that it was a cool autumn morning. The water was so still, so green and clear. And then he saw it. At first he thought it was the passing shimmer of a swerving fish, but it remained stationary. The yellow light looked as though it had been embedded into the reef, hidden by the shadows of weed and conge. After a few minutes of squinting through the water, Best knew what he was looking at: the *Black Swan's* sunken treasure. He fell back into the boat and began hyperventilating. This could solve all his problems. No longer would he have to cower to the

Telford family. He would have his own fortune. He could do whatever he liked. Be whatever he liked. Maybe move away from Thurrough with all its scarring memories? He rubbed the sweat off his brow. All he had to do was dive out of the boat and claim it. That's all he had to do. It was so easy, so very easy. Since the Pelegranettis, no one had even entertained the thought of this bounty being a reality. And now here Best was, hovering over it, ready to strike it rich.

As he was leaning over the dinghy about to force himself to jump through the glass-like surface of the water, he began to feel an overwhelming ache in the pit of his stomach, which then gurgled and began forcing its way up his oesophagus. He suddenly felt excruciatingly sick, which was only relieved by vomiting. And then he had an epiphany; an overpowering, blinding vision of what he was about to become, of what he was turning into, even now, as he was hanging over the side of the boat throwing up. He was prepared to conquer his extreme fear of water, to push that phobia aside, in order to gain whatever lay below the surface, when he had been unable to enter the sea to try and save Elizabeth. He stumbled back into the boat. He had made himself physically sick. He was revolted by his own thoughts, by his own behaviour. Is this what riches do to someone, he asked? Is this what they turn men into? He quickly grabbed the oars and began rowing away before he could try and talk himself into diving in after the gold again. He no longer wanted anything to do with it. The gold was no longer an option he wished to pursue. He would rather go through life like he was, unhappy but true to himself, rather than gain the whole world but lose his own soul.

Best Douglas never mentioned the gold of the *Black Swan* shipwreck to anyone. Although he had turned his back on significant riches, his guilt over Elizabeth's death was compounded by the fact that feelings of anger and greed had almost helped him conquer his fear of the ocean where feelings of love had failed.

ELIZABETH'S drowning continued to eat at the very soul of Galbraith

Telford. It was he who had taken his daughter down to the beach to swim ever since she was a child, and it was he who wiped his hands of her as soon as she had married Best Douglas – the public servant. He could not humble himself enough to condone their union, and the only time after their marriage that he ever saw his daughter was over the ever-dilapidating dunes, which separated the lighthouse from his sand-mining operations. Not willing to face his own guilt, which was gnawing its way through to his marrow, he vowed to finally destroy the lighthouse. Not long after the war ended, he negotiated the sale of another large parcel of land which neighboured his sand-mining operations. This time the buyer was the Bell Oil Company, which subsequently built an oil refinery. Galbraith Telford was slowly turning the historic Thurrough Peninsula, where the Gweagal once feasted on abundant seafood and plentiful fruits, into a grotesque human carnival where nature would be slowly but irrevocably altered.

As *Norah* stood proud and weathered the Telford storm, Best became a virtual recluse, only leaving the lighthouse to buy parts and equipment needed for repairs and maintenance. Even his groceries were delivered by government service. As he watched the construction of the oil refinery, a permanent knot formed in his stomach. He felt like he was waiting; waiting for someone to take his final prized gift away.

*

ORION jumped up with all the energy of youth. He looked up at the lighthouse. "I can help you," he said confidently. "We can do it together. I'll help you find him, and maybe he'll help save the lighthouse?"

Best smiled weakly. He wasn't sure anymore. He was feeling tired. He was starting to feel tired all the time now. He didn't know if he still believed in the Keeper. He wasn't sure what he believed. Even as he told Orion the story, it didn't seem quite real to him. Maybe Richard Tipody was right after all? Orion was a young boy, still infused with the kind of naivety that the passing of years finally steals. But he was certain of one thing: *Norah* was one of the only symbols left in his life that meant anything to him.

*

DR Richard Tipody's Voluntary Assisted Expatriation staff consisted of himself, an anaesthetist, and two assisting nurses. At first, the Superintendent of the Thurrough Nursing Home expressed some surprise when Tipody informed him that their establishment had been selected by the Government to be the initial test sight. But Tipody went on to make it sound like it was an honour – a privilege.

"And of course," added Tipody, "the name 'Thurrough Nursing Home' will figure prominently in the expatriation."

The Superintendent tried to sound composed. "I must say this has all come as quite a shock."

"I know it must." Tipody was sympathetic, his tone soothing, almost as if it was the Superintendent who was to be expatriated.

"Who's the subject?" the Superintendent asked.

"Best Douglas."

The Superintendent's face was blank.

That was a good sign, thought Tipody. "Do you know him?" he asked, knowing full well that there was a good chance that, not only did the Superintendent not recognize the name, but that he never came out of his office just in case he had to look upon any of the frail old prunes who were wasting away under his care.

The Superintendent nodded. "Vaguely," he answered honestly.

The expatriation manual made a dull thud as Tipody planted it on the Superintendent's desk. "This will outline the methodology. You will note on page forty-three that nobody except my staff will be allowed to discuss the procedure with Mr Douglas. I must be insistent on that point."

"Is he permitted to have any contact with others?"

"Only a religious minister of his choice."

"Where will the procedure take place?"

"In Mr Douglas' room. It's important the subject be in a surrounding familiar to him."

"When do you plan to perform this test of Voluntary...?"

"...Assisted Expatriation."

"Right... Thank you."

"In approximately two weeks."

"Approximately?"

"Page seventy of the manual. Nobody except the expatriation staff will know at what time the VAE is to take place. We'll merely walk in one day, and walk out an hour later with his body. The procedure has been designed to have as minimal an impact as possible on the other residents around him. And the two week window is there so I can adequately prepare Mr Douglas."

"Will I receive notification from the Department of Health?"

Tipody thought the Superintendent was a meddler. "Yes, of course."

Five days later, the Superintendent received a letter from the Department of Health. It was all official. He slumped back into his chair, opened up the desk drawer and took out a packet of cigarettes. He selected a stunted one, which had been half-smoked, and went outside, resting against the frangipani tree whose buds were starting to bring forth summer flowers. He lit the cigarette and drew back long and hard before incessantly coughing. Ever since he was struck off the medical register, he had tried to keep to himself and just do his job – and now this. What kind of practical joke was life playing on him, he wondered. He had been stripped of his license to practise medicine after accidentally killing someone during a surgical procedure, now he was a party to killing someone else, but this time the DOH and the NSW Government were telling him it was all right. He snuffed out the cigarette after only four puffs and tucked it back inside the packet. Since he was struck off and his wife had divorced him, he had become a frugal smoker – he was a frugal everything. He went back inside and walked past Best Douglas' room, only to see him and Dr Tipody sharing a laugh. He shook his head as he made his way back to his office, telling himself to stay beneath the radar.

CHAPTER TWENTY-NINE

B EST hadn't been outside the Home in close to twelve years. The last time was part of an excursion to the art gallery. Best was so disillusioned with what he saw that he took no further part in such ventures. Picasso, thought Best, what a joker!

When Best announced to Nurse Selby that Orion was taking him for a walk, she was pleasantly surprised. It was good for the residents to get some fresh air, and the only virgin air Best got was when he opened his window. Normally, family were the only ones permitted to take their relatives outside the Home, but as she was so well acquainted with Orion, she was happy to let him take Best for a stroll, especially as minimal staffing ratios prevented the staff from taking him themselves.

Nurse Selby told Orion to make sure that Best was warm. It was all about layers, she lectured. Best had wanted to dress himself but didn't have the range of movement in his left shoulder to complete the task. So Orion slipped on Best's cotton singlet, then a flannel pyjama top, and on top of that his cardigan. Orion was careful with the fragile cardigan.

After passing Nurse Selby's inspection, Orion pulled out a blanket from his bag and laid it across Best's lap. Wrapped in the blanket were a small shovel and two flashlights.

Best felt invigorated to be outside of the clinical environment of the Home. Even the litter gathering in the road's kerbside gutter looked good to him. He hadn't seen garbage in such a long time. As Orion wheeled him along the esplanade, which wound up towards *Norah*, he embraced the salty air like a long lost friend. It was liberating. He should have gotten out sooner. Inside the Home, it seemed he only breathed short, stale breaths. Outside, he felt as if he could breathe full, deep, satisfying breaths, as if the salt air was some kind of asthmatic drug that opened and expanded his lungs.

It took them forty-five minutes along the esplanade to get to the lighthouse. When they arrived, Orion saw that Best was disturbed.

"This is terrible," Best said.

When Orion looked around at the construction site – the waterlogged, cratered land where towering sand dunes used to be, and the blight of the nearby oil refinery – he shook his head in agreement.

Norah was under siege. Trucks and bulldozers surrounded her like devouring monsters waiting to feast on her. Best looked up at the lamp room. How many times had he stared up there and seen his father? How many times had Elizabeth waved to him up there? The noble lighthouse had saved countless lives. It didn't deserve to be felled into rubble along with its gallant history.

Orion peered sceptically down at the steep uneven path leading to the beach. "We're not going to be able to get your chair down there."

"I know." Best had already confronted that reality. "There's only one thing to do… Grab my arm."

Orion looked worried. "Are you sure?"

"No, I'm not sure. But I can sit here and not be sure or I can get my old numb bum out of this chair."

Best tried lifting himself out, relying on the strength of his good right arm, which fell hopelessly short of the task required of it.

"Lean on my shoulder," Orion advised, as he attempted to heave Best from the snare of the wheelchair.

"I can't lift you up," gasped Orion, his face red from the effort.

"Hang on. I'll try to help you."

Once Best felt his two feet planted securely on the asphalt, he rocked forward and brought himself upright, relying on Orion's support to keep him there. With his left hip carrying weight for the first time in years, he experienced a sharp pain. He winced and gave out a low moan.

"Is it your hip?" asked Orion.

Best mustered all the strength he had. "It's all right... I've got another one."

Orion took firm hold of Best as they made their slow, cautious descent down a path that, seventy years earlier, Best used to sprint down. After finally reaching the bottom, Orion sat Best on a rock. Best let out a relieved sigh. His face was glowing from the exertion.

Orion laughed. "You look like you're sunburnt."

Best gave out a relieved and somewhat victorious chuckle. "I feel like it!"

They stared across at the fifty-metre long by twenty-metre wide trench that had been carved out of the sand. The Hole was ten times as big as Crenshaw's Hole ever was, and yet few passers-by stopped to wonder at it. In the days of huge shopping malls, theme parks, and reality TV, a hole in the ground was something of a non-event.

Best and Orion hobbled over to the edge. The drainage ditch was located in the top left-hand corner of the pool. The pool's construction workers made their descent into the Hole using a series of steps that had been carved out of the side of the trench and then reinforced with steel and concrete. Once construction was completed, these same steps would then serve as access to the pool.

Orion went first. He stepped carefully backwards as he helped guide Best down the stairs. On the pool floor, they rested briefly again before moving on. The sand was wet underfoot as they made their apprehensive way to the corner of the trench with Orion's two flashlights helping to guide their passage in the failing daylight. Best took another moment to rest. He looked skywards as he often had as a boy. The first of the stars were visible in the dusky firmament. He approached the edge of the two-metre wide drainage tunnel. He peered down it. It was dark. Orion came along side him.

"This is the spot," said Best. "This is Crenshaw's Hole."

"How deep do you think it goes?"

"I don't know. We'll have to measure it." Best looked around. He spotted a cord running the length of the pool, which the workers were using as a plumb line. He scratched his head. "How many feet is fifty metres?"

Orion shrugged his shoulders. "They don't teach us that at school. It's all metric stuff."

Best tried to remember. "I think there's about two and a half centimetres to an inch... so that means there's about thirty centimetres in a foot... so there's three and a third feet in a metre... three and a third times fifty is...?"

"One hundred and sixty-six!" chimed Orion proudly.

Best looked impressed.

"I'm pretty good at maths."

"If we stick that cord down we should be able to tell how deep the tunnel is already."

Orion fetched the cord. They tied a rock to the end then lowered it down the tunnel. The cord went down a third of the way.

Best did some quick calculations. "The Hole was around about ninety feet deep when the army covered it in. We're already ten feet down – and the cord went down about fifty – that means we have to dig another thirty feet."

"Why don't we let the workers just keep digging?" suggested Orion.

Best shook his head. He had already considered that possibility. "I've watched them from when they first started. They've been digging at a rate of fifteen feet a day with their machine. If, for some reason, they were to go quicker, they'd find the bottom tomorrow. We have to start digging tonight."

Orion resigned himself to the task. "I'd better get going then."

They grabbed one of the ladders, which the workers had left lying on the bottom of the pool, and lowered it into the drainage tunnel. Orion grabbed his shovel, and within seconds had sunk the tip of it into the cold, wet sand. Best sat as comfortably as he could manage at the edge of the tunnel, shining both flashlights down to provide illumination for Orion, who was digging as fast as he possibly could given that he had to remove the sand from the Hole using two buckets, which he had to carry up the ladder when full.

As he watched Orion dig, Best was struck by feelings of *déjà vu*. But he *had* been here before. Nigh on eighty years ago, he had been in much the same spot watching Dirk Crenshaw dig furiously. He laughed out loud as he thought of Dirk. What a goofball! To distract Orion, he shouted down tales about Dirk Crenshaw; how he liked to have a brown stomach, and how he had to take up smoking for the sponsors, and how he couldn't read or write.

Three hours later, Orion was exhausted, and had dug seventeen feet. Best told him to stop.

"Shouldn't I keep going?" asked Orion, who was fighting against the urge to lie down and sleep.

"No," answered Best, who could see how tired Orion was. "That's enough. They might start to worry about me back at the Home. We'll come back tomorrow night."

"But the workers will be digging here tomorrow!"

Best smiled. "Orie, you've done a grand job. Now it's my turn."

Once back at the Home, Best wasted no time in calling the phone number he had copied down from the pool construction contractor's sign erected beside the trench. There a recorded message. He crossed his fingers.

"Yes," he began, adopting an officious voice. "This is Best Douglas from the Pollution Control Board. I'm calling to notify you that we have discovered high readings of faecal matter and coliform in the ocean water off Thurrough Beach. We strongly advise against working in the Crenshaw Pool site until a change in the wind direction. We will notify you when levels have decreased. Thank you."

After Best left the same message on the workers' union's machine, he thanked the reigning New South Wales Government. After all, it was they, in a misguided attempt to rid the inner city Sydney beaches of pollution, that had built two ocean outfall pipelines three miles out to sea, which carried the pollution not further out into the ocean, but in the event of a strong north-easterly seabreeze, down the coast to beaches like Thurrough.

Best dreamed like a young boy all night. He dreamed about breaking through to the chamber to see the Keeper smiling gloriously at him. He woke up early the next morning. He was anxious. He grabbed his binoculars. At seven-thirty, the time the workers normally commenced work, two men walked down the beach and stood above the Hole. They talked for several minutes then one shook his head and walked off, leaving the other man staring blankly into the void of the trench. The union representative had just notified the contractor in charge of the pool's construction that his members would not work under the threat of infection, and that they would only come back after that threat had passed.

Best kept an eye on the hole all day. The tides went in – and went out. Nobody came near it. As the day wore on, his apprehension grew. He was nervous – exceedingly so. He could barely contain himself. After all the years, this would be the night. When Orion came by at three o'clock on his paper run, he too was anxious. And Orion's excitement only served to fuel Best's. They both could hardly wait.

As Orion practically barged Best's wheelchair through the doors of the home, Nurse Selby asked in surprise, "Off on another walk?"

"I enjoyed myself so much yesterday," answered Best with a youthful sparkle in his eyes, "that I just couldn't wait to go again!"

As they passed through the shadows cast by Telford Towers, Best shivered. Orion stopped and wrapped the blanket tighter around Best's shoulders.

"I could never understand how it works," Best said pointing up at the top of the Telford Towers.

"What works?" asked Orion.

"The lighthouse on the top of the hotel. No one tends to it."

"All done by computers," stated Orion simply, his young mind much more able to accept the concept. "It doesn't need anybody."

In 1965, Galbraith Telford's parting gesture before he died had been the renovation of the historic hotel, Telford Towers. It was only when he was staring distastefully towards the end of the Thurrough Peninsula at *Norah* during one of his many walks amongst the dwindling sand dunes that he was struck with the idea. Due to the deteriorating condition of the old Thurrough Lighthouse, he had little difficulty convincing the New South Wales Maritime Commission that a new, unmanned lighthouse should and could be built atop his restored twenty-five storey hotel complex. Technology had finally negated the need to have a lighthouse keeper. Computers could now monitor conditions and then dictate the lighthouse's response accordingly.

Best was cleaning *Norah*'s lens when the representative from the Government ascended the stairs to break the news. He never could quite understand how they could shut her down; how they could do without her. They allowed Best to remain at the lighthouse for a period of two years while the hotel was being renovated, and he took it upon himself to maintain the gardens and lawns surrounding *Norah*, not willing to let her succumb to age quite so easily. Even when Telford Towers' unmanned lighthouse was completed, he still religiously followed *Norah*'s maintenance routine, never fully convinced that an unmanned lighthouse could possibly replace her. Surely it would not be long before the New South Wales Maritime Commission would be back to see him, saying it was all a big mistake, how could we ever think that we could do without a lighthouse keeper? But that day never came. And in fact, in less than twenty years, technology advanced so much that, with global positioning systems linked to orbiting satellites, vessels no longer had to rely on the guiding lights emanating from coastlines. The role of even the unmanned lighthouses became reduced to that of a warm comforter to sailors, in much the same way as the soft glow of a young child's bedside lamp lulls a child to sleep.

The day before Neil Armstrong landed on the moon, six months after the first rays of light shone forth from the roof of Telford Towers, Best Douglas was evicted from his cottage home of sixty-two years. His lowly retirement pension meant that the only thing he could afford to rent was a small one bedroom apartment sandwiched between two high-rises, which dwarfed his stout apartment block and kept his apartment in perpetual darkness. Best went from the magnificent views of *Norah's* lamp room to the blunt site of a morose, monstrous, red brick wall, which stood between him and the ocean. As Best shut the door to the cottage that his father had built, he was convinced that, with no one left to care for her, *Norah* was destined to be claimed by the sea in much the same fashion as her namesake.

*

CRUICKSHANK slowly got up from his haunches and lumbered past the door to the sacristy. He still prayed kneeling, although arthritis in his knees prevented long petitions. His prayer today didn't concern himself. It was for Best, and contained Cruickshank's hope that he would be able to adjust to his post-lighthouse keeper life. He looked up at the western stained glass window, whose image of the resurrection was now brilliantly backlit by the afternoon sun. He nodded thankfully. It was Ben Douglas who suggested the aspect of that window. Such a visionary, thought Cruickshank. He could see structures even before they rose from their foundations. If he'd been born in earlier centuries, he would have built great cathedrals. They both would have. Cruickshank, the abbey monk, and Ben Douglas, the Master Builder. Still, they had done all right: a lighthouse and a church – both shining beacons.

He walked through the large oak doors down the sandstone passage towards the rectory, past the fishpond beside the spot where his faithful Lab, Sheba, had been buried many years ago. To the east, just visible between two new multistorey apartment blocks, Saint Bede's respite home was getting a new name and a new coat of paint courtesy of the NSW Department of Health, which had recently purchased the facility from the Catholic Church who had decided to bow out of caring for the old and infirm. Priests, Brothers, Sisters – they were all drying up, and employing lay people was too expensive. A dismembered front page of the *Daily Chronicle* nudged along by the afternoon sea breeze swept over his shoes. He knew the headline. There was another war: a civil war in Vietnam. To Cruickshank, there was nothing civil about war. Soldiers were still killing one another. He sighed heavily. He had lived through sixty-five years of the 20th century and man had learned nothing. It wasn't very encouraging, and as he looked around at the apartment blocks sprouting haphazardly, it seemed as if things were becoming more confusing. At approximately two-fifteen the following morning, he no longer had to worry about any of that. Bill Cruickshank passed away in his sleep aged eighty-five.

*

THEY were ten minutes faster reaching the trench than the night before. Best knelt by the drainage tunnel as if praying and shone the two flashlights down at the digging Orion. The plan was that, when Orion broke through to the chamber, he would help Best lower himself down the ladder and they would enter the chamber together.

Best was shaking in anticipation. The flashlights were moving all over the place.

"Can you try to keep the lights still?" Orion yelled in exasperation.

"Sorry. I'm jumping out of my skin up here!"

Two and a half hours after Orion started digging, Best heard him stop suddenly.

"Best," Orion said slowly, "you'd better come down here if you can."

Best leapt down the ladder as though he was the same age as Orion. The drainage tunnel was tight, but when he got to the bottom there was just enough room for him and Orion to stand side by side. A small, tennis ball-sized hole separated them from another section.

"The chamber," Best whispered. "Dig a larger opening," he directed eagerly.

Orion chipped away what was left of the brittle, wet sand that formed the dividing wall between tunnel and chamber.

Best poked his head through the opening. He couldn't see much. "Hand me the flashlight." Best shone the light in on the chamber. It was no bigger than a walk-in wardrobe and the light was rebounding against the walls to such an extent that Best found it hard to see anything. "I can't see much. Let's try to get in there."

Orion carved away a larger opening, and within five minutes, they had both climbed through and were standing in the middle of the chamber. Best frantically darted the flashlight around. It soon became apparent that there was no one in there except him and Orion.

Best's shoulders slumped.

"Maybe there's something here?" suggested Orion, still trying to be positive. He shone his flashlight into a corner and spotted something. "What's that over there?" The beam from Best's torch bisected the one from Orion's. "It looks like a lump of sand with something on it."

Orion went over. The clay figurine was half-covered in the brittle sand, which had continually fallen away from the ceiling of the chamber over the decades. He picked up the angelic figurine and handed it to Best who stared despondently at it before numbly dropping it to the sand. He grabbed hold of the rungs of the ladder and laboriously heaved himself up.

Orion turned back to pick up the figurine and then quickly followed Best up the ladder in order to make sure he didn't slip.

Best hardly talked as Orion pushed him back to the Home. He felt depressed and deflated, and it wasn't like him to feel either of those things. Nothing Orion could say would lift his spirits. Best only replied that the Keeper had said he would be there, and he wasn't. Best thought back to the time when he had tried digging, when Elizabeth was missing. For years he had blamed himself for not being able to swim, and for not being able reach the Keeper. But what did it matter? He wouldn't have been there anyway. He was just a foolish old man clinging to an absurd dream that he'd once had as a boy. Richard Tipody was right: he had been deluding himself for years. He had no one to blame but himself. His personal misfortunes should have been in his power to remedy; he did not need some mystical "man of sorts."

Best didn't get out of bed the following morning, or the next. He saw no point. He had nothing to look forward to. He couldn't bear to get up and catch a glimpse of the old lighthouse trying to resist the destructive intentions of men who could never appreciate what she represented. At ten o'clock, Orion phoned to say that he was going surfing. Best said he might look out for him if he felt like it. He soon recognized that he was turning into the very thing he despised – a bitter, old man. He had to resist that. He reluctantly got out of bed and went to the window. He put the binoculars to his eyes just as Orion was paddling out to the break. The waves were a solid six foot. No place for the inexperienced.

Best saw Orion catch one wave but lost sight of him when he turned away to stick his false teeth in. There weren't many surfers out, and after searching for close to half an hour, Best concluded that Orion must have left the beach. Still, a niggling feeling ate away at him. He called Barclay House. Was Orion there? No, was Mrs Packham's reply. Best went back to the window. He checked the other breaks. He still couldn't locate Orion. Two hours passed. He called Barclay House again. Had Orion returned yet? No, he hadn't. Best started to worry. Orion hardly ever surfed for more than three hours. Best called for Nurse Selby, and told her that he'd been watching Orion in the surf and that he'd disappeared. He asked if she could notify the lifeguards. Nurse Selby didn't seem concerned. As a surfer's girlfriend, she told Best that she often had to wait for her boyfriend, who would go and eat three Big

Macs and two vanilla thick-shakes at McDonalds after surfing. When Best insisted, however, she did as he asked just to help put his mind at rest. Three hours later, one of the lifeguards contacted the nurse. He'd thought she sounded attractive when she'd rung them so he tried to be as helpful as possible. He said that they remembered the surfboard, but hadn't yet found it, or anyone surfing one like it, and by the way, would she like to visit the lifeguard tower?

At two o'clock in the afternoon, Best again called Barclay House. Orion still hadn't returned. Best waited anxiously for three o'clock, hoping to see Orion's cherub-like face coming through the door carrying a smile along with his papers. But, at five to three, another boy walked past Best's door pushing the familiar yellow barrow.

"Hey?" shouted Best.

The boy craned his head inside Best's room.

"Where's Orion?" asked Best, beginning to shake nervously.

The boy shrugged his shoulders. "He didn't turn up for work. I'm doing his run instead."

Best started hyperventilating. He felt a sharp, knife-like pain in his chest.

"Are you all right, Mister?"

Best could only gasp an incoherent reply. He was having a heart attack.

*

HE slipped the tiny cassette inside the envelope and tried reaching through the rosebush. He felt a sharp prick and quickly withdrew his hand. The tip of a thorn broke off and half-embedded itself in his finger. Normally, there would have been droplets of blood, which might have trickled onto the envelope. But when he plucked the offending barb out, there were none. A welt appeared as he sucked the tip of his finger. Physical pain – such a necessary sensation – but he'd learnt that emotional wounds were far more scathing and long-lasting. Injured soldiers, crippled old men, disfigured boys – their physical disorders paled into insignificance against the scars they bore inside.

He delicately deposited the letter inside the slot of the letterbox, this time avoiding the protective thorns of the rosebush. As he walked away down the middle of the quiet country road, he looked skyward and allowed his face to bask in the warm rays of the noon sun. Wisps of cloud lay strewn across the sky like spun, white fairy floss. He glanced at the maple trees that lined both sides of the street like a guard of honour and watched mesmerized as the higher branches swayed gently with the breeze as if waving their friendly arms at him. The beauty of creation always inspired him: the cleansing tang of seawater; the towering sand dunes; the kaleidoscope of trees in autumn. As the lipstick-coloured maple leaves crunched under his feet, he felt that, at this moment, even mankind was in unison with the Creator – their introduced Maples mingled harmoniously with the indigenous Flame trees, creating brilliant leaf combinations of pinks, oranges, and reds. He smiled as he continued to move slowly down the hill, and as the natural surrounds began to fade, he gradually disappeared.

*

WHEN Dr Richard Tipody heard Best's name mentioned in the same breath as "heart attack," he instantly dropped what he was doing and charged towards Best's room.

Nurse Selby and the rest of the nursing staff later said that Dr Tipody's response to Best's heart attack was exceptional. He personally administered the treatment and hovered around for days to monitor Best's condition. No one knew, of course, that Tipody was keeping Best alive just so that he could kill him.

Best was placed on a respirator and was being fed intravenously. He could barely talk.

"Richard?" he wheezed. "Is that you?"

Tipody took Best's hand much like a loving son would. "Yes… How are you feeling?"

"Better."

"Glad to hear it. I was very worried about you." Which, as strange and insincere as it sounded, was the truth.

But Best had meant to say that he *had* felt better.

For a week, Best was listed as being in a stable but critical condition. Orion never came by once. After Best was taken off the intravenous drip, Nurse Selby came to help feed him his first solid-food meal.

She probed the soggy mashed potatoes. "No wonder you had a heart attack with this food."

Best smiled weakly. "Have you seen Orion?"

A solemn expression marked her face, which she attempted to hide. "I called Barclay House just like you said. They reckon he buggered off. They said it happens all the time."

Best didn't believe it. He thought Orion had drowned. Otherwise, he'd have been by his side. Yes, Orion had drowned. That was the fate of everyone he had ever cared for.

Tipody loved Best's depression, welcomed it, tried to foster it. Depression was fantastic. Depression led to feelings of despair and hopelessness. Tipody knew Best was ready. His physical condition had stabilized. He was now out of that critical zone. He was now ready to die.

"So," Tipody said as he looked out Best's window, "They're moving the old lighthouse next week. That should be something to see."

Best sighed. "It'll never stay together."

Tipody wasn't listening. He leaned closer and lowered his voice to a whisper. "I can end it for you."

"What?"

Tipody glanced around. "The pain... I can end it for you."

"The drugs are fine, Richard."

"I mean *forever*."

Best went silent. He suddenly understood. He was in constant pain, and the physical was the easy part to bear. At ninety-four years old, there was always physical pain. It was the mental pain that was proving unbearable. Hope had kept him alive. But now that had been torn away from him. Oak Legs was gone, not able to extract himself from Garrawarra. Orion was gone. The lighthouse was going to be destroyed, and no one was lifting a finger to do anything about it. His wife was dead. His father was dead. Orion was dead. The Keeper was some perverted figment of his imagination.

"How?" asked Best.

"As simple as a tiny prick... A friendly little needle."

"Like a dog being put down?"

"Just like that... A simple injection... Painless."

Richard Tipody made it sound so soothing. Best wanted to be finally free of the pain. The decision wasn't a hard one in the end. He would get to do what both his mother and wife were denied: he would get to say goodbye – like his father did. He remembered how his sorrow was softened by those three days in the lamp room with his father.

Best was defeated. He could now accept that. "All right, Richard."

Tipody's face lit up. He couldn't prevent the broad, beaming smile. "You won't regret it," he replied, but he meant, "You won't live to regret it."

*

THE 1964 bottle of French champagne crashed against the hull of the largest ship ever built. The friends and relatives of those on board stood on the dock cheering exuberantly, as the frothy, bubbly, wine dribbled down the side of the *Queen of the South Pacific*. Three thousand six hundred and seventy passengers were setting sail on her maiden voyage, which was to take them from the Winston Line's home port of Southampton, England down the French coast through the Bay of Biscay, where Captain Marcus Swanson had successfully completed her sea trials three months previously, down the Portuguese coast through the Strait of Gibraltar, across the Mediterranean, through the

Suez cannel, across the Indian Ocean, and then down the east coast of Australia through the Whitsunday Passage, all the way down to terminate inside Port Philip Bay, Victoria.

When the travel press in the public relations preamble to the voyage interviewed Captain Marcus Swanson, the atmosphere was light-hearted and jovial until someone asked him if the Queen was invincible.

Swanson's smile faded. "Nothing's invincible."

The CEO of the Winston Line was quick to cover for his Captain's sobering reply. "But she's close to it," he declared as he put a unifying arm around the Captain.

A travel reporter grinned. "Before the Titanic's maiden voyage they said that even God couldn't sink her."

Under the hot television lights, the Captain shifted uncomfortably in his seat. "And now she's lying at the bottom of the North Atlantic."

Winston's Marketing Director laughed nervously. "Luckily there aren't any icebergs along the way – just the beautiful Great Barrier Reef."

After Marcus Swanson returned to his hotel room, he called France. "I want you beside me on this trip."

"Winston's have already booked me a tourist berth," replied Jese Sommer.

"You don't think I'm letting you have a holiday do you? You're riding on the bridge with me."

*

CHARLEY Pelegranetti had been a regular visitor since Best's heart attack. For Best, the visits were a welcome distraction. He would just lie there and listen to Charley who would sit for hours at a time and just talk – about everything. Sometimes, Best would lapse into sleep, but Charley didn't seem to mind.

Best's eyelids were weighting heavy. He was just in that twilight state between drowsiness and sleep when Charley gave a hearty laugh, making him more alert. He just managed to catch Charley's distant words, "Yep, we thought we'd struck it rich with the *Black Swan,* my old man and me."

Best opened his eyes fully in startled surprise, which half surprised Charley who was used to Best falling asleep during his visits.

"The *Black Swan?*" asked Best, who had now propped himself up on his right elbow.

Charley nodded. "John Selby's pirate ship. My dad was obsessed with it… convinced it'd gone down on the reefs with a hull full of the Telfords' gold just off the northern headland." Charley glanced out of Best's window where he could just make out the breaking white water which, on bigger swells, would often swirl and bear down on the jagged outer reefs. He pointed his finger east. "He reckoned the gold was definitely down there, but we never found anything." Charley laughed again. "In fact, your old man rescued us one night when we were out trying to find it."

"You didn't look hard enough," said Best simply.

Charley looked at him. There was a pause. "What do you mean?'

"It's there."

"What's there?"

"The gold. It's there."

"How do you know?"

"He saw it… the night he pulled you both from the water."

Charley whistled. "And for years I thought my old man was crazy, but he knew. That crazy wog knew. Why didn't you ever do anything about it?"

Best glanced away, embarrassed by what the gold had nearly turned him into. "It can change a person."

Charley nodded his head, not completely understanding, before laughing again. His age made him wise enough to feel humour, not regret, in this new knowledge. "Well, I'll be!"

Best nestled his head deeper into his pillow. "I'm getting tired now, Charley."

Charley rose to leave. "I'll be on my way then."

"Goodbye, Charley. You've been a good friend."

For a second, Best's remark seemed conclusive to Charley; the kind of passing comment that precedes something monumental. "You too," Charley finally stumbled out, unusually lost for words. "I mean... a friend... a good friend, Best."

CHAPTER THIRTY

THE morning of Best's Voluntary Assisted Expatriation came quickly, and he looked forward to it with a quiet resignation. Life had finally defeated him. After all those years, it had done him in. It was the victor, and he was going to accept his loss without protest. The atmosphere in his room was almost like that of the Home's Bingo room. It was light, relaxed, and sometimes even humorous, but focused nevertheless. There had never been more people crowded into his tiny room: two nurses, a cameraman, an anaesthetist, and Richard Tipody. Best wasn't lonely. It seemed like these people cared. He started to feel almost content.

Events were proceeding more smoothly than Tipody had ever anticipated. He had neglected to tell Best that he could have a clergyman of his choice. And since Best never asked, in his report, he would just fudge the details. He couldn't force a member of the clergy on Best. Best's decision was final and binding. After all, this was a voluntary procedure.

Richard Tipody leant over Best and touched him tenderly on the shoulder. He pointed to the anaesthetist. "The procedure gives you an option to receive a pre-VAE injection to relax you."

Best smiled. "I am relaxed."

Richard Tipody waved the anaesthetist back. "Do you wish to forgo your right to receive the relaxant?" he asked officiously.

"What do you want me to do?" Best asked, not wanting to inconvenience anyone.

Tipody gave out a nervous laugh that helped ease his tension and bring some informality to the process. "It's not about me. It's about you. How about we just administer the VAE?"

Best nodded obediently. "That sounds fine."

Tipody placed a pistol grip on Best's chin and pried his mouth open with such force that it seemed as if he had forgotten that Best was still alive. He brought a glass to Best's bed. "You will need to take your teeth out. Just so you don't choke."

For expediency, Tipody took the liberty of reaching inside Best's mouth and pulling out his false teeth. He placed them in the glass and handed it to the nurse who didn't quite know what to do with them.

Dr Richard Tipody tapped the needle. He squirted some of the deadly serum into a beaker. He smiled inwardly. With this newly-developed drug, there did not need to be an intravenous drip to administer the lethal blow, which would have made the procedure too hospital-like. Instead, the highly-concentrated dose could be delivered by just one needle. It was beautifully simple.

Tipody signalled for the cameraman to take up a position over Best's bed. He had issued the cameraman with strict instructions: if Best's face begins to contort and he looks like he is in pain, divert the camera to his body to show how his muscles relax. If Best's face looks peaceful, just keep filming. Above all, try to capture the calm peacefulness of death.

The nurses took up their positions on either side of Best's bed. One of them prepared Best's arm for the needle, which was to be inserted into his brachial artery.

Tipody aimed the needle at the site of entry. "Just relax. It'll all be over soon. So very soon."

Tipody's hand was shaking. He couldn't control his excitement. Adrenalin was flowing through his veins like the death serum that would soon be flowing through Best's. This was what medicine was all about – braving and creating new frontiers. He was going to be famous.

Best exhaled softy. He was relieved. It would all be over soon. He had dwelt on this moment for days – what would be his last thoughts? He turned his head ever so slightly to look out the window. He couldn't see *Norah* from this position, but he could view the surfers dancing on their boards to the music of the waves. He had always loved the ocean even though it had taken from him. He forgave it like as anyone would a life-long friend. He saw a boy walking hand in hand with his mother and father – like he used to do all those years ago, before she was taken. Strolling slowly the other way were two lovers; the woman's head listed to one side to find the shoulder of her partner. He had experienced all this. He was grateful. He had tasted love. He had partaken of its fruits, though he had been starved of it when Elizabeth left him. The questions he had asked of God had never been answered, and he had never returned to water; never again experienced its cleansing wash – like the waters of baptism. That was his regret. The water. And he couldn't see *Norah*.

Tipody brought down the needle.

The tip was about to break the skin.

Tipody steadied the death-blow hand.

Best nodded away from the beach to study the needle as it bore down on his arm. So small, so innocent, so unobtrusive, he thought. His death was gentle. He was thankful for that. He looked back towards the endless expanse of the blue ocean and the point where it touched the sky – the meeting of two worlds. He slowly closed his eyes, content to take in the sea as his last earthly vision.

Sweat from Tipody's glowing forehead dripped down onto Best's white pristine sheets.

The door to Best's room suddenly flung open.

Richard Tipody turned around. "What the hell's going on?" he barked on seeing the Superintendent.

Dr Fiona Chalice charged into the room behind the Home's Superintendent, a police sergeant, and a representative from the Department of Health.

"Get away from him!" she cried.

Tipody reared up like a big red kangaroo and pointed the needle threateningly towards the three intruders. "This is supposed to be a private procedure. Get out!"

Fiona Chalice was not intimidated. She moved into the room and stood beside Best's bed. "We're not going anywhere. And this procedure is not going ahead."

"Evidence has come to light to suggest that this event is not sanctioned," interjected the official from the Department of Health.

"On the contrary," responded Tipody. "This VAE has been approved at the highest level. Now remove yourselves. You are violating the sanctity of this expatriation!"

"I'm sorry," began the Superintendent almost forlornly, not convinced that he was in the right. "I just couldn't condone this after receiving Dr Chalice's information."

"It would seem, doctor, that this procedure may not be entirely voluntary in accordance with the legislation," added the Officer, not backing down from his position.

"I'm warning you all. You are in breach of a highly delicate social experiment. Now for the third time, get the hell out of here!"

Best's tranquil thoughts were turning upside down. He was back on the slippery rock of the northern headland, and he was being dragged towards the ocean, towards his drowning mother. It was so violent. Death was so violent. His death couldn't be serene. Death and serenity were contrary to each other.

Fiona Chalice held up the dictaphone she had removed from her handbag. "This is the real conversation you had with Best Douglas, not the edited one you manipulated for the Committee."

"Where did you get that?"

"Does it matter?"

"It can't be!"

Fiona Chalice hit the play button and aired enough of the evidence to convince Tipody of its genuineness.

Tipody looked anguished, as if he was the victim of the cruellest practical joke. "But I destroyed it?"

The burly sergeant moved cautiously towards Tipody, who was backing away, pointing the deadly needle menacingly.

"Stay away from me!" Tipody yelled.

"The needle contains the serum," warned Fiona. "Don't go near him."

The police officer was used to such situations when confronting drug addicts most Saturday nights in the city. He slowly cornered Tipody.

"I'm warning you," screamed Tipody. "Stay away from me!"

The sergeant moved closer and Tipody lunged at him with the needle. The officer grabbed Tipody's arm and they both fell to the floor. There was a muffled struggle. When the officer got up, the needle was sticking out of Tipody's jugular vein. Fiona Chalice ran to him, but she was too late. The contents had already been squeezed into his bloodstream. And as his bulging eyes glared horrifically up at her, she suddenly recalled Tipody's leering presence in medical school all those years ago. His heart stopped within two minutes. Dr Richard Tipody had gotten his wish. Unfortunately, the Assisted Expatriation was his own, and wasn't very Voluntary.

TWO days later, when Best's condition had improved, Fiona Chalice sat by his bed and explained the whole history of Richard Tipody's hidden agenda.

Best felt no malice towards the deceased doctor. He had always thought Richard Tipody a little strange. "But if he destroyed the tape of our conversations, where did you get it?" he asked.

Fiona Chalice fluffed up a pillow and slipped it behind Best's back. "In my letter box, inside an envelope with a letter saying that I should play the tape. Whoever recorded it must have overheard the conversations in your room. I knew then that Richard Tipody had coerced you into the procedure over many months."

"Where did the letter come from?" asked Best. "One of the nurses?"

Fiona shook her head. "No. The envelope had no address or stamp so it must have been personally delivered. The letter was quite curious. It just ends with the letters OK."

Fiona Chalice handed Best the letter and offered him her own reading glasses, which Best gratefully accepted.

"I think the letters are a signature," said Best as he returned her glasses.

"You think so? I just thought they were saying OK."

"OK," Best mouthed softly. "OK?" he asked himself again, struggling with his assumption. "OK?" He looked outside the window. He spotted a gaggle of surfers. "OK... Orion...?"

Fiona Chalice looked bemused. "Orion, that's quite an unusual name."

"Orion was the paperboy here. I never knew his last name. I tried to read it once on his nametag... but I couldn't... my glasses... but I'm sure..."

A solitary tear trickled down Best's cheek as his voice trailed off. Fiona Chalice touched him tenderly on the hand. "I'm sorry if I upset you. You've been through enough."

Best grabbed one of his forty-year-old handkerchiefs and rubbed his eyes. "It's not you."

"I should let you get some rest," she remarked.

But Best wasn't listening. He glanced across at the clay angel doll that Orion had left on his bedside table the day they returned from the Hole. He suddenly remembered Oak Legs Finbar and asked her about him.

"It's all been taken care of. He'll be back here sometime tomorrow.

The Superintendent confirmed that Dr Tipody was intent on getting him away from you." She got up gingerly. "I should be going now." She suddenly clutched at her stomach and groaned.

"Are you all right?" asked Best.

"Oh, yes," she replied as she made towards the door. "Just a tiny bit of nausea. Think I might be coming down with a mild stomach bug. Haven't quite felt myself for the last couple of weeks."

CHAPTER THIRTY-ONE

OAK Legs Finbar, Charley Pelegranetti and Best sat by the window taking turns to look through the binoculars as the Telford Industries crew readied themselves to remove the lighthouse from its foundations.

"It'll never stay together," grumbled Oak Legs. "Any idiot would know that."

Best nodded sadly.

"But we're not just dealing with any idiots up there – those guys specialise in it!" chimed in Charley.

It was when it was Best's turn to look through the binoculars that Oak Legs noticed the figurine perched on Best's bedside table. He limped over to examine it. "What's this?"

Best looked over. "Don't know exactly... Orion found it."

Oak Legs turned it upside down and studied the imprint underneath. "I'll tell you what it is – it's a clay angel, and it's got the imprint *JP* on the bottom – that's James Perry! Struth! This must've been made by the local black fellas nearly two hundred years ago! Where did he get it?"

"Out of a hole up by the beach."

"Whereabouts exactly?" asked Charley.

"Where they're building the new pool," replied Best.

Charley gently took it from Oak Legs in order to study it closely. "They won't be building anything if the local Aboriginal tribe gets a whiff of this. They'll label that land a sacred site quicker than you can say boomerang."

"You think so?" asked Best

"Think so? I know so," answered Charley. "I've seen developments stopped by a bone the size of a thimble, let alone something as special as this."

With that, Charley made a hasty phone call to the chapter of the local tribe, the head of which happened to be a lawyer whose firm used to handle all of the Pelegranettis' real estate transactions. Fifteen minutes later, a hundred Aboriginals swarmed onto the construction site. The lawyer, Jonathon Perry, put a sudden stop to the lighthouse relocation as soon as he got word of the sacred relic. Two hours later, he dropped by the Home.

"May I see the piece?" he asked.

Best handed it to him.

Jonathon Perry studied it with quiet reverence as he read the letters imprinted on the bottom. "This was made for Jamesperri by our Gweagal Tribe. We've never been able to find much by them. We think pirates in the early 20th century plundered their sacred relics from the old Tin Town. How it ended up in Crenshaw's Hole I have no idea."

"Maybe it came in with the tide?" suggested Oak Legs.

Jonathon Perry handed the doll back to Best. "Maybe."

Best studied it thoughtfully for several seconds. "You keep it."

"But it's yours."

Best stroked the angel affectionately before handing it back. "It's what it represents that's important to me." He tapped his head. "And I've got that all up here. Besides, it really belongs to you."

"You must accept something for it?"

"If you can save *Norah* that'll be good enough for me."

"*Norah?*"

"The old lighthouse."

Jonathon Perry smiled. "Ah yes, *Norah*. I haven't heard that name in quite a while. I believe she was named after your mother?"

Best nodded.

"Don't worry... We'll give it our best shot."

Jonathon Perry was able to secure a court injunction that prevented Telford Industries from going ahead with any kind of construction until the NSW Government reached a decision on whether the parcel of land was to be handed back to the local Aboriginal people. Thurrough Council was furious. In a recent move, power had been taken away from them and given to the State regarding the ability to resolve Aboriginal land claims. All Thurrough Council could do was to sit and wait in the wings while the issue was resolved.

Geoffery Certi, representing Telford Industries, lobbied hard. His Telford defence was passionate and impressive. He had six generations of outstanding Thurrough citizens to fall back on. But Perry was a formidable opponent. He had nearly two centuries of history behind him. And the mix of a twenty-one-year-old convict who washed up one day in 1787 on the shores of Thurrough Beach and his beautiful Aboriginal wife had created a fascinating, passionate, highly intelligent young man two hundred years later. In the end, Perry was victorious, obtaining the section of Thurrough Beach that included the entirety of the site where the resort, new pool, and golf course were to be located. But the State Government didn't want to crush the toes of Thurrough Council and Telford Industries, even if they had stepped on them a little. In a similar decision to other Aboriginal land rights cases, such as that of Ayers Rock, they decided that the Gweagal could lease the land back to Thurrough Council if they so desired, who could in turn lease it to Telford Industries. The resort development could still go ahead.

Geoffery Certi was quick to seize upon this new angle. He arranged a meeting with Jonathon Perry at the lighthouse.

Certi raised his arms as if embracing the land. "This, Mr Perry, is going to be a huge money earner for your people. You'll be able to buy the best wine money can buy. No more sniffing petroleum fumes from the refinery for your mob!"

Jonathon Perry motioned for Certi to look around. "Take a good long look at this land. It'll be the last time you'll be stepping foot on it."

And that was the Aboriginal decision. No development. The lighthouse and cottage would remain. The trench built for the new Crenshaw Pool would be filled in. Thurrough would take a step back into its past, not into its future.

*

AT five o'clock in the afternoon, the *Queen of the South Pacific* sailed out of Sydney Harbour. Most of the three-thousand-odd passengers were tired. They had made the most of their time in Sydney: walking around the Opera House, climbing the Harbour Bridge, riding the ferry to Manly, dining atop Centrepoint Tower. Weather conditions were relatively calm. Captain Marcus Swanson had been briefed on the intense low-pressure system that had developed in the Tasman. He wasn't too concerned. An increase in swell was to be expected. But the *Queen* would handle it with ease. The only casualties would be some seasick passengers who had whooped it up a little too much the night before in Kings Cross – Sydney's red light district.

At seven o'clock, a cool south-westerly ripped through Thurrough sending sand and salt spraying across the beach. Best's window rattled. He and Oak Legs looked out at the ocean in awe. They had heard reports of a low-pressure system in the Tasman, but didn't anticipate the dramatic increase in seas. They had been playing Gin Rummy until the relentless rising of the ocean magnetized them both.

Best noticed the sea creeping insidiously up the beach. "It's a king tide. It looks like it's going to reach the road!"

Oak Legs looked worried. "That must be some low-pressure system."

But the low-pressure system hadn't raised the level of the ocean on its own. An earthquake in the Tasman Sea measuring 6.6 on the Richter scale had done the rest. Twelve feet belonged to the low-pressure system, the remaining twelve to the earthquake. The seas had not been this big in over eighty-eight years.

THE reception staff on the Front Desk of the Telford Towers Hotel did not pay much attention to the courier. They were busy, and Friday night was a hectic time. The hotel was ninety percent booked for the weekend. One of the staff glanced fleetingly at him. His uniform looked official enough. And he was polite. He could see they were all busy. He volunteered to put the package in the back office. The front office staff were grateful. He got a quick signature then scurried out before any of them could get a good look at him. Telford had received a lot of bad press over their resort proposal. Riding roughshod over an Aboriginal sacred site had been a public relations nightmare for them, and groups of environmentalists had begun constantly protesting in front of Telford companies, where they made their objections known through loudspeakers and large red placards, but generally in an innocent, non-disruptive fashion. But Tindall Pemberton was not so passive. Telford Industries had dragged his reputation through the mire until what was decent and credible about him was barely recognizable behind the mud. He had been dismissed from the Council, and labelled a crackpot drug addict. Not only that; his grandmother had been dispatched to the nut house for repeating his left-field philosophies. His life had been decimated, and he was determined that someone was going to pay. He cut his hair and shaved his beard. As he groomed himself in the mirror, he felt satisfied in the knowledge that he was gaining back some control over his destiny. He could just lie down and accept what had happened to him, or he could strike back. Nothing too drastic, nothing to cause too much anguish for innocents: he just wanted to chip away at the Telford business, to be a thorn in their side.

The staff heard a muffled bang. It could well have been a car backfiring, or a round of thunder. Then, all five of the front desk computer terminals went blank. When the Duty Manager went to check the main server computer, he saw a large basketball-sized dent in the metal casing. Employing new electro-magnetic explosive wave technology, Tindall Pemberton had planted an electro-magnetic bomb near the hotel's mainframe computer, which amongst other things, coded door keys with the ability to open computerized locks. The effect of such a bomb was remarkable. It was totally safe to humans, but if the outfall waves bombarded computers it would send them into a frenzy of electric confusion, and in the worst-case scenario, completely corrupt all hard disc data rendering them useless.

The computers that ran the unmanned lighthouse situated on top of the twenty-storey Telford Towers had never been in error. They regulated the lamp down to the tiniest degree. The computers used an array of sensors in order to adjust and regulate the beam over a wide range of weather conditions. Telford had not only wanted to supersede *Norah* but completely jettison her into Thurrough's past. However, not only did the explosion wipe out all the hotel's computers, preventing many patrons from entering their rooms for the night, it also wreaked havoc on the unmanned lighthouse located within the hotel's top floor, whose computers were connected to the hotel's by an auxiliary power supply in the event of a blackout. The result was a safeguard shutdown of the lighthouse, plunging that area of the coastline into navigational darkness.

*

THE *Queen* was four nautical miles past Thurrough Beach. Three of the crew had confirmed sighting of the Thurrough lighthouse. As the *Queen* began to distance herself from the coastline, Captain Marcus Swanson recognized that the seas were abnormally high long before he got a report from the Point Leo Seismic Station in Victoria regarding the ocean quake in the Tasman. As a Captain, he always erred on the side of caution. It was the only way to sail, especially with a ship full of passengers.

Jese Sommer had remained on the bridge following the *Queen's* majestic exit from Sydney Harbour. Both men had experienced the tumultuous, often bone-chilling seas of the North Atlantic where fierce storms would swoop down from the Artic and whip up the ocean to monstrous heights. Now, as they both looked out from the bridge, they realised they were confronting the biggest seas they had ever seen. After consulting with Jese Sommer, Captain Marcus Swanson decided to turn the massive *Queen* around and make back for the sheltered safety of Botany Bay.

Both men were checking that the systems were working according to normal parameters, when something totally unexpected happened: the ship veered hard to the starboard side. Captain Marcus Swanson checked the navigational computers, and then asked Jese Sommer to do likewise. For some inexplicable reason, they had suddenly altered their course. Following several more drastic, seemingly erratic manoeuvres, a complete check of the ship's operating interface revealed that the ship's on-line computers and back-ups had been inexplicably thrown into disarray. What both men could not possibly realise was that the waves of Tindall Pemberton's parcelled bomb, with no landmass to block them, had effortlessly travelled out to sea to wreak havoc on the heart and soul of the *Queen.*

Jese Sommer was at a loss to explain the extreme nature of the computer confusion. "It seems as if all the systems have been affected by some type of electrical interference."

"Like the Bermuda Effect?" Captain Swanson asked, recalling the phenomenon that sometimes influenced vessels within the Bermuda Triangle.

Sommer nodded. "Perhaps. It may have something to do with the approaching storm."

Marcus Swanson glanced down at the ship's four main compasses:

north was east, east was south, and south was west. He didn't think for too long. He didn't have time. "Disable all her automatic navigational systems."

Jese Sommer looked at him, almost painfully. He knew it was the only decision to be made. "Yes… yes of course."

The ship's entire voyage up to this point had been achieved with the use of autopilot navigational systems. Now, the order had been given: Captain Marcus Swanson was going to take complete control of the *Queen*. His hands alone would guide the destiny of the massive liner. After Jese Sommer disenabled the autopilot systems, he signalled to the Captain that the ship was all his. Marcus Swanson was now the true Captain, not just a computer programmer. The crew looked to their leader as he gripped the controls, the four bars on his jacket shimmering with authority.

The storm had closed in. Torrential rain was shutting down visibility to less than a hundred metres. And due to the downfall of the navigational computers, Marcus Swanson had no way of knowing their exact position. He was sailing blind. He glanced down at his wristwatch, which contained its own compass. It was static, unaffected by whatever magnetic forces had gripped the *Queen*. He corrected their heading back to the north then craned his head out the window in a futile attempt to search for the stars. They were hidden behind a blanket of angry clouds. The only way he was going to be able to possibly determine their position was by sighting one of the lighthouses on the shore, barely visible through the curtain of rain.

The three crewmen sent out on the deck could not locate Thurrough's lighthouse. The Captain did not think for one moment that it had been extinguished, not when the same three crewmembers had sighted it just ten minutes earlier, and not when it was desperately needed in huge seas like these. No. There could only be one explanation: the rogue computers had increased the *Queen's* speed. That dark void was the large, secluded entrance to Botany Bay, just north of Thurrough Beach.

Mountainous waves were buffeting the impenetrable steel hull of the *Queen,* sending vibrations throughout the frame of the ship, which absorbed the charge and groaned loudly in response. The ship was crying out like a harpooned whale, but its construction was designed to withstand such an assault.

Marcus Swanson glanced nervously across at Jese Sommer, masking his apprehension with a forced smile. "You've built her well, Monsieur Sommer."

Sommer nodded, but was too consumed with analysing the ship's computers to bask in the compliment.

Captain Swanson checked the compass and adjusted the *Queen's* heading to due west. Without their global positioning systems, at that heading, the *Queen* would hit the treacherous outer reefs of Thurrough Beach in less than thirty minutes. In the tumultuous seas, and in spite of the superiority of the design and construction, the giant liner would crack like an egg on the jagged reefs. And, although they were relatively close to the coast, few of their numerous lifeboats would remain seaworthy in such a strong-willed ocean. Most of the passengers were going to drown. Jese Sommer's beautiful, mammoth luxury liner was going to perish, along with him and most of her passengers.

IT was Oak Legs who first noticed the lack of light coming from the roof of Telford Towers. He quickly pointed it out to Best. They rang the hotel. Their observation was soon confirmed: eighty guests couldn't get into their rooms. The powerful beams of the lighthouse had been rendered inoperative. By this time, rain was falling in buckets, along with hail the size of macadamia nuts, which was smashing against Best's window with such intensity that he thought the glass was going to shatter.

Oak Legs shook his head. "If there's anybody out there, the're gonna be in real trouble. I've never seen a swell like this in all my sorry life."

Best picked up his binoculars. He could barely see to the edge of the shore where the swelling sea was clawing its way further up the beach, lunging for the road. And yet, somewhere in his mind, with that innate sense that sits somewhere between all the physical senses but which cannot be called either sight, smell, touch nor sound, somewhere in this ambiguous realm, which transcended what was physically possible, Best detected it. He was able to perceive the bow lights of a ship heading towards them.

He handed the binoculars to Oak Legs. "Can you see that?"

Oak Legs peered through Orion's gift. "I can't see anything."

"Look closer," prompted Best.

Oak Legs pressed the glasses firmly against his eyes, so much so he could feel them tugging at his eyeballs. "Why? What do you see?"

"Something."

"Can you be more specific?" asked an exasperated Oak Legs.

Best almost snatched the glasses back. He took another look. The experience of ninety years of studying the ocean now confirmed what he had previously felt. "There's a big ship out there... A mighty big one."

"Are you sure?"

"Take a look for yourself. Her size is causing a shadow in the storm on the ocean."

Oak Legs looked again. He looked hard. Then he saw it. "You're bloody-well right! And it's coming right for us. Why would it be doing that?"

Best shook his head. "I don't know, but there's no light to warn her off. She'll just keep on coming. She's heading right for the reefs."

Oak Legs whistled. "Sheiiiiiiiiit!"

Best went to his wardrobe and pulled out his old grey cardigan. "We've got to get to the old lighthouse."

Oak Legs jumped up, knocking his legs together in the process. "Are you crazy? It's raining cats, dogs and cows out there!"

"If that ship hits the reef in these seas, you know what will happen to her and anybody on board her."

Oak Legs knew a good deal about the pre-*Norah* days – the litany of shipwrecks whose fates were sealed by the destructive, insatiable appetites of the outer reefs of Thurrough. He helped Best wrap the cardigan around his shoulders. "I should've stayed in Garrawarra. That's for crazy bastards like us."

Nurse Selby blocked their paths. "You fine old gents can't go outside in weather like this. You'll both catch your death of cold."

Best was just beginning to explain their quest when Charley Pelegranetti arrived right on cue to distract her.

"We're all dying anyway," barked Oak Legs as he bulldozed Best past Nurse Selby, who Charley had latched onto.

"There's water leaking through my window," said Charley, looking back and winking at Best. "Can you come and check it out for me?"

As Charley led Nurse Selby away, Oak Legs shoved Best out the door of the home.

Oak Legs laughed at the thought of what they looked like: a crippled war-veteran pushing another cripple over a path of hail. Oak Legs fought against the howling wind and driving rain, propelling Best's wheelchair along the esplanade, which was being bombarded by waves. As Best took in the bulging ocean, his breathing became more laboured. He was scared. The fear of the sea, which had first been ignited in him as a boy, and which had often haunted him, rose in him again now, much like the waves. He felt he was back on the rock shelves, clinging tenuously as the dark ocean dragged away his mother. The sea was now coming for him.

But Oak Legs pushed that much harder, shielding Best by turning his wheelchair away from the waves, enduring the brunt of their force himself. When they were within a mere eight hundred metres of the lighthouse, they were confronted by the awful reality of the fiercest weather to hit Thurrough in many years. The waves and extreme rain had flooded the Thurrough Peninsula, isolating it from the rest of Thurrough. In order to reach the lighthouse, Best and Oak Legs Finbar would have to negotiate a fifty-metre-wide body of water that was now three metres deep. Tindall Pemberton had been right after all. The Peninsula had flooded.

Drenched and shivering madly, Best was horrified as he stared at the intruding water from the Pacific Ocean, which was flowing across the Peninsula and disgorging itself into Botany Bay. Oak Legs Finbar barked out hacking coughs, trying to catch his breath as rain pelted down all around them.

"I can't go any further," Best uttered hopelessly.

"One of us has got to!" yelled back Oak Legs above the loud, ceaseless clatter of the deluge.

"I can't swim!" Best screamed back, as much to himself as to Oak Legs.

Oak Legs collapsed to the ground and began to remove his legs. "I'll go!" Oak Legs pointed to the other side. "There's a dinghy over there that's come off its mooring. I'll bring it back for you!"

Best watched helplessly from the prison of his wheelchair as Oak Legs patted his legs affectionately and gently placed them beside each other.

Oak Legs grinned. "You can keep 'em if I don't make it back. They're not much good to me in there… Just dead weight!"

Oak Legs dragged himself to the edge of the torrent. Without another word, he plunged into the swirling water. He thrashed madly to stay afloat, but the current was strong and determined to sweep him away. He put up his hand in a vain attempt to muster help. But none could possibly be forthcoming.

Best watched in anguish as Oak Legs drifted further and further away. He turned and clenched his eyes shut. But he could not avoid the pain. Images of his mother and Elizabeth bobbing helplessly in the ocean, horrifyingly vivid, played out in his mind, heightened by the hopeless plight of Daniel Finbar – the war hero. He dropped his head into his hands and moaned. He could not watch Oak Legs drown – to witness a noble life cruelly ended in a manner so sickeningly familiar. The anguish was overwhelming. It made him angry; angry with himself.

Best's downcast eyes found Daniel Finbar's oak legs lying lifeless by the edge of the water divide. "Oak wood," he muttered to himself. "It floats," he said then, struck by his revelation, he repeated, "it floats!"

He leant on his good right hand and, with all his might, forced his soaking form from the snare of the rusting wheelchair. Once upright, he carefully bent down and grabbed hold of the prosthetic legs. He forced himself not to dwell on what he was about to do. There was no time for self-pity or self-doubt. His mind was made up. If Oak Legs was going to drown, then he would finally drown too. They were in this together, and if fate decreed it, they would both go down together. Why should he be immune from such a fate? It had happened, seemingly indiscriminately, twice in his life; why should he escape? Best quickly undid his old leather belt and slid both wooden legs down the back of his trousers before tightening it again in order to fix to himself two wooden buoys. For the first time in over ninety years, he gently glided into the water, prepared to succumb to its will.

As he tried to keep his head afloat, he madly paddled his arms to direct his path towards Oak Legs Finbar, whose head was barely remaining above the surface. Best began to accelerate with the current, his torso perched up like a hydrofoil, the oak legs providing him with remarkable floatation.

"Grab onto your legs!" yelled Best as he rallied beside Oak Legs whose mouth widened in amazement on seeing him.

Best wasn't sure if Oak Legs was shocked from nearly drowning, or by the fact that Best was wearing his legs as floaties. Either way, he had to yell the instruction no less than three times. In the end, the astonished Oak Legs did as Best insisted and took hold of the two life preservers. As Best kicked with his one good leg, and paddled furiously with his one good arm, aided by Oak Legs with his two good arms, they made their slow progress towards the other side of the newly-created river.

As they pulled themselves up onto the sand bank like beached whales, Oak Legs tightened his hug affectionately around Best. "You crazy son of a gun!" he yelled. "You just saved my life with my own two legs!"

Best nodded furiously. "Wood floats!"

"It bloody-well does!"

They both looked up towards *Norah*, then out to sea, only to witness the approaching lights of the colossal ship. Oak Legs' smile disappeared. "There's no time to put my legs back on. That ship's gonna hit the reefs in no time at all."

Best undid his belt and handed Daniel Finbar back his two wooden legs. "I'm the only one who can operate her. I'll go from here by myself."

Oak Legs adjusted the straps on his legs and quickly began the task of reattaching them. "I'll be right behind you!"

Best limped away shivering madly. "I'll have a cup of tea ready for you!" he yelled back.

"Best?" Oak Legs cried after him. "Godspeed!"

Best dragged himself the seven hundred odd metres to the old lighthouse. He arrived exhausted. He rested briefly before he swung open the old door on its rusty hinges and exposed the first of fifty-three steps he had to climb in order to reach the lamp room. He took a deep, cleansing breath then began his arduous ascent. It was slow and laborious. Just after halfway, he started experiencing chest pains. "Not now," he protested as he struggled to climb onwards.

Despite the nagging pain, he persisted. He climbed the last fifteen stairs at a snail's pace, barely able to get enough air into his lungs to fuel his tired legs. After eleven gut-wrenching minutes Best entered the lamp room. He dusted off the old Fresnel lens and instinctively proceeded to embark on the same checklist he had last done thirty years ago. He breathed a sigh of relief. The lamp seemed to be in working order. He reviewed the electrical supply. Some of the wires had been disconnected at the power box. It had been a long time since he had done any kind of electrical work. He attached the wires and flicked the switch that operated the lamp. Nothing. He re-routed the wiring and tried again. Again, nothing. He looked out the window. It seemed as if the huge liner was coming right for him. He knew that it was only a matter of minutes before it hit the reefs.

Best shook his head. "Come on, think. What could it be?"

He bent down and looked under the lamp at the electrical points into which the wires inserted. Some of them had rusted and corroded due to years of exposure to the salt air. He spat out his dentures and used the wire connecting his false teeth to scrape the points clean. He crossed his fingers then turned on the lamp. It shone out brilliantly.

"You beauty!" he screamed.

But his excitement was premature. He flicked the switch that operated the rotating apparatus. Nothing happened. The lamp was pointing directly south. If it remained in that position, there was no way that the ship was going to see it. The problem that had afflicted his father had come back for him.

There was no other way. Best would have to rotate the lamp manually. He gingerly perched down on his haunches. He paused. He wasn't sure whether he had the strength. He reached up and grasped the two handles. He saw the signature of Harry Heath and was instantly reminded of the strength of his father. He half-smiled as he began tugging on the handles. It wouldn't rotate. Time's rust had seized the bearings. He pulled harder. The rotator let out a protesting groan. It was tight. Best tugged with all his might, but he still couldn't manage to move the lamp any more than a couple of degrees, and it needed to rotate close to ninety. The pains in his chest were returning; this time with more intensity.

"Best?" said the voice.

Best looked around. "It's you?"

The Keeper stepped out of the shadows.

Best knew then that the Keeper hadn't lied. He had been there when Best needed him. He had been there all along. It was he who had kept Best alive for the last two years. It was he who had given Best hope. And it was he who was down in the Hole with him when Best had sought him out. The Keeper had been true to his word.

"It's stuck. I can hardly move it. And my chest…"

"You can move it. I know you can move it."

"I don't know… It's so tight."

"I waited in the Hole for you, Best, for this purpose. I know you can do it. You're the only one to do this."

Suddenly, Best heard other voices – all urging him.

"For the love of the dearly departed saints," said his father, who seemed to have placed his own hands over Best's, "you can do it."

"We know you can do it," said his wife Elizabeth, who had appeared to massage his shoulders. "I whispered something into your ear one day when we were up here together. Do you remember what I said?"

Best had never forgotten those words, even though he believed he had never fulfilled them.

Elizabeth leant down and whispered into his ear. "You're going to do something remarkable one day, Best Douglas. This is that day, my love."

"The *best* thing to happen to me, my son," said Norah softly as she ran her motherly fingers through his hair. "You can do it. You can do anything."

Best stared up at the Keeper in disbelief. He was now much older than all of them. It was strange to be considered a young man again after all the years that had gone by.

The Keeper moved closer. "They're part of who you are. Part of who you've always been. Although taken from you, they lived to give you the strength to do this."

As their images faded, Best began pulling on the mechanism with all his might. The rotator resisted. He mustered more strength from somewhere. He knew he could do it now. He was sure he could do it. Suddenly, it jerked. It began giving in. He was fighting against time and winning. The brass mechanism swivelled slowly, reluctantly, along the corroded bearings.

"It's moving!" cried Best in jubilation. "It's moving!"

It felt like somebody had plunged a knife into his chest. He clutched at his ribcage with his arthritic left hand but kept pulling the lamp with his right until it was facing the ship. He could hardly breathe when the pain vanished as quickly as it had begun. When he collapsed backwards against the cracked wall, the lamp continued to rotate of its own volition.

Best had done it.

The Keeper reached down and gently picked Best up like a father carrying a child to bed. Best felt intense warmth in the Keeper's arms. The Keeper's body gave out a glorious white light, which filled the lamp room. With Best nestled securely in his arms, he rose straight through the lighthouse window, which remained intact as they passed right through it. Looking down from night sky, Best could easily see the ocean liner.

"Three thousand, seven hundred souls on board," remarked the Keeper soberly. "You just prevented that Captain from making a tragic error. He was about to enter Thurrough Beach by mistake. The ship would have crashed on the reefs. The huge seas would have tipped the lifeboats. Two thousand, seven hundred adults and three hundred children would have drowned in less than five minutes."

"The poor fella had no light to guide him," remarked Best.

"Do you remember when you asked me what my name meant all those years ago when we were in the Hole?"

As Best looked upon the Keeper's strong, majestic face, the memory seemed but yesterday. "I remember."

The Keeper's smile was punctuated by gleaming white teeth. "Best, you and I are the same. We are Keepers. We are *Keepers of Light.*"

Oak Legs gave out a triumphant hoot as he hobbled in front of the lighthouse and craned his head up at the lamp room. Just as the light shone out, he saw another strange beam that looked like it was coming from two bright floating images moving through the air away from the lighthouse. He was not to know that Orion Keeper was giving Best one final breathtaking view of the lights of Thurrough before whisking him away from his mortal life.

WHEN paramedics found the body of Best Douglas the next morning on the floor of the lamp room of the old Thurrough lighthouse, the lamp was burning bright and still rotating. Captain Marcus Swanson of the *Queen of the South Pacific* said that he was about to navigate the giant ship into Thurrough Beach, thinking it was the entrance to Botany Bay, when Jese Sommer suddenly spied the glow of the old Thurrough Lighthouse. People were quick to label Best a hero, but Best would have argued that there were many heroes. Jese Sommer was not to know that both his life and his reputation had been redeemed by his Uncle – the eldest son of his unknown grandfather, Ben Douglas.

Oak Legs Finbar came down with a nasty cold, but it didn't develop into anything worse. And, after a few weeks, he was back to his cantankerous self. Orion's roommate from Barclay House, Justin, took over Orion's paper route, and began to spend quite a lot of time with Oak Legs Finbar. Oak Legs would entertain Justin with stories from the war, and Justin would tell Oak Legs how Orion was really a celestial being that had flown away. Oak Legs chuckled. Kids, he thought, such imaginations. Still, the image of Orion often came to him in dreams about the war, when his mind would conjure visions of the paperboy sitting by his bed in Cologne reading to him in French as his wounds mended, the persona of the French Private all but fading into the image of Orion's angelic face. Dreams, he thought, always merging images of one being into another.

After a comprehensive report submitted by a heavily pregnant Dr Fiona Chalice, the Federal Parliament overturned the legislation enacted by both the Northern Territory and the New South Wales Governments and removed the State's power and authority to create legislation surrounding the delicate issue of euthanasia.

OAK Legs Finbar and Charley Pelegranetti beamed the smiles of proud new parents as the first of the gold broke through the surface of the water and on board the cruiser that the pair had dubbed *The White Swan*. Sixty million dollars later, they had salvaged all the gold that the waters of Thurrough had held captive for all those years.

As the last of it was stacked onto the vessel, Oak Legs put his arm around Charley and cried out in jubilation, *"The night too quickly passes And we are growing old,*

So let us fill our glasses
And toast the Days of Gold;
When finds of wondrous treasure
Set all the South ablaze,
And you and I were faithful mates
All through the Roaring Days!"

After Daniel Finbar passionately quoted from Henry Lawson's stirring poem, he took hold of Charley and hugged him. They both couldn't stop laughing for days.

The money had been ear-marked for a specific purpose long before Oak Legs and Charley had begun the salvage attempt: the complete restoration of *Norah* and the development of the Thurrough Lighthouse Historic National Park; a site designed to reflect the best of indigenous and white societies, and perhaps represent some form of reconciliation. It celebrated the harmonious meeting of the two cultures when, two hundred years before, an exhausted convict had washed up on the shores of Thurrough Beach and been assimilated into the Gweagal tribe.

Jonathon Perry was only too pleased to grant Oak Legs' request. After all, the old Thurrough lighthouse had been Best's home for many years. So, on the edge of the Peninsula, just up from where Crenshaw's Hole used to be, one more hole was dug, and in it, Best's body was laid to rest. The new President of the Friends of Thurrough Lighthouse, Oak Legs Finbar, placed a tombstone at the head of the grave. The inscription simply read:

Best Douglas
Born March 6th 1904 – Gone Surfing May 2nd 1998

Three months later, Justin found Orion's surfboard washed up on Thurrough Beach. Although the reef had made deep gouges in the top of the board, the mural on the back was virtually un-scarred, except in one spot. Justin wiped the surfboard clean and studied the picture of the lighthouse with wings overlooking a beach bulging with perfect waves, but as he did so, he noticed that the reef had carved what looked to be a small image in the left-hand corner of the picture. At the bottom of the design, barely visible, was an uncanny portrait of a surfer with a beaming smile etched onto his tiny face as he and his surfboard were tucked into one of the mural's epic waves. As Justin looked closer still, he discovered that the surfer looked remarkably like a vibrant, nimble, now ever-youthful Best Douglas.

THE END

www.ingramcontent.com/pod-product-compliance
Lightning Source LLC
Chambersburg PA
CBHW060401260626
47160CB00006B/2394